CHEVY CHASE

OR,

THE BATTLE ON THE BORDER.

"BOYS OF ENGLAND"

PUBLISHING OFFICE, 173, FLEET STREET, E.C.

CHEVY CHASE:

OR,

THE BATTLE ON THE BORDER.

BEAUTIFULLY ILLUSTRATED.

COMPLETE.

LONDON :

" BOYS OF ENGLAND " OFFICE, 173, FLEET STREET, E.C

AND ALL BOOKSELLERS.

COMBAT BETWEEN EARL PERCY AND DUGLAS AT THE FIGHT OF CHEVY CHASE.

CHEVY CHASE;

OR,

THE BATTLE ON THE BORDER.

"'STAY! HOLD YOUR HANDS, RASH BOYS. PERCY, DOUGLAS, FORBEAR!'"

CHEVY CHASE;

OR,

THE BATTLE ON THE BORDER.

CHAPTER I.

NEWS FROM THE NORTH.

OD prosper long our noble king,
  Our lives and safeties all ;
A woeful hunting once there did
  In Chevy Chase befal.

To drive the deer with hound and
  horn,
  Earl Percy took his way ;
The child may rue that is unborn,
  The hunting of that day.

FIVE hundred years ago, the period at which our tale commences, London was very different from the city of this present year of grace. In those days the city was enclosed within walls, and to enter it the wayfarer had to pass through one of the many gates which afforded the good citizens the means of ingress and egress when they wished to issue out into or return from the surrounding country.

The immense suburbs which now enclose the city were then fields, meadows, and woods ; Islington had fewer inhabitants than a modern joint-stock hotel ; Bloomsbury was unheard of ; while, if Westminster could boast a larger population than either Finsbury or Marylebone, it was because it had an abbey, and the king sometimes held his court there.

The mean-looking sheds or shops in which the city tradesmen displayed their goods were strangely mixed up, in those times, with the frowning mansions in which powerful and wealthy nobles resided when they came to attend the king's court at Westminster, or the Tower of London, and conspicuous among these substantial buildings was one that stood in gloomy majesty nearly at the end of a narrow thoroughfare known then as now as Bull and Mouth Street, near the Aldersgate entrance to the city.

The building was of grey stone with a turret at each angle of the roof, and what added more to its sombre appearance, was the scarcity in number and narrow limits of the iron-barred windows which served to give light and air to the inhabitants of the mansion.

An archway, guarded by strong iron-bound gates of oak, led to the interior of the building, but those gates were seldom opened save to allow some member or retainer of the family to pass in or out.

One stroke of the pen, however, will prove quite as useful as the porter's key in revealing the interior of that jealously-guarded mansion.

The archway led to a large, square court-yard, surrounded on every side by buildings ; one side of the quadrangle being a kind of barrack, in which the followers of the owner were lodged during their lord's stay in town ; a second side consisted of store-houses ; the third side, that facing the street and pierced by the archway, was devoted to the exclusive use of the family and their friends ; while the fourth side of the square was a huge stable, in which some scores of horses might find stall and manger room.

On that June morning in the year 1375, the great mansion, with its court-yard, its stores and stables, seemed almost tenantless, the only persons to be seen being the porter who kept the keys of the great gate, and a lazy groom who loitered listlessly in front of the stables, glancing at the shadows on the pavement that told him that the hour for dinner was nigh.

Ascend the narrow stone staircase that leads to the western turret, ascend higher and higher till you reach a low-arched doorway immediately beneath the roof.

Open the door and enter.

The apartment has a bare look, the furniture is of that wooden, uncomfortable kind with which our ancestors were obliged to make shift, the roughness of the walls was in some measure hidden by pieces of gaudy and coarsely-executed tapestry, while the two windows were nothing but open loop-holes.

Three persons were seated within this apartment.

A man, whose dress and shaven head proclaimed him a member of one of the religious foundations with which England was then plentifully blessed, while his companions were tall, well grown boys, costumed in such a manner as to show their noble birth.

The elder of these two youths appeared to be between fifteen and sixteen years of age, the other being about two years younger.

That they were brothers was evident from the striking similarity of their features and dress.

These two youths were the young lords—Henry and Ralph Percy—sons of Henry, sixth Lord Percy, and first Earl of Northumberland.

The young nobles were richly dressed in the fashion of the period—tunics of purple velvet, with long, wide sleeves, lined with white silk, crimson hose, and boots of dark green leather with long points extending some inches beyond the toes of the wearers.

Richly ornamented daggers, and caps of velvet, surmounted by heron's plumes, completed the dress of the young lords.

The monk was nearly fifty years of age, with a countenance expressive of the love of good cheer and hatred of anything like physical exertion; his position in the establishment was that of family chaplain and confessor, and tutor to the two young lords.

The boys had each a parchment volume before him ; but their eyes were much more frequently directed towards the loop-hole windows, through which the sunlight streamed merrily, than upon the crooked black letters of their books.

They sighed to be away—to dash through the streets on their fiery horses, or to fly their falcons at the heron or plover in the fields at no great distance.

And as Father Abel was engaged in an abstruse calculation as to the amount of good things he would eat and drink at the coming meal, their thoughts were allowed to roam unchecked.

Presently a loud knocking was heard at the outer gate, so clamorous as to reach the turret-room in which the lads and their tutor were seated.

"Now, who, in the Virgin's name, can this be who knocks so loudly ?" exclaimed Ralph Percy. "All our varlets are within, I know, except old Adam Houghton, and he, like the good father here, loves no noise save that of trencher and flagon."

"I know not who it may be," replied Harry ; "but I'll not long remain in doubt."

So saying, he started up, overturning the bench on which he had been seated, and dashed out of the room, followed by his brother.

"Ho! young lords, do you leave your tutor thus?" exclaimed Father Abel ; but his pupils were too far down the staircase to pay any attention to his remonstrance.

"A pair of fiery youths, and will make fine warriors, I'll warrant. Well, well, thanks be to the Holy Virgin, my pious parents had the good sense to place me in the bosom of a peaceful monastery where no warlike sounds can ever come. Ha, ha, ha! such young gallants as these are only too happy to draw their swords at the bidding of holy church, and think themselves well repaid by promises of speedy release from purgatory. Now I should have made but a very poor man-at-arms, I love feasting so much better than fighting."

With these words the holy man slowly descended the staircase and made the best of his way towards the offices of the clerk of the kitchen.

As he crossed the court-yard, he cast a glance towards the gateway, and beheld his two wayward pupils conversing with a mail-clad trooper, whose dusty, jaded appearance seemed to denote that he had travelled a long distance.

The boys had reached the great gates just as the new comer was admitted, and seeing at once, by his dress and badge, that he was a retainer of their family, began to ply him with questions.

"What Fenwicke de Fenwicke!" exclaimed Harry Percy; "and what brings you to London?"

"Your noble father's commands, my lord; though much I wish he had laid those commands upon some other person. I never feel in the mood to journey south of the Humber while any Scots remain north of the Tweed."

"And how is our father, the Earl of Northumberland?" asked Ralph.

"Well enough, Lord Ralph, with the exception of a slight scratch he caught in a fray with some of the Scots free lances last week. But I'll warrant he has paid the score in full ere this; for, e'en as I started, there was a great furbishing of lances and sharpening of swords amongst the retainers of the noble Percy."

"A murrain on these Scots!" exclaimed Harry Percy. "Would that I were there!"

"Patience, my lord. Another year or two and you may flesh your sword on their kilted carcases."

"Patience! Talk you to me of patience, caged up in yon old owl-roost of a turret along with the sleepy, blinking old monk and his musty parchments! I long to be in the saddle to couch my lance by my father's side, and charge these Scottish freebooters. Who knows but I might meet the Douglas and win my spurs? Younger nobles than myself have been knighted ere now."

"Bravo, my lord! Well they may call you Hotspur in the tilt-yard; you breathe the spirit of a true Percy. As for your meeting the Douglas, though, he is far too powerful a champion for you; besides, he does not often take the field in these border forays. But I hear he hath a son

a few months older than yourself, and a cock of the gamest breed."

"Ha! say you so? Then Harry Percy knows no peace till he meets this crowing gallant face to face and cuts his comb."

"Good lord! how I love to hear the lad talk," exclaimed John de Fenwicke, of Fenwicke Tower. "But, my lord, while talking to you I had almost forgotten your most noble father's messages."

"And what are they?"

"He bids me greet you with his best love, and bids you hold yourselves prepared to set out for the north about a month before the holy-tide of Christmas begins, when he will send another message. He also charged me to deliver certain letters to your confessor and tutor, Father Abel."

"Whom you will find yonder in the kitchen offices," said Ralph Percy, with a smile.

"Come hither, Ralph," said Harry, who had gained the nickname of Hotspur on account of his impetuous temper.

While John de Fenwicke strode towards the kitchen to search for the friar, as well as to refresh his own thirsty throat, the two boys walked up and down the court-yard conversing earnestly in a low tone of voice.

What the subject of their talk was will be found hereafter.

Father Abel, of the holy order of St. Benedict, as Ralph Percy rightly stated, was found near the kitchen.

The monk was in the act of raising a flagon of good ale to his lips, when the soldier entered.

"A fair morrow to you, Father Abel. When you have betowed your blessing on the measure in your hand, I pray you let me taste the contents."

"John de Fenwicke, thou shalt have my blessing but not my ale. Master Steward, bring another cup, I pray thee. And now, good squire of Fenwicke Tower, tell me what brings thee hither. Have the Scots invaded our land from the south?"

"They have not; and in their north ern forays they have been driven back

But, my noble lord, the Earl of Northumberland charged me with certain letters to thee.''

With these words the soldier laid upon the table the packets with which he had been entrusted.

Father Abel broke the seals and glanced at the contents of the documents, while John de Fenwicke applied himself to the task of swallowing the liquor which had been placed before him.

"Know you aught of the contents of these letters?" asked Father Abel.

" Not I, holy father."

"The noble Lord Percy tells me that ere long he will take my pupils from me."

"Aye, I have heard him say as much."

The good monk's face grew pale, or, rather, it became less purple, as he heard the squire confirm the intelligence conveyed in his letters.

"And know you, good John of Fenwicke, doth he intend to deprive me of mine office as chaplain? In what have I angered him, good Fenwicke?''

"Angered him! Why, good father, his words regarding you have always been those of love and regard. Nay! If you have given offence, it must have been since I left the goodly towers of Warkworth Castle, for his last words were, ' Tell Father Abel not to cease to say a prayer for us, for while these beggarly Scots range our hills, and harry our cattle, we have little time to attend to our own devotions.' "

"Thanks be to the Holy Virgin for such news ; I should be loath to quit the service of the noble Percy."

" Or the society of his cook and butler. But the hour for dinner must be nigh at hand. Do your pupils take their meal in the great hall ? "

"They do ; and I care not how soon they take it in Warkworth or Alnwick, since I am not to lose my holy office of chaplain and confessor. But, come, to the hall, to the hall, for my nostrils do smell a goodly odour.''

CHAPTER II.

JOHN DE FENWICKE.

In the dining-hall was a long oak table stretching down the centre of the apartment, with a smaller and higher one crossing it at the upper end.

At the upper board sat Ralph and Harry Percy, while from all parts of the building came flocking a number of hangers-on of the establishment, who crowded the benches round the lower table.

Harry Percy, as the eldest member of the house, took the chair of state occupied by the earl on his visits to town ; Ralph sat on his right hand, John de Fenwicke on his left, while the monk and a young squire, whose duty it was to attend upon the lordlings, took their seats at the two corners of the board.

Father Abel hurried through a Latin benediction on the meal, and then began a general attack on the mountains of solid food that decked the board.

The brothers appeared to be more intent on watching the countenance of the monk and John de Fenwicke than on the food before them ; but, as all the rest of the diners were blessed with good appetites, their abstracted looks were not noticed.

"When dost thou return, De Fenwicke?" asked Harry Percy, in a low tone, when he had succeeded in catching the attention of the jovial Northumbrian squire, who, though of gentle blood and ancient family, deemed it no disgrace to wear the badge, and serve beneath the banner of the powerful Northern baron.

"To-morrow morn an hour after daybreak, my lord. In good truth, I like not this great town of London; there be too many Jewish pedlars and wolfish lawyers in the streets, and if a man do but walk abroad with helm and breastplate on, a score of saucy 'prentices are sure to follow him with their idle jests and gibes."

"This is but short resting time after your journey."

"Long enough, my lord, long enough; John de Fenwicke is not easily tired, and would as soon be in saddle as out."

Then the young noble whispered a word in the ear of his brother, who nodded, and nothing more was said.

The dinner over, the guests dispersed, and the two young Percys were seen no more till it was near the hour at which the household retired to rest, and then they merely showed themselves for a few minutes at the table, at the evening meal.

The great gates were finally closed, and sleep was supposed to visit the eyelids of all in that great mansion.

True to his word John de Fenwicke arose with the sun—and that luminary is up betimes in the month of June—and, saddling his good steed, soon issued forth on his journey. His first act was to call at an inn close at hand, where he had left a dozen troopers; and, having marshalled these, and given the word of command, the whole party passed through Aldersgate at a trot.

They passed through Islington, and were just congratulating themselves on having left the town behind, when a sound of horses' hoofs galloping rapidly after them was heard upon the wind.

The little party wheeled about, for in those times little parley was made when the partizans of one house attacked those of a rival, and, for aught John de Fenwicke knew, these galloping horsemen might be retainers of the Duke of Glocester, or some other foemen.

"Only two, unless my ears deceive me," he muttered. "Surely they do not mean to attack *us* thus short handed. Who can they be?"

In another minute De Fenwicke's doubts were set at rest, though his mind was considerably astonished; for the two horsemen was seen to be none other than Harry and Ralph Percy.

"You here, my lords! Is this prudent or safe to venture beyond the city without one or two stout men-at-arms at your back?"

"Is there danger, good De Fenwicke?" asked Harry.

"Aye. The sons of the lord of Northumberland were a prize that might tempt many a bold knight to run the risk of the king's displeasure."

"Then I am right glad to be here, for where should Percy be if not where danger most threatens?"

"Well said, Sir Hotspur! But, my lord, your ride will seriously delay my journey, for I cannot suffer you to return unattended, and must perforce accompany you back to that hateful city."

"But we do not intend to return, De Fenwicke; I, for my part, am as heartily tired of London as you, and long to be chasing the deer along the Cheviot side."

The stout soldier scratched as much of his poll as was left uncovered by his armour, and looked at the two boys in considerable astonishment. That they fully meant to go with him to Northumberland there could be little doubt, for both were armed and fully equipped for a journey.

"Forward, De Fenwicke; we do but lose time," cried Harry Percy. "Our minds are made up, and we will see the fair river Tweed ere we return to Father Abel and his black-letter books. Faugh! the very thought of the old missals makes my head ache!"

"Then forward, my lords," replied De Fenwicke; "but, hark ye, Sir Hotspur, you must use all your influence with your noble father to shield me from his anger."

"Have no fear, good squire of Fenwicke Tower. If his displeasure visits you now, my favour shall find you out when I am earl."

So saying, the hot-brained youth

touched his horse's sides with the spurs, and the whole band set forward, the troopers shouting for joy to see their gallant young lord riding at their head.

The journey from London to the northern boundary of England was not accomplished with such ease and swiftness as it is now. There were no express trains with comfortable first class carriages, nor even a stage coach with four fiery horses and a change of cattle at every twelve or fourteen miles.

Those who made the tremendous journey, travelled on horseback, or, still more perilous adventure, trusted themselves to one of the few rude merchant vessels that carried on a little commerce between the north and south of this island.

The journey on horseback was a wearisome and dangerous task, for robbers were numerous, and well organised in large bands ; in fact, many men who wore gilt spurs, and called themselves knights, were little better than captains of banditti, and lived principally from the plunder they obtained from their neighbours and the travellers who passed by their fortresses.

The young Percys well knew all this, but danger could never daunt the heart of the fiery Hotspur, or his calm, though equally courageous brother Ralph.

Eight days after setting out from London, they came within sight of the castle of Warkworth, where the Earl of Northumberland then resided, for the better superintendence of certain repairs which the fortifications required.

The castle presented a grand and striking figure as they approached it from the south.

Their road lay up a gentle hill, and on reaching the top of it, John de Fenwicke reined up his little party to point out to the youths the strength and beauty of the building.

The great gates—the chief entrance to the castle—lay before them, defended on each side by strong circular towers ; a deep moat, crossed by a drawbridge, lay before it, while on each side was a strong and high wall pierced with loop-holes.

There was no wall on the north side, for the great tower, or keep, was placed on the very edge of a steep cliff, which an enemy would have been puzzled to scale.

The keep itself, as it rose above the surrounding buildings, was a most lordly-looking piece of architecture.

On the top of this waved a banner, bearing emblazoned on it the *Lion of Brabant*, while a similar grim-looking animal was carved over the principal gateway.

As De Fenwicke and the two young Percys approached, some commotion was visible in the castle.

Armed men were seen gathering on the towers each side of the gateway, and the drawbridge was raised.

" What a strong castle, and what ready soldiers ! " exclaimed Ralph.

" Aye, but not so strong as Alnwick," replied Harry. " What say you, De Fenwicke ? "

" Why, my lord, it is strong enough to keep us out all night ; so, by your leave, I will ride forward and say who 'tis demands admittance."

With these words, John de Fenwicke rode up to the gate, and was soon in conference with the warder.

That officer, as soon as he heard that the two young lords were with the party, hastened to have the portcullis raised, and the drawbridge lowered, while he himself marshalled his men to greet the youthful nobles as they rode through the archway.

As their horses' hoofs clanged upon the iron bridge a thrill of joy shot through Harry Percy's bosom ; he had cast off the thraldom of Father Abel's tuition, and henceforth was resolved to live as a soldier.

Neither he nor Ralph had been in Warkworth Castle since infancy, so that it seemed to them like entering a new home ; and a very pleasant one it promised to be, though Harry would have preferred Alnwick, with every turret and paving-stone of which he was familiar.

They dismounted from their horses, and followed John de Fenwicke up a flight of stone steps, which led them into a kind of outer hall or vestibule, around which were ranged stone seats for the convenience of the servants in attendance on the earl in the great hall.

Into his presence they were quickly ushered.

At the upper end of the room sat Henry, sixth Lord Percy and first Earl of Northumberland.

The earl was a stern-faced warrior, slightly marked by age, for his hair was beginning to assume that grisly appearance which is a mark of maturity of years.

His dress was a loose robe of velvet, trimmed with furs; but close at hand were breast-plate, helm, gauntlets and sword, as though he knew not how soon he might be called upon to sally forth and repel some invading party from the north.

"How is this, truant lordlings?" he exclaimed, as his eye fell upon his sons. "John de Fenwicke, you have not done well in bringing these lads from their books."

"And it please you, my lord, I did not bring them. I had left London some way behind on my homeward journey when Sir Hotspur and his brother came riding after me and refused to return."

"Pardon us, noble father, but we heard that the Scots had been burning, killing and destroying, and I felt anxious to draw sword against them. Surely I did no wrong in wishing to fight my father's enemies."

The earl was silent for a few moments, and then replied—

"Well, be it so, Hal. 'Tis but a month or two before I intended; and perhaps thou hast already as much book learning as is needed to make a good lance. But the Scots have retired, and so thou shalt hunt deer on the hills to-morrow instead of riding down followers of the Douglas on the Marches."

So saying, he motioned them to retire, and resumed his conversation with the knights and squires who surrounded his chair.

"If the Scots have retired, I doubt not they will cross the border again ere long, for, as I crossed the hall, I heard it said that the Witch of Wooler had been seen, and she generally brings hard blows behind her.

"And who is this witch, De Fenwicke?" asked Ralph, turning to the speaker.

"A fearful hag who lives up in the hills. Whenever any of our people see her we are pretty sure to have some rough riding soon after."

"Then may she show her face every day!" exclaimed Harry Percy, grasping his sword.

"So say I, my lord, for I am growing rusty for want of a downright good skirmish. But if you hunt to-morrow I would advise that you take a good train at your back."

"That I will, and thou, John de Fenwicke, shalt be of the number, unless my father orders otherwise."

And then, after making a few brief arrangements for the morrow's sport, the two lads sought their respective couches, happy as larks at the prospect before them.

But lords and nobles in those days did not lie till ten or eleven o'clock as many of our modern aristocrats do.

The Percys of the fourteenth century usually dined at about the hour the nineteenth century fop rings for his valet, and the two youths with whom we have already made acquaintance were in the saddle, ready for the chase, by the time it was fairly light, just about the time when the aforesaid modern fop thinks of retiring to rest.

John de Fenwicke was with them, and a chosen band of twenty of the best archers in all Northumberland.

Such a force would be quite competent to deal with any straggling party of Scots that might be abroad.

Away they rode right merrily, taking the northern route, till, at length, they arrived at a steep woodland, through which it was impossible to proceed on horseback, so each man sprang to the ground, and prepared to hunt on foot.

Harry Percy and Ralph were both good archers for their age, and carried bows and arrows.

Then the hounds were uncoupled, the foresters blew their horns, and the whole party dashed forward into the greenwood, encouraging the dogs with their voices, and making the grand old woodland glens ring again with their cheerful shouts.

"Look out, my lord, a stag's afoot!" cried De Fenwicke. "Make to the right, and you will intercept him as he goes towards the Raven's Glen."

Off dashed young Percy, and after him a dozen of the foresters.

They gained the entrance to a ravine called the Raven's Glen; but had scarcely taken up their stations when a crashing sound was heard amongst the underwood, and a gallant stag bounded proudly into the mouth of the pass.

The dogs were baying behind, but he seemed to sniff danger before, and suddenly halted in a listening attitude, tossing his branched antlers back, and pawing the ground with his hoof.

That moment's hesitation sealed his fate, for Harry Percy's arrow whistled through the air, and, after one high leap, the splendid deer lay dead.

The young huntsman placed his horn to his lips and blew a loud note, which, to his astonishment, seemed echoed back from the adjacent woods.

"Can Ralph have been successful too?" he said. "I heard another horn!"

"I much doubt that it was English music you heard, my lord. Bend your bows, my men; it were best to be prepared."

Even as De Fenwicke spoke voices were heard, and, in an instant after, another party of hunters appeared.

The dress of the new arrivals showed them to be Scots, and they seemed under the leadership of a youth a trifle older than Harry Percy.

"How now," said this lad, stepping forward. "Who gave you permission to kill the deer I was in chase of?"

"In these woods I kill what deer I list, without asking permission of any kilted savage," replied Harry Hotspur. "The deer is mine, killed by my arrow, so claim it if you dare."

So saying, he placed one foot on the body of the animal, and half drew his sword, while the Scottish youth laid his hand upon his claymore.

But, ere blood could be shed, a figure appeared standing betwixt them—a weird, mysterious figure, clothed in sombre apparel, and, in harsh tones, addressed the two youths—

"Stay! hold your hands, rash boys! Percy Douglas, forbear! Ye are yet too young to fight! but the time will come when ye shall meet face to face, and hand to hand, and blood shall flow down this glen like water. And hunting the stag shall be the cause of this. For mark the prophecy—

"Woe for the day when in the dark Chevy Chase,
Douglas and Percy shall meet face to face ;
Blood like a torrent shall flow down the glen,
Death be the hunter, his quarry be men."

"It is the Witch of Wooler! Come away, my lord!" whispered De Fenwicke.

Harry Percy retreated a few steps, but when he again looked towards the spot the figure had vanished, and along with it the forms of the Scottish hunters, who, as if awed by the strange words and weird gestures of the sorceress, had suddenly retired through the underwood.

Harry Hotspur laughed a loud laugh of scorn and derision, and drew his sword with intent to pursue them.

But Fenwick de Fenwicke instantly caught him by the arm.

CHAPTER III.

ESPERANCE! PERCY!

HARRY PERCY kept his eyes fixed upon the spot where he had seen the apparition, scrutinizing it with all the keen accuracy of young eyes and excited feelings.

"What dost thou think, De Fenwicke? Should we obey the injunctions of the weird woman, and let the Scots depart in peace, or follow them sword in hand?"

"Why, my lord, you know I am no coward, and am ever ready to strike for England; but when the Witch of Wooler says 'no fighting,' why, 'tis time to sheath swords."

"What, you fear a woman, then?"

"No woman, my lord, but a being of more than mortal mould."

"Then, what, in the Virgin's name, doth she on this mortal soil? By the rood, if she appear before mine eyes again, I will see if her 'more than mortal mould' be proof against the teeth of my good hound."

"Harry Percy, beware!" cried a harsh voice, and, looking up, the young noble again saw the form of the Witch of Wooler.

"Hi, Don! seize her, good dog! Drag her down!" cried the hot-blooded youth.

But the hound moved not a step, though his low, deep growl and displayed fangs showed plainly that he was aware of the presence of the being at which his master cheered him.

"Then, by Heaven, this shall prove if thou art mortal or not," cried Hotspur, drawing his sword, and rushing forward.

But his intention of testing the supernatural qualities of the hag was frustrated, for his foot caught in the branching antlers of the dead stag, and he fell forward to the earth.

The witch, with a harsh laugh, darted behind an oak tree, and was seen no more, although the young chief made a strict search as soon as he had recovered from the confusion occasioned by his fall.

"This is witchcraft with a vengeance. Are you much hurt my lord?" said De Fenwicke.

"Not hurt, but much grieved that yon hag hath escaped us. Give a blast on your bugle, De Fenwicke and call hither our brother with all speed."

De Fenwicke did as commanded, and made the merry green woods echo again with the shrill notes of his horn.

The sound was repeated at no great distance, and in a few minutes Ralph Percy, with those who had followed him, appeared on the scene.

"What sport, brother Hal? By my word, a right noble stag! But I have as fierce a wild boar as ever ranged Cheviot side to add to the tale of game."

"There is likely to be other sport. Scots are ranging these woods, backed up, as De Fenwicke says, by the powers of darkness. But what say you, Ralph, shall we defy the Evil one, and unharbour his kilted imps?"

"With all my heart; I long to strike a blow in right good earnest."

"Then forward, my merry men. De Fenwicke, do thou stay, if afraid."

"I afraid! By the holy saint of Lindisfarne, the man who calls me a coward shall eat his words from the point of my sword. I am not afraid, Lord Henry Percy, of any living soul, and did the fiend himself confront me face to face, in mortal shape, I would not show him my back."

"I did not doubt your courage, De Fenwicke. What I said was but in jest. But will you go forward with us, and hunt up these Scots, who seem to be under the special protection of this Witch of Wooler?"

"Aye, my lord. It shall never be said that a De Fenwicke *dared not*."

The brothers Percy rushed forward with all their followers in pursuit of the Scots; but no sign of them could be perceived save a few indistinct and scattered footprints on the soil. Which way they had gone, and how they had managed their retreat so noiselessly, were equal mysteries.

"Let us scatter; we may fall in with them then," exclaimed Ralph.

"No, no!" cried John de Fenwicke. "Keep together, if you value life and liberty. I should never be able to show myself before your noble father again did aught of evil befall either of you."

The counsel of the experienced warrior overcame the headstrong valour of the two youths, who little cared what happened so that they had a chance of a skirmish with the Scots. John De Fenwicke, however, assumed the command of the party, and under his directions, the search for the intruders was resumed, though they saw no more of the Douglas or his followers.

It was late at even when they returned to Warkworth Castle, bearing six fat deer and two boars as trophies of their success in the chase. The news that they had seen and met with Scots in the woods was hardly credited by the Earl of Northumberland or his knights, who could scarcely believe that any intruders would dare show themselves on the border hills after the chastisement they had so recently received.

"'Twas the young Douglas himself at their head, my lord," said De Fenwicke.

"And you, Henry Percy, shunned him," said the earl, turning with a severe look, towards his eldest son.

Up jumped the youth in an instant; but, so full of anger was he that the words refused to flow from his mouth, and the only sound heard was an inarticulate stammer.

Luckily John de Fenwicke came to his young lord's aid and gave a better account of the affair than Harry Hotspur himself was capable of doing.

"Not so, my lord. Our young gallant here at once defied the Douglas to the combat, and blows would have been exchanged had not the Witch of Wooler appeared and carried the young Scot away in her apron. The heir of Northumberland lacks not courage; though perchance, we may see his mettle put to the proof ere long."

"My son, forgive me that I doubted you," replied the earl. "I should have known you better, but you have been from me so long."

Henry Percy bowed his head and would have replied, but that an uncouth sound, in some respects resembling the bellowing of bulls, was heard outside the castle.

"To arms!" shouted the earl, springing from his seat upon the dais. "The Douglas dares attack us is our very halls. Up, up, my merry men, to the ramparts!"

At this instant the earl's conjecture that the sound had been made by a party of Scots blowing on cow's horns was confirmed.

A man came rushing into the great room, crying out—

"To arms, friends! The Scots have attacked the western gates!"

The earl looked towards his eldest son, and saw that the impetuous youth had, in that short space, donned the greater portion of a suit of light armour that had been made for him at a great price in Milan.

He then spoke.

"My son, yours be the task to drive back these invaders from our hearths. Retainers of the house of Percy, follow your young lord to the gates. Cry Esperance! Percy! and lay on like men! John de Fenwicke, keep your eye upon my boy, and give aid if the Scottish blows are likely to prove too weighty for his young head."

"Esperance! Percy!" was shouted from a hundred throats till the vaulted roof rang again with the echoing notes; then in swift time, but orderly array, the retainers streamed out of the hall, headed by the young heir of the house, and made their way towards the point of attack.

"Stay by me, Ralph," said the earl, to his youngest son; thou art too young yet to take part in these broils."

"May I not look from the loopholes

"THE LOVER'S VISIT."

of the ante-room, and see how it fares with my brother and his followers?"

"Go then; but not beyond the door-way."

There is scarcely any old proverb which has so much truth in it as that which tells us—

"None are so deaf as those who will not hear."

Ralph Percy was a living example of this, for no sooner did he catch the words "Go, then," than he darted off, resolutely closing his ears to the remainder of the sentence.

In the outer hall or ante-room were a quantity of swords, bucklers, helmets, and other offensive and defensive arms which had been brought from the stores when the first alarm was given.

Ralph Percy seized a light, but well-tempered blade, and a stout bull-hide buckler, bound with brass, with which he deemed himself sufficiently accoutred to take part in the combat which raged.

"Esperance! Percy!" he shouted, rushing to the western gate, and lending his youthful voice to swell the war-cry which sounded high above the clanging blows of the conflicting parties, and the agonised cries of those upon whom the keen sword, barbed shaft, or crushing axe had descended.

In the meantime, Harry Hotspur and his men maintained a desperate combat for the possession of the drawbridge before the western entrance of the castle.

The Scots had seized upon it ere it could be raised, by advancing along a slightly uneven ground from the north side of the building, and were thus close upon the gate ere seen by those who kept watch.

Conspicuous amongst the Scots was one tall warrior clad in black armour of the simplest kind.

His weapons were a broad claymore, and a Lochabar axe, which latter he wielded with great strength and dexterity; and, as though to add terror to the might and dexterity of his arm, his helmet, instead of being decked with a plume of feathers or horsehair, was surmounted by a human skull!

Harry Percy had marked the Knight of the Skull, and, impatient to win a glorious name for himself, he rushed forward to bar the progress of the Scottish champion, who raised his ponderous axe on high, thinking to crush the English youth with a single blow.

Down came the weapon; but Harry Percy saw the danger, and leaped aside nimbly, while the point of his sword found an entrance beneath the breastplate of the "Knight of the Skull," as the Scottish Champion was called by the English soldiers.

The wound, though severe enough to cause pain, was not sufficient to stay the warrior's arm, and a second blow would, in all probability, have numbered young Hotspur with the slain, had not his brother Ralph dealt the black knight a timely thrust in the arm, which caused him to drop his weapon; and before he could recover it, John de Fenwicke dealt him such a blow on the helm with the heavy iron mace he bore that the valiant Scot fell to the earth devoid of sense or motion.

This event quickly decided the fight, for the attacking party, being few in numbers, quickly withdrew when they saw their leader overthrown.

Hotspur was for following; but De Fenwicke advised to the contrary, for it was nearly dark, and the Scots might possibly have had a reserve force near at hand; so the young chief reluctantly gave the word to retire within the gateway, and then the drawbridge was raised.

Four prisoners besides the Knight of the Skull had been taken, and, with these trophies of success in their midst, the victors marched towards the great hall, where the earl sat, confident in the valour of his men-at-arms and the strength of his castle.

"My lord, we have vanquished the enemy, and taken five of their number prisoners," said the young leader, bowing low. "One of them seems, by his helm and spurs, to be a knight, but is too sorely wounded to give any account of himself."

"Remove his helmet, De Fenwicke," said the earl. "Let us see if we know the warrior who wears so strange a crest."

In a few seconds the features of the fallen knight were uncovered, and an exclamation of surprise echoed round the hall.

" Does this surprise you, gentlemen ? " continued the earl. " Surely, the war-like character of Sir Alexander Ramsay would lead him on to more daring deeds than an attack on our castle with a mere handful of men ; but pour a goblet of wine down his throat, and see if you cannot revive him in some measure."

The rich juice of the grape wrought the cure which it had been expected to do.

The knight sighed deeply, opened his eyes, and looked around.

" Where am I ? " he asked.

" In the hall of Warkworth Castle, though you came not hither of your own free will," replied John de Fenwicke.

The wounded knight made no reply for a few moments ; but his eyes wandered round the apartment till they rested upon the forms of Harry Percy and his brother, who stood side by side some little distance from where the earl sat.

He then advanced towards them, and spoke thus—

" To you, brave youths, I owe my defeat, and, therefore, to you do I yield myself a prisoner, rescue or no rescue, on the word and faith of a true knight."

" Be it so, Sir Knight," replied Henry Percy ; " but touching the ransom, we leave that to our noble father, the Earl of Northumberland, whose guest you must be for this one night at least."

" Sir Alexander," said the earl, " ere we speak more on that subject, your wounds must be attended to. Go, Witherington, attend the knight to a chamber, and call the surgeon to dress his hurts."

The wounded knight was then led from the hall ; the inferior prisoner after ad placed in the guard-room, and after additional sentinels had been placed on the ramparts, the castle once more assumed a quietude befitting the hour.

CHAPTER IV.

THE SCOTTISH PRISONER.

THE day following the attack on Warkworth Castle, Sir Alexander Ramsay remained in the chamber that had been prepared for him, being too ill in body as well as vexed in mind to show himself amongst the elated, victorious retainers and allies of the house of Percy.

The Scottish knight was a prisoner for the first time in his life, and, although everything was done to make him comfortable, the want of perfect liberty proved excessively irksome.

On the second day after his defeat, however, he felt in better health, and, therefore, in better spirits ; and about an hour before noon descended from his apartment to the court-yard of the castle where Henry and Ralph Percy were walking.

" A fair morning to you, Sir Alexander," said Hotspur, as he saw the prisoner approach. " Your wounds are healed, I trust ?"

" So far that I can walk without much pain, thanks to your skilful leech. Had I known you were so well prepared for attack, I should not have ventured my body nigh enough your walls to receive such injuries ; but the young Douglas misled me by saying that you, with half your garrison, had gone a hunting on the hill side.

"We certainly did hunt two days ago, but returned from the sport in time to welcome our unexpected guests! Had it not been for a certain hag, whom men call the Witch of Wooler, we might have tarried awhile to exchange words or blows with Douglas."

"Had it not been for his information I would rather have paid a visit to Alnwick, where your noble mother, and the Lady Katherine Mortimer, hold their court."

"The Lady Katherine Mortimer!"

"The same, fair sir."

"I knew not she was at Alnwick, or ——"

"You would have been there. Is it not so?"

Harry Percy made no reply, but coloured slightly. He had once seen the lady spoken of, and her beauty had made a deep impression on his young heart.

"If you knew not that the fair lady was at Alnwick, some thanks are due to me, I fancy, for bringing the information. Young Douglas, your rival——"

"Douglas my rival! What mean you?"

"From the colour which flushed your cheek a few moments ago I judged that you loved the lady, and the Douglas has vowed in my hearing to win her at all hazards."

"Then is the Douglas a perjured knight, for Lady Katherine Mortimer shall never be his. Henry Percy says so, and a Percy's word was never broken."

"Ah, well; little care I how the lady bestows her hand or her heart. *My* heart has little room to spare for other people's love affairs. But, my wounds begin to pain me anew; I will retire, and leave you to devise what schemes you will to win the fair Katherine."

With these words, Sir Alexander took his way towards the great hall, leaving Harry Percy in a very curious state of mind.

The English youth was just of that age when the heart begins to come under the influence of Love's emotions, and since the day he first saw Lady Katherine he had loved her with all the wild ardour of boyhood's first love.

Lady Katherine was about the same age as young Hotspur, fair to look upon, and heiress to great wealth, though the young lover little thought of the advantage that might be obtained from possession of her gold. The fond heart and the fair face were all that he desired, and he began to feel a tenfold hatred for the young Scot who seemed inclined to contest the prize with him.

"I have never told her my love; she thinks I care not for her, and perhaps will listen with pleasure to the fine speeches of this Highland gallant. Oh! what a dolt was I not to declare my suit."

There was no response to his words, uttered aloud, for this reason—there was no one at hand to hear them. Ralph had gone to see John de Fenwicke break in a young colt, and the other members of the household were variously engaged in different parts of the castle.

No one being at hand to give advice, the young lord was compelled to act according to his own inclinations, and, indeed, he was not sorry that no listeners had been at hand to overhear the conversation between himself and Sir Alexander Ramsay.

A project flashed through his brain which he at once resolved to perform; it was romantic in the highest degree, and, to a certain extent, dangerous.

To think and to act were almost the same with Harry Percy; indeed, so impetuous was he by nature, that there were times when he rushed on to action without first taking the trouble to think.

The name Hotspur was well bestowed upon him, for even in his youthful days he displayed much of that headstrong, hasty valour which, in after years, gained him so much renown—and a bloody death.

He ran after Sir Alexander Ramsay, and overtook the knight as he was ascending the stone steps leading to the hall.

"One word in your ear, Sir Knight," he said.

"A dozen if you will," replied the Scot. "But what have you to say to me?"

"Let that which has passed between us be kept a secret."

"Willingly. I have no inclination for more tattling."

"On your word?"

"On my knightly word. Does that satisfy you?"

"It does. Thanks, Sir Alexander."

To not a soul did the youth impart his scheme; but when he saw that the castle court-yard was free from idle loungers, he made his way to the stables, quickly saddled the brave steed that had borne him from London to Northumberland, and when he had thrown a mantle of plain stuff over his dress, led the animal through a narrow gate in the castle walls, where only one warder was usually posted.

"Now, good sentinel," said he, "listen to my words. No matter what questions you hear, tell no one that I have passed out of the castle until thy comrade comes to relieve thee."

"As to that, my lord, it is not likely that I shall be asked. By our Lady, I think it is a full week since the gates were opened."

"Here is a piece of silver to spend in ale at the tavern; but be silent in unbarring the postern."

The soldier nodded and opened the gate.

Harry Percy led his horse through, and then rode off rapidly towards a grove of trees which lay at the distance of about a quarter of a mile from the battlements, and where the road from the main entrance took an abrupt descent into a valley, along which the young rider would be able to pass unseen.

"Now, then, Bay Raby," he muttered, addressing his steed when he had gained the shelter, "bear me as swiftly as thou canst; for the road is long, and many dangers lie between us and our halting place."

CHAPTER V.

LADY KATHERINE MORTIMER.

HARRY PERCY began to fancy that all the dangers of his journey were over. The steed had done his work bravely, and it wanted at least an hour to sunset when the rider drew rein before the door of a little hostelry at the outskirts of a group of cottages, which then represented what is now an important town.

Host and groom came bustling out when they heard the horse stop, and made very reverential though clumsy bows to the youthful cavalier.

"Holy Virgin save you, fair sir!" exclaimed the landlord. "Will it please your honour to alight and taste the best my poor house affords?"

"Aye. Let me have a private apartment and a flask of good wine. And knave, groom, look well to my horse."

So saying, young Percy leaped to the ground, threw the reins to the ostler, and followed the landlord through the low doorway.

"Does your honour prefer the wines of France, or the more fiery liquor brought from Spain?"

"Nothing but good Canary for me, mine host. The light wines of France are but thin tipple for an English throat."

In a few seconds the innkeeper placed his liquor on the table, and then in obedience to the young cavalier's wish, quitted the apartment.

"Here I must remain until it is dusk" thought the young noble. "It would not be wise to be seen roaming round Alnwick Castle while the sun is yet up in the sky."

And being well aware that he had a full hour to wait, he threw himself at full length on a bench, and began to muse on various things; Lady Katherine

Mortimer being, however, the principal subject of his meditations.

But ere long his thoughts were interrupted.

Voices were heard in an adjoining room, and a name was mentioned by the talkers which at once arroused young Percy's attention to the keenest pitch.

"They say, father, that the young Earl Douglas has been seen on the border," said a soft, female voice. "Surely he will not be bold enough to attack the castle. We are in no danger of being killed or carried away as prisoners?"

"'Tis true, wench," replied a man's voice which Hotspur recognised as that of his host; "young Douglas has been in this neighbourhood; but he will not attack the castle with armed men, fire and sword, as you fancy. Ha! ha! I warrant me he'll summon the garrison to surrender in a very different style."

"What do you mean, father?"

"What do I mean? Ha! ha! ha! You must have grown marvellously deaf of late, wench; but that is a family failing, for your mother—Heaven rest her—was a little hard of hearing, thank the Virgin; but you must be deaf, wench, or you would have heard the grooms and serving-men from the castle talk of the beautiful Lady Mortimer, who is staying up there with the noble countess. Ha! ha! ha! No wonder young Douglas wanders about Alnwick woods like a Highland ghost, for they say the young lady—she's not so old as you—is beautiful enough to tempt a saint."

"And does Douglas love her?"

"Ha, ha, ha! What in the Virgin's name, do you know of love? I warrant me, the young rascal, Hugh Witherington, the page, has stuffed thy silly head with a lot of nonsense about love and troubadours. But they do say that the young Scottish earl is most often seen roaming about the south-east tower where the lady has her apartments. And now ask me no more questions, for I must away to see that Jack Groom has properly tendered the cavalier's horse."

There was a moment's pause, and then the voice of the innkeeper's daughter was again heard.

"Father! do you think he can be the young Douglas?"

"No, silly wench; no."

Then the landlord's heavy step sounded as he left the room, and for a short space of time there was silence.

But ere long there arose, instead of the sound of voices, the sweet notes of a guitar, stealing in soft, gentle, plaintive cadence upon the young noble.

The strings were touched by no unpractised hand, though it seemed as if the musician's fingers wandered at random over the instrument in search of notes whose sweet sounds had hitherto laid dormant and undeveloped.

Henry Percy leaped to his feet, and cried out in a loud voice.

"Host! Come hither, host, I say."

The music abruptly ceased, and in a few moments a young girl, about sixteen years of age, entered the room.

"My father is not in the house, noble sir. What is your good pleasure?"

"I would have asked him whose hand it was produced the sounds of music I heard, but I doubt not I see the musician before me."

The girl cast her eyes to the ground.

"And now, my fair damsel, I have a favour to ask."

"Name it, gallant sir."

"I would beg the loan of your guitar for an hour or two."

The girl smiled, and asked,

"For what purpose, noble sir?"

"Doubtless you have heard of the fair lady who at present resides in Alnwick Castle. I love her, and would serenade her with a love ditty."

The innkeeper's daughter could not refrain from lauging at the youth's confessions.

"I will lend it you most willingly, gallant sir," she replied. "But," she added, in lower and more serious tones, "take heed that you are not seen by the sentinels."

"But keep all knowledge of this from your father."

"I will, noble Scot. Your life would be in danger did any of our people know of your presence here."

"Noble Scot. What mean you?"

"Are you not the young Earl ? Douglas "

"I am not. My name is Henry Percy."

The girl stared, and then made a low curtsey, as she said,

"Oh! forgive me, my lord."

"Not a word. But the guitar, quick."

The instrument was brought, and placing it under his mantle, Hotspur leaped through the open window.

In the south-east tower of Alnwick Castle was a pleasant apartment. At the window sat a fair girl, dressed in a robe of pale blue silk, trimmed with ermine, gazing pensively at the waving trees that grew almost up to the ramparts.

This was the Lady Katherine Mortimer, daughter of a powerful northern baron, and by him intended to be the bride of the young Douglas.

The lady had seen Harry Percy some two years previously, when he was a mere boy, and had thought him one of the most dashing, daring lads she had ever met ; but at the present time the young Scot was uppermost in her thoughts, for Douglas had carried his courtship to such a pitch as to meet her in the walks and rides she took round about the castle.

As Lady Katherine was wondering when she should next meet her Scottish lover, her ears were greeted with the sound of a guitar, and in another moment a clear, but evidently unpractised voice, singing a ballad which in that day was very popular.

"It must be Douglas," thought Katherine. Then she looked, and beneath a tree saw a figure, evidently that of the musician.

"I dare not descend to the lawn at this hour, and if I answer him I shall be overheard."

Then her eye caught sight of a rope-ladder, that had recently been used for repairs on the battlements, before her window.

"There can surely be no harm in his meeting me here—I cannot descend this ladder."

A moment she hesitated, then threw the end of the ladder ropes over. Her white handkerchief was waved in the air as a signal.

The mantled figure rushed forward, when Lady Katherine perceived it was not the face of young Douglas, but a noble-looking youth whose features she could not recal to mind.

"Stay, gallant sir, the signal was not for you," she said, in a low, though distinct, tones.

"For whom, then ?" asked Hotspur in a hasty manner.

"For one whom I expected. Ah! I see him yonder coming out of the wood —fly, fly, for heaven's sake."

Percy turned his head to see if he could discover this cause for alarm, and saw a male figure emerging from the shadow of the trees.

The youthful form, the jewelled bonnet and the tartan dress, all told him that it was his foe, the young Earl Douglas.

A moment he hesitated, then said—

"Fair lady, yon Scot is my mortal foe ; he dares cross my path, and must abide the conquences."

So saying he withdrew his foot from the ladder and rushed to meet the Scot, who came forward to the contest.

But both the foemen stopped, as a voice upon the castle ramparts shouted.

"Who goes there ? Speak, or I shoot."

CHAPTER VI.

THE FLIGHT AND THE CAPTURE.

A Sentinel's challenge caused both Douglas and Percy to halt for an instant. Hotspur had no particular wish to be taken prisoner in the grounds of his own father's castle, or to be discovered lurking about the neighbourhood—while the young Scot at once perceived that it would be folly to continue his onward course now that he had been observed.

Harry Percy was the first to regain his presence of mind—perhaps because he was in least danger. He returned his sword to its scabbard, and hurried forward to meet young Douglas; being quite as resolved to save the Scot from harm as he had been before to kill him.

"Douglas!" he cried, our quarrel cannot be decided now ; away with you to a place of safety—your life is in danger."

The Scottish youth glanced towards the castle, from which lights and armed men were seen to issue, and then with a sigh replied,

"Percy—foeman—I trust thee. But our quarrel ends not thus!"

"To-morrow—at sunrise, if you will—let the truce expire. But, for to-night, a place of shelter and security is required. Come this way."

Douglas followed Hotspur as readily and unhesitatingly as though they had been sworn friends instead of hereditary foes ; but the Scot knew how strictly the laws of honour and chivalry would judge any attempt at treachery or foul play on the part of his guide.

They had not moved three paces together when again the stern voice of the sentinel was heard—"Stand, or I shoot!" but as they thought proper to disobey the injunction, the archer kept his word, and discharged an arrow, which, after cutting one feather from Harry Hotspur's plume, buried itself in the trunk of a tree, not two feet from the Douglas.

"Had Tim of Tylmouth shot that shaft one us would have felt its barb," said Percy.

"And who is Tim of Tylmouth, good Percy ? "

"An English archer, who, at three hundred paces, never missed his mark. Let us hasten into the thicket ere he sends a second arrow."

So saying, they hurried forward with such rapidity that in a few seconds they were free from all immediate danger.

The wood began to grow more dense in its growth, and Douglas began to fear that his young guide had mistaken the path—a thing which would not have been very surprising, as the thick branches overhead completely shut out all light.

"Whither dost lead me, Percy ? " he asked, when some distance had been traversed in silence.

"To the habitation of a holy friar who dwells in these rocky glens ; in his cell you may rest in safety. But hark ! By Heaven, we have no time to lose ! Do you not hear the bay of dogs ? They have set the bloodhounds on our track ! "

"I hear them. Come show me the cell of this holy man ; and to-morrow—"

"We will measure swords."

Without another word the two youths hurried forward through the greenwood, while each moment the deep-toned voices of the bloodhounds sounded more distinctly on their ears. At length young Percy paused at the top of a cliff, saying, in melancholy tones—

"I have wandered slightly from the path ; there should have been a flight of rude steps here, in the face of the cliff leading down to the banks of the river Aln. We must retrace our steps."

"To do so would be to rush into the hands of our pursuers, it seems," replied

Douglas. "Is there no other means of escape?"

"None—unless you like to risk a leap of twenty-five feet, with the certainty of alighting on the sharp-pointed rocks at the bottom of this glen."

"And if I do so, where shall I find this hermitage — this abode of the friar?"

"His cell lies about a quarter of a mile to the right—on the opposite side of the stream you may hear pouring along its rocky course below."

Young Douglas peered over the precipice ; but all was darkness, save where in one or two places the moonbeams found their way through the overhanging foliage, and cast a gleam of light upon the bosom of the rocky stream.

"Twenty-five feet you say?"

"Aye, and rugged rocks to light upon."

"Then we can yet manage to evade the bloodhounds. See ; I have a rope which will reach the bottom ; we can descend by it."

As he spoke, young Douglas drew from beneath his doublet a coil of cord which he had intended should aid him in ascending the battlements of Alnwick Castle, and fastening one end of it, by means of a hook, to the root of a tree, allowed the other to drop over the precipice. But whether it reached the bottom or not was more than either of the lads knew.

"Over with you—quick!" cried Percy. "But stay ; there is danger beneath ; let me make the attempt."

"A Douglas fears not danger," replied the young Scot, as he grasped the cord between his hands and slid over the precipice.

Hotspur gazed anxiously as he saw his foe disappear into the darksome abyss ; but the bottom of the cliff was beyond the reach of his eye, and in another moment his attention was called to a danger which threatened himself.

One of the bloodhounds came rushing furiously through the wood, and, with a fierce growl, sprang upon the young noble.

"Holy St. Cuthbert be my aid ;" exclaimed Hotspur, as he saw the hound leap, and at the same time he jumped

aside or his throat would have been torn by the fierce dog.

The growl of the anger changed into a yell of dismay as the animal, having missed its victim, and unable to save itself, fell heavily over the precipice and was heard to beat against the rocks beneath.

"Thank heaven! Art safe, Douglas?"

"Safe at the end of the rope ; but I can find no resting place for my foot."

"Thou art safe, at all events, master jackanapes," cried a third voice, and at the same instant a stalwart man-at-arms sprang forward and seized young Percy by the shoulder.

"Unhand, me, knave! What means this insolence?"

"Insolence, forsooth! Nay, good master, your insolence in disturbing the castle must be accounted for before our noble lady, the countess. Ho! Edward, secure this other springall at the end of the rope."

A second man then came forward, and after glancing a moment at the cord which sustained Douglas, shouted,—

"Up, there! up, I say, quickly ; for by the rood, an' I have to drag thee up, thy back shall feel the end of the rope."

"Sirrah knave! how dare you use such language to one of noble blood?" cried Hotspur. "The young Earl Douglas is at the end of that cord!"

"Ha! sayest thou so? Then, by the mass, I will rid Northumberland of the pestilent Scot!" exclaimed the soldier, and ere Percy or his captor could raise a hand to prevent him, had cut the cord with the dagger.

A half-smothered cry was heard as the rope parted, and then, for a moment, all was silent.

The man who had done this act of wanton barbarity broke out into a loud laugh.

"Rest you, merrily, fair Scot. An' your bones be not broken you owe me some thanks for saving you time and trouble in reaching the end of your journey ; though it would have been better had you thought of the old proverb, which says—' Look before you leap.' "

"Dastard!" exclaimed the enraged

Hotspur, dealing the fellow a blow on the face which sent him to the earth.

"Fool!" cried he who had captured Harry Percy, giving the fallen one a kick which quickly raised him to his feet again. "Fool, I say, how are we to catch the runaway now thou hast cut the rope?"

"An' I be a fool you may catch him yourself. But he's safe enough; we shall find so much as the wolves, foxes and ravens spare of him in the morning. So let us return to the castle."

"He is safe enough beyond our reach," said he who had first spoken. "But who are you, fair sir, who have led us this weary dance through the woods?"

I am called Henry Percy, and am the son of your noble mistress, the countess."

"By the mass, 'tis so! I thought the voice seemed familiar to my ears."

So saying, the man uncovered his head and made a low bow, in which he was imitated by his companion who had felt the force of young Percy's fist. By this time, two other men had arrived on the spot, and a word from the leader soon made them aware that the prisoner was none other than the young lord.

"Pardon, my lord, if I did my duty somewhat roughly; but Captain Witherington will be obeyed."

"You need not ask pardon for doing your duty; but the Saint of Lindisfarne, yon knave whose face hath hurt my hand shall suffer, if any harm have happened to the young Earl Douglas. Can you not procure lights and see if he has escaped or not?"

The last comers had torches in their hands, and these were soon burning brightly. By their light the whole party gazed down into the ravine; but nothing was to be seen save the body of the bloodhound, which remained where it had fallen among the rocks. They even threw one of the torches down in order the better to make certain; but not a trace of the Douglas could they see.

"My lord," said the man-at-arms, "my orders were to kill or make prisoners the persons seen by the sentinel on the south tower; you will accompany us to the castle, therefore, I doubt not, in order that all may be explained."

"Right willingly. But how are you called, friend—what is your name?"

"I am called Anthony Risingham, my lord."

"Then Anthony, lead on by the shortest way, for I am weary; and when we reach the castle send down to the hostelrie for my steed."

The man bowed, and, after marshalling his comrades in order, gave the word to march homewards. To Percy the journey seemed twice the length it had appeared when he traversed the same path with his young foeman; but at length the party reached the postern-gate of the castle, where they found a strong body of men-at-arms drawn up in military array to receive them.

CHAPTER VII.

THE ABDUCTION.

THE Countess of Northumberland was seated in a chair of carved oak at the upper end of the great dining-hall of Alnwick Castle. The room much resembled that at Warkworth already described. There was the same kind of antique, rude furniture, the same quantity of mail-clad warriors standing upon the rush-strewn floor.

In one respect it differed, for on either side of the countess a number of female attendants were grouped, and their presence lighted the otherwise sombre appearance of the apartment.

When Anthony Risingham and Harry Hotspur with their followers entered, the noble lady broke off the conversation in which she was engaged, and addressed the retainer.

"So, good Anthony, you have captured

the young masquer whose songs disturbed us? Holy Mary! who have we here?" she continued, as her eyes fell upon the youth's face. "Our son!"

"Your son, dearest and noblest mother," said Hotspur, stepping forward and dropping on one knee before her.

"But our good captain of the guard, Hugh de Witherington, swore there were two. Where is the other—and who is he?"

Harry Percy coloured slightly.

"Speak out, boy, who was your companion, and where is he hidden?"

"My companion was the young Earl Douglas; but where he now is I know not."

"Douglas! You with a Douglas and did not sheath your sword in his bosom?"

"That would I have done had not the sentinel interrupted us as we were about to cross weapons."

The countess smiled in a sarcastic manner, as though she doubted the truth of her son's words. The enmity she bore the whole Scottish nation was deep and undying; and when we consider that more than once the bold northern warriors had ravaged the whole country with fire and sword, even to the very castle gates, we cannot wonder at her hatred.

"And if you would have killed him why conceal or aid him to escape?"

"That I may kill him in the morning. Twice he has defied me; but by the holy rood it is the last time! One of us shall fall ere the sun sets to-morrow."

"Pardon me, noble lady," said a grey-haired old warrior, whose body was covered with steel from head to foot; "pardon me; but Dickson Draw-the-Bow, the sentinel, affirmed that he saw naked swords in the hands of both the youths, and at first thought that it was two of your ladyship's pages going to settle some dispute by moonlight. It may be that, as the young lord says, he intended to kill the Scot."

"But what did the young Douglas roaming around our castle at night, and alone?"

"That I know not madam," replied old Witherington, the warrior who had before spoken.

"Can you explain this, Henry?"

"I think I can, noble mother: but I would say what I think privately."

The countess made a motion with her hand, and both soldiers and females drew back half-a-dozen paces.

Young Percy then told his mother how he had heard that Lady Katherine Mortimer was resident in the castle, and had resolved to win her affection, but found he had a rival in the person of young Douglas.

"I pledged my word for his safety to-night," he added, by way of conclusion; "but to-morrow he shall answer to me for his presumption, I may have acted in a foolish manner, but I am neither coward nor traitor, therefore do I hope dearest mother, that my fault may be forgiven."

"You did foolishly, but no dishonour taints your name, Henry, therefore you are forgiven. Janet," she continued, addressing one of her women, "go tell the Lady Katherine Mortimer we wish she would grace the hall with her presence. Methinks she must feel melancholy with no companions save the moon, or the bats and owls of the old tower."

Ere the woman could leave the hall on her errand another female came rushing in, and fell upon her knees before the countess in a wild and distracted manner.

"Oh! your ladyship! Oh! holy virgin! Oh! mercy on us!" she exclaimed, and then burst into a torrent of tears.

"What ails you, silly girl? Have you seen a spirit?"

"No, your lordship. Holy saints above preserve us! Oh, there's nothing but wickedness in this world!"

"What new act of wickedness have you to relate?"

"The Lady Katherine Mortimer is gone!"

"Gone! Whither and with whom? Answer, woman, quickly!" exclaimed Harry Percy.

"Carried off by a thousand Scots in armour, who broke into her chamber ten minutes ago."

"ONE OF THE BLOODHOUNDS, WITH A FIERCE GROWL, SPRANG ON THE YOUNG NOBLE."

At that moment a commotion outside announced that the guard of the castle had found some new cause for alarm, for the hoarse voices of the sentinels were heard challenging, and the clatter of mailed feet sounded upon the courtyard pavement.

A dozen swords glided from their sheaths, and the soldiers who thronged the hall ran hastily out to take part in the fray.

Harry Hotspur was among the first to spring to action, but a word from his mother recalled him.

"Stay, Henry."

"But, dear mother, they have carried off the lady——"

"Stay a moment; and you, good Hugh de Witherington."

The old captain bowed respectfully, and advanced a few steps nearer the oak chair.

"The damsel's tale was told in so wild a manner as to be incomprehensible, except that we understand our fair guest has been carried away. Speak out, girl, and tell us all you know."

"May it please your ladyship, the Lady Mortimer was sitting in her chamber with her back to the window, and I was doing my work at the other end of the room. I heard a noise which made me turn my head, and I saw the lady struggling with two men, who must have been Scots, while another stood hard by the window. As soon as they saw me the one by the window came and brandished his sword over my head, swearing most horribly, by all the saints, he would kill me if I made any noise."

"But the lady—how is it that she made no outcry? Did she go willingly?" asked the countess.

"No, my lady, she struggled with them; but they had wrapped a thick cloak round her head, so that she could not cry out. I was so frightened at the man with the sword that I fainted, and when I recovered they were gone."

"What manner of men were these? Did you see their faces?" asked Hotspur.

"No, my lord; their faces were hidden."

"Here be three Scots only. What of the nine hundred and ninety-seven who go to make up the thousand?" muttered Witherington.

"Hugh de Witherington, the lady must be recovered from the hands of these bold, audacious robbers. To you I give charge, while I myself will command in the castle during your absence; women ere now have gained great victories."

"Trust me, madam, we'll give a good account of these rascals," replied the warrior.

"And I, noble mother, shall I be compelled to remain here while others are giving and taking blows?" asked Percy.

"Go, boy, go, if thou art so impatient; but be obedient to the command of Hugh de Witherington. Look to him well, good Hugh, and put a curb upon his hasty temper."

"Trust me, noble madam. He shall have fighting enough, but it must be only when I give the word to strike."

The old soldier then made a low bow and left the hall, followed by the impatient Hotspur.

In the courtyard all was bustle and commotion; men were seen, some armed, some half dressed, some few on horseback, but most on foot. Torches were waving, horses prancing, and confusion reigned supreme. The voice and presence of De Witherington soon restored a little order and discipline.

"Arm yourselves, and to saddle quickly!" he cried. "Let the drawbridge be raised. Anthony Risingham, go bring me hither the rogue sentinels who have been sleeping at their posts. Thou knave, go ring the alarm bell to rouse the sleepers and skulkers from their dens."

The loud clang of the bell was soon heard, and in such deafening style that the old captain soon wished he had not given the order to ring it.

Then came Risingham with two sentinels, who, from their stations, should have seen and given notice of the approach of those who had carried off the lady.

"How now, rascals, what means this negligence? By the mass, an ye keep not better watch, your shoulders shall taste the stirrup leathers! Whence came these foul robbers and whither went they?"

"I know not, good sir; I saw nothing till they were going away," replied one.

"Nor I," said the other.

"There were two of ye ; could you not have sent two cloth-yard shafts through their Scottish jerkins ?"

" Aye, but we feared we might harm the lady."

" And which way went they ?"

" They mounted on horseback when they reached the edge of the wood, and rode off towards the north-west."

Witherington stood a moment in silent thought, and then dismissed the archers with a wave of his hand.

Percy called loudly for his steed, and while it was being saddled walked up and down the courtyard in a most impatient state of mind.

" Douglas, if thou hast done this foul deed, in every camp, castle, and court of Europe I will proclaim thee a false, treacherous and felon knight," he muttered. " Yet, who else can it be ? We are at peace with our neighbours of England, and the little chiefs on the border know our power to punish too well to give such provocation. Douglas it must be, or his minions ; but, by the mass, I swear, that should I meet him face to face, Scotland shall, from that hour, lack one more gentleman of high birth !"

" To horse, to horse, there !" shouted old Witherington. " What ho! ye laggards, brace on your breastplates, set your steel caps firmly on your heads, and mount. Sirrah sentinel, come ride by me ; thou must act as guide and point out the way these Scottish thieves took in returning to their rocky dens."

By dint of hard swearing, the old trooper managed to marshal his men in order, forty in all—but the best men of Northumberland, and in his opinion a fair match for any three score of Scots. Torches were flaring brightly, for the moon had passed behind a cloud. The gates were thrown open, and the band passed out in pursuit of the abductors.

CHAPTER VIII.

SEEKING HIDDEN TREASURES.

WHILE Witherington and his men are following the lady and her captors, let us use the fictionist's privilege of annihilating time and space, and return once more to Bull-and-Mouth Street, London, where we first met the brothers, Harry and Ralph Percy.

The worthy chaplain and tutor was sitting in his room, a few days after the abrupt departure of his pupils, when an unusual noise at the gateway informed him that some visitor had arrived.

The holy father grieved for a moment at being disturbed in his studies, which at that moment happened to be how to compound a savoury stew which should excel anything the cook of the establishment had ever concocted.

Spurs rattled, and armour clanked, as a mailed man ascended the staircase, and the good friar was again compelled to lay down his imaginary spoon, and let the ideal soup remain in an unfinished condition.

Then came a knock at the door of his chamber, not a cheerful tap, such as might be given by a serving-man come to call him to dinner, but an imperious summons from the dagger-hilt of a man-at-arms, who would hear of no delay.

" Open, holy father, open, I say, and let a poor sinner into this owl's nest of yours."

" It is not Fenwicke ; who, in Heaven's name, can it be ?" muttered the priest.

The knock was loudly repeated.

" Put up thy beads, holy father, and

welcome a sinful, warfaring man into thy cell."

"Enter, my son, enter, though I know not what a man of war would have with a peaceful priest. This is no time or place for confession, save in the case of a man on the point of death; but enter, and peace be with you."

The stranger entered, and after making a bow to the monk, seated himself in a very comfortable chair, from which the holy man had just risen.

"You know me not, good father, but you will find my name and business duly set forth in this scroll, the contents of which I would have mastered if I could. But you monks and priests do not let poor soldiers such as myself share the wisdom you possess."

So saying he tossed a small packet to the chaplain, who forthwith seated himself upon a wooden stool that had in former times been used by one of his pupils.

"Too much wisdom is not good, my son; it leads to heresy and other deadly sins."

And the monk gave a loud groan, not at the thought that even then new doctrines were undermining his hurch, but in sorrow at being compelled to place his plump body on so hard a seat.

While he was opening his letter and slowly reading its contents, the soldier amused himself by picking his teeth with the point of his dagger, being apparently quite unconscious of the fact that he had put the monk to considerable bodily torture by depriving him of his easy chair.

"When saw you the writer of this?" asked the churchman, looking up suddenly.

"What, Sir——"

"Hush! mention no names. The walls may have ears for aught we know. I mean the man who gave you this for me."

"Two days ago, good father. But if these walls have ears, as you say, by the rood, I should like to crop them with my dagger."

"Never swagger or boast in the lion's den, my son; if the lion himself be out the jackals will guard his house."

The soldier struck his dagger into its sheath in an angry manner, and was silent while the monk finished reading his letter.

"Ha, well saith the psalmist that the mighty shall be brought low and the poor lifted up. Now we have our enemies on the hip. Where is the writer of this?"

"He must be in Northumberland or near it by this time. He was riding as fast as spurs could urge his horse forward."

"Hath he seen the young Douglas?"

"No."

"What folly is this? He should meet the Scot fairly and parley with him."

"That he vows by all the saints he will never do."

"And wherefore?"

"I know not more than this, father— there is some fair lady whom they both love, and so they are not so good friends as they should be for the success of our enterprise."

"I know the young lady you speak of, but she can soon be removed from our path. But tell me, good son, have you no idea of the contents of this letter?"

"None, save that I was to answer all questions asked, give advice if required, and receive at your hands certain articles he names within the scroll."

The monk nodded, and then sat in perfect quietness for a short time, evidently revolving some scheme in his bald pate.

The man in armour watched him in a listless manner, as though such chamber conferences were not to his taste, and he would rather perform his part of the business in an open field, with an adversary before him whom he could plainly see.

"I must have those keys," said the priest, at length, speaking more to himself than his companion.

"What keys?"

"A bunch that hangs at the girdle of our good house-steward. They are necessary to our project."

"I will go ask him, father, if you bid me."

"And be laughed at for thy pains."

"Then will I plunge my dagger into his throat, and take them without his consent."

"And be hanged from the battlements for thy trouble. No, no, good Archie, they must be obtained by a stratagem. What is the hour?"

"It wants not more than two hours of sunset, father."

"Then listen to me," and he dropped his voice to a whisper. "Go thou to the kitchen, and thou wilt see this same house-steward: greet him from me, and say that I desire thy throat should be washed out with good ale and wine ; ply him with the flagon—for he loves good liquor, and when a cup or two hath passed into his stomach, find a means to pour two or three drops of the fluid contained in this phial into his drink. In a few minutes he will sleep so soundly that you may even take away his hose, an you will, without awakening him. But harm him not, for he is a good man and loveth good liquor."

Archie, as Father Abel called the soldier, took up the phial and gazed at it curiously.

"I have cut many a throat," he said, "but never yet poisoned a man's drink."

"It will not harm him if you put no more than I said. Go, my son."

The soldier departed, and the priest, when he had once more ensconced himself in his easy chair, began to write.

For nearly an hour he continued to wield the pen, and only ceased when his former companion returned.

"See," cried he called Archie, "I have the keys, and the foolish fat rogue lies on a bench snoring like a drove of fat hogs in clean straw."

"Silence, madcap. The ale hath somewhat affected thy own brain, I fancy. If thou canst walk without noise, follow me ; if not, remain."

"I'll go, father, for I am anxious to see what nook or corner of this old house you are going to explore with all that rusty iron."

He then took off his spurs, and laid aside one or two of the loose portions of his armour, retaining his dagger in his belt, and carrying his sheathed sword in his hand.

Half down the staircase, they came to a little arched door, which appeared to be very seldom used, as was, indeed the fact.

Father Abel, however, soon found a key that fitted the lock, though it was more than his fat fingers could do to turn it.

Archie, however, performed that task, and the door flew open.

Before the worthy pair was a long passage with a flight of stone steps at the extreme end guarded by an iron grating.

This difficulty too was overcome by one of the keys, and turning to the right another door appeared.

For some time there was a difficulty in making either of the keys move the rusty bolt that secured the door, and the impatient soldier suggested breaking through it by sheer force.

"You know not the strength of this door, my son," answered the priest. "The oak of which it is composed is two inches in thickness and well bound together with plates and panels of iron. See, here is the key, the last one that we shall have to use."

Archie snatched it from Father Abel's hand, and in a very short space of time opened the door, which led to a small room looking out upon the street.

"Six times before have I endeavoured to penetrate to this apartment, and each time have I been foiled. Now the Virgin hath given me success."

With these words the monk crossed himself and then looked curiously round.

The furniture of the room seemed more fitted for a scrivener's office than a nobleman's private apartment.

There were tables, wooden seats, inkhorns, pens, and slips of parchment scattered about in profusion, but no arms or anything to denote that the lordly owner of the house was a great warrior.

In one corner of the room was a strongly made iron-bound box.

No sooner did the priest perceive this than he pointed to it with a smile, saying—

"What we seek must be there."

CHAPTER IX.

THE IVORY TABLET.

OUR readers have already been informed that Lady Katherine Mortimer was taken from her chamber and carried away, and that young Percy followed hard behind with a goodly band of retainers.

While the youth remains in saddle let us recount the various misfortunes that befell the lady of whom he is in search.

Lady Katherine gazed anxiously from her window when she saw her rival lovers hasten towards each other, racking her brain to devise some means of preventing the conflict which seemed inevitable.

She heard the sentinel's challenge, saw the youths pause for a moment and then make towards the wood, heard the twang of the archer's bow on the battlements, and the noise made by the guard turning out in pursuit of the fugitives.

The fair one was in a state of mind much more easy to imagine than to depict with the pen.

The gallantry and devotedness of young Douglas had made some impression on her soft heart, while the glimpses she had caught of Hotspur's handsome face and figure had recalled some portion of the affection she had felt for him long before seeing the Scot.

Her heart being thus divided by love was agitated by fear that one or both of them would fall in the combat which seemed certain to take place.

Then she dreaded lest it should be known she had encouraged the Scottish noble's visits, and so incur the anger of the stern countess, who certainly seemed better fitted to wield warrior's sword than housewife's needle.

"Heaven grant no blood may be spilled by the hot-headed youths. How could I be so imprudent? Holy Virgin! should the countess hear of this I shall feel the sharpness of her tongue."

Then again she looked out.

But both the young warriors had disappeared.

"Ah, me!" she sighed. "I fear trouble is at hand. The old fortune-teller said as much, and even now the moon goes behind a cloud, leaving the earth in a darkness emblematical of my fate."

Was it the wind that caused that low murmuring rustle amongst the trees and bushes, or was it the near approach of her unseen troubles?

Lady Katherine knew not.

But the sound disturbed—disquieted her.

She touched a silver hand-bell, and a female servant entered.

"Light the taper, Martha," said Lady Katherine, "and then when the room is set in order sit by me for a short time, I am lonely to-night."

"Ah, my lady, I'll warrant there is a handsome young knight not far off who would give the world to be your ladyship's companion," replied the woman.

"Peace! peace!" exclaimed the lady. "Do your office, and say no more of knights or gallants."

The woman lighted a taper, and then turned her head to put away sundry ornaments that lay scattered about.

Lady Katherine still sat with her eyes towards the wood, fancying in her mind that there Percy and Douglas were fighting furiously.

Suddenly a steel cap rose above the level of the window, quickly followed by the armed body of a man, who entered the chamber with rapid but noiseless motion.

Two others followed in swift succession.

"Holy saints!" exclaimed she, as they stood before her. "What means this intrusion?"

"Hush! not a word," said the leader, in a stern low voice, drawing his dagger as he spoke. "Secure that serving woman," he added, turning to his follower. " See that not a word escapes her lips."

The man with fearful frowns and gestures, brandished his sword over the poor frightened servant's head, threatening instant death if she ventured to make the slightest sound.

But violence was not needed, for the first sight of the glittering weapon caused her to fall upon the floor in a swoon.

The principal ruffian who wore on his heels the gilt spurs of knighthood, then turned his attention to Lady Katherine.

" Fair lady, you must come with us. If you resist, force will be employed, so you had better descend the rope ladder quietly."

" False, felon knight, know you where you are ?"

" Aye, right well, and that if we are not quick a whole swarm of Northumbrian archers will be buzzing around us. So, fair lady, by your leave——"

As he spoke the knight wrapped a thick mantle round her face, and lifting her in his arms, descended the ladder followed by his two men.

The serving woman recovered from her swoon just in time to see the last man leave the chamber.

And then after collecting her scattered senses ran off to give the alarm.

The knight and his companions took it in turns to carry Lady Katherine until they emerged from the shadow of the huge building and came out into the full view of the sentinels.

Then the leader himself once more caught her up, and disregarding the challenges of the archers on the battlements, hurried forward to reach a spot on the outskirts of the wood where his horses were concealed.

On reaching that spot half-a-dozen other armed men were seen, all mounted, and holding four spare horses—those of the knight and his two immediate followers, as well as one harnessed for a lady, Lady Katherine Mortimer.

Not a word was said until the whole party had mounted and proceeded some little distance when the knight spoke—

" Come hither, knave," said he, beckoning one of his grooms.

The man rode nearly up to his master's side and made a low bow.

Lead the lady's horse while I prepare for a skirmish with those who may pursue us. Pardon my rudeness, fair lady, in thus leaving you to a groom," he continued, removing the mantle from Lady Katherine's face, " but you are far too precious a treasure to be surrendered when once gained without trying the force of arms."

" And should the pursuers overtake you," replied she, " they will hew the spurs from your heels and hang you to the highest oak in this wood."

The knight laughed a discordant laugh as he pulled on his gauntlets and took his lance from his squire.

" Little care I for Earl Percy's rage now I have gained the shelter of these green woods."

" The vengeance of Earl Douglas may overtake you beyond the border and prove as terrible as that of Percy."

The knight made no immediate reply to this, but it was evident from the manner in which his hand trembled that Lady Katherine's words had made some impression on his mind.

After a little while, however, he said—

" And suppose I should have the authority and warrant of Douglas for what I have done ? Why, then, should I fear ? But no more of this. Ask no questions, lady, or I shall be compelled to stop your tongue in a somewhat rude manner."

The knight then rode on a few paces before the rest of the party, leaving Lady Katherine to the society of grooms and soldiers.

Doubtless he imagined that would be the best way to keep his fair prisoner silent, for a lady of such high rank could scarcely be expected to hold conversation with the low-born men who conducted her steed.

The expedient answered, and the journey was continued in silence though the fair prisoner frequently looked back over her shoulder to catch a sight or sound of those who should be speeding to her assistance.

The road became steep and rugged, in fact it scarcely deserved the name of a road, being merely a path made by the flocks of the mountain shepherds.

The soil was bare, though huge rocks and stones were plentiful enough ; the herbage was coarse and scanty.

At length the panting horses after toiling up a steep ascent stood upon the topmost ridge of the Cheviot Hills, and after a moment's breathing space began to descend on the Scottish side.

The strange knight turned to Lady Katherine, and in a triumphant tone exclaimed—

"If the Percy would rescue his fair guest he must now come at the head of an army. We are on Scottish soil, and every shepherd on these slopes would take up arms to resist the invader."

"The Earl Douglas has been known to punish ere now. And methinks the men of Roxburgh have seen English archers at their gates in days gone by when a Percy has ravaged their fields and burned their towns."

"I much doubt the Northumbrian's inclination to visit the good town of Roxburgh now, so thither will we take our way. The walls have been repaired and strengthened since Percy's last visit."

Lady Katherine once more became perfectly silent, and with good reason.

She now knew whither her captors were leading her.

And the thought that most occupied her mind was how to convey that knowledge to her English friends.

Her hand instinctively travelled to the pocket of her dress, and there she found the means—her ivory tablets.

On one of these, with a sharp-pointed bodkin for pen, she scratched her name and the word Roxburgh, then dropped it on the pathway they were traversing.

The action was not noticed.

The ivory tablet lay on the earth, glittering in the cold moonbeams.

And when a few hundred yards more of the journey had been accomplished Lady Katherine repeated the stratagem.

CHAPTER X.

THE CRUCIFIX.

THE pursuing party, at the head of which rode Witherington and Harry Percy, had not got very far from the towers of Alnwick, when Hotspur abruptly, and without word of explanation, rode off on a path which skirted the banks of the River Aln.

"What, ho, my lord, whither away at such speed?" cried Witherington.

The young noble answered not, save by urging his horse on at full speed.

"The enemy have gone this way, you have taken the wrong path, Sir Hotspur," shouted the old soldier.

No reply came, and in another second the headstrong youth was out of sight.

"A wild youngster," muttered old Witherington. "I wonder on what mad errand he is gone now? and," he added, after a moment's pause, "how long will he be gone?"

These weighty questions the old soldier was not able to solve, so he halted the troop to await the return of the headstrong Percy.

The minutes glided away, and as nothing occurred to announce the return of the young lord, Hugh de Witherington began to grow impatient ; for he had been sent out on a certain business, namely, to rescue Lady Mortimer from the hands of her captors, and not to wait in attendance on all the whims and caprices of his master's eldest son.

"It will not do to leave him behind, nor dare I linger any longer on the track of the cursed Scots," he growled. "Is there ever a man among you can write?" he continued, raising his voice.

There was no reply. Writing was in those days an accomplishment possessed by few. Even the Captain de Witherington himself could no more sign his name than fly to the moon ; so therefore it is not very surprising that none of the men-at-arms stepped forward to avow themselves more learned than their leader.

"Then we must e'en leave somebody here to let him know which way we have gone," continued the old warrior. "*You* and *you* remain on the ground, and tell our young lord to ride hard by way of Eglingham towards Wooler, if he would ride with us."

The two men old Witherington had indicated with his finger, dropped out of the ranks, while the others hastened forward, anxious to make up for lost time.

In the meantime Harry Percy kept upon his headlong course, until he entered a deep ravine, fringed at the top of either bank with dark-looking pine trees. Even in day-time this pass was gloomy enough, but at night its aspect was dismal beyond conception.

As he rode on, the rocks on each side the path became more lofty and more fantastic in their outlines ; assuming in places the appearance of columns, towers, and battlements, while in other spots the shadows of the trees falling on the side of the cliff resembled huge, dark, and yawning caverns, where robbers might be supposed to lurk or where grim goblins stalk about to scare the timid. And, to add to the wildness of the scene, in some places the face of the rock bore rude inscriptions, carved in the letters of an unknown tongue, which, according to the popular belief, gave the man who could read them control over the evil spirits that are supposed to haunt this earth. But Harry Percy cared neither for robbers nor demons. A band of Scots or a troop of fiends would not have turned him from the path he had made up his mind to pursue.

He reached a point where the glen curved to the left, and then drew up his horse. Before him was a twinkling light, which apparently burned in the face of a smooth mass of rock ; but on approaching nearer, a rude flight of steps could be seen leading up to an archway hewn in the solid stone.

"So here lies my journey's end," exclaimed Hotspur, putting his horse again in motion when he had gazed a moment on the light. As he rode forward he loosened his sword and dagger in their sheaths, and clenched his teeth firmly, as though resolved to do battle with whatever might be opposed to him.

The noise of his horse's hoofs had apparently alarmed the inmates of the cavern or grotto. A second light appeared in the shape of a torch, held by a venerable old man, dressed in a long gown of coarse grey stuff. He stood bareheaded, his long hair and beard streaming in the wind, and waved his torch as a signal to the wayfarer, whoever it might be.

Young Percy leaped from his horse, and drawing his sword ran hastily up the steps which led to the hermit's cell.

"My son, put up that angry weapon and be welcome to my humble cell. See you not above the door the sign of the cross—symbol of peace and love ?"

"Holy father, stand aside, I pray you ; there is no peace for me ; nor can there be love in my heart till I have slain the cursed Scot who harbours in your cell."

"Of what Scot speak you, my son ?" answered the hermit, still barring the doorway with his body.

"Of a Scottish youth who sought refuge in your cell this evening. His name is Douglas."

"But, my son, is it likely a Scot would seek shelter on Earl Percy's lands ? Doth the lamb fly for safety to the den of the wolf ?"

"Holy father, this is no time for equivocation. I am Henry Percy, commonly called Hotspur, therefore I say stand aside lest injury befall you."

The hermit took up his crucifix and stretched it out before the impatient young noble.

"By this holy symbol I command you to forbear, nor seek to force an entry into my cell. Scot or Englishman who gains its shelter must be secure from all foes ; the holy church gives him sanctuary."

"Then is your sanctuary a den of thieves," replied Hotspur ; but he made no further attempt to force his way into the cell. "This very evening, holy Sir Hermit, have the cowardly Scots crawled like rats into Alnwick castle and carried away the Lady Katherine Mortimer, the guest of my noble mother, the Countess of Northumberland."

"It grieves my heart to hear it, son ; but be assured that he who rests within this cave had no hand in the foul deed."

"Would I could believe your words, good father, but suspicion points too strongly to him. Ho! Douglas! come forth, I say ; come forth, gallant assailant of defenceless women!"

"Who calls Douglas?" replied the voice of the young Scot from within the cell, and in a moment the Highland youth made his appearance. "What would you with Douglas?"

"What would I with Douglas? I would the restitution of Lady Katherine Mortimer to the friends from whom she has been so vilely snatched."

"Vilely snatched! what mean you, fair Percy? Your words are a riddle to me."

"It is well to plead ignorance when the avenger demands justice. I mean that by your arts and by the hands of your minions, the lady has been stolen. Therefore, I say, restore her, or come forth from the sanctuary and face me, sword to sword."

The Scottish chieftain instantly unsheathed his sword.

"By Heaven!" he cried, "you accuse me wrongfully ; but a Douglas needs not twice bidding to battle. Down to the glen, Sir Hotspur ; this ledge is too narrow."

"Hold! hold! rash youths," cried the hermit, "I forbid the fight."

"For the once your pious commands must be disobeyed," replied Hotspur. "Now, Douglas, confess yourself a per-

jured villain, or prepare to die like a brave Scot. The good hermit will hear your confession and perform the last offices of his priestly calling."

"I need no priest. My time has not yet arrived, proud boaster."

They reached the glen at the foot of the hermit's cave, and drawing their swords put themselves in position to commence the combat.

Their swords glittered in the moonlight, clashed together, and descended upon a hard wooden object.

It was the hermit's crucifix which he had interposed between the angry combatants, and which had thus received both their blows.

The sight was so sudden and unexpected that by instant and mutual consent the youths drew back and lowered the points of their weapons, while the hermit placed himself between them.

"Kneel, kneel, rash boys," he exclaimed, "kneel humbly, and ask pardon for your great transgression. Were I to do what the holy church commands me, I should pronounce you both excommunicate and accursed. But I am willing to make some allowance for the rashness and hot temper of youth."

The young nobles prostrated themselves bareheaded before the crucifix, which the hermit now held on high, and muttered a few rude petitions.

Such was the superstition of the age, that a deed like that which they had done was looked upon as one of the most heinous crimes a man could commit, and only to be expiated by a severe penance.

Percy and Douglas were both to a certain extent believers in the church of Rome, and the hermit's words filled them with dismay.

CHAPTER XI.

THREATENED VENGEANCE OF THE EARL OF NORTHUMBERLAND.

THE news of what had taken place at Alnwick was quickly conveyed to the Earl of Northumberland at Warkworth.

The stern old gentleman stormed and raged most furiously when he heard that Lady Katherine had been carried away as was supposed, by young Douglas, or those in his employ.

It would have been difficult though to say whether he was most angry at the loss of the young lady, his ward, or the loose state of discipline which allowed such a loss.

"By the bones of St. Cuthbert the Scots shall rue this! Ho, there! Hugo, Albert, Robert de Ridley, to horse, all three of you instantly, ride south, east, and west, call up all my vassals and retainers, bid them assemble the day after to-morrow at Alnwick, fully armed and equipped. You, De Fenwicke, ride first to Sir Ralph Nevill, and then to Sir Thomas Musgrave, tell them what hath happened, charge them assemble their forces and join me at Wooler. By the Holy Rood I will lay waste the whole of Scotland."

"My lord," said an old squire, stepping forward, "an it give your lordship no offence I would urge that a herald should be sent first of all to the enemy's camp to demand justice. The calamities of war usually fall most heavily on those who are least guilty."

"A herald shall be sent; but in the meantime let our men-at-arms assemble as I have said, that the foe may see we have force to back our demands. Come hither, Sir Herald, and do thou, Master Secretary, write."

The herald—an officer in those days found in the courts of all the most powerful barons—approached the table at which the earl was sitting in company with his secretary.

The latter individual dipped his pen into the inkhorn and slowly inscribed on a fair sheet of parchment the words as they fell from the earl's lips—

To Thomas, Earl of Moray, the Earl Douglas, or others commanding the Scottish armies on the English borders.

GREETING, We, Henry Percy, Earl of Northumberland, do hereby demand restitution of the persons of several captives taken from our territory during term of truce, and, notably, the Lady Katherine Mortimer, stolen from our castle of Alnwick. Failing compliance with our demands and the restoration to liberty of all English prisoners now in your hands we shall not fail to exact justice in person and at the head of our troops, so we pray you give speedy heed to this.

Given at Warkworth, on the sixteenth day of July, in the year one thousand three hundred and eighty-five.

"See to it, Sir Herald, deliver my message quickly. And harkye, take good note of the position of their camp and of the points where they may be attacked with most advantage."

The herald bowed, took up his credentials, and withdrew.

But when he had gained a safe distance from the castle walls, he turned in his saddle, and shaking his fist towards the building, exclaimed—

"May all the fiends of hell combine to plague me if I obey your behests, proud earl. To Scotland I go, but my going shall be a sore thorn in your side, haughty Percy."

With these words he drew the parchment from the breast of his doublet, and cut it in two with his dagger.

"Yet," he muttered, "I will not destroy it. Its contents may afford some little matter for mirth to our friends. They shall see and judge for themselves."

The man said no more, but with all haste spurred onwards towards the town of Berwick-on-Tweed, though he knew well enough that the Scottish commanders were encamped near Kelso.

This Tale will be completed in about Twelve Numbers.

"'HOLD! HOLD! RASH BOYS—I FORBID THEE FIGHT.'"

The way was long and full of dangers.

But his herald's robes protected him, or many a bold borderer would have made an effort to gain possession of the noble and powerful horse he bestrode.

For heralds were almost as sacred in their office as priests.

To strike one entailed on the offender the loss of his right hand and a long term of imprisonment.

It was early morning when the herald left Warkworth, but the day was far advanced when he halted his reeking horse at a little collection of mud huts, about three miles from Berwick-on-Tweed.

That town was then, as now, a kind of neutral ground between the two countries. It had been taken by the English, retaken by the Scots, who again had been driven out by the English under Percy of Northumberland. In fact, wherever war might break out, the inhabitants of Berwick-on-Tweed were pretty safe to come in for a fair share of the fighting.

The herald stopped his horse before the largest of the huts which the half-civilized inhabitants of that neighbourhood called an inn, and dismounting, strode into the building.

In a room at the back of the building five men were seated ; none of them very far advanced in years, but all of them having the appearance of soldiers who had seen plenty of rough work. They were all partly armed.

"Welcome, brother," they all exclaimed, as the herald entered the room. "What news from Warkworth?"

"The Earl of Northumberland hath sworn by at least fifty saints that he will ravage Scotland with fire and sword ; and hath sent me with a certain cartel to the leaders of the Scottish forces."

So saying, he produced the parchment, and in a formal voice read its contents, amid the laughter of his companions.

"Ha, ha! Old Northumberland has been rarely fooled. The Douglas accused of carrying off a lady! this is rare sport. But you said he SWORE BY THE SAINTS ?"

"Aye ; But more from custom and habit than belief in their sanctity. But what news from London, lads? Has good Father Abel succeeded in his share of the business ?"

"Nay, but we have rare letters from his grace the Archbishop, giving the Church's sanction to our undertaking."

"Good. But what have ye done with the young lady ? I should much like to set eyes upon this paragon of beauty."

"Bold Sir William hath her, I doubt not, but he hath not yet returned."

"But should our enterprise be delayed for these loiterers ?" demanded the herald, throwing his robe of office on the floor. and taking from the corner of the room a steel cap, breastplate, and sword. "Methinks the time for action has arrived."

As he spoke footsteps sounded in the passage. Instinctively the six men laid their hands upon their weapons, but their alarm passed away as the door opened, and the man who had carried off the Lady Katherine Mortimer entered the room.

"A cup of wine, for the love of the Virgin !" exclaimed "bold Sir William," as the others had called him, sinking on a seat.

The wine was instantly poured out.

"What ails you, my bold knight ?" asked the herald, as he presented the cup. "Are you ill ? wounded, perchance ?"

"What ails me ? ha, ha, ha! Why, a perpetual and unquenchable thirst, inherited from both father and mother—rest their souls ! Fear not, I have received no wounds to-day but this will go a great way towards their cure."

So saying, he tossed off the wine, and held out the goblet to be refilled.

"And what of the lady ?" asked one of the conclave. "We hear you succeeded in bearing her off."

"Aye, faith ; and no very difficult task either. I will wager that I will bring away the standard from the topmost tower of Alnwick an they keep no better watch. As for the lady, she is safely bestowed in the nunnery of St. Agnes, though not before I had carried her through the Scottish camp. She raved and threatened me with Percy and Douglas both, but I care little for either. I serve neither England nor Scotland."

"Nor I! nor I!" exclaimed every one in the room.

"Let us drink the health of our own lawful lord," said the herald.

"Hold thy foolish tongue. Our worthy host may overhear," said Sir William Graham.

"And if he betrayed us, I would cut his tongue from his mouth," replied the herald, drawing his dagger.

"What advantage would that be when all our schemes were betrayed? When we have the keep of Berwick Castle in our hands, thou shalt drink healths enough, I warrant. But now let us to business. Archie hath not yet returned from London?"

"He hath not, though we may well look for him to-night."

"Then, if he comes, our attempt shall be made just at daybreak in the morning, when the sleepy sentinels begin to close their eyes and slumber as they walk. The countersign for this night is known to me, and we shall have no difficulty in passing the gates; once within the walls, our arms and our swords must do the rest. But, my friends, Berwick must be ours!"

"It shall be ours," responded all the others, in emphatic tones.

"It must, it shall. Holy Church permits, and our lawful lord, the King of France, commands it. But now listen while I explain to you the method of attack."

Sir William Graham then showed them a plan of the fortifications of the town of Berwick, and explained to them the part each was to take in the attack. The garrison was not large, but still it outnumbered, in the proportion of ten to one, the seven bold daring men who intended to capture the town and there establish the foundation of a third monarchy within this island. Such was their design. The French king had given the scheme his sanction, being willing to do anything that would injure the English and withdraw their attention from him; and for reasons which will be seen in a future chapter, the high dignitaries of the Church had approved of it for the sake of undermining the power of the Earl of Northumberland, who was well known to be a favourer of the Lollards and other sects of religious reformers of that early period.

With which brief explanation we will leave the conspirators to their devices.

CHAPTER XII.

THE PRIEST AT WORK.

WHAT we seek must be there!" So said Father Abel, as with a gleam of triumph in his round eyes he pointed to the old chest in the Earl of Northumberland's private apartment.

"An it be there we'll soon have it elsewhere," said Archie, the man-at-arms, taking two long strides towards the piece of furniture. "Do you keep the key of this as well as of all the doors, good father?"

The priest for a moment returned no answer, and the stalwart man-at-arms, imagining from the silence that his clerical friend was at a loss how to proceed, lifted up his foot and bestowed a terrific kick upon the lid of the box.

The noise made by the soldier's iron-armed heel falling upon the chest aroused Father Abel from his reverie.

"Hold, my son! Hush!"

"What now, father? If you have not the key, we must find some means of forcing the lock, and I doubt whether your fat fingers could achieve the task."

"Hush! Hark! do you hear any one?"

The soldier listened, but could perceive no sound that might give cause for alarm.

"I hear no one, father. I'll warrant you no disturbers will venture near me. But touching this old box; what is to be done with it? Shall I carry it off on my shoulders?"

"That perhaps were best. Yet, stay; we could not convey it out of the house. It must be opened."

"The key, then, good father—quick!"

"I have no key; but there is, I know, a spring, the slightest pressure on which will cause the lid to fly open."

The soldier bent down and pressed his heavy fingers on every projection and ornament of the iron binding which seemed likely to be the spring mentioned.

"Here, father, your back should be more accustomed to stooping than mine; try your hand at it, for may the fiend seize me if I see any way of opening it, save with my dagger."

"Patience, my son; patience, good Archie."

"Talk of patience to a soldier!"

"Aye, good Archie. Many a lost battle would have been won had the commanders been possessed of patience as well as valour. Let me try the box."

The stout priest dropped upon his knees before the chest as if he were about to say mass to the unseen treasures it contained, and with his fat soft fingers explored such parts as the soldier had overlooked.

On the edge of the lid was a nail which seemed to have been imperfectly and carelessly driven into the wood.

Father Abel's eyes again assumed a triumphant expression as he saw it.

"Now, my son, you'll see the value of patience," said he. "It saves time and is noiseless."

With these words the priest pressed his finger upon the little piece of iron, and as if by magic the lid of the box flew up.

"Oh! oh! oh!" roared Father Abel, as he fell back upon the floor.

"Why, what is the matter, good father?" asked the soldier.

"My malison on the box and its contents!" groaned the priest, as he wrapped a corner of his robe round his jaw.

"Curse it by bell, book, and candle, if it so please your holiness; but by Becket's bones, I know not why these sounds of anger and sorrow in the moment of our triumph."

"The lid hath well-nigh broken my jaw," replied Father Abel, in melancholy tones.

"Ha, ha, ha! This comes of curiosity and patience, Sir Priest. Had you allowed my impatient foot to force its way through the oak, your teeth would not have been broken. But there is still some consolation; no modern Sir Samson will now be able to use your jawbone as a weapon with which to slay the Turks. Ha, ha, ha!"

Father Abel was waxing wroth most rapidly, under the influence of the soldier's bantering language.

"Revile not the Church or its ministers, friend Archie, or by virtue of mine holy office, I will presently pronounce thee accursed."

"Well, well, father, pardon me; but we soldiers are always so near death, that we must laugh when we have the chance, as there is no laughing in the grave. But the box is open; let us take from it what we want."

The box contained a few parchment scrolls and some few heavy volumes bound in vellum.

"Clerks' toys! What have I to do with these?" exclaimed Archie.

"You have much to do with them, my son," replied Father Abel, as he lifted rolls and volumes from the chest. "These are the evidences that shall prove Henry Earl Percy both traitor and heretic."

The man-at-arms half drew his sharp, glittering dagger.

"Beware, priest, beware!" he said, in stern tones. "A jest may cause anger, and most assuredly he who, in play or in good earnest, casts dishonour on the name of Henry Percy will feel the weight of my displeasure."

Father Abel stared with all the surprise his round, fat-embedded eyes were capable of expressing.

"What! Are you not then a friend of our cause, Archie?"

"I was and still am a friend to the cause of the Holy Churbh, but I am not yet convinced that the Earl of Northumberland is either traitor or heretic."

"You will not desert our friends?"

"No; nor will I do aught that may

injure one who in my hour of need befriended me."

The monk sat himself down upon the box, and reflected on the course he should pursue, which was nothing less than to compass the death of his companion, the bold man-at-arms.

"Archie," said he, after some minutes' silence, "Archie, you must ride to-morrow at early dawn."

"Whither?"

"To Sir William Graham."

"But why not to-night, good father?"

"The night is close at hand; it will be dark ere long."

"And pray how many of these mouldy old parchments do I carry at my saddle-bow?"

"None. I myself will see to them."

"What, do you ride with me then?"

"Heaven forbid that my bones should be endangered by galloping through the land along with a hasty soldier, whose spurs would not be idle one minute. No, good Archie, my neck is too precious for such an adventure, and besides, my easy-going palfrey would never be able to keep pace with your headlong charger."

"As you list, father. You would only be an encumbrance should we meet foes on the road."

"Rest, then, to-night, Archie, and in the morning hie thee away to announce to our friends that ere long I will be with them."

"Then by your permission I will seek some refreshment for myself. An empty stomach is by no means the best foundation for a sound night's rest before a journey."

"Go to the hall with me, Archie. You will fare all the better for being in my company."

The soldier carelessly nodded, and strode towards the door, while Father Abel, after collecting a number of bulky manuscripts from those he had taken from the box, led the way through the corridors and passages which led from the secret chamber to the inhabited portions of the mansion.

The monk in his progress carefully closed and locked every door through which they had to pass, in order that no trace of their clandestine visit might be visible to the eyes of the household servants.

That done, he carried the parchments he had stolen—for we can use no milder term—to his own apartment, and then conducted Archie to the hall.

The supper set before them comprised almost everything that people in those days thought dainty eating.

Fish, fowl, and flesh, in the shape of mountainous masses of beef, smoked upon the board.

For some little time both monk and man-at-arms were two busily employed in satisfying their hunger to hold any conversation. To the astonishment of all the menials who waited at table, Father Abel was the first to break silence.

"This is but dry work, friend Archie. Holy Virgin, how I thirst!"

"My throat is as dry as the road I travelled this morn. A cup of good wine would be no slight improvement to the flavour of this venison."

The priest immediately called for wine, and full goblets were placed before them.

The two friends were seated side by side, and at the moment the liquor was set upon the board, Father Abel endeavoured to remove Archie's eyes from the cups.

"A small slice of that partridge pasty will finish my meat. Plunge your knife deeply into it, good Archie, and seek me out the daintiest bits from its bowels."

The soldier at once did as Father Abel requested, and while so occupied the priest poured a few drops from a phial into the goblet which had been placed at Archie's elbow.

The action, though dexterously performed, was noticed by the spearsman, whose suspicions were at once aroused.

"It must be the same stuff that he bade me put in the drink of yon poor butler who even now has not overcome the effects of the potion," thought Archie. "What can be his object in poisoning me? I have no letters, no keys."

Then, swift as lightning, another and a still more fearful suspicion crossed his brain.

"It must be poison. He dares not use sword or dagger, but does his foul work by drugs."

For an instant the soldier was resolved to plunge his own weapon into the monk's throat, but on second thoughts he resolved to play trick for trick.

"As a sweetening to this good wine I pray you hand me some of those confections that grace your right hand, father," said he. "Not those, the others wrought in curious shapes and devices."

While thus speaking he removed the monk's wine cup and substituted his own, the deed being done with greater dexterity and better success than had attended Father Abel's manœuvres.

The priest was unconscious of the change, and when he had helped his guest to the desired sweets, pledged him.

"Your health, good Archie. May you never lack better wine than this."

"Your health, father."

In a few seconds the goblets were placed upon the table empty.

"Beshrew me," said Father Abel, "my palate must be strangely out of order, or yonder idle Jack-o'-the-Bottles hath gone to the wrong side of the cellar."

"The wine was good enough to my taste. Ho, there, another draught!"

One of the attendants replenished the goblets, and the priest, with renewed appetite, attacked his partridge pasty.

But in a few minutes he laid down his knife and yawned in a sleepy manner.

"Heigh-ho-ho! I know not what should give me this drowsy feeling."

"Too much study, too many masses in the chapel at midnight."

The chaplain's head dropped upon his breast.

He breathed heavily.

But in a few minutes he roused himself and exclaimed—

"Archie, I believe you——"

What the good monk believed was not at that time to be made public, for ere he could conclude his speech Father Abel was in a sound sleep.

After regarding his defeated adversary with a grimly sardonic smile, the man-at-arms continued his meal with good appetite, while some of the servants looked to the priest and deposited his fleshy body on a soft well-padded seat by the open window overlooking the courtyard.

His supper concluded, the soldier at once proceeded to the stables, saddled his horse, and in a few minutes was once more on his road.

The evening was balmy, and the sun about to set.

Both man and horse were invigorated with rest and food.

The road was—for those times—good, and at least two hours' hard riding were performed ere Archie drew rein at the door of the hostelry where he intended to pass the night.

Archie was thoughtful, as well he might be.

He had been befriended by the Earl of Northumberland against whom the priest wished him to plot along with others, and he was sworn to aid the Holy Church, which, according to Father Abel, had pronounced the earl traitor and heretic.

From the priest himself the soldier had in bygone days received many benefits.

But the remembrance of those favours was now effaced by the attempt to poison or stupefy him by drugging his wine.

So that when he alighted and entered the inn mine host set him down as a surly knave, and one who would be likely to pay him with steel weapons instead of silver coin.

CHAPTER XIII.

THE PURSUIT.

THE solemn manner and reverent appearance of the hermit made great impression on Hotspur.

The holy man, after a brief homily, of which anger formed the subject, reconducted young Douglas to his cell.

Hotspur, after asking forgiveness, which was accorded him, again mounted his horse.

"You are forgiven, my son," said the old man, "but beware of giving way to the rash tempers of youth. Go in peace."

"And be assured, Percy, on the word of a Scot who never had a false tongue, that I am innocent of the abduction of the lady from your castle," said Douglas, from the mouth of the cave.

"I would fain believe it, though suspicion strongly points towards thee," replied Percy.

With these words he mounted his horse and galloped back to the spot where he had parted from his friends.

There he found waiting him the men whom Witherington had left there for the purpose of directing him.

A few brief words sufficed to explain to him the road which the old squire and his troop had taken.

And setting spurs to his horse's flanks he galloped rapidly along the moonlit road after them.

Of course during the time that Hotspur had been engaged in his senseless, needless controversy with Douglas at the hermit's cell, Witherington with his men-at-arms had been pushing forward in haste after the Lady Katherine and her captors.

It was a long time ere the young noble could overtake them, and his steed was covered with foam when he once more joined their company.

"You have ridden hard, my lord," said old Witherington, "and your horse will be unable to travel much further. Shall we halt awhile?"

"As you please, worthy squire."

"In another hour it will be daybreak, and then we shall be able to proceed faster, so, by your leave, we will quit our saddles."

"An it please you, sir," said one of the soldiers, "there is a little inn just beyond the next turning of the road where we can refresh ourselves as well as our horses."

"Ah, well, a cup of good ale will do us no harm. What say you, my lord?"

"Drink as much ale as thou wilt, good De Witherington, but trouble me not, nor delay our journey longer than is necessary."

"Trust me for that," muttered the old warrior, as he again set his horse in motion.

In about a quarter of an hour they reached the little inn, and found the host, as might have been expected, in bed.

A few loud knocks at the door with sword and lance handles dispelled his slumbers, and his night-capped head was seen protruding from the window over the door.

"Oh, spare me, spare me, I pray you, good gentlemen," said he, in piteous tones. "I am only a poor peasant."

"Open the door, knave!" roared Witherington.

"I do assure you, worthy sirs, I am only——"

"A lusty innkeeper, to whom I owe a score," said the man who had informed Witherington of the existence of the inn. "Open the door, good Tim-o-the-Tap, and see the spigot runs freely, for we are athirst."

The voice sounded friendly enough, and the frightened man descended to open the door.

His alarm entirely vanished when he saw that his unexpected visitors wore the badge of the Percy family.

For some little time he was busily engaged in satisfying the wants of the thirsty troopers, but, at length, young Hotspur found an opportunity of inquiring whether he had seen any horsemen pass that way with a lady.

The man had heard hoofs about an hour since, but fearing lest an assault should be made upon his house, had not looked out to see who the riders were.

They had gone on the road to the north at a fair speed.

Percy asked no more questions, but paced up and down before the house while his men were drinking and attending to their horses.

Eager and impatient as he was, the youth knew well that he could not proceed until his horse had rested, and endeavoured to curb his natural impatience by thinking of the terrific onslaught he would make upon the foe when he should overtake them.

The hour, though to the troopers short enough, to him seemed an age; but, at length, to his great joy, Witherington pronounced the horses fit for the road, and the order was given to mount.

It was a lovely morning, but the beauty of smiling nature had little effect upon our young hero.

His eyes could not see the waving trees and the dew-spangled grass.

The only vision he was capable of perceiving was that of Lady Katherine Mortimer struggling in the hands of her rude captors.

The soldiers amused themselves by singing merry songs; but their harmony jarred upon his ears, which, in fancy, heard the screams of his lady love.

They reached the hills, and gazed down upon Scottish soil; but no sight of the party they were in pursuit of gladdened their eyes.

"Now, by the saints, I have a prize for my sweetheart!" exclaimed one of the soldiers, leaping from his horse to secure something he saw by the roadside.

"What is that thou hast found?" asked his companion.

"St. George! I know not. It is a dainty ornament, and seems to have letters upon it."

"Then show it to our captain; it may be news of the foe."

The ornament, which was none other than the ivory tablet which Lady Katherine had dropped, was handed to Witherington, who, after looking at it from every point of view, gave it to young Percy.

"Do you read it, my lord. My eyesight is none of the best of late."

The old warrior might have added that his education, excepting in warlike exercises, was as defective as his eyesight; but he cared not to let his lack of scholarship be known.

Harry Percy took the tablet, and thanks to Father Abel's hateful books, managed to decipher the inscription without much difficulty.

"Here, fellow, a piece of gold will rattle in thy pouch much more merrily than this bone," said he, tossing the soldier a coin. "Forward, Witherington, we are on the right path, and shall find them at Roxburgh, if we do not overtake them ere they reach that town."

"Roxburgh? Why, we need five hundred good soldiers if the lady is to be dragged from thence."

"It is too late to turn back now. We must do the best we can."

They rode forward, and in due course found the other tablets which Lady Katherine had dropped to direct her friends.

But when they had found the last they were still some miles distant from Roxburgh.

"The lady's scheme seems to have been found out and prevented," said old Witherington, when some miles had been passed without finding any more of the welcome ivory tablets.

"But we know whither she has been taken."

"Be not so sure, my lord. The rascals may have altered their course; but there is a man tending cattle yonder. Ride, some of you, and bring him hither. He may perchance be able to give us news."

Half-a-dozen of the troopers at once left the main body, and in a few minutes the luckless herdsman was dragged before the grey-headed old English captain.

"Hast seen any horsemen go past

carrying a lady with them?" said Witherington.

"I know nothing of your lady," answered the man, with a Scotch accent, so peculiar, that it would be impossible to give an idea of it on paper.

"That's false, I know by the look of his eye," exclaimed Percy.

"The truth, man, the truth, and that quickly, or by Saint George of England, I swear that in five minutes thou shalt hang from the highest branch of yon oak !" continued Witherington.

The herdsman looked doggedly in the old soldier's face, but made no reply.

Witherington took a lance from one of the soldiers, and stuck it upright in the ground.

The slender piece of wood threw a thin, dark shadow upon the ground.

Parallel to this shadow, and but a short distance from it, the captain of the English troop traced a line with his scabbarded sword.

"We have no dial here to mark the flight of time ; but mark me, knave, if by the time the shadow of the lance reaches this line thou hast not truly told us how long it is since the horsemen passed with the lady, and which road they took, thou diest."

"I can die but once, and my death will be avenged."

To this Witherington made no reply, but with arms folded gazed first upon his captive, and then upon the line which marked the length of the poor man's life.

There was a deep silence for some minutes while the space between the shadow and the line grew less and less.

An inch—half an inch—quarter !

Surely the poor wretch has not long to live !

"Speak, man, speak and save thy neck from the cord," cried Hotspur.

No reply.

The shadow reached the line !

Witherington gazed sternly on the herdsman for a moment, and then motioned to his soldiers.

"Away with him ! hang him up to yon tree as a warning to all others who may be in league with these robbers."

The troopers who held the herdsman hurried him towards the tree.

A rope was fastened round his neck, and the end thrown over a branch.

But before the noose could be tightened the man's courage failed him.

"Mercy, mercy, gallant sirs ; I will tell you all I know," he cried.

"You should have spoken sooner," replied Witherington. "Up with him, men—we can learn all what we want to know elsewhere."

"Not so," said Hotspur. "Let his life be spared."

"Mercy, mercy, noble sirs. I can tell you more than you think."

"Then speak out, and that quickly."

A few hurried words informed the English that Sir William Graham was the knight who had stolen away the Lady Katherine, and that they had not taken her to Roxburgh, but to a convent about three miles to the right of that town.

The abbess, he added, always kept a band of armed men, fifty in number, to defend her and the convent against all enemies, foreign or domestic.

"Then to the convent we go. But hark ye, knaves, tie up this rascal by the arms and put a gag in his mouth so that he cannot betray us."

"That is folly, I fancy," said Hotspur. "Let one of your men take charge of him and bring him along with us. Then we can ensure his silence, and punish him if he has deceived us."

"Good, my lord, it shall be done."

It took little time to arrange the means of conveying the herdsman, and once more the party moved onwards.

Amongst the men-at-arms were many who had taken part in forays into Scottish territory, and who knew the road to Roxburgh as well as they did that to Alnwick, so that there was no necessity for the employment of a strange guide.

By the most unfrequented paths they neared their destination, and at length halted in a large wood, which extended in one direction nearly up to the walls of the convent.

In fact from the open glade in which they drew bridle the roof of the building which was perched on a hill was plainly visible.

Having come to a standstill, a council of war was held, of which the members were old Hugh de Witherington, Hotspur, and Witherington's son, who for the first time in his life was engaged in the serious business of war.

An open attack, they all agreed, would be useless against strong walls defended by armed men, and after a little consultation Hotspur resolved to go alone and demand admission as a weary traveller who desired food and rest.

At Witherington's desire the project was deferred till night, as it did not appear probable that such a request would be granted in the daytime while the supposed traveller was near the town of Roxburgh.

CHAPTER XIV.

WITHIN THE CONVENT.

EVENING came, and with it dark clouds.

The sky presaged that the night would be a stormy one.

The wind moaned heavily amongst the old trees of the forest, and in the distance thunder muttered heavily.

Hotspur was to be accompanied, so it had been agreed, by young De Witherington, the old captain's son.

As they were about to set forth, a sound was heard—neither the wind nor the thunder, but proceeding from the hoofs of a horse urged at a rapid gallop through the forest glades.

"To your arms," said De Witherington, "it may be the enemy."

The well-trained soldiers at once seized their weapons, and stood upon the defensive.

But in a few moments the cause of their alarm appeared.

A single horseman, mounted on a white steed, approached.

Both horse and rider seeming of gigantic size as they entered the glade.

"It must be the Wild Huntsman," said young De Witherington, crossing himself. "I have heard that he haunts these forests."

The superstitious boy, though he would have fought single-handed with any number of Scots or Frenchmen, trembled as he gazed on a being he supposed supernatural, and began to mutter all the prayers of the Church that he could remember.

But his supplications availed nothing, for the white horse and rider continued to advance, and in a few minutes was in the midst of the troop.

Its gigantic and supernatural proportions had diminished into nothing more formidable than Ralph Percy on his favourite white charger.

"Welcome, brother, welcome," said Hotspur, as Ralph sprang lightly from the saddle. "We little reckoned on your aid."

"I am here, nevertheless, and sorely vexed that you should have started on such a foray without my knowledge."

"You are too young, Lord Ralph, to meet such heavy blows as we are likely to find. Now, if we beard old Douglas himself we must e'en stand the encounter of a sword two ells in length."[*]

So said old De Witherington, as he leaned in a thoughtful manner upon his own weapon, which had sufficient metal in it to construct a couple of modern sabres.

Ralph Percy paid no attention to the grim warrior's warning, but questioned his brother as to his plans.

"I will go with you, Hal. I am young and innocent in appearance, but

---

[*]Vide Froissart's Chronicles.

can wield a sword as well as one of older years."

"You shall. But how did you find us ?"

"Sir Knight of the Skull—Ramsey—hinted that you might be found at Alnwick. From thence the path made by your horses was plain enough."

A few words of caution from De Witherington fell almost unheeded upon the ears of the daring lads as they commenced their journey.

They had laid aside all appearance of defensive armour, but beneath their doublets they had close-fitting shirts of mail of steel rings, cunningly and closely linked together.

Their swords they carried as a matter of course.

In those turbulent times no one who had a right to wear weapons went abroad unarmed.

Thus equipped they had the appearance of three wayward pages who had wandered from the castle of their lordly master.

Of course they stripped themselves of every badge or sign that could betray their relationship to the Earl of Northumberland.

The night increased in darkness as they proceeded on their journey, and had it not been for the twinkling lights in the convent chapel they would most probably have lost themselves in the wood.

After a tiresome journey they reached the gates just as the forked lightning began to play, the thunder to reverberate and echo through the surrounding solitudes, and large drops of rain to patter down upon the dry, thirsty earth.

They knocked loudly at the gates.

What was more natural than that benighted travellers should seek shelter from such a storm as that which had just commenced?

A light appeared at a little grating in the gate, and a harsh voice asked—

"Who is there ? Who knocks ?"

"Travellers, who desire shelter from the storm," replied Hotspur.

"How many are you in number ?"

"Three."

"Then wait a minute while I call the captain."

The grating was closed, and the three lads were allowed to remain waiting in the rain for fully five minutes, until it pleased the robber chief, who protected the abbess, to come and survey the applicants for admission.

"Speak not a word either of you," said Hotspur. "You shall appear to be pages from the French king's court, who have come hither in attendance on his envoys."

"And if we are questioned I trust we both know our native Norman tongue sufficiently well to evade suspicion," answered Ralph.

The porter returned, and with him the captain?

"Whence come ye, gentlemen ?" asked the latter.

"From Edinburgh," answered Hotspur.

"And whither are ye travelling ?"

"To Berwick."

"That is a long journey. How is it you are on foot ?"

"We had dismounted, and foolishly loosened our hold on the horses' bridles, a loud clap of thunder startled them and away they galloped."

The gates were then thrown open.

"Enter," said the captain.

Within the gates were about a dozen of the most bandit-like soldiers Hotspur had ever set eyes upon.

The light of their torches fell upon the faces of the three lads, and a most ferocious-looking warrior stepped forward, sword in hand.

Hotspur said, "My companions are French, and unable to speak our language. "I will interpret aught you have to say."

"Then tell them I hope their king will soon join us in a war upon the English."

In his heart Hotspur loathed and detested the false character he was assuming ; but it seemed necessary for their safety.

"Come along, my dainty gentlemen, come along to the hall. You must be presented to our good abbess ; but I can well guess the errand on which you ride to Berwick."

"If you can guess, then, I need not tell," said Hotspur.

"WHEN THE SHADOW REACHES THE LINE ON THE SAND YOU DIE."

"You need not ; Sir William has been here, and from a word he said I know the scheme."

Hotspur did not know the scheme, nor the Sir William mentioned by the rude soldier.

He nodded and smiled, however, as though fully informed of everything.

"You will see the lady Sir William brought with him—a rare beauty!" continued the soldier.

"A lady?"

"Aye ; but here we are at the door."

In a moment, the lads found themselves in the presence of the lady abbess of the Convent of St. Agnes.

A tall and stately dame was she, with an eye that told plainly enough that if she had renounced the world, the devil still had some command over her fiery temper.

The soldier briefly stated the account the three youths had given of themselves, and then left them.

"Sit, gentle sirs, for gentle I judge you to be by your dress and mien. Though vowed to be apart from the world, I may still afford shelter and rest to those who need it."

So saying, the abbess pointed to some hard uncomfortable seats.

"In the name of my companions, I thank your ladyship," said Hotspur as he seated himself.

There were six persons in the room— the three lads, the abbess, a hard-featured, ancient, female servant, and a lady whose face was hidden by her hands, and who had taken no notice of the entrance of Hotspur and his companions.

At the sound of the young nobleman's voice, however, she lifted her face, and fixed her eyes upon the speaker.

It was, as he had surmised, the Lady Katherine Mortimer.

CHAPTER XV

ATTACK ON BERWICK CASTLE.

WE left the Earl of Northumberland's treacherous herald with Sir William Graham and others, planning an attack on the castle of Berwick.

The non-arrival of Archie, who, as the reader already knows, had been sent to London, caused them some anxiety, and some of the inferior spirits of the band began to counsel delay.

"No!" exclaimed the herald ; "if we delay, we are lost. Instant action, on the other hand, wins us a lasting reward and a rich booty."

"I see no reason for delay," said Sir William Graham ; "but I doubt not that if we be not in Berwick by morning, we shall be in the hands of Percy ere the sun again sets. Forward, my friends ! Courage ! and the castle is ours !"

"Another flask of wine, then !" continued the herald, Arthur du Bois by name. "Good liquor sharpens our swords and nerves our arms. We shall find wine enough, though, in Berwick castle, for Sir Robert Boynton hath a rare mouth for the flagon."

The wine was brought and speedily swallowed ; sword-belts were tightened, armour donned, and the conspirators left the inn with as little noise as possible.

The castle being on the outskirts of the town, they were able to approach it without observation, and were within about a hundred yards of the building when Graham gave the signal to halt. The whole party at once came to a stand-still, and concealed themselves behind some stunted bushes, to escape the eyes of the sentinels on the ramparts.

"Wait here a while," whispered Du

Bois ; "I will creep forward and see what watch they keep."

Graham nodded, and the herald crawled forward till he was actually in the trenches or dry ditch of the castle. All was quiet ; not a sound could he hear ; not a soul was visible ; and satisfied from this observation that the sentinels were not doing their duty, he crept back to his companions.

"All is well ; the castle is ours, if we advance silently."

"On, my friends," said Graham. "See, Du Bois, we have procured a ladder from yon outhouse since thou hast been away."

No more was said ; the whole party entered the ditch, and, without being seen or heard, placed their ladder against the castle wall.

"These are the steps that shall lead us to fame's highest pinnacle," said Graham, placing his foot on the ladder, "and I will be first to mount."

"Nor will Du Bois be far behind ! Lead on, valiant Graham !"

One after another the men mounted the ladder and gained the ramparts. The sentinel was in a sound sleep, but in another moment his sleep was changed to death ; for the dagger of Du Bois pierced his heart, and without a groan the luckless man expired.

This foul murder, which the conspirators looked upon as necessary, having been accomplished, they ran as fast as possible to the tower or keep, in which dwelt Sir Robert Boynton, the governor of the castle.

There was no sentinel before the gate, but it was securely locked.

"Axes to work," said Graham ; and two of the party, who bore those terrible weapons, began to batter the door. The timber soon gave symptoms of yielding, and the sound awakened the governor.

"It must be my servants," thought the latter individual. "Those knaves I chastised three days ago have resolved to revenge themselves by killing me."

He snatched up his sword, with the intention of defending himself ; but on listening again, it seemed, from the sound, that his adversaries were too numerous for him to cope with, and he was the only man in that tower.

"Better self-destruction than the assassin's steel," he muttered. "A man can die but once."

To throw open a window overlooking the dry moat and to leap out, was the work of but a moment.

The rash man fell upon his head ; the spine was broken, and life was extinct.

"In with you ; heed not yon rash fool, who hath spared us the trouble of killing him. If we gain not the keep we are lost !" shouted the herald, Du Bois.

Crash ! Crash !

The stout oak yielded to the heavy blows from the Lochaber axes, and in a few minutes the doorway was clear.

"Go you, bring planks, tables, anything with which to barricade the door. I and Du Bois will defend it in the meantime.".

So shouted Graham, and four of his men immediately applied themselves to the task commanded by him.

By this time the sentinels began to rouse themselves, under the impression that all was not well.

They ran to and fro, having no leader, and hardly knew where to collect themselves.

At length they gathered together on the ramparts, at the spot where Graham and his comrades had ascended.

The frightened trumpeters at length found their instruments, and breath with which to blow them.

A great shout rent the night air. It was a cry of "Treason ! treason !"

With the planks and articles of furniture brought, Sir William Graham quickly barricaded the doorway of the great tower or keep, in such a manner that it could not be carried by assault.

"Now let us see how we are provisioned for a siege," said Du Bois. "Famine is of all foes the most persevering, and the only one that cannot be vanquished by sword-thrusts."

"Therein I differ from you," said Graham, "but we will be careful of our necessaries."

A blank look overspread all their faces, when two of the party returned and reported that the only provisions in the tower were a small quantity of salt beef and a few loaves of bread.

They stood and looked, and the more they looked the less they liked the starvation prospect before them.

The leader of the expedition, Sir William Graham, was the first to speak.

"There is sufficient here to last us a week, with proper care ; it will be strange if we have no assistance by that time."

"So say I," said Du Bois. "We are here and must abide our fate. Besides we may procure food from the enemy, or from the town——"

"Where we have enemies also," said Graham.

"And friends. Do you imagine, Sir William, that all these honest citizens are anxious to cut our throats ? By the rood, an I thought so, I would save them the trouble, and perform the operation on my own windpipe."

"I doubt that we shall find many friends ; and how are we to bring them hither that will espouse our cause ?"

"First of all we must clear the ramparts of these archers," replied Du Bois. "Have we no bows and arrows in the keep ?"

"Plenty, good sir," responded one of conspirators. "The bow-staves are of good Spanish yew, the shafts a clothyard in length, and tipped with bright steel. I for one know how to draw a bow with any border archer."

"Then, in Heaven's name shoot. Shoot, and spare not. Strike me down those rascals one by one. Stick thy shafts in their buff jerkins till they resemble pins in a housewife's cushion. The castle and town may still be ours, an you shoot with good aim and lusty strength."

The words of Du Bois stimulated every one to exertion, and the shafts began to fly swiftly from the loopholes of the tower.

Sir Robert Boynton's men fell one by one.

Having no leader they had no plan of attack or defence, and knew not how to defend themselves from their resolute adversaries.

"Hurrah, hurrah ! Berwick is ours ! Hoist the French flag from the highest tower. Shout for King Charles of France, who should also be King of England."

As Du Bois uttered these words a shaft came from the town, which, passing through the loophole at which he was standing, buried itself in the mortar of the wall behind him.

"Sound thy trumpet, Sire Du Bois. let the good burghers of Berwick know that we hold the castle, and demand their assistance," said Sir William Graham.

The herald, traitor though he was, proved himself no coward.

He at once made his appearance on the summit of the keep, and in a loud voice made proclamation to the people of Berwick, who began to gather around the castle walls.

The castle, he told them, had been taken by the Scots, and would be held by them on behalf of the French king.

All good citizens who hated the English rule were invited to join the garrison holding the castle.

About three dozen men responded to this invitation, and these were men principally from more northern climes —Scots who hated England and everything pertaining to it.

The day was beginning to break slowly over the eastern sea as they had accomplished their task, and the whole town was soon alive with men and women, all of whom thronged up towards the castle.

Strange rumours were afloat.

Some said that the French king with a large army had entered the town during the night.

Others vowed that thousands of Scots had taken the castle.

But there were a few amongst them who had a better knowledge of the state of affairs.

Amongst these was John Bisset, the governor of the town, a man who had passed his early days in the Earl of Northumberland's service, and even now was devotedly attached to that nobleman.

This worthy gathered together all who were capable of bearing arms, and arrayed them before the castle.

His trumpeter then sounded, and he himself advanced to the gates to parley with those within.

"I charge you, whoever you may be,

to lay down your arms, surrender the castle into my keeping, and trust in the clemency of the noble Earl of Northumberland," said he, when he had succeeded in obtaining a hearing.

"That we may not do," said Du Bois, speaking for his companions. "We have taken the castle and by Heaven's aid will keep it."

"Then shall ye all hang from the castle battlements as a warning to false traitors, of whom thou, Du Bois, are the blackest and most false."

"Ha, you are known then ?" exclaimed Sir William Graham.

"So it seems. I thought yonder rogue would have lost all recollection of Arthur Du Bois."

"A word in your ear, Sir William," said one of the subordinates.

And a consultation took place in such low tones that the herald, Du Bois, was unable to overhear them.

"Shall we surrender if they allow us to depart with our arms in our hands ?"

asked the knight, afterwards. "With our small force we can hardly maintain the place."

The herald looked around, and saw that the place was already invested on all sides by hundreds of men, whose looks showed that they were anxious to avenge the defeat the regular garrison had sustained.

He again demanded a parley, and in the name of himself and companions offered to deliver up the castle on condition of being allowed to leave the town.

"Not so, fair sirs," replied Bisset ; "you came hither and surprised our castle without asking, and now, by the mass, ye go not hence without our leave."

"Then do I defy ye one and all, burghers of Berwick," replied the herald. "An ye desire to have the castle, come, take it. A warm welcome ye shall have, I promise."

To this Bisset made no reply, but retiring to his men, sent off mounted messengers in haste towards the south.

CHAPTER XVI.

HARRY PERCY IN THE CONVENT GARDEN.

WHEN Henry Percy saw that the lady who sat alone in the convent parlour was indeed Lady Katherine Mortimer he could hardly restrain his hasty spirit, and would have rushed forward to her side had not Ralph seized his hand and held it.

"For Heaven's sake, dear brother, be not rash," whispered the latter. "A word or a look may destroy us."

The hot-headed young noble loved his brother, and for his sake remained silent, though he could not withdraw his eyes from the fair form of her he loved.

Lady Katherine had recognised him as well as young Witherington the page, and at once guessed that the object of their presence in the convent was to effect her liberation.

She, too, was well aware of the danger of hastiness, and from her seat a little behind the abbess made a rapid signal for them to remain silent.

Of all this the lady superior of the establishment was ignorant, being too deeply engaged in writing in her journal the events of the day to notice any looks or signals that passed between her voluntary guests and her fair prisoner.

Hotspur was in a state of the greatest anxiety, and it was quite a relief to his mind when supper was served, as it partly diverted his thoughts, and enabled him to move, speak, and look with less fear of arousing suspicion.

The three youths were hungry, as boys always are when in good health.

The supper was a dainty one, and they

did justice to the various delicacies set before them.

Even Lady Katherine found an appetite, having eaten nothing since the previous evening, and having hitherto refused all offers of food.

But much as he enjoyed the meal, Hotspur was as impatient for its conclusion as he had been for its commencement.

After a time his wishes were gratified.

The abbess gave the signal for retirement.

"Sister Dorothy," said she, "conduct this fair lady, our guest, to her apartment in the north corridor, and then call one of the men from the outer court to show these noble youths where they are to rest."

Lady Katherine rose, and with a stately bow to the abbess, followed her guide from the hall.

Again Hotspur was upon the point of bringing affairs to a climax by his hastiness.

He would have rushed after her had not Ralph and Witherington detained him.

"Hold, my lord," whispered the page. "We can find out her lodging well enough, I'll warrant, when the abbess and her robber soldiers are asleep. She has recognised us, and I doubt not, will show some signal in her window."

The young lover was compelled to be silent, and, in a few minutes, one of the male servants of the convent entered.

"Conduct these youths to their lodging," said the stately lady, "and see that they are properly furnished with all that they lack for their comfort. If there is anything you require, gentle sirs, be not afraid to make your wants known. And, in the meantime, accept my blessing."

The lads bowed reverently and passed out of the hall.

They found that the chamber they were to occupy was on the southern side of the building.

It was a large room with stone walls and floor, the furniture being but scanty.

But as they had no intention of occupying it for any length of time, they were not disposed to find fault, and expressed themselves perfectly satisfied with the accommodation provided for them.

Their guide, after placing a torch in a bracket over the fire-place, bade them a surly good night, and left them.

"Now, let us to action!" said Hotspur, when they were alone.

"Fair and softly, good brother; there are too many people stirring yet."

"What, then, would you do?"

"My advice, my lord, is, that we hide the light, so that they may fancy we have retired to rest, and then in an hour's time when they fancy we are asleep we can issue forth with the greater security to seek the lady," said Witherington.

"And I am of the same opinion," said Ralph.

Very little more was said, and they sat themselves down to await the time when they might venture to commence their bold enterprise.

The storm seemed to have nearly passed over, though the thunder still rolled, and occasional flashes of lightning gleamed through the casement.

The clouds began to break, and the moon showed a few glimpses of her countenance.

The sentinels who kept watch by the gates of the convent could be heard as they paced up and down—sometimes conversing in rough voices.

Then came the trampling of armed men and the hoarse challenge as the watch was changed, after which a deep and profound silence reigned.

"Now is our time," said young Witherington. "The new sentinels have fairly settled down for their watch, and we shall escape notice."

"But how are we to find the lady?" asked Hotspur.

"Why, by the signal which she will show from her window. Surely she will aid us as much as lies in her power," replied Witherington.

Hotspur led the way, and they all three advanced cautiously to the door of their chamber.

They had bolted it on the inside but on quietly withdrawing the bolt the page was surprised to find that the door had been secured on the outside.

"We are prisoners, my lord," said he, in a low whisper.

"Your hastiness has caused us to be suspected, Harry," said Ralph.

"Then shall my sword free you. I will carve through this oak with my dagger."

"The noise would bring the guard upon us."

For a minute Hotspur said nothing, but at length he turned to Witherington and said—

"Come, Witherington, thou hast as keen wits as either of us. Set them to work to devise some plan by which we may escape from this hole."

"The window might be tried with success, my lord. It is not very high from the ground."

"A good thought. Help me to drag hither that hard, wooden bench, without it we shall have some difficulty in reaching the window."

The casement in question was fully five feet from the ground, and the walls of the building being very thick, they were unable, standing on the floor of their chamber to see what was beneath them outside.

On mounting the bench, Hotspur exclaimed, after a glance—

"If we descend here we shall be in the garden of the convent. This will not do, Witherington."

"It will do, my lord. They have no sentinels there, I should judge."

"Then follow me."

With these words Hotspur forced himself through the window, and dropped to the ground about eight feet beneath.

Alighting on a soft turf, the lads were not heard as one after another they followed their headstrong leader.

"Keep under the shadow of the building, my lord, until you reach the angle," said the page. "Then we can easily run to those thick bushes yonder, and from

their shelter survey the other side of the house."

Silently, yet swiftly, they crept along, Hotspur leading the way, Ralph following, and the page Witherington forming the rear guard.

They passed the corner of the building and found themselves on the east side of the nunnery.

Several groups of bushes were planted about in many places, growing to a considerable height, and fancying that these would conceal their movements better than the shadow of the house itself, the three adventurers sought their shelter.

For some few yards they proceeded safely and pleasantly enough.

The adventure smacked of the romantic, and pleased all three of the lads engaged in it.

Suddenly Ralph Percy laid his hand upon his brother's arm.

"See, Henry ! we are watched ! There is a man amongst those bushes before us."

Hotspur's sword flashed from its sheath, and he darted forward.

The others followed though they could not overtake him.

The headstrong youth reached the cluster of bushes, amongst which both he and his brother had seen a form, though so indistinctly that they could hardly be sure, whether it was male or female.

They searched around and amongst the thick laurels, Hotspur thrusting his sword into every bunch of foliage he judged large enough to conceal a human being.

But their search ended in disappointment, for no trace of anyone could they find—not even a footstep on the soft wet turf.

"This is strange, passing strange," said Hotspur. "Who can it have been ?"

"Some spirit, my lord ; they haunt all these abbeys and convents," replied Witherington.

CHAPTER XVII.

THE RESCUE OF LADY KATHERINE MORTIMER.

THE seriousness with which young Witherington spoke was not without effect upon Henry and Ralph Percy, who were both, to a certain extent, believers in the superstitious tales and legends inculcated by the priests of the Romish Church.

That spirits of deceased bodies did actually walk by night in solitary places with no apparent object was part and parcel of the belief of nearly every English man, woman, and child of that age, from the king in his palace to the meanest peasant in his hut.

Hotspur was the first to break silence.

"Spirit or not, I will not turn aside from the object I have in view. The foul fiend himself would not shake my resolution."

"I am with you, Hal," said Ralph. "Whither thou goest I will go."

"And you, Witherington?"

"I am no coward, my lord, and will follow where you lead; but be cautious, I entreat."

Again they pushed forward, and in a few minutes found themselves on an open lawn, before the north side of the convent.

On this side the boundary wall came up nearer to the building than on the east and west sides.

A grove of trees stood in the centre of the lawn, and in the midst of this grove was a fountain, which sent up a tiny column of water into the foliage.

Towards this grove the youths took their way, intending to watch the various windows for some signal—such as a light, or an open casement by which they could ascertain the presence of Lady Katherine Mortimer.

As they came beneath the shadow of the trees, a tall figure was plainly seen standing by the side of the fountain.

It was draped in a long cloak, which enveloped the body, while a hood concealed the head.

Once more Henry Percy rushed forward, with the intention of demanding the stranger's name and business; but as he approached, it glided behind the marble basin of the fountain and disappeared.

When his brother and Witherington once more joined him, he was engaged in a terrific effort to overthrow the marble basin, pedestal, carved dolphins, sea-nymphs and all.

"It disappeared here," he said; "it must have gone into the fountain. Help me, Ralph—help me Witherington, for I am determined to unearth this mystery."

"It is useless," said Ralph, when they had rendered themselves almost breathless by their exertions.

"Said I not that it was a spirit?" exclaimed Witherington. "What mortal being could disappear from before our very eyes as this has done."

"I know not why a spirit should trouble us," replied Hotspur, who began to grow intensely angry with the whole ghostly realm. "If it comes within reach of my sword I will question it."

"But see!" said Ralph. "There is a light in yonder window. The Lady Katherine must be the inhabitant of that chamber."

In a moment Hotspur forgot the strange appearance, and leaving the ghost or goblin to its own reflections, strode off towards the window from which gleamed the light of a solitary lamp.

The form of a lady was plainly visible.

"It must be the Lady Katherine," thought Percy.

"Hist! Lady Katherine, I am here!" he said, in a loud whisper, as soon as he arrived beneath the window.

The curtain was drawn aside, and Lady

Katherine's fair face appeared at the window.

"Who calls?" she said, in the same low tones.

"I—Henry Percy."

"Thanks, good cousin. I doubted not that you would follow. But the door of the cell is locked ; I am a prisoner."

"You must descend from the window."

"It is a fearful height."

"Not quarter so high as the tower down which you were borne on a rope ladder."

"There is a ladder yonder, my lord," whispered De Witherington. "I will bring it."

He departed, and in a few minutes returned with the article in question, which had been left standing against the garden wall.

It was sufficiently long to reach the window, and in a moment Percy was at its summit.

"Brave Percy ! And have you undertaken this perilous adventure unattended, save by your brother and a stripling page ? Is this prudent ?" asked Lady Katherine, as Hotspur stepped from the ladder into the cell.

"Fear not, dear lady ; our men-at-arms are in the wood, and a blast on young Witherington's bugle would soon bring his stout old father to our aid. But come, descend the ladder, and we will conduct you back to Alnwick,"

Lady Katherine approached the window, but suddenly started back,

"Hush ! hark ! I heard footsteps in the corridor. It is my jailer coming to see that the prisoner is secure. Fly ! hide yourself, Harry !"

"Descend and save yourself rather," replied Hotspur. "I will keep all intruders at bay in the meantime."

So saying, he bolted the door inside, and stood by it, sword in hand.

The footsteps came nearer.

A hand was heard endeavouring to unfasten the door, and then came the voice of the lady abbess.

"Open the door, I pray you, dear lady ; open the door without fear."

"Fly, fly, quick ! begone, ere she suspects treason !" ejaculated Hotspur.

"By the mass, if she succeed in forcing the door, I will pass my sword through her, though I be burned afterwards for slaying a nun."

His voice was heard by the abbess, who at once began to suspect that all was not right.

She rushed into the adjoining cell, and looking from the window, at once saw sufficient to convince her that a plan was on foot to carry off the fair prisoner committed to her charge by Sir William Graham.

"Help ! treason !" she cried, running along the corridor, and rousing the inmates of the other cells, who added their shrieks to those of their lady superior.

"Down with you," cried Hotspur, and in an instant Lady Katherine was received safely by Ralph and young Witherington, who stood at the foot of the ladder.

Hotspur followed, disdaining the use of the steps by which he had ascended, and leaping from the window to the ground beneath.

"This way," he cried ; "To the grove ! It may be that the goblin we saw will scare away those who will doubtless pursue us."

That they were pursued there was no room to doubt, for the clatter of heavy feet sounded loudly upon the gravel walks of the garden, and the guard, roused by the abbess, appeared.

The fugitives ran towards the grove, but no sign of the strange figure was to be seen.

When within three yards of the fountain, however, it suddenly started up, and casting the long cloak from it, revealed to the eyes of the astonished youths the form of the Witch of Wooler.

The sudden appearance of the weird woman, clothed in her uncouth garments, with long, snaky-looking tresses waving in the wind, was too much for Lady Katherine's nerves.

With a half-suppressed scream she fainted, and would have fallen to the earth had not the stalwart arm of Harry Percy sustained her.

CHAPTER XVIII.

A WARNING FROM THE NORTH.

TO be deprived of sleep is to be deprived of health and peace of mind.

Macbeth speaks of sleep as knitting up the ravelled sleeve of care, and certainly, in most instances, it does refresh the spirits as well as the body.

But when the father confessor, holy Friar Abel, woke up out of the senseless state into which he had been thrown by the drugged wine intended for Archie, he felt no benefit from his heavy slumber.

His head was hot, heavy, and confused, his tongue parched with thirst, his eyes lustreless and bloodshot.

"A cup of strong ale!" was all he could find words to say.

The potent liquor was brought, nor did it tarry long in its journey down the priest's throat.

But though it quenched his thirst, it had an effect which Father Abel did not anticipate—it acted as an emetic, and made him the laughing-stock of the household.

Looking around, and seeing nothing of Archie, the priest imagined that he had retired to rest, for it was past the usual hour.

He was too sick and ill to ask any questions, and was assisted to his own apartment.

Morning came, and Father Abel was awake betimes, though not quite recovered from the effects of the drug.

He sat up, anxiously expecting a visit from the man-at-arms, but Archie did not make his appearance.

Hour after hour passed—no sounds were heard save those usually made by the menials in the performance of their duties.

The loud horn was heard calling them to breakfast.

"I shall surely see him at table," thought Father Abel, and forthwith he assumed his gown and sandals.

To the hall they repaired—there were cooks, scullions, grooms, and other retainers, but the tall figure of Archie was not to be seen.

"Why comes not my friend, the gallant soldier?" he asked. "Surely ye have aroused him from his sleep?"

"He slept not here, good father," replied the man addressed.

"He slept not here? Where, then?"

"I know not, father. He left the house soon after you—you—you—were—asleep."

"A thousand fiends torment ye for this news, sirrah. And wherefore did ye suffer him to depart, after seeing him drug my wine?"

"We knew not that, holy father, craving your pardon and indulgence. We only fancied that—that——"

"That what, rascal?"

"That you had taken too much."

This enraged the priest more than ever.

Rising from his seat in a torrent of wrath, he cursed the unhappy wretch who had offended him by every formula of his creed.

Saints and fiends alike were invoked to consign to eternal torments the miserable being who had been guilty of the fearful sin of suspecting his priest of intoxication.

This religious duty, for so Father Abel deemed it, being discharged, the enraged ecclesiastic withdrew to his own chamber, ordering one of the servants to prepare breakfast there.

For some hours the priest remained secluded from the public eye, during which time his reflections were not of the most pleasant kind.

He had been outwitted by the man he thought his dupe, and that man had departed, but he knew not whether as friend or foe.

His meditations were disturbed by a footstep which ascended the stair, and then came a knock at the door of his apartment.

At first the priest's eyes brightened.

He thought it might be Archie returning like a penitent.

But on second thoughts he knew it could not be the soldier-wearer of jingling spurs and clanking armour who ascended so softly, and knocked so humbly.

"Enter!" said he.

The door was thrown open, and a youth of about seventeen or eighteen years of age appeared—the lowest of all—the household drudge's drudge and domestic slave in general.

"What is it?" demanded the priest, in no very pleasant tones.

"Heaven save your holiness——" humbly began the lad.

"Heaven will take care of me without your asking. Say what you have to say, and begone."

"A stranger brought this letter for your reverence."

So saying, he deposited the document upon the table, and, making a low bow, was about to retire, when the voice of the priest stopped him.

"Who was it brought this?"

"An it please your holy reverence, I know not."

"Did ye not ask?"

"Marry, yes, your reverence."

"And what said he?"

"He said 'Give this letter to Father Abel ; tell him it comes from a friend.'"

"What then?"

"He turned away from the gate and vanished."

"Vanished, knave, blockhead?"

"Even so, holy father. We looked down the street after him ; but he was not to be seen."

The priest looked at the lad very hard, but he at least meant what he said.

Father Abel cut the silken thread that secured the billet, and was about to open it when he recollected that the household drudge before him could read.

The holy man who had held the office of domestic chaplain before Father Abel, had actually so far departed from precedent as to wish to give the servants and retainers some little learning, and had commenced with this overgrown lad. But all this had been put a stop to when Father Abel took charge of the souls of the household.

There was danger, however, that the poor drudge might see the letter, so with a stern voice, he ordered the drudge from his presence.

When once more alone, he ventured to open the billet conveyed to him in so mysterious a manner.

Its contents were brief ; and to add to the strangeness of the affair, there was no signature or seal attached to it, nor any mark by which he might discover the writer.

It ran thus :—

"A warning from the North. Take heed, good father, and be more circumspect. Your wishes and designs are known, and will be thwarted. One who has more power than you watches over those you seek to destroy. Did not the writer of this bear you some love your life would pay the penalty of your foolish treason. As you love life tamper no more with Archie."

"Now, who in the foul fiend's name can have written this?" muttered the priest, as he turned the slip of parchment in every direction in a vain effort to discover who the writer might be. "Archie himself knows not a letter, so he, at least, is innocent."

He thought of Sir Willian Graham, and likewise of Du Bois, the herald ; but neither of those persons bore him sufficient love to refrain from betraying him if it suited their purpose, or would benefit them. The other conspirators were all in Archie's state of ignorance, unable to decipher a letter much less form one.

He racked his brain in vain—the seal gave no clue, nor could he guess who had discovered the secrets he supposed were known only to himself and comrade.

"One thing is certain," thought he, as he held the parchment in the flame of a taper. "If we are discovered my gown will not shield me from Percy's vengeance. I must save myself."

But then he reflected that in order to do so flight would most probably be necessary, and our priest's list of friends, save those with whom the reader is already acquainted, was rather a scanty one.

"THE ENCOUNTER WITH THE WEIRD WOMAN."

Good fat livings were not to be picked up every day, nor without some influence and patronage.

"I know what I will do," he exclaimed, when he had watched the parchment crackle and curl till only a black, charred, greasy mass remained, "I will hie me to Scotland ; there, at least, I shall be safe."

To resolve was not difficult, but to execute the journey was an entirely different affair.

Our priest, as before said, was a man of corpulent rotund build, loved his ease, and always most carefully studied how to keep his body out of danger.

But as Father Abel never stuck closely to the truth when it suited him to depart from it, he had no difficulty in convincing the servants of the house that the message came from their master, the earl.

By these means he obtained everything he considered requisite—servant, horses, and provisions, and thus equipped, commenced his journey.

CHAPTER XIX.

A SEARCH FOR THE WISE WOMAN.

METHINKS I hear the reader say, "Gramercy! Marry come up I' fackins! An the author tell us not what happened young Douglas in the hermit's cell, by the rood, we will most soundly cudgel his buff jerkin!"

Patience, gentle reader, deal gently with all our sins ; lay not the blows of your censure too heavily, and your curiosity shall be gratified.

Douglas returned to his cell after his combat with Percy had been prevented by the interposition of the hermit's crucifix.

The holy recluse had himself been a warrior in his younger days—had fought to wrest the holy sepulchre from the hands of the Saracens—had marched with the English army into the heart of France, and well knew how difficult it was to restrain the fiery passions of youth when fairly aroused.

But for all this the good hermit could not refrain from doing what he considered his duty, and forthwith read the young Scottish youth a homily, which Percy would have shared had he not taken himself off.

"Holy father, I ask forgiveness," said Douglas. "Shall I plead in vain?"

"Assuredly not, my son. You are forgiven so far as I can forgive, nor sha my prayers be lacking to make the atonement complete. But rest, my son, for you must need it ; partake of such poor food as my lonely cell can afford, and then sleep in peace, for here no foe will molest you."

A rude meal was placed upon the table, but the hermit tasted it not.

A couch of fresh heather and ferns was spread for Douglas, but the hermit kept his seat at the door of his cell gazing heavenward into the star-decked sky.

In the grey of morn the young Scot awoke to find his pious host still keeping his self-appointed watch.

Day was dawning, grey mists curled up from field and wood, the eastern sky assumed a lovely orange tint, while in thicket and grove a thousand feathered songsters piped their joyous chorus to greet the rising sun.

Douglas arose and stood by the hermit's side.

"Good morrow, holy father. Have you passed the night in watching?"

"Aye ; like the wise men of eastern climes I would fain read wisdom from the face of heaven."

"What, are you an astrologer?"

"I know the stars in their courses, and

can tell what they presage. But wherefore do you start and shrink back ?"

"A magician ?" muttered Douglas. "One versed in dark mysteries and black arts ?"

"I know no art that I may not practise, so that it be done in humble spirit and to no man's harm."

"But do you not converse with the fiend ?"

"Foolish boy, think you that one who held conversation with evil spirits would bear the weight of this sacred symbol on his breast ?"

The argument at once convinced the youthful heir to the earldom of Douglas that, however learned his host might be, his knowledge was not of that class which both church and state deemed criminal.

"Your pardon again, father. But, pray, tell me what saw you in the stars last night ?"

"I saw a sign of danger."

"To whom ?"

"A young Scot of noble birth. The stars revealed his name."

"It must be me. But is the danger to be averted ?"

"It is."

"In what manner ?"

"By instant departure to a place of safety, at least so I read the heavenly signs."

"I will depart," said Douglas.

But instead of at once setting out on his journey he seated himself on a grey mossy rock by the side of the door, and gazed up into the same sky on which the hermit had looked.

The stars had vanished, and in their stead the glorious summer sun was shining brightly.

For a long time he sat thus, and the hermit, absorbed in his own meditations, did not disturb his young guest's reverie."

Douglas was the first to break silence.

"Father !" said he.

"My son."

"You can read the stars, you say ?"

"Their voices are known to me."

"One so learned should possess still more knowledge."

"It becomes me not to boast, son."

"Can you foretell the future ?"

The hermit cast a look of sorrow upon the anxious countenance of the young Scot as he awaited his answer.

"Foolish, rash youth ! Why wouldst thou pry into the secrets which Providence has hidden ? Is life too bright and joyous that thou must needs mingle the gall of future sorrows with the cup of present happiness ? Forbear, forbear ! nor seek to know the bitterness of coming woes."

The Scot was silent for a few moments, and then again spoke.

"I have heard," said he, "of clever men and wise women who could show the future as in a picture."

"Some few there be. I have heard of a young Welsh prince who boasts such knowledge * ; and then there is the strange, weird woman who sometimes ranges this Northern country, called the Witch of Wooler. I have heard that she pretends to foreshadow coming events ; but with what truth I know not."

Again Douglas sat moody and silent for a long time, with arms crossed over his chest.

His brow was contracted and stern, his lips compressed, and his whole appearance was that of a man working himself up to the requisite pitch of daring for some desperate undertaking.

The sun rose higher and higher and higher ; the waters of the stream shone more brightly, the dewdrops faded from grass and leaf, and at length Douglas rose.

"You say that danger threatens ; to avert that danger I go. Many thanks for your hospitality, holy father, and pray accept these gold pieces in repayment."

"Nay ; keep your gold, son. The hermit is no innkeeper, nor can he take payment for the roots from the earth, the water from the rock, or the couch of heather. Farewell, my son ; the saints protect thee."

Douglas bent his bonnet over his brow, and strode off rapidly.

"Little does the hermit know whither I go," he murmured.

---

* We suppose the hermit alludes to Owen Glendower, afterwards Percy's friend and ally.

He paused, and then asked himself the question—

"But whither do I go?"

He stopped abruptly in his walk, and bent his eyes upon the ground.

"A Welsh prince, and the Witch of Wooler, whom I have already seen. Wales is too far; to reach it I must cross the enemy's country, and after all there may be no truth in the rumour; but the witch—I have seen her once. Methinks she should be able to tell me, if there lives mortal man who can—I will seek the witch!"

He took two paces onwards, when an obstacle presented itself in his path.

A hideous viper, half-coiled up, though with head elevated above the ground, was hissing, darting out its forked tongue, and gently moving its head backward and forward in readiness to make a spring if the young noble advanced.

A moment's hesitation, and then, with a blow of his broadsword, the reptile's head was severed from its writhing body.

The young noble proceeded onwards, and soon passed into a dense thicket.

A rustling noise was heard, and a gaunt, fierce-looking wolf stood before him in the path, seeming inclined to dispute the passage with him. *

Again the good broadsword flashed in the air.

The wolf growled, showed its teeth, and erected the hair on its neck and back like an angry dog.

"Well said the hermit that danger besets me," said the youth. "A new one presents itself at each step; but hey for Scotland. I have faced a man, and shall I fly from a wolf?"

So saying, he leaped forward, aiming a heavy blow at the animal, which, in turn, sprang forward at the Scot.

Douglas grappled the animal by the throat, though he could not prevent it from seizing him by the shoulder.

His left hand was free, and in a moment it sought the dirk or dagger he wore.

A few deep, desperate stabs, and the savage brute lay dead upon the path.

Douglas wiped his dagger upon its hide, replaced his weapons in their sheaths, and proceeded on his journey.

But his shoulder was painful from the effects of the bite, and blood slowly trickled down his arm.

The young Scot, however, was not to be daunted by such trifles.

His body could show scars of wounds received in desperate combat with armed men, and the bite of the wolf, though painful, was not dangerous.

Some time then passed as he walked along a solitary path, through a gloomy forest.

The arching trees overhead shut out the light of the sun; no sweet flowers were there to waft fragrant odours up to his nostrils; the song-birds were silent in that darksome grove.

Upwards and onwards, though the ground became more uneven and the trees less thickly planted by the hand of nature.

At length he stopped, for a deep precipice lay before him, much like the one down which he had lowered himself the night before.

But now he had no friendly rope to aid his descent; not even a vine or a creeping plant was there; and the precipice was much too high for a leap.

Wearied and angered at the succession of obstacles thrown in his path, he flung himself on the short mossy turf which bordered the edge of the rock, and began to bind up his wounded shoulder with large cool leaves.

His mind was still bent upon the desperate project he had formed.

He would seek out the witch, and from her learn the secrets of the future.

Almost unconsciously he uttered his thoughts aloud—

"Shall I turn back when once I have commenced an enterprise? Shall it be said that one of the race of Douglas was baffled by a snake, a wolf, and a cliff? Never!"

He leaned over the edge of the rock and gazed along up and down the ravine of which it formed a wall.

No break or place of descent was visible.

"I will find this witch, I have sworn!"

* There were a few wolves still remaining in Great Britain, though they were much hunted; but that circumstance would render them the more ferociou

"Then seek her in Scotland, near the convent of St. Agnes," a voice seemed to whisper in his ear, and, at the same time, a shadowy form seemed to glide before his eyes.

Douglas leaped to his feet and gazed eagerly around.

Not a living being was visible save a solemn old raven sitting on the tree beneath which Douglas had been lying, and even the bird of ill-omen flew off with a dismal croak as the young Scot rose to the ground.

Douglas shuddered as he heard the mournful sound.

"Who spoke ?" he said, in a low voice, but no answer came save the whispering of the light breeze among the trees. "Who talks of the convent of St. Agnes?" he continued, as he sent keen glances into every thicket or bush that could conceal a human being.

He was much agitated, but the brave lad considered his honour at stake, and forthwith commenced a search along the precipice for some place where he could descend.

It everywhere presented the same smooth, perpendicular aspect, though he observed with joy that it grew less and less in height.

When he had proceeded half a mile it ceased, and he was enabled to go forward.

The forest gradually cleared away, and he soon found himself on a tolerably open heath, where thousands of gay blossoms sent up a sweet perfume, and thousands of busy insects sucked honey from the bells.

This, however, was nothing to Douglas.

He took no note of bell, bee, or butterfly.

But he was glad to find himself on the heath, because it reminded him of his native home, and also because he knew its situation, and saw at a glance which direction he must take.

With a sickly smile upon his lips, he strode onwards.

He had half crossed the plain when, on casually stopping and turning his head, he was surprised to see four men on horseback following on his track.

They had evidently just issued from the wood and caught sight of the Scottish youth.

"They must be Percy's men," thought he. "He is not with them, and my fate is sealed. I will make an effort to gain yon thicket though."

Off he started at headlong speed, while at the same time a shout from one of the strangers echoed across the waste.

"I cannot stop to answer," he muttered, as he sped onwards.

But he turned his head and saw that they were spurring their horses in pursuit.

A deep fissure in the earth yawned beneath him.

He crouched, and, reckless of his imminent peril, made a mad bound through the air.

CHAPTER XX.

THE BOWELS OF THE EARTH.

MAY the holy saints watch over us," exclaimed young Witherington, as he saw the soldiers advancing on the one hand, while the weird woman of Wooler stood on the other.

"We are surrounded by enemies," said Ralph Percy, unsheathing his sword.

"Cut them down ! Down with the spies, the sacrilegious traitors !" shouted the soldiers of the convent.

Harry Percy drew his weapon, though he continued to support Lady Katherine.

"You cannot resist, they are too many for you," said the witch, in a deep voice.

"I, for one, will never surrender," said Percy.

"Why endanger your lives when I can save you?" replied the weird woman. "The power I possess is greater than that of yon robber chieftain, and all his free lances. Trust in me."

"It shall never be said that a Percy entered into a league with the evil one."

"Foolish boy! What evil have I done thee or thy kindred?"

"Trust in her, brother," said Ralph, "she is but one, and we can easily overcome her."

The last words were spoken in a low whisper, but an angry flush on the woman's cheek told that she had overheard them, but she made no remark.

"I will trust in you, then," said Hotspur. "Lead on, but beware of treachery."

The witch pressed her hand upon a portion of the carved marble of the fountain.

In an instant the jet of water ceased to throw its sparkling spray aloft, and a harsh grating sound was heard like the rattling of rusty wheels in motion.

The cumbrous stonework began to move from its pedestal, revealing a flight of steps, which descended deep into the bowels of the earth.

"Descend," said the weird woman, pointing to the yawning cavern.

Harry Percy hesitated a moment, not for his own sake, but for the safety of the precious burden he bore in his arms.

"I will be the advance guard," cried Ralph, stepping forward. "Follow me."

"Haste, haste, or you will be too late," said the witch.

The youths hurried down the steps, bearing Lady Katherine between them, and the strange being who had so suddenly provided the means of escape followed close behind.

When she had descended about a dozen steps she stopped and turned a little iron knob which projected from the staircase wall.

The harsh rumbling noise was again heard, and the huge stone basin resumed its former position, shutting out the pursuers and the light.

They were in total darkness, but their strange guide soon remedied that.

She produced a lighted torch from a recess in the wall, over which a covering had been hung.

"Now let me be your leader—follow me," said she, as she led the way down the staircase.

Down, down, down, far beneath the foundations of the convent, below even the spring that fed the fountain overhead.

The walls grew more damp and slimy, the air more foul.

At length they reached the bottom of the staircase, and there found a passage or corridor on each hand.

"Step not beyond the left hand archway," said the witch, "if you wish to avoid sudden and horrible death."

She then turned off abruptly to the right and walked swiftly forward.

At least a quarter of a mile must have been traversed when suddenly they came upon what appeared to be a rapid river flowing across the pathway.

The water burst out of one side of the wall, and through a low dark archway on the other side.

It seemed as though the infernal river Styx had burst its banks to leap madly over a cataract, and plunge down into the bowels of the earth.

The noise was so great that it was with great difficulty the youths could distinguish each other's voices.

"How can we cross this stream?" demanded Percy, turning towards the witch.

"Do you fear to wet your feet?" was the ready response.

"But the lady?"

"You love her?"

"I do."

"You have borne her so far in your arms, a few yards more will see you at the end of your journey."

So saying the woman stepped into the water, and turning to the left stooped down to pass through the archway.

Hotspur fearlessly followed, finding to his surprise that what appeared a deep and dangerous stream was only a shallow underground brook of a few inches in depth.

When through the archway, the witch paused, and held a torch aloft.

It was a strange and grotesque scene.

The roof above was a vault of Nature's own building—wild and rough to the eye, yet, in its grand proportions and noble height, impressing the beholder with admiration and awe.

Hotspur, Ralph Percy and young Witherington gazed around in wonder at the stupendous grandeur of the scene.

The witch waited till they had satisfied their admiration, and then led on to a little nook in the side of the cave.

A stout oaken doorway barred their progress, but the weird woman had only to touch a spring in the woodwork to overcome the difficulty.

"Enter," said she, "enter the witch's chamber."

Hotspur hesitated, but only for a moment, and then walked into the apartment.

"I wonder not that you should hesitate to put faith in me," said the weird woman, "for well I know the false tales that are told. But let those who malign me produce evidence of my evil deeds."

"But," said Witherington, "I have heard that you blight the peasant's crops, spread dire diseases among his herds, and take delight in thwarting man's industry."

"The crops and the herds are under the control of one mightier than I. No power of mine can change their destiny."

"But do not you and your companions meet in strange places, perform strange rites and ceremonies, and worship the Evil One?"

The woman's brow grew stern, the flush of rage was on her cheek.

"How, when, and where we meet matters not to any one, neither does our worship, since we seek no converts to our faith."

"But you have spirits at your command?" said Hotspur, who had deposited the helpless form of Lady Katherine on a couch.

"I have control over unseen agents."

"You can foretell events that are to come?"

"Behold the mirror of the future."

As she spoke the witch drew aside a curtain which hung against the wall, and pointed to what appeared to be a dull, tarnished plate of glass.

Then she let fall the curtain again, and turned her eyes towards Lady Katherine.

"It is time the fair one was recovered from her swoon. Stand aside, and let me apply some effectual remedy."

Hotspur moved away a pace and the woman, after feeling Lady Katherine's pulse, began to uncork a small phial.

"Hold!" cried the youth, "no philters nor fiendish potions shall pass her pure lips."

"You mistrust me?"

Hotspur made no audible reply, though his look plainly answered in the affirmative.

"Foolish, thoughtless youth! had it been my intention to injure you, how easy it would have been to have left you to the mercy of the ruffian soldiers above, or even when you had safely entered the cave, could I not have hurled you into pitfalls and dark chasms in which your bodies would have been dashed to pieces?"

So saying she applied the phial to Lady Katherine's lips, and poured a few drops of its contents down her throat.

The effect was soon visible.

The colour began to return to her cheeks, her bosom showed signs of life and motion.

Then the large, lustrous eyes were opened wide, and fixed in wonder and amazement on the strange form and features of her physician.

"Where am I?" she asked.

"With friends," replied the witch.

"Where is——"

Her tongue hesitated to pronounce the name.

"I am here," said Hotspur, stepping forward.

Lady Katherine gave him a look of love and confidence, and sat up.

"You are better?" said the strange woman.

"Thanks, yes. But who are you?"

"They call me the Witch of Wooler."

Lady Katherine could not repress a shudder.

"Fear not, gentle one, you are safe

enough. You have three gallants to protect you. But rest awhile, you must not leave this place till morning."

She sat down in a curious old chair, and Lady Katherine looked round the strange place to which Fortune's freaks had brought her.

A strange-looking apartment, strangely furnished.

As before said, at one end was the mirror veiled by a dark curtain.

The other walls were hung with tapestry, on which strange figures were embroidered.

Before the mirror was a table on which stood two candles, between them was a book supporting a skull.

On the floor before this table was traced a circle of about six feet in diameter, the circumference of which was decorated with the signs of the Zodiac and a variety of heiroglyphics.

In one corner was a furnace, with crucibles, retorts, and various chemical instruments.

And last of all, on a kind of bracket over the magic mirror, was perched a large horned owl which stared with its large round eyes, ruffled its feathers, and hissed with evident displeasure at the presence of the intruders.

This was the only living creature visible, with the exception of the five human beings who sat silently in that strange apartment.

Hotspur's thoughts were roving over the past, and speculating on what was to come, while the other youths regarded with awe the gloomy-looking apartment and its mysterious owner.

The witch was buried in a reverie from which neither of the young people cared to rouse her.

CHAPTER XXI.

THE MAGIC MIRROR.

A SLIGHT noise was heard, which seemed to proceed from some distant part of the cavern.

On hearing it the witch started to her feet, and exclaimed—

"Some human foot has penetrated the mysteries of this cave. Be on your guard; be prepared."

"Should it be a foe he returns not," said Harry Percy, drawing his weapon.

"Hush! your blade is of little worth."

The owl began to ruffle its feathers, and hiss with greater violence than before.

It had heard the approaching intruder.

Ralph Percy and young Witherington followed Hotspur's example, and stood, sword in hand, prepared for any emergency.

Then a tinkling sound, like a small bell, was heard close at hand, and the witch's brow became still more agitated.

"They have entered by the secret cave in the woods," said she. "Remain you here while I discover the number and purpose of the intruders."

With these words the woman glided behind the tapestry and disappeared.

Hotspur began to suspect treachery, and fancied that the bell they had heard was a signal.

"Trust in the weird woman still, my brother; hitherto she has befriended us," said Ralph.

"What object can she have in betraying us into the hands of our enemies after helping us to escape from them?" asked Lady Katherine. "Surely our foes are not divided into two parties."

"Ah, lady, you little know the malignant nature of these strange beings," said Witherington. "But hush! she returns."

It was evident, from the fact of two voices being audible, that the witch was returning, and in company with some one.

In a few minutes the tapestry was again drawn aside, and she re-entered, followed by a youth clothed in Scottish tartan.

The English youths could scarcely believe their eyes, for it was none other than the young Earl Douglas himself.

"Once more we meet, then, mine enemy," exclaimed Hotspur, springing forward, sword in hand. "Draw your blade, Douglas ; defend yourself!"

"Not yet, gentle Percy ; in any other place and presence I would not baulk your humour."

And, folding his arms, he gazed intently on the form of Lady Katherine, whose face was covered with blushes.

But though he thus looked, the Scot spoke not, nor even made any sign of recognition.

"Coward!" shouted Hotspur ; "I will pierce your worthless body with my sword."

And the hasty youth made another step forward, brandishing his weapon as though about to strike.

Still Douglas heeded him not.

His eyes had wandered from Lady Katherine's face to the curtain which shrouded the magic mirror, and on it his thoughts seemed centred.

His cheek flushed, and his breath came more quickly as he heard the word "coward," though he remained motionless.

"Percy, put up your sword," said the witch, in stern tones of command.

"Not so. I will slay the vile Scot," replied the youth, lowering the weapon in preparation for a thrust.

Another moment would have sealed the fate of Douglas had not the witch again interposed.

With her fingers she sprinkled some drops of a liquid on Hotspur's face.

In an instant all colour left his cheeks, his limbs became stiff, his feet rooted to the earth ; not even a pulsation remained to show that life existed within that gaily-dressed and handsome body.

Like a cunningly carved image, there he stood, sword in hand.

The others were for a few seconds speechless with astonishment at this exhibition of the strange woman's power.

Ralph Percy was the first to break silence.

"Vile witch !" he exclaimed ; "you have slain my brother, the hope of Northumberland. Your own body shall answer for it."

As he finished speaking the gallant boy aimed a blow at the woman.

But he, too, was as instantly rendered motionless by her.

But in each of the brothers every principle of life was in full action, save speech and motion.

They could hear what was said, and see what took place.

Young Witherington, though much more superstitious than his noble companions, was not less brave, and determined to make an effort to avenge them.

After a brief prayer to his patron saint, the page raised his weapon to strike.

"Hold, hold, rash boy ! what is it you would do?" said the witch. "Of what advantage would my death be when no power of yours could undo the spell that binds their limbs? Return your sword to its sheath."

"True—true !" replied the page, despondingly. "Strange being, whatever you may be, I beseech you restore life to the inanimate forms of my friends."

"In good time they shall depart as easily as they came."

"And think not, sir page, that the fierce looks and haughty words of your young lord have made my heart know fear," said Douglas. "Had I known who was concealed within this apartment my tongue should have grown to the roof of my mouth ere I swore the oath which binds me not to draw weapon until I return once more to the open air beneath the canopy of heaven."

"Then what brings you here, Sir Scot ?"

"I care not to reveal my thoughts, wishes, or motives to every English lad who asks; but as my business has not been told to the owner of this mystic dwelling, I will state it. I would know the future, and see what shall happen me in future years," he continued, addressing the dark woman.

"You would know, then, what had better far be hidden from your sight," replied the Witch of Wooler. "Why seek to know what would render your young life a misery, and blight every bright hope and aspiration of youth?"

"Such knowledge is not hidden from you. I pray you reveal it to me?"

"Then so be it."

"And I too would know my doom," said young Witherington.

"Thou! Why does not the fair lady seek to know her fate? Has all the curiosity of her sex departed from her?"

"I feared to ask what I would wish to learn," said Lady Katherine.

For a few moments the witch was silent.

Then, suddenly rising to her seat, she exclaimed—

"The mirror shall be unveiled—the future brought before your view. But if the sight strikes terror to your hearts, blame not Gunara, the Witch of Wooler, as men call her."

The woman—or Gunara, as we shall henceforth call her—then blew a shrill blast on a small silver whistle.

It was answered by a black dwarf dressed in the fanciful picturesque costume of a Moor or Morisco, as he would have been called in that time.

His mistress spoke some words to him in a language unknown to any of the others, and the dwarf began to place on the table certain phials, caskets, and bunches of herbs which he procured from a recess behind the furnace.

Then, having opened the book, he placed on the table a brazier full of burning charcoal; after which he made a low bow to Gunara and retired.

"Stand all of you within this circle; stir not from it as you value your lives," said the sybil when these preparations were completed.

Gunara herself conducted Lady Katherine within the charmed line, where the fair girl stood supported on either side by Hotspur and Ralph Percy.

The brothers were already within the circle, having ventured over its limits in their hostile movements towards the Scot and the enchantress.

"Speak not—stir not, till I bid you," said Gunara, who then, with stately step, walked towards the table.

The red charcoal glowed brightly in the brazier as she threw on it some few of the herbs, and sprinkled some drops from one of the phials.

Then, in a low tone, she began to read from the volume before her, in what appeared to be the same language that she had used in addressing the dwarf.

Dense clouds of smoke curled up, so that the mirror and its curtain were almost hidden from view.

The cave itself was filled with a sickly perfume.

Suddenly, Gunara left off reading, and directed her gaze towards the fire.

Blue sparks were rapidly flying from it with a hissing sound, and the brazier seemed surrounded by a lurid light which did not emanate from the burning coals within it.

She opened a casket, and threw more spices upon it, after which she sprinkled the curtain before the mirror with the contents of one of her phials.

Then, changing her language to the vernacular understood by her audience, she recited in clear, measured tones, the following incantation—

"Spirits that dwell on cloud-capped mountains,
    Where the foot of man hath ne'er been seen;
Spirits who haunt the sparkling fountains,
    That rise in the midst of forest green;
Spirits who dwell in earth's deep caves,
Spirits who dwell 'neath ocean's wave;
Ethereal beings, I summon ye all;
Hasten hither—obey my call!"

The cavern was then filled with a sound as though thousands of winged beings were cleaving their way through the air.

The fire crackled and emitted more vivid sparks than before, while the owl rising from its perch with an unearthly scream sailed away through the archway into the outer cavern.

The face of the weird woman, lit up by the fire, assumed an unearthly hue.

Her glowing eyes appeared to outvie in lustre the lamp on the table.

She held up one hand as though to enjoin silence.

Then a voice was heard thundering and echoing through the gloomy vault.

"We are here. Why have you called us? Speak, potent mistress."

"Weak-minded mortals have wandered hither, and seek to pry into the future. Can you show it them?"

"We can; we can; we can."

It seemed as though a hundred voices had united to answer the question, and it was some seconds ere the echoes of the unearthly sounds had died away.

"Will you show them?" asked Gunara.

"We must if you command."

The sybil then turned to the young people and said—

"Do you still desire, or shall I dismiss the spirits I have called?"

"That would be sorry courtesy to call them for no purpose," said Douglas. "I am as fixed in my desire as when I first entered the cave."

"And you?" she continued addressing Lady Katherine.

The fair girl, though half fainting with terror, bowed her head to signify that she wished the ceremony to proceed.

Witherington said nothing, but began to fumble at a bunch of consecrated beads which he carried at his belt.

The page's devotional movements were suddenly brought to a conclusion.

The owl came sailing back with another of its unearthly cries, and plucked the beads from the lad's girdle.

Ere Witherington could recover from his surprise, the bird was gone, while a sound that much resembled laughter echoed through the cave.

"Silence, fiends! I command you—and disobey me at your peril," said Gunara.

"You command us now, but a time will come when we shall be free," replied a deep harsh voice.

And then all became silent, save the crackling fire in the brazier.

The cheek of the sorceress became livid with rage as she heard the voice.

With a stern voice she continued—

"Spirits, I command you by the mighty spell which gives me power over all of you, by the name which fills you with dread, by the torments you fear to endure, by the labours you seek to shun, show these prying mortals as much as is known to you of the events that shall be."

As Gunara uttered these words a loud peal of thunder reverberated through the cavern, and the curtain before the mirror was rolled up by some invisible hand.

"What seek they to know?" asked the same voice that had before spoken.

"Speak—ask what question you will," said Gunara, turning towards Douglas.

"I would know the manner of my death," said the young Scot, in firm tones.

The smoke gradually cleared away from before the mirror, and its surface became radiant with light.

Then came shadowy figures and grouped themselves upon its polished surface.

The figures became more and more distinct, till the young Scot could discern a form which appeared to be his own, lying on the ground in the midst of a number of fighting soldiers, Scottish and English.

A long feathered arrow appeared to have pierced the bosom of the recumbent figure.

Close by were two knights in armour, whose crests showed them to be of the Percy family, surrounded and made prisoners by a number of Scottish soldiers.

"Behold your fate!" said Gunara.

The youth gazed on it for a minute, and then, heaving a deep sigh said—

"If that be my fate, I will meet it as a true Scottish knight should."

The figures became indistinct, and vanished from the face of the mirror.

"Now, lady, look upon your doom," cried Gunara, turning to Lady Katherine.

Once more the mirror brightened, and a different scene presented itself.

There was an altar and a robed priest.

Before it knelt a youthful couple, whose hands were united by the holy man.

Their features were those of herself and Henry Percy.

A grateful smile passed over her lips, and Lady Katherine signified that she had seen sufficient.

"THE PRECIPICE."

Again the vision faded.

"Percy," said Gunara, sprinkling him with a new distillation, "speak and answer me. Dare you look upon what shall befall you in future years?"

"A Percy dares all!" exclaimed the youth, speaking in hollow tones without moving a muscle.

Again the face of the mirror was filled with forms.

Another battle-field was presented to the eye where the dead lay piled in heaps.

Knights, grooms, bowmen, pikemen, all in one mass of mangled humanity.

A group approached, the leader of which wore in his helmet three ostrich feathers.

A second group comes from the opposite direction, the leader of which lowers his lance and tilts down upon the knight with the ostrich plumes, who, nothing loth, spurs forward to the combat.

The knight with the ostrich feathers proves the victor, and in the features of his vanquished, slain opponent, Percy recognised his own.

Then the living ones went their way, and sorrowing females, among whom he recognised the form of Lady Katherine, came to wail and mourn over the dead.

"Such shall be the fate of Northumberland's eldest son," said Gunara, and as she spoke the glass again became clouded.

"And I?" said Witherington, after a pause.

The first picture that appeared on this mirror then again became visible, though the principal actors were gone.

In their place the page discerned a mutilated man, whose legs had been hewed off, trying to crawl towards a brook.

The face was his own.

"Do you seek to know more?" asked Gunara, fixing a stern gaze upon him.

The youth shook his head, and the vision faded, while screams of unearthly laughter echoed through the vaults, and, the owl sailing in again, with one sweep of his wing extinguished the lamps.

The whole vault was filled with stifling fumes, which gradually cleared off as Gunara, in louder tones than before, chanted another incantation in that strange eastern tongue.

In a few minutes all was still, and the dwarf appeared with lights which he placed upon the table.

CHAPTER XXII.

THE PRIEST'S ADVENTURE.

IT is now time that we should once more turn our eyes towards Father Abel, and see how the industrious plotter fared on his travels.

He had, as the reader knows, provided himself with everything necessary for the journey, at the expense of the patron he was deserting, and so managed to progress very comfortably.

As they began to reach the north country, however, the servants wondered that the friar made his way towards Westmoreland, instead of taking the road that led to Alnwick.

But they attributed this to some Scottish invasion of which they had not rightly been informed.

Three nights before the scene which we have just described as taking place in the cave of the witch, they reached a little inn, and Father Abel announced his intention of remaining there for the night.

He dismounted, and the servant led the horses to the stable.

"Ho, host ! Come, man, stir thyself, and provide good cheer," said he, entering.

"Aye, that will I, good father. I crave pardon for not attending on your reverence myself."

"Thou hast pardon, man, and shalt have my blessing, if thou speedily provide a dainty meal."

So spoke the priest, in such jovial style, that no one unacquainted with the incidents of his life before mentioned, would imagine such a merry yet holy man could carry about thoughts of murder in his heart.

Mine host set him down as one of the jolliest specimens of humanity he had ever seen, and publicans should be good judges.

His wife and himself did all that lay in their power to please the dainty taste of their holy guest, and mine host began to consider whether it would be profitable to let the priest have a bottle of very rare old wine at the price of more ordinary tipple.

The priest thought that he had lighted upon very comfortable quarters, where the host was civil and his wife not bad looking, when a horse was heard clattering along the road at full speed.

A warrior, fully armed, sat upon the back of the steed, and Father Abel thought he was familiar with that coat of mail and the well-worn, dingy plume on the somewhat battered helm.

Before he had time to indulge in many speculations as to who the warrior could be, his spurs were heard jingling in the passage, and the next moment he entered the room where Father Abel was sitting.

The priest almost fainted as his visitor threw up his helm and revealed the well-known features of Archie !

"Holy saints !" he exclaimed, holding his hands before his eyes.

"Call rather on the evil one, father ; he is more likely to come to your aid than any saint in the calendar," replied the soldier, as he threw himself into a seat, and stretched his long legs across the doorway.

"Archie, let the past be forgotten," said the priest, after a pause.

"What ! forget all the vows of friendship we have sworn—all the kind deeds we have performed for each other—the cups we have drained to each other's health ?" and Archie fixed his fiery black eye upon the countenance of the priest. "Why good father, you must surely have taken leave of your senses !"

The priest mumbled some reply which was quite unintelligible, and Archie smiled as he witnessed the fear and dismay of his treacherous friend.

"Shall we sup together, father ?" asked the warrior. "I can promise you rare viands, and wines that have not their match."

"I—I am ill ; I would fain lie me down and rest," groaned the wretched priest, who only sought some excuse to leave the society into which chance had thrown him.

"Will it please your reverence to retire ?" asked the host, who, in passing the door, happened to overhear the last words spoken.

"Aye, that it will ; lend me thine arm, good fellow."

The landlord approached, and assisted by him, Father Abel staggered to a bed chamber, Archie making no effort to stay him.

In a few seconds the host again made his appearance, saying, as he quitted the priest's chamber—

"Very well, your reverence ; supper shall be served up in a few minutes."

"Host !" shouted Archie.

"Coming, good sir ; coming !"

"Haste, then."

There was something in the warrior's voice that told he would brook no delay ; so the landlord, with a low bow, inquired—

"What is your worship's pleasure ?"

"What hath the priest ordered for supper ?"

The host stared and hesitated.

"Speak out, man ; quick !"

"A brace of fresh trout from the brook, a fat capon, and sundry confections."

"Then serve them *here* as soon as maybe."

"But his reverence hath ordered it to be served in his chamber."

"What care I? Shall I eat in a priest's room? Not I, forsooth, so serve it *here*, and quickly, too."

"But, gentle sir, there is not another capon to be procured for miles, and old Peter the fisherman hath disposed of the remainder of his wares."

"Thou hast bread, and the spring hard by produces water of the purest quality. Such fare is good enough for a perjured villain who would betray his patron and slay his friend."

The host lifted up his eyes in amazement, but the warrior, with an imperious gesture, again commanded him to serve up supper, and lose no time in doing so.

The viands were placed upon the table, and Archie fell to with a good appetite.

"Hath the priest any companions?" he asked, after a few minutes.

"Two grooms, your worship."

"What badge do they wear?"

"They wear the livery of the Earl of Northumberland."

"Then send them hither to me."

The host obeyed, and in a few minutes the two grooms stood before the soldier.

"Now leave us, sir host."

The door closed behind the cringing landlord, who, however, remained outside, with his ear to the keyhole.

From this position he was called by the voice of Father Abel.

"Coming, holy father, coming!" he cried.

"What delays my supper?" asked the priest, in fretful tones.

"Your reverence, I—I crave pardon."

"Thou hast it."

"But, your reverence, the gallant warrior——"

"What of him?"

"Hath ordered it to be served, and is now eating it."

"My curses light upon his head and wither his brain. Bring me some wine, and send my grooms hither."

"Holy sir, they—they——"

"Well, what more ill news?"

"They are now with the warrior."

"Maledictions on them! Bring me some wine, and the best food thou hast left after providing for yon cormorant of a soldier."

The landlord bowed and retired.

Father Abel began to calculate the chances, and found that they were against his reaching his destination, unless he took speedy and decisive measures to secure his own safety.

But how was that to be done?

If he remained at the inn, perhaps Archie, or even one of his grooms, might feel disposed to cut his throat—or, still worse—deliver him up as a traitor.

The villain judged of all humanity by his own heart, but therein he judged wrongly, for Archie, though bold as a lion, never took life save in fair, open combat.

"I must fly then, and on foot," he muttered; "for the noisy horse would betray me to mine enemies."

The very thought was a source of misery to the priest, who, as before said, had a deep-rooted aversion to pedestrian exercise.

He sighed deeply.

As his eye despondingly roamed about the room, he caught sight of a Scottish dress that lay folded carefully beneath the bed.

A bright idea struck the priest.

He resolved to assume the tartan, and in that disguise to make his escape.

He knew he was not many miles from the boundary between the two kingdoms, and, when once fairly across the border, the dress would be a protection to him.

He hastily slipped off his gown, clothed his body in the plaid and kilt, and set the plumed cap upon his shaven head

Then, throwing open the window, he slipped out, and made his way down the little lane congratulating himself, as he proceeded, on having so easily escaped.

But as he walked on he reflected that he had done a very foolish act.

He had left his pouch and money behind him at the inn!

It would be very dangerous to return, so he walked on, cursing his ill-luck, and trusting to meet with a hospitable reception at the first house he should see.

The land on each side became more wild in appearance.

There were no signs of human habitation, and darkness coming on apace, began to obscure the horizon.

Suddenly the lane terminated on a wild, desolate heath, and at the same moment the last spark of daylight vanished.

Father Abel little relished the idea of passing a night in such a dreary place ; but there seemed no choice.

Anxiously as he scanned the horizon, not a sign of any glimmering light met his eye to cheer him with hopes of food and shelter.

He stumbled on, scratching his face and limbs with the brambles and furze bushes through which he passed.

Suddenly a most dismal sound met his ear.

Again—again !—nearer each time so that its hoarse notes echoed through the night air.

Father Abel's legs trembled so violently that he could scarcely stand.

It was the howl of a wolf, and there could be no doubt that the fierce brute was on the priest's track.

For a few minutes he hurried on, but as the moon began to rise, he halted, and looked back.

The dark form of the animal was dimly visible as it came over the crest of a little hillock.

The priest uttered a cry of dismay, and fled as fast as his legs could carry him, while the wolf howled loudly behind him.

CHAPTER XXIII.

THE GUIDE.

WE left Douglas in a preceding number bounding at full speed over a rocky chasm in the earth, to escape from the spears of pursuing foemen, and now we have brought him before the reader again as an inmate of the cave of Gunara, the Witch of Wooler.

It behoves us now to explain how he passed from the one scene to the other.

When the young Highland chieftain made the leap before described, he had no very distinct idea of the breadth or depth of the chasm across which he had to jump.

All he knew was that three men, fully armed and mounted, were behind him, and that, on foot, it would be impossible to cope with them.

Douglas was no coward.

Had his limbs been clothed in armour —had he been mounted on his favourite steed, with one well-armed follower behind him—he would have been well-content to abide the trial of strength ; or even by himself, boy as he was, he would have dared the fight had he been on horseback.

But three mounted men against one unarmed lad on foot were odds he felt justified in declining, nor should the boldest of Britain's sons condemn him for running as he did in this case.

He reached the chasm, and leaped high into the air.

The opposite bank was fully fifteen feet from the one from which he jumped ; but, being a little lower, he was able to clear it, and alighted without injury upon a soft and fragrant bunch of blue bells.

The very sight of the favourite Scottish flower revived hope in his breast.

He rose to his feet, ran forward a few

yards, and then glanced back over his shoulder.

His pursuers had reined up their horses at the brink of the precipice, fearing to take the fearful leap over which he had bounded unharmed.

The young Scot gazed at them with scorn upon his lofty brow, and shook his fist in defiance.

"Cowards!" he cried, "come one at a time. I dare ye all!"

There was no immediate answer to this fiery challenge.

But a few seconds afterwards, the soldier who seemed to be the leader exclaimed—

"By St. George, we have left the buck to chase the fawn. Yon is no shaveling priest."

"You speak right, fair sir, by the rood!" replied one of his companions.

"A plague on all tartans, kilts, and broadswords!" exclaimed the testy leader.

"These Scots bear no cognisance, and dress so much alike, that I wonder much they do not cut each other's throats.

"To the right about. We need follow yon stripling no further."

They reined back their horses, wheeled round, and in a few seconds were lost to view.

"The cowardly rascals;" muttered Douglas. "They dared not accept my challenge, and meet me man to man."

He continued to look back for some seconds after they had disappeared beyond the ridge, and then, in listless sort, continued his journey.

To our readers it will be hardly necessary to explain that these men were Archie and the two grooms he had enlisted on his behalf to pursue the fugitive priest.

Archie had shown the Northumbrian retainers in what treacherous company they were travelling, and had persuaded them to aid him in following and killing, or capturing the false Father Abel.

Hitherto, it seems they had not succeeded in overtaking him; but of the priest's further adventures we shall speak again ere long.

Douglas proceeded on his way for nearly an hour, but the fatigue of travelling began to overpower him, and he looked around for some place where he could rest and refresh himself.

A thick wood was before him, but there were several tracks, made by rude carts and cattle, which showed him that he must be at no great distance from some human habitation.

At length he saw before him a small rudely-cultivated field, in one corner of which was a rude hut.

He walked towards it, knocked, and without waiting for any reply, entered.

The dresses of the people within at once assured him that he was amongst his own countrymen.

There was a brawny peasant with long hair and rough beard, feet guileless of shoe and stocking, and herculean limbs clothed in a rude homespun tartan.

There was a fair-haired wife, and three half-naked children, all clad in the national dress—coarse, rudely-made and rugged, but still of the true Gaelic type, fashion and colour.

The peasant at once doffed his bonnet as his visitor entered, for there was sufficient in the dress as well as in the mien and bearing of the young Douglas to assure the owner of the cot of his rank.

"Welcome to my cabin, sir, if ye be a true Scot," said he, pointing to a rough seat.

"A true Scot in heart and by birth," replied the young noble, with a weary smile. "My name is Douglas."

"A cadet of the house of *Dhu Glas?*"*

"His eldest son!"

At these words the peasant and his wife fell upon their knees before the illustrious guest."

"Thrice welcome, noble chief!" cried the peasant.

"Thanks; rise, my friend. But you look sad; have you any more tales of English barbarity and oppression for my ear?"

"My curse upon the Saxon tyrants! And may St. Andrew rot my bones if my father's broadsword drink not deeply of their blood ere long."

The peasant then related how he had been captured by the party under Wither-

* The dark grey man.

ington's command, and threatened with death as the penalty for refusing to answer their questions.

The blood of the young Scot boiled as he listened to the recital of the indignities his countryman had been compelled to endure.

"Which way went these proud, boastful invaders ?"

"Towards the convent, my chief."

"Then gird on your sword, and follow me."

The Scot hesitated a moment.

"I dare not," he replied, in low tones.

"Coward !"

The fiery herdsman laid his hand upon his dirk as he shouted his reply—

"Coward! Not I! No living being does Oswald the herd fear, though he dares not face the dread being who lives among the dark recesses of the forest which surrounds the convent. I am no coward."

"What dread being do you mean ?"

"A weird woman known to men as the Witch of Wooler."

"Dwells she in the forest you speak of ?"

"She does."

"Then you shall conduct me to her."

"I cannot."

"A Douglas will have his commands obeyed. On my head shall all the danger of the enterprise descend. Do you know her dwelling ?"

"By accident I discovered it. A deep cave, the mouth of which is hidden from view by ivy and briars."

"Prepare for the journey," said Douglas, rising, and walking to the door of the cabin.

After a few seconds' hesitation, the peasant put on his bonnet, and with a low bow to the young chieftain beckoned him to follow.

The way was long and weary.

Hours passed, and still the journey came not to a close.

At length they reached the wood ; but not before the shades of night had wrapped the whole scene in perfect darkness.

The guide, however, knew his way.

After scrambling through bushes, and up steep hills, the guide at length halted in a deep ravine and pointed to a narrow crevice between two rocks.

"There dwells the witch," said he. "I dare not accompany you further on your journey, Sir Chieftain."

"Nor do I require your presence. Take this gold piece to requite you for the trouble you have taken, and hie homewards."

With these words the youth strode forwards into the cave, which was dark as Erebus.

But ere he had gone many yards a light appeared, and in another minute the Witch of Wooler stood before him.

Ere the strange woman could speak the young Scot had explained the cause of his visit.

"Granted," said she, "on condition that you draw not your sword till you return to the light of heaven."

"I swear," said the youth.

The witch led him into the cave, and our readers know what happened there.

CHAPTER XXIV.

HOMEWARD BOUND.

WHEN quietness once more reigned in the mystic cavern, Gunara spoke though her voice was husky with emotion.

"You have seen enough, Sir Douglas, you know that which you desired to learn, go—go hence and trouble me no more."

"I go, but take this as a reward for thy pains," said Douglas, placing a purse upon the table.

"Keep the gold. I need it not. It would do more good if bestowed on the peasant who conducted you hither."

The young Scot started in alarm.

"Who told you of my guide?"

"It matters not. Few secrets are hidden from me."

So saying, she again motioned him away, and the dwarf, torch in hand, ushered the young Scot from the cavern.

As he reached the door he turned, and, with a low bow, addressed Lady Katherine.

"Farewell, lady, farewell for ever!"

A deep sigh followed, and he passed from her sight.

The three English youths and Lady Katherine still stood motionless within the mystic circle, from which Gunara showed no haste to release them.

"May we not depart now?" asked Lady Katherine, after a long pause.

"What, are you so eager to fall into the hands of those from whom you have just escaped?"

"No, indeed. But the sight of yon mirror troubles me."

"Then follow me."

"But these gentlemen?" said the fair girl, pointing to the brothers, Henry and Ralph.

"Shall soon regain the use of their limbs."

Gunara then took another of the numerous phials her lavatory contained, and sprinkled the contents upon her motionless prisoners, if we may so call the youths.

As though waking from a dream, they stretched their limbs in a listless manner, not feeling at all certain that they had regained the power of motion.

"Thank the holy saints!" exclaimed Witherington, as he saw the change. "By the holy man of Lindisfarne! I feared you had been changed into pillars of stone, my lords."

Hotspur made no answer, but gazed upon the witch with looks so hostile that it might have been thought that he intended to vent his anger upon her.

Perhaps he would have done so had not the imploring looks of Lady Katherine restrained him.

Gunara took no notice of his angry glances, but repeated her invitation—

"Come—follow me."

Taking the light, she led the way into another apartment; indeed, the cave seemed to be divided into many such recesses.

Here a number of seats were ranged in a circle, though no other furniture was visible.

Gunara motioned her young guests to sit down.

Wondering what new mystery was about to be performed, they obeyed.

The witch then stamped three times upon the floor, which immediately gave way, and in its place appeared a table filled with the richest viands and wines.

"Eat," said she, "and fear not that the food thus strangely served will injure you."

For a moment they hesitated; but Hotspur was at length bold enough to seize a goblet of wine and drain it of its contents.

The superstitious young Witherington crossed himself expecting to see Percy fall back senseless, or perhaps lifeless; but no such evil results ensued, and it was long ere the whole party proved by experience that the viands were harmless and wholesome.

The witch excepted.

She alone touched neither food nor drink, but sat beseemingly wrapped in thought.

The meal came to a conclusion, and then the strange woman rose.

"Your armed men wait for you in the wood," said she. "Rejoin them, and return to your homes in peace and safety. Follow the dwarf, he will conduct you to them."

As she spoke the Moor made his appearance.

"Farewell," said Lady Katherine, who felt impatient to regain the society of her friends. "Though men may speak evil of you I shall ever remember Gunara as a friend."

Hotspur and Ralph Percy, lifting their caps, bowed slightly, while Witherington crossed himself.

The dwarf led the way, and they passed from the presence of the Witch of Wooler.

The passage through which he led them out was not that by which they had entered, nor was it the one by which Douglas had found his way to the witch's presence.

It was smooth and more easily traversed than the other paths, and in a few minutes the dwarf opened a door which allowed them to step out into the air.

But without stopping to allow them to see in what manner this door was concealed, the dwarf hurried them forward for a few yards until they reached a thick grove.

"There," said he, with a foreign accent, pointing forward. "Soldiers there."

Then with a bound the mannikin leaped into the midst of some thick bushes, and was out of sight in a moment.

"What shall we do now?" asked Witherington.

"Go forward. Not that I have much faith in the word of yon stunted ape, but if we stand here we shall never find those we seek," said Hotspur.

"Hark! what sound is that?" exclaimed Lady Katherine.

The youths laid their hands upon their weapons instantly.

But there was no cause for alarm.

"I know the sound well," Ralph. "Those are our horses snorting, and our men conversing in low tones as they wait for our return. The dwarf was right."

"On then," exclaimed Hotspur, though he did not as usual take the lead, but walked by Katherine's side.

His brother, however, pointed out the way, while Witherington took upon himself the task of guarding against any attack from behind.

They mutually agreed to say nothing whatever respecting their adventures in the cave.

Before they had walked very far a voice was heard hailing them.

"Who comes there?"

"Friends."

"Give the countersign, friends?"

"I have it not," replied Hotspur, "but methinks you should know my voice."

"Saint George! It is our young lord," exclaimed another voice, which Hotspur recognised as that of old Witherington, and in another instant his scabbard was heard rattling against his mail-clad legs as he made his way towards them.

"Welcome, welcome back, my lord. By my patron saint I was just on the point of launching my forces against the convent walls, and scaring up the old abbess and her nuns. What! and ye have brought back the lady?"

"We have, good Witherington."

"By Heaven! what a dolt I must have been that one of your house could possibly fail in any expedition. I had hopes of rescuing the lady myself, but you young gallants have robbed me that chance of gaining honour."

"Nevertheless I thank you from my heart as much as though you had stormed the convent and rescued me from its burning ruins," said Lady Katherine.

"By the mass, an' I have a great mind to set a torch to it now. Did they illtreat you, lady?"

"No; except that they refused to give me liberty."

"Shall we return, my lord?"

"As you like," replied Hotspur.

"Father, it would be sacrilege," said the page, laying his hand upon the old warrior's arm.

"Hum!"

"The most deadly of all crimes, father."

The warrior twirled his moustache, and looked very much as though he differed in opinion, but said no more.

"Let there be no violence, I pray," said Lady Katherine. "Enough misery has been caused already through my being carried away."

"Your word shall be law, my lady," replied Witherington. "To horse, my men, to horse, and let us be returning."

The men-at-arms leaped to their feet.

Saddles were placed on the backs of horses, girths buckled, and bridles arranged.

Another word of command, and every beast bore a living burden.

One horse had been especially prepared for Lady Katherine's riding, and as soon as everything was in readiness Hotspur helped her to its back.

"Forward," said Witherington.

And they began their homeward march just as day was breaking, and the eastern horizon began to show a grey light which heralded the approach of morning.

CHAPTER XXV.

KNIGHTHOOD AT LAST.

HOW long it took Hotspur and his companions to accomplish the journey to Alnwick it matters not, but certain it is that they were sorely fatigued when they reached the portals of the grand old castle.

Lady Katherine was so overcome by want of sleep that more than once she would have fallen from her horse had not Hotspur's arm supported her.

The countess was waiting at the gate, and tenderly welcomed the fair girl and her two sons.

Hotspur pretended to despise the fatigues and dangers he had recently passed, and professed himself ready for another adventure immediately.

Nor was his active mind kept waiting long.

The news of the preparations made by the earl for the recapture of Berwick Castle had reached Alnwick, and the retainers were in a high state of excitement.

Some of the more turbulent of them were for going at once to Warkworth to join the English army, but the measures taken by Witherington soon checked these intended desertions.

The morning after their return, however, Hotspur and Ralph, attended by young Witherington and half a dozen picked men, rode from the castle with the intention of "forming a junction," as military men would say, with the forces gathered by the Earl of Northumberland.

This movement was very successfully executed, and the brothers had the satisfaction of riding on their first real campaign beside their noble and warlike father.

Then the men moved forward, and Hotspur almost shouted with joy as his war horse snorted and neighed, and pranced along the road.

They reached the neighbourhood of Berwick, and by the earl's command entered the town by three different roads so as to surround the place.

The townspeople hailed the advancing army with loud cheers; but Graham, Du Bois, and the others within the keep of the castle, were not so well pleased at the prospect before them.

"At all events," said Du Bois, "it would be perfectly useless to contend against this host. Five hundred to one are fearful odds."

"What alternative have we?" asked Graham.

"Negotiation with the townspeople before this proud earl and his vassals entirely surround us."

"Then try what your persuasive tongue can do in the matter."

The English army had still more than a mile to march ere they could reach the castle, so that there would be just sufficient time to escape could Du Bois prevail on the townspeople to allow him to depart.

The ex-herald walked out upon the ramparts, holding in his hand a little white flag to announce to the townspeople who surrounded the castle that he desired a parley.

The head-borough, or chief man of the town, advanced, holding out a similar white flag, and desired to know what the defenders of the castle had to say.

"Friends and townsmen," said Du Bois, "we have conquered and taken your castle, but would save you from the horrors of war. We have provisions, arms, and a strong garrison with which to hold what we have taken ; but you have wives and children whose eyes are not accustomed to the sight of bloodshed, and whose tender bodies may by chance fall as victims in the strife which must take place. Why should this be ? Why should you expose those you love to the chances of battle, sword and fire ? It may be prevented ; they may rest in peace, and they will rest in peace if you allow us to depart at once, unharmed and without opposition. Reflect on what I have said, and return me an answer speedily."

The bombastic eloquence of the herald was entirely lost upon the hard-headed citizen, who happened to be pretty well informed as to the strength of the garrison and the resources they possessed.

Five minutes' conversation with his associates was sufficient to empower him to return the following answer—

"It may not be, fair sir. You came hither without our invitation, and, by the mass, you go not hence without our permission ; and that permission we, acting for the most noble Earl of Northumberland, do refuse to accord."

"Then on your head be the responsibility of all the carnage that may follow. But one minute more I give you for reflection."

"We need it not ; we have decided."

"We are rightly served !" exclaimed the proud, haughty Graham. "Yet methinks the honour we have done you in condescending to parley with hucksters and mechanics might have ensured us a different reply."

So saying, the two chiefs of the besieged garrison retired from the ramparts, and took up a position at one of the loopholes of the keep, from which they could observe all the motions of the advancing enemy.

The English advanced, and in a short space of time the castle was closely invested on every side. There seemed to be no hope that even a bird might escape, for the English archers sent their shafts high over the topmost turret of the keep.

"We must defend ourselves," was the word passed from mouth to mouth ; and they *did* defend themselves right bravely against the overwhelming forces sent against them.

For seven nights and seven days did those forty desperate men resist the attack of the English host of at least four thousand.

"We may yet hold out," exclaimed Du Bois, as he fought on the ramparts, discharging arrows, hurling down large stones, and encouraging the little band of defenders by word and gesture. "If Earl Douglas knew our desperate situation, he would perhaps move to our assistance."

"There you err. He cares not the value of a rush for us or our enterprise."

"But some other circumstance might perhaps induce him to aid us."

"I know not of any such circumstance."

"See you yon tall knight, who seems to command the east attack, and who is accompanied by a fair, gallant-looking youth ?"

"I do ; but what have they to do with bringing the Douglas to our aid ?"

"They are Earl Percy and his son Hotspur. If Douglas knew they were here, five thousand Scottish lances would speed to the border."

"But there is no method of conveying the news to him."

Du Bois shook his head mournfully.

"We must trust to our own valour, and to the chances of a friendly tongue conveying him the tidings."

A desperate hope, certainly, but, such as it was, these men clung to it with the energy of despair.

The eighth morning of the siege dawned, and an unusual activity prevailed in the camp of the Earl of Northumberland. The defenders of the castle imagined that reinforcements had arrived during the night, but they little knew the nature of those reinforcements.

"' BEHOLD YOUR FATE,' SAID GUNARA."

The Earl of Northumberland and his two sons were seen busily superintending the troops. The old noble looked triumphant, as though he expected to annihilate the little body of men opposed to him.

Hotspur, on the other hand, looked gloomy.

Presently a signal was given, and huge clouds of smoke enveloped the English lines, while loud reports were heard. Heavy missiles struck against the walls of the castle, and huge blocks of stone were shivered to atoms.

"At last, then, we see the cannons* of which we have heard so much," said Du Bois. "What think you of the new weapon, Sir William ?"

"Milan steel would be but a poor protection against these thunderbolts," replied the knight, as he pointed to the corpse of a poor fellow whose body had been cut in two by a ball. "Down, down, my men ! it is folly to expose yourselves to the certainty of death."

The men obeyed the injunction, and sought behind the walls a protection against the iron missiles. Ere long a loud crash was heard.

The door of the keep had been smashed in, and there was now nothing left to oppose the progress of the Northumbrians, who, with loud shouts, leaped over the ramparts and hurried towards the tower.

At their head was young Hotspur, and close by him John De Fenwicke.

The young noble was no great admirer of the artillery practice he had seen, but when a charge was to be made—when man was to be opposed to man and sword to sword—he determined to be foremost in the fight. Nor was the old earl averse to his son's proceeding ; he knew that the youth was bent upon winning renown for himself, and resolved upon giving Hotspur a good chance of winning his spurs.

The youth and his followers reached the gateway, and began to ascend the staircase, when they found themselves opposed by Du Bois, Graham, and the greater number of the little garrison.

"What ! do I see a young Percy in battle at last ?" cried Du Bois. "Come,

* Gunpowder was invented and first used in warfare about this period.

then, my boy, let me end your sufferings in this world by a speedy passage to the next !"

"Traitor!" exclaimed Hotspur, striking fiercely at the herald ; "I will slay you without one regret, save that my sword should be stained by such base blood."

In an instant they were engaged in mortal combat, while Fenwicke, without wasting time in giving vent to his anger in words, attacked Graham. The less important combatants on both sides soon found antagonists.

The fight was long and fierce.

Du Bois had all the advantage of mature age, greater height, and more experience in the use of his weapon ; but, on the other hand, Hotspur was young, active, and full of high aspirations. The youth felt, in fact, that the eyes of all England were watching his career, and, anxious to maintain the high name of his ancestors, he fought with the utmost bravery.

He received one slight wound in the left shoulder, which only served to render him more wary, though not an atom less determined ; his sword had found its way through a joint in the armour worn by Du Bois, and was reddened with blood.

A slight movement by his side caused him to half turn his head, and with sorrow he saw the brave Fenwicke fall to the earth, pierced through the heart by Graham's sword.

"There, you see your own fate pourtrayed," said Du Bois. "Yield, Percy, and I will be merciful !"

"Yield to a traitor ? Never !"

And with a sudden blow he drove his sword up to the hilt in the breast of the false herald, who, with a deep groan, fell dead ; and at the same time an arrow pierced Graham's brain, and he dropped beside his companion.

"Esperance ! Percy !" shouted the retainers, as they pressed on, to find themselves opposed by the remainder of the small but desperate garrison.

The combat was sharp, short, and decisive ; in less than five minutes after the death of Du Bois and Graham, the remainder of their followers were numbered with the slain, and Hotspur was hailed master of the tower.

A loud shout rent the air as the men of Northumberland heard of their young lord's achievement ; but it seemed as though the shout had been echoed back. A thick cloud of dust was seen advancing, and from the midst of it were seen glittering spears and waving pennons. High above all floated the royal standard of England, announcing that the king himself was at hand.

That Richard the Second should come in person was a thing not to be wondered at ; for Northumberland had, on first hearing of the capture of Berwick by Graham and his followers, sent a special message to the young monarch, who happened to be at York.

In the midst of the youthful nobility of England, the young king approached the spot where the Earl of Northumberland stood.

"Heaven preserve your majesty," said he, kneeling on one knee.

"Rise, earl, rise, and accept our thanks for the active measures you have taken to punish these bold aggressors," said the king. "But do they still hold out ?"

"Thanks to St. George we have just regained the keep, your majesty. But, to judge by the sounds, it must have been a stubborn fight."

"Ha ! See to it, Brember ; see how many of our brave subjects have fallen, and whether any of the enemy have been taken alive."

The courtier thus addressed hastened away ; but in a few moments returned to make his report.

"Your majesty has lost fourteen loyal subjects, while the traitors have been destroyed to a man."

"And what brave knight commanded the attack, my Lord of Northumberland ?"

"No knight, your majesty ; but a youth who would fain qualify himself to wear spurs of gold."

"He hath well earned them. Bring him to our presence, Sir Nicholas."

Brember hurried away again, to return accompanied by Hotspur.

The gallant youth flushed.

His brow was warm with perspiration, and stained in one or two places with blood.

In his hand he carried a sword, the point of which he dropped to the earth as he stood before the king.

"Young sir, you have done well and nobly," said the king. "Kneel at our feet, and receive the reward of your valour."

Hotspur dropped on one knee.

"Your name, fair sir ?"

"Henry Percy," replied the youth, directing a smiling look towards his father and brother Ralph.

"My son," said the earl.

The king started, changed colour, and for a moment appeared strongly agitated.

But recovering himself by an effort, he laid his sword on the youth's shoulder saying—

"In the name of St. George and St. Michael I dub thee knight. Be ever valiant, loyal, and constant. Arise, Lord Henry Percy."

Hastily kissing the king's hand, Hotspur rose to his feet with a proud, elated expression of countenance.

Loud shouts resounded through the air of "Long live the king !" mingled with cries of "Esperance ! Percy !"

As King Richard heard these last words his brow grew more flushed than before, and he motioned his courtiers to gather more closely round him.

The Earl of Northumberland, taking his son by the arm, stepped forward.

"I thank your majesty for the honour you have conferred——" he commenced.

"It was well earned, my lord. But spare your thanks, we pray you, for our thoughts trouble us."

So saying he moved away, and without deigning to take further notice of the earl, entered an apartment which had been hastily prepared for his reception in the keep of the castle.

From this retreat he sent an order to the earl, who, with Hotspur, remained standing in the courtyard, to put a proper garrison in the castle, and then to disband his forces.

Then, without any explanation of his strange conduct, he rode off with his knights and returned to York.

"What means this?" asked Hotspur.

"I know not," was the curt reply.

"By the bones of my ancestors!" replied the headstrong youth, "had I dreamed he would treat you so discourteously, his sword should never have touched my shoulder."

The earl smiled, and then proceeded to give orders as to the number of men to be left in the castle.

This was soon arranged, and three hours after the departure of the king to York, Northumberland and his son were on their way returning to Alnwick.

CHAPTER XXVI.

THE TOURNAMENT AT ALNWICK CASTLE.

THE old castle of the house of Percy was reached in due time, and great were the rejoicings among both young and old when it became known that the earl's eldest son had been knighted by the king's sword.

The behaviour of the king on that occasion seemed forgotten or unheeded—in fact, the sturdy Northumbrians looked upon the earl as equal in power and dignity to the sovereign, and would willingly have followed him to battle against Richard.

So that, when they heard that the monarch had retired to York, the news cast no damp whatever upon their festivities, but rather increased their joy, as proving how much King Richard feared the noble Percy.

Partly in joy at the successful issue of his expedition, and partly to prove how little he valued the king's unmerited anger, the earl announced that a grand tournament would be held at the castle of Alnwick, at which all gentle knights of north country were invited to try their skill at jousting.

All was bustle and preparation in the castle.

Carpenters and artizans were busily engaged in erecting barriers and galleries.

Cooks toiled and perspired as they endeavoured to provide beforehand for the crowd of guests expected to assemble.

Grooms and pages toiled at the polishing of armour, and curried down steeds till the animals' coats shone like silken fabrics.

The butler sighed as his assistants drove spigots into casks of ale and wine, for he well knew the thirst produced by a tournament.

A similar activity prevailed in the apartments devoted to the use of the ladies.

The dear creatures then, as now, were much addicted to the wearing of fine raiment, and the staff of needlewomen employed to prepare the garments in which the countess and Lady Katherine intended to grace the tournament, would have performed all the work of a moderate-sized modern millinery establishment.

The two ladies themselves were very industrious, Lady Katherine Mortimer especially being actively engaged in the embroidering of scarves and favours, with which to decorate the victorious knights.

The old earl moved hither and thither, directing and ordering, and, at the same time, keeping a good look-out for any hostile movement either from the north or the south.

At length the appointed day arrived, and, by way of commencement to the festivities, the earl, at Hotspur's request, restored to liberty Sir Alexander Ramsay, the Knight of the Skull, who had been taken prisoner in the attack on Warkworth Castle.

Arms, armour, and steed were restored, so that, if inclined, he might take part in the tournament.

The Scottish knight was delighted and assumed his harness with a pleasure he had never before felt.

At length the castle gate was thrown open, and the people of the town began to flock in to see the tournament.

Several knights and nobles of lesser rank took up their stations on each side of the principal gallery.

Then came a loud flourish of trumpets, and this sound admonished the spectators of some important arrival.

A bevy of fair ladies was seen entering the gallery and seating themselves on each side of the throne reserved for the Queen of the Lists.

Again the trumpets sounded, and the fair lady destined to hold that important station, took her seat, while loud shouts and acclamations rent the air.

The queen was Lady Katherine Mortimer.

Then a herald stalked forth into the arena, and, after another loud blast of brazen music, announced that the noble lord, Henry Percy, claimed to be the appointed champion of the Queen of Beauty, and would, in that capacity, hold the lists against all comers.

At the conclusion of this announcement the young knight rode forth from a little tent that had been erected under the gallery, attended by young Witherington, who had been appointed his " esquire."

The young noble was attired in complete armour of exquisitely polished and inlaid steel.

On the top of his helmet was the lion crest of the house of Brabant, from which he claimed to be descended.

A scarf of white silk, richly embroidered, was thrown across his left shoulder, while his horse was barded with a covering of azure velvet, fringed with silver tissue.

His handsome countenance was radiant with gaiety as he conversed with his esquire, who was also richly dressed ; and the appearance of the young cavalier seemed altogether deserving of the admiration he excited.

Behind him rode two pages, one of whom bore his painted lance, to the shaft of which was attached a bow of white ribbon, the colours of the Queen ; while the other carried a shield, on which was blazoned the armorial bearings of the house of Percy.

Old Witherington was among the spectators, and gazed with pride upon the gallant bearing of his pupil.

" By the seven champions !" he exclaimed, " I have never seen a more handsome knight, and he will bear himself right well in the course, too, or Witherington is no judge !"

Percy's herald then stepped forward, and in a loud voice proclaimed his master's readiness to defend the fair fame of the Queen of the Lists.

As the noisy trumpets concluded this bold challenge, a young knight named De Watherston rode into the lists and took up a position opposite Hotspur.

His lance and helmet were decorated with crimson favours received from some fair damsel he considered better fitted for the throne of the lists than Lady Katherine.

As his adversary rode forward, Percy drew down his vizor and grasped his lance.

The charge was sounded, the steeds started, and the champions met.

De Watherston's lance was shivered to atoms against Hotspur's helmet ; but the young Percy kept a firm seat in his saddle.

Not so with the other, for Percy's lance struck him on the throat with such violence as to lift him clean out of the saddle and hurl him half-stunned to the earth.

His esquire and the attendants removed him ; while Hotspur took his station beneath Lady Katherine to await the next comer.

Five other youthful warriors in succession presented themselves, but not one could keep his seat before the impetuous Hotspur's charge, and loud shouts greeted him after each successive victory.

Then there was a pause, no other champion seeming to think fit to dispute the title of the Queen.

At length there was heard a solitary trumpet, and following its blast came a young warrior, whose golden spurs betokened his rank, though he wore no cognizance by which his name might be known.

Addressing the marshal of the lists he begged permission to pay his respects to the Queen, and to be appointed her champion.

The request was granted, and he rode forward to lift his vizor.

A film overspread Lady Katherine's eyes as she recognised the young Earl Douglas, who bowed to his saddle bow.

But ere her heart ceased throbbing the two champions were riding at full speed towards each other, lance in hand.

CHAPTER XXVII.

THE RESULT OF THE COMBAT.

WITH a fierce shock the two champions, Percy and Douglas, met at the barriers.

Their lances shivered to atoms with the force of the shock, yet neither horseman was unseated.

Hotspur knew not who was the champion who so suddenly had appeared in the lists; but his young blood boiled as he looked round and saw that his friends were actually trembling lest he should be vanquished.

No! death itself would be preferable to defeat at the hands of an unknown champion.

Douglas, on the other hand, knew he was watched with intense interest by the only spectator who had seen his face—the lady who presided as queen.

He felt that the combat ought to be to the death to satisfy the intense desire he felt to accomplish the ruin of his adversary, and regain favour in the eyes of Lady Katherine Mortimer.

A trial of skill with blunt lances hardly satisfied him.

The antagonists reined up their horses as the spears shivered, and wheeled back each to his respective end of the lists for a fresh course.

Fresh lances were given them, and they opened their gauntlets to show that no injury had been sustained.

Again the trumpets sounded.

Lady Katherine fearfully, and with a shudder, opened her eyes to watch the result.

Her heart was a prey to conflicting emotions, for while there could be no doubt that Hotspur had gained her whole heart, the regard she had once felt for the gallant young Scot was sufficient to fill her with terror for his fate should any unlucky event betray him to the adversaries into whose midst he had so bravely yet incautiously ventured.

Again there was a fierce rushing of horses' hoofs, and a sharp clang as lance splintered against helmet and breast-plate.

"Brave knights! good lances!" cried the spectators, and expectation was raised to its highest pitch as the combatants prepared for a third course.

So evenly matched did they seem, that even the Northumbrians—whose belief was that a Percy must be next of kin to a deity—were beginning to feel doubtful whether their young lord would gain very much success.

A third time the trumpet sounded, and from the manner in which the antagonists grasped their lances, it was evident that they meant to put forth every particle of muscular strength and skill with which they were endowed.

The third charge would be the final and decisive one.

Even Lady Katherine felt convinced of that, and trembled for the result.

The excitement of the spectators was raised to the highest pitch.

They watched the movements of the combatants with intense interest.

Again the trumpet sounded, and as the blast echoed through the air, Hotspur struck the spurs into his steed's flanks, at the same time bringing the truncheon of the lance within a few inches of his thigh, in readiness for the career.

This action was performed with great grace and dexterity, causing much applause.

For the third time they started on their career.

The lance held by Douglas struck with such force upon the crest of Hotspur's helmet, that it carried away the plume ; but the blow could not shake the firm horseman.

Worse luck, however, attended the young Scot himself, for although he withstood the shock of the lance himself, his saddle girths gave way, and he rolled to the ground.

"A Percy ! Esperance ! Esperance !"

The triumphant shout was heard on every side of the "listed plain," and, with voices unanimous, the young knight was hailed victor.

"Not conquered !" shouted Douglas, striding towards the spot where sat the judges of the tournament ; "I claim the right of combat with swords."

"By the laws of the tourney you are held as vanquished, sir knight," replied the earl.

"Nay ; I entreat you decide not so. Let it be as my brave adversary desires, and let a combat with swords decide who shall be the victor."

So said Hotspur, riding up hastily to second his adversary's request.

The earl consulted for a time with the other judges, after motioning the champions to retire ; the Lady Katherine fervently prayed that the joint request of the hot-headed youths might be refused. She feared that blood would be spilled, and although that was not an unusual consequence of the tournaments of the period, our heroine had no desire to behold so sorrowful a spectacle.

"If I could only convey a message to the Scot, he would retire from the lists," she thought ; and acting at once upon the impulse, she hastily wrote a few lines.

"These to the unknown knight," said she, addressing a young page who stood close by her chair. "Give the packet into his hand—say nothing more than to bid him take heed of my words."

The sprightly youth, proud of being thus entrusted with a commission from the Queen of the Lists, concealed the paper in his doublet, and vaulting over the arena, approached Douglas.

"What would you with me, fair youth?" asked the Scot.

"A letter from the lady who sits yonder. Take good heed of its contents."

In an instant the impatient Douglas had severed with his dagger the thread that secured the packet, and in another moment the contents were firmly impressed upon his mind:—

"As yet you are unknown, but should you be discovered your life will be forfeit. Be advised, and retire while there is time."

There was no signature, but he could well guess whose hand had traced the lines. He refolded the paper, and placed it within his gauntlet.

"Return to your lady," was his brief reply.

The herald at that moment stalked out into the midst, and in a loud voice proclaimed that the combat should be decided by swords.

The young warriors placed themselves at opposite sides of the lists, the barriers were removed, the swords drawn, and with breathless anxiety every one awaited the signal.

The trumpets sounded, and grasping the reins firmly in their left hands, the youthful warriors speeded from their posts. As they passed, they dealt heavy cutting blows, and then wheeling suddenly, the strife commenced in downright good earnest.

That one or both the champions must perish seemed written in the book of fate, and sick at heart, Lady Katherine left the balcony, pleading illness as the excuse for neglecting the duties of her mimic throne.

As the horses pranced and plunged, each knight discharged a succession of heavy blows upon his adversary's helmet and breast-plate. No attempt was made to thrust, as that had been forbidden by the marshals, on account of the danger to both person and weapon.

At length the Douglas raised his sword and made a sweeping blow at Hotspur's crest. The young Percy raised his own weapon to beat off the stroke, but it fell with such force that the blade was shivered at the hilt, while that of Douglas, diverted from its aim by the attempt to parry, sunk deep into the neck of the horse which bore the heir to Northumberland.

The brave steed staggered, and before the seemingly victorious Douglas could deliver a second blow to complete his triumph, fell to the ground, bringing his rider with him.

The marshals of the lists raised the fallen one to his feet, and his squire brought forth a second horse and sword.

But ere the combat could be resumed a man dressed in the garb of a monk stepped into the place of combat, and whispered a few words in the young Scot's ear. This action was noticed only by a few, the great majority of the spectators having their eyes fixed on Hotspur, who was in the act of mounting to renew the combat.

Those few who saw the monk, wondered at the strange influence he seemed to possess over the unknown knight, who at once leaped from his steed, passed through the crowd, and followed his clerical conductor through a side door, which led to an unfrequented part of the castle.

The heralds then made their usual charge, and the trumpets once more sounded. Hotspur was anxious to avenge the fall he had received.

But no trace of his adversary remained, save the steed standing motionless at the extreme end of the lists.

Consternation was visible on every face.

Was the unknown knight one who considered discretion the better part of valour, or was he a magician, who, after hurling horse and rider to the ground, had suddenly conveyed himself from the place of combat?

Those who had seen him depart soon explained matters, however, and messengers were sent to follow and demand an explanation of his conduct.

But after a time these messengers returned with the news that, though they knew not how the strangers had escaped, neither knight nor monk could be found.

CHAPTER XXVIII.

THE SECRET PANEL.

THE reader will, no doubt, have guessed that the priest, whose whisper thus suddenly put a stop to the tournament, was their old acquaintance Father Abel.

But we left him flying from a hungry wolf; how happens it, then, that we find him at Alnwick?

The monk, when he saw the huge, gaunt animal coming over the hill, was for a few moments stupefied with fear; but the love of life was strong within him, and he soon found means to use his legs.

As he rushed forward, with all the haste of fear, he suddenly stumbled over some object which lay stretched in his path.

"How now, hasty sir?" said a rough voice; "have you no eyes in your head, that you must needs fall over me, like a stricken deer over a fallen tree?"

"Oh! save me—save me! The wolf!"

"Ha! then by Saint Hubert I must have fallen asleep," replied the voice, and at the same time a big, burly forester arose from the turf, on which he had been lying. "I must have fallen asleep, I say, or I should have heard the howling of the four-legged robber."

"Save me, I am a priest," muttered the father, as he pulled off his bonnet to show his shaven head.

The forester doffed his cap in a reverential manner, as he replied—

"Fear not, holy sir ; my crossbow and its bolt shall give good account of the villain wolf."

As he spoke the man drew his weapon, and fixed its bolt in the proper position.

On came the wolf, but stopped when it perceived that instead of one flying man it had to do with two men at bay.

The beast hesitated, and the hesitation cost it its life. The forester's crossbow twanged, the iron-headed "quarrell" struck the wolf on the forehead, and knocked him to the ground senseless.

"His skin will procure me a good bottle," muttered the man, as drawing his knife he at once proceeded to cut the beast's throat, and drag the skin from its carcase.

While so occupied he was compelled to place his crossbow on the ground as well as the bolts, which he drew from his belt to enable him to kneel with greater ease beside the dead beast.

The monk saw, and for a short space his mean soul meditated treachery. "How easy it would be to kill this man, and take possession of his weapons," he thought.

But just in the act of stooping to raise the crossbow another reflection came upon his mind. Without the aid of that forester he would never be able to find his way to the place of rest, shelter, and food, of which he stood so much in need.

That one thought alone saved the life of the rude forester.

"Can you inform me, friend, how far it is to any inn or house at which I can procure some food ?" he asked.

"There is an inn within two hundred yards of this spot, but men speak ill of it."

"Nevertheless, I will proceed to it if you will show me the way. Why is it ill-spoken of ?"

"Men say that it is infested by robbers, and that the landlord himself is no more than a robber in disguise of an honest tradesman."

"Can this be true ?"

"I know not, in faith, good father."

"Then you have not been within the walls of this hostelry ?"

"Aye, many a time, to sell skins as I am now going to sell this. Come with me then if you would see this den."

"How is it called? Hath it no sign ?"

"It is called the 'Wayfarer's Home.'"

While this conversation was going on the two men were walking onwards, the countryman bearing on his shoulders the warm skin of the wolf.

They plunged down a deep ravine, and turning sharply round to the left hand came in sight of a house or hut, in the window of which gleamed a dim, solitary light.

Father Abel, indeed, so little liked the look of the house that he would have retreated had he dared. He resolved to question his guide.

"Is there no other house hereabouts ?" he asked.

"My own cot is two leagues and a half from this spot," replied the wolf-killer.

"Then I must even rest here," replied the disguised monk with a sigh.

As they approached the inn the noise of their footsteps seemed to give notice to the host, who was at the door to meet them ere they reached the threshold.

"Will it please you to enter, good sir ?" said he. "My house is but a humble one, but our ale is not the worst on Cheviotside."

"I would follow my journey," replied Father Abel, "if it were possible."

"Whither do you journey, sir ?" asked the forester, bending a searching gaze upon the priest.

Father Abel hesitated a moment, and then replied—

"I would reach Roxburgh if it were possible."

"Roxburgh? Why that is five leagues at least from this spot."

"Then I must perforce remain."

"Aye, indeed, good sir," exclaimed the

host, "unless you would spend the night in wandering over the hills and moors."

At that moment something struck Father Abel upon the back, and as he turned to see what it was he resolved that he would sooner dwell in a cave of robbers than go forth again during the hours of darkness.

The object which had touched him was the skin of the wolf, whose jaws the monk had so narrowly escaped.

"I will remain. Provide me with food and drink."

The landlord bowed and left the room into which they had walked on reaching the inn, and at the same moment the stranger said—

"By your leave, sir, I will now depart and sell my prize to the rogue ostler who purchases such wares."

Could the monk have seen what took place outside the door his fickle mind would have changed, and a night with the wolves would have been risked rather than a sojourn in that inn.

The host stopped in the passage till he was joined by the forester.

"We have the man now," said the latter.

"What man?"

"The monk—Father Abel."

"Well?"

"He must not leave this house."

The landlord trembled and changed colour.

"What would you do with him?"

"He will be a useful tool. He must be one of us."

"Then I must not place him in the new room?"

"Certainly not—the oaken chamber."

"It shall be done."

"Are George the pedlar and the others here?"

"They are."

"Bid them be in readiness at midnight and they shall have due instructions. Place the monk—for such he is, though in disguise—in the oaken chamber, say nothing, and leave the rest to me."

"But if he should take a fancy in his head to continue his journey?"

"You must prevent him."

"How?—by force?"

"No. He fears wolves. Persuasion will suffice."

The forester then threw the wolf-skin over his shoulders and departed, while the landlord brought food and drink for the refreshment of the monk.

"Know you yon forester?" the latter asked, as the host returned.

"A little, good sir; he has departed now."

"How is he called?"

"I know not his name, but people call him the moody hunter."

"Why?"

"That I cannot tell you."

"Where does he live?"

"I know not."

"Does he live in this locality?"

"No."

"Where then?"

"I have never asked."

Father Abel thought that his host was one of the most reserved men he had ever met, but attributed it to his supposed connection with the banditti he had been told of.

He was resolved to eat his supper in silence and to retire, trusting in the events of another day to clear off the score, which he himself had no means of paying.

The meal finished, he arose from his seat, and said—

"Show me my chamber."

The landlord obeyed this injunction without a word.

Taking a lamp in his hand, he led the guest up a flight of steps and along a corridor which led to the priest's room.

The oaken chamber before alluded to was a tolerably large, but very sombre-looking apartment, better furnished than the priest imagined.

Its name, "oaken chamber," was due to the wainscoting around the walls, which were of that timber as was also the furniture.

The landlord placed the lamp on an old-fashioned mantel-piece above the hearth and withdrew.

Father Abel looked and listened with the greatest attention as he did so.

As the door closed behind the host it struck the traveller that the creaking of a bolt immediately followed the closing of the door.

The monk hastened to assure himself on this head, but found that his suspicions were too well founded.

The door was bolted on the outside.

"What can this mean?" thought he. "It must be a device of the robbers the forester spoke of."

A cold perspiration stood upon his brow.

He felt in his belt for weapons and in his pouch for money, but neither were to be found.

Urged by a strong natural impulse—that of self-preservation—he hastened to the window to discover if there were any means by which he could escape.

"Strong iron bars," he muttered. "Treachery—the direct treachery—must be meditated."

He sat down on the bed and began to moan and weep.

Death was, in his opinion, the only thing that could happen, for he knew that the robbers of that time knew the worth of the proverb which says—"Dead men tell no tales," and he knew also that they did not hesitate to act upon it.

After a time he became more composed, and, taking a lamp in his hand, proceeded to view more narrowly the room in which he was thus imprisoned.

It contained a bedstead of oak, a table of the same material—over which was a crucifix—and a few other articles of furniture.

The priest's eyes glistened as he saw the crucifix, and, taking it in his hand, he threw himself upon the bed.

"With this on my breast, I shall be safe," he exclaimed. "The dagger of a robber cannot touch me now. The rascals fear the power of the Church."

As he spoke, his eyes rested upon one of the panels of the wainscot, and, to his great astonishment, he perceived that the wood glided back, revealing a little trapdoor, through which a naked arm presented itself and placed a letter upon the oaken table before described.

The hand and arm were then withdrawn, silently but speedily.

The panel glided back into its place, and all was silent.

This was but the work of a single second.

The priest rushed forward, and—half maddened by the events of the night—endeavoured to force back the panel, but in vain.

It resisted his efforts, and Father Abel then turned his attention to the letter which had been so mysteriously thrust into his apartment.

It was addressed to him, and this fact made him feel secure while breaking the seal, which had nothing on it that could reveal who they were who had adopted this strange method of communicating with him.

The priest's face became white with terror as his eyes gazed upon the lines—

"Fail not, at your peril, to follow, in silence and without resistance, the person who will enter your chamber at midnight. Death will follow disobedience of this mandate."

The paper dropped from the priest's nerveless hands, his jaws fell, and his eyes became fixed upon vacancy.

But the striking of a bell aroused him from his stupor, reminding him that only one hour more was allowed him.

And a hoarse voice shouted beneath the window—

"It is eleven o'clock!"

"THE TOURNAMENT."

CHAPTER XXIX.

THE FEAST OF THE PEACOCK.

SOME little disappointment was visibly expressed on the faces of spectators when the tournament at Alnwick came to such an untimely end.

But those who principally regretted it were the people of the little town—the hosiers, cordwainers, smiths and carpenters, who could hope for no share in the feast which was to follow.

As for the squires, pages and retainers at the castle, they little cared, for was not their young lord still in the lists, ready to undertake a course with any comer ; and was not a most gorgeous feast being prepared by cooks, scullions and grooms of the kitchen ?

Many of the more convivial ones hoped that no other adventurer might appear, in order that the feasting might at once commence.

They knew that the newly-made knight was to take the vow of the peacock, and that rare times would follow that most regal ceremony.

For of all the delicate dishes set before the gourmands of the middle ages, there was not one that was more esteemed than the peacock—"The food of lovers, the noble bird, the meat of lords," as an old writer expresses it.

Scarcely any noble or royal feast was deemed complete without it.

A little description of the manner in which it was prepared would perhaps, not be out of place.

The bird was stuffed with spices and sweet herbs, while the head was covered with a cloth, kept constantly wet to preserve the crown.

It was roasted, and when cooked, served up whole, covered, after dressing, with skin and feathers, the comb or crown entire, and the tail spread.

Some covered it with gold leaf instead of its skin, and placed in its beak a piece of cotton dipped in spirits which was fired when the dish was set upon the table.

The honour of serving it up was reserved for some one of noble birth—the pages or esquires who aspired to reach the dignity of knighthood.

On very rare occasions it was served up by the ladies of the court, who brought it to table in a gold or silver dish, followed and preceded by musicians.

It was always set before the knight who had most distinguished himself in the tournament, or in actual warfare, who was expected to display his skill in carving the favourite fowl, and was expected to take oaths on its head of valour, loyalty, and fidelity to the ladies.

Any of our young readers who have read "Lancelot" will remember the passage which represents King Arthur as performing this task to the complete satisfaction of five hundred guests.

But to return to our tale.

No other claimant appeared to contest the honours of the arena with Hotspur, who was thereupon declared the victorious knight.

The barriers were removed, the throng slowly dispersed, the townsmen to the inns, where entertainment had been provided, and the retainers to their various offices.

The same page who had conveyed the note from Lady Katherine to the unknown knight now informed her of the mysterious disappearance of the stranger.

Lady Katherine was on her way from the hall to her own room to prepare herself for the feast when she received the tidings.

"Thank Heaven he has escaped !" she murmured and passed on.

Hotspur, on the other hand, was not so well pleased.

He felt nettled that his adversary should have departed without bringing the fight to a decisive termination, and, hearing how the stranger had disappeared resolved to search for him.

Whispering to his esquire, Witherington, he left the throng and passed through the side door by which Douglas had departed.

The way was narrow and dark, for the afternoon had become cloudy.

But the two youths well knew the path.

It led to a chamber in the very heart and centre, as it were, of the massive keep, and which had a gloomy look befitting its position in the strongest, best secured part of the castle.

The walls were in part hidden with tapestry, as much for the purpose of concealing the doors as for any other purpose.

The floor was covered with rushes, and the furniture was of a very solid, cumbersome description.

The chamber was in fact seldom used, but was designed for habitation in the event of any foe gaining possession of the outworks of the castle, and so rendering the other apartments uninhabitable.

For the keep itself was strong enough to resist a stubborn siege, even if communication with other portions of the vast building should happen to be cut off.

"We must surely find him soon," exclaimed Hotspur. "He cannot go much farther, unless he be a magician."

"See, see, there, behind the tapestry," cried Witherington, pointing to a spot where the hangings seemed agitated, though not a breath of air was stirring.

"Step forth, sir knight," said Hotspur, "surely you will not leave the feast as you left the lists."

There was no response to this invitation, and, without a word, the two youths strode to the spot resolving to unmask the stranger.

With a hasty hand Hotspur tore the curtain aside and there beheld neither monk nor knight, but Gunara, the Witch of Wooler.

The young knight started back, and laid hands upon his sword.

The esquire crossed himself.

The woman held up her hand, and in low tones, said—

"Remember, violence avails not with me. But those you seek have departed."

"And you aided them?"

"I did."

"Wherefore?"

"To avoid spilling blood at the feast which graces these halls."

"His name?"

"Ask me not, for I cannot now reveal it."

"And the monk ; methinks I recognise his sleek visage and smooth poll. Is he one of your emissaries?"

"He is not. As you love your life, Percy, beware of that man, he is a dangerous plotter, and, if only half as brave as he is mischievous would be an enemy by no means to be despised. But return now to the hall, the knights and nobles await your coming, the dainty bird is dished, and only needs the presence of the successful knight before whom it is to be placed."

With these words the weird woman once more ensconced herself behind the hangings.

Percy turned upon his heel, and took two steps towards the door by which he had entered the chamber.

But a thought flashed across his mind and he resolved to seek more information.

But on drawing aside the tapestry Gunara was not to be seen, nor had she left any sign of the manner in which she had so suddenly disappeared.

With an exclamation of surprise and disappointment, he took his way towards the great hall in which the feast was prepared.

The room has already been described with its raised dais, its long tables, and its high arched windows.

On the present occasion four huge brazen lamps were suspended from chains attached to the vaulted roof, and their somewhat smoky flames served to dispel the fast thickening glooms of twilight.

On seats around the table at the hall might be seen the towering form of the earl, dressed in costly robes of rich velvet and cloth of gold; there was the countess, attired as became her dignity, and numbers of gallant warriors and lovely damsels; pages and servants flitted hither and thither! in fact, the hall might have been taken for the banquet of a great and powerful sovereign rather than that of a subject lord.

But the Earl of Northumberland, though a subject, was a rich, powerful, and at times a troublesome one.

Two chairs were occupied, one being destined for Hotspur, the other for the Queen of the Lists.

The young Percy seated himself, and a moment afterwards Lady Katherine took her place by his side.

The earl then raised his hand, and the trumpets sounded.

Two armed men with drawn swords appeared, and behind them the most highly-honoured pages and servants, bearing a huge silver dish, on which was the bird, dressed and decked according to custom.

The procession marched straight to the principal table, every one rising to receive it.

The servitors on their knees placed the dish upon the board, the guard of honour waved their swords, and the trumpeters sounded their loudest blasts.

Then, when the clamour had in some measure subsided, the chaplain rose and recited a benediction in Latin.

This finished, Hotspur arose with a blush on his countenance, and, holding his right hand over the dish, said—

"By the head of this noble bird, and by the faith of a Christian knight, I devote myself to deeds of arms, to the service of fair ladies, and to the succour of the distressed."

At this moment some of the menials uttered cries of surprise, and every eye was directed to the opposite end of the vast hall.

CHAPTER XXX.

THE PINE-TREE FOREST.

WHEN the priest heard the fearful voice beneath his window proclaiming the hour, his soul was filled with terror.

As before said, escape was cut off; even a monkey would have found a great difficulty in quitting the apartment, so close were the bars across the window and at the back of the fireplace.

Time passed.

Midnight came, and found Father Abel trembling with fear.

Horrible visions of dungeons, daggers, racks, and tortures arose before his distracted mind.

The door was opened slowly, and a man, armed to the teeth, entered.

His face was concealed by a kind of mask.

Without a word, he approached the priest, and tied a handkerchief over his eyes.

"Make no noise, hold my hand, and do not attempt to remove the bandage till I give the word," said the unknown.

Father Abel was too agitated to utter a word.

His knees trembled, his teeth chattered, and it was with great difficulty he could summon up sufficient physical strength to follow his mysterious guide.

They passed down the staircase, out of the house, and Father Abel soon perceived that they were ascending a steep hill.

But they soon came once more to level ground.

The stranger then removed the bandage from the priest's eyes, and Father Abel stole a furtive glance around.

The darkness prevented him from seeing much; all he knew was that he found himself on a strange wild heath, near which was a gloomy-looking pine forest.

The guide noticed the look, and spoke—

"You would hardly find your way back to the inn without my assistance, so that an attempt to escape would be useless. The bandage was removed in order that you might make your way between these blocks of stone with greater ease."

Then the journey was resumed in silence, till they neared the trees before mentioned, when a kind of instinct compelled Father Abel to halt.

That grove, he doubted not, was the place of sacrifice where he was to be slain to satisfy the malice of some one he had unwittingly offended.

"Whither do you take me?" he asked.

"To the presence of those who summoned and expect you."

"Who are they?"

"I may not divulge their names."

"What want they with me?"

"Your services."

"In what capacity or office?"

"They will inform you. Forward, they will be angry if kept waiting."

So saying, he laid his hand upon Father Abel's shoulder, and pushed him forward.

The shadow of the pine trees reached, the unknown guide motioned Father Abel to stop.

The ground was tolerably level, and free from bushes.

In fact they seemed to be traversing a well-worn frequented pathway.

"There are no obstacles in our way now; you can have no use for your eyes. I must bandage them again," said the guide.

"Is it necessary?"

"It is," was the reply, and in another moment the handkerchief was bound over the priest's face.

For at least a quarter of an hour they continued their walk, the guide holding Father Abel by the hand, and warning him when the path was rough, or any obstacle stood in the way.

But in spite of this friendliness the priest stumbled several times, and fell heavily once, though luckily without receiving any very serious injury.

Then, after journeying for some yards, a loud voice, not that of the guide, said—

"Halt!"

The priest instantly stood still, and the bandage fell from his eyes.

Father Abel glanced around with surprise and terror.

A little open glade, surrounded on all sides by the tall pine trees, formed the scene.

The actors being, besides himself and the guide, some half dozen of well-armed men, all of whom wore their visors over their faces.

"I have conducted hither the expected guest," said the guide, raising his hand to his brow in military salute.

"You have done well, and performed our bidding faithfully," said a voice, which the priest at once recognised as that of the forester from whom he had so recently parted.

"I need not address you by name, holy father, though you are well known to me. Even these tall trees might waft away an echo of the sound; and our business requires secrecy."

He paused awhile, and the priest, thinking that he was expected to make answer, said, in faltering accents—

"What is the reason I have been brought here, worthy sir?"

"That you shall know ere long; but, first of all, listen to a recital of the crimes of which you are accused.

"You are accused of conspiring, with others, to bring ruin upon the most noble Earl of Northumberland; and to endanger his life by means of false charges of treason and heresy.

"You are furthermore charged with having attempted to poison a certain man-at-arms, who paid you a visit at the mansion of the Earl of Northumberland; and also with stealing from the aforesaid mansion four valuable steeds with their furniture, and sundry other articles of lesser value."

The monk trembled so, that his lips refused to utter the words he had in his mind.

At length, by means of a great effort, he managed to stammer out—

"Guilty, I acknowledge; but be merciful."

"Guilty, you acknowledge yourself, and the plea shall be remembered. Now comes the punishment. You shall choose whether you shall be delivered up to the Earl of Northumberland, who, no doubt, will deal gently with you, for the sake of old acquaintance, or whether you shall be given into the hands of the sheriff of London, who respects your cloth a little; or finally whether you will devote yourself to our service, and faithfully obey such commands as we shall impose."

There was a long pause.

Father Abel knew full well that the powerful earl would no more hesitate at hanging a priest than a pauper.

The sheriff of London was one of the the new sect—the Lollards—and, therefore, had very little fear for the thunders of the church; the service of this strange forester might lead him into fearful dangers, and perhaps to death.

Which, then should he choose?

"What if I refuse all three of your propositions, what would follow?"

"A short rope and a tall tree, from which to dangle," was the stern reply, as the forester—for so we must call him till his name is revealed—pointed to one of the lofty pines close by.

This answer decided Father Abel's choice.

Death was a certainty in three cases; in the fourth case lurked unknown dangers.

"I will be your faithful servant," he replied. "Only lay not upon me commands which it is impossible to execute."

"Your tasks will be suited to your abilities, and to your holy profession; but think not treachery will avail you. The slightest attempt to deceive or betray will be punished with instant death. Our eyes can pierce the gloom of the darkest cave, our hands strike through the strongest breastplate. Do you listen?"

"I do," replied Father Abel, and, in truth, the words of the unknown were well calculated to sink deep into his mind.

"Then repeat this oath after me."

So saying, the unknown held towards the priest a book, between the leaves of which was a dagger, and, in clear, distinct tones, pronounced the following words, the monk repeating them as well as his fear would permit—

"I swear by this book, emblem of everlasting life, and by this dagger, symbol of death, to render true and faithful service to those in whose presence I now stand. I swear to execute all their commands without hesitation or reservation, and to preserve inviolate every secret entrusted to me!"

The book and the dagger were then pressed to his lips, and Father Abel had pledged himself body and soul to the service of a cause of which he knew nothing.

"You have taken the oath, see that you keep it, or the dagger will be your portion; and not all the powers of earth can screen you from our vengeance. The hand that could place a letter on your table, could, with equal ease, plant a poignard in your heart, even if you filled the Papal throne. But take this scroll; in it you will find your instructions."

The monk glanced at the document, which contained orders for him to proceed to Alnwick and prevent Douglas from entering the lists with Hotspur.

A sealed packet was also handed him to be given to the young Scottish chief in case the encounter had already taken place.

"Go; conduct him from the forest, and point out to him the road he is to follow," said the unknown, the "Moody Forester," as he had been called by the landlord of the inn. "Provide him with the dress fitted for his holy calling, and put money in his purse to defray his expenses. Stay, though; let him rest till day begins to dawn, so that he can travel without fear."

The guide bowed, and conducted Father Abel to a spot beneath the pine-trees where the embers of a fire glowed, and, motioning him to sit down, placed food before him.

Father Abel was not so destitute of sense as to imagine that the men who were about to employ him would poison him, and made a hearty meal.

A monk's dress was given him, differing very little from the one he had left behind, and the poor confessor once more had the satisfaction of seeing himself clothed in the garb of his profession.

" You can sleep for an hour or two," said the guide. " I will rouse you when it is time to commence your journey."

The monk stretched himself at full length upon a bundle of heather and endeavoured to sleep.

But his mind was in such a state of confusion from the strange scenes through which he had passed, that it was a long time ere he could succeed.

At no great distance out in the open forest he could dimly discern the forms of the men who had bound him by oath to their service, and could hear the hum of their voices as they conversed.

Amongst other things the names of Sir William Graham, Dubois, and others with whom he was acquainted, fell upon his ear.

What could all this mean?

Who were these strange men who sought to link his destiny with theirs?

While endeavouring to solve this riddle he fell asleep, nor did he wake until his mysterious guide shook him by the shoulder.

" It is daylight, father, rouse yourself."

The priest assumed a sitting posture, and his companion once more produced the handkerchief.

" You must be bandaged for a short time ; such are the orders of our chief."

The priest for a moment meditated resistance, but, fancying he saw dark forms moving amongst the trees at no great distance, changed his mind.

His guide performed his office, took him by the hand and led him away.

" This caution seems needless," said the father, when some distance had been traversed. " If I am not allowed to see the road how can I find my way hither if my presence is required ?"

" By the same means as you did in the present instance. But you will not often be called upon to appear in the pine forest. Your instructions will be forwarded you by a sure hand, and so long as you obey them all will be well. However, we have now left the forest some distance behind, so let me unfasten the bandage."

As soon as his eyes were free Father Abel perceived that he was standing in an open heath with a forest on each side.

His unknown masters had taken care that he should not be too intimately acquainted with their haunts, nor could the monk form the least idea as to which of the woods had been the scene of his strange adventure.

" There lies the road to Alnwick," said the guide, " and here is the money. Hasten forward, or your errand will be useless."

The monk bowed, and raised his hands as though in the act of bestowing his benediction.

He hastily walked on, not deeming it prudent to look behind for some time, but when he did venture to glance back over his shoulder the guide had vanished.

" Not a sign of him left. I shall go on with good speed lest evil overtake me."

In due time he reached the castle, but, as the reader already knows, the tilt had commenced.

Nor is it necessary to recapitulate how he succeeded in inducing young Douglas to leave the lists.

CHAPTER XXXI.

BEFORE THE ALTAR.

THE feast of the Peacock was interrupted by a frightened menial, who, with pallid face and distended eyes, rushed into the hall, crying—

" The witch ! the witch !"

Every one rose and looked towards the door, expecting to see the wierd woman enter.

But she came not.

" Bring hither yon frightened rogue," exclaimed the earl, angry that the festivities should thus be marred.

Half-a-dozen men at once seized the poor fellow and dragged him to the platform on which sat the earl and the other great ones of the feast.

" What witch is this you speak of, villain ?"

" The Witch of Wooler, an' it please your lordship."

" Well—and what of her ?"

" She is in the tapestry chamber, my lord."

" You dream, fellow. This is no witch's cave, no place where the fiend can hold unhallowed revels."

" 'Tis true, my lord, true as I stand here. Oh, holy Virgin ! what a fright it gave me."

" Go you, Witherington, and search the tapestry chamber. If you find this witch confine her in our deepest dungeon, if you find her not lash this rogue from the castle."

" I go, my lord," said the old warrior. " I fear no witch, for the hilt of my sword contains a precious relic, which renders the powers of darkness of no avail."

So saying, the bold, stalwart trooper left the hall followed by a number of men.

Not one of whom would have moved a step had they not heard Witherington's boast of the virtues of his valuable sword hilt.

When the stout old captain entered the apartment known as the tapestried chamber, he was rather surprised to find standing there a woman answering in every description to the accounts he had heard of the Witch of Wooler.

" Ho ! what want you here, my good woman ? Know you that you are an intruder ?"

" If I intrude, I do so in such a manner as to annoy no one ; and am now ready to quit the castle."

" Nay, nay, that may not be. You came hither without invitation : and you go not hence without giving some account of yourself to our noble lord."

" Who shall prevent me from going whithersoever I will ?"

" I !"

" You !" said the woman, with a contemptuous look.

" Aye, I !" roared the old captain. " Witch as you are, your spells have no power over me ; for there is that in my sword-hilt which will preserve me from your malice."

So saying he held out the handle of his weapon, from which Gunara started back, in evident alarm.

" Now perhaps you are convinced," said Witherington, with a look of triumph.

" I feel your power," replied the woman.

" What would you with me ?"

" I would have you come with me to the stone room, beneath the keep, where you must abide till morning."

Gunara made no reply, but motioned that she was ready. Witherington was in no humour to be long absent from the feast, and hurried her forward.

In less than five minutes he had locked her in a strong dungeon, and full of the superstition of the age, nailed a horse-shoe to the threshold to prevent her leaving without permission. He had no fear that she would leave by any other means ; for it seems, in all ages, to have been believed that witches must leave every place by the way that they enter. He then gave orders that a man should enter the cell to look after the prisoner once every three hours, and returned to the hall.

"I have her, my lord," said he ; "I have her safe under lock and key, with such a spell laid upon the threshold of her dungeon that she will not dare cross it. You can see her in the morning, my lord."

"Good, Witherington. You have acted well."

The feast then proceeded. The wine cup passed round, the minstrels sang their best songs, jugglers and morris dancers performed their antics, and all was merry. Only old Witherington took an occasional walk round the ramparts as the night advanced to see that the sentinels were awake and performing their duties.

It seemed, however, that no foe felt inclined to attack the castle ; at all events the inmates of the castle were not aroused from the sound sleep which succeeded the day's pleasure.

Morning came ; life and activity once more reigned throughout the castle ; knights, squires, pages and grooms were seen hastening hither and thither.

The earl sat in the great hall to give judgment in the several little disputes which had arisen over the strong ale consumed the previous night. These however, were soon disposed of, and the great event of the morning anxiously expected.

Witherington and his men proceeded to the dungeon to bring the witch before the earl.

The horseshoe still remained upon the threshold, the bolts were secure, but when the door was opened the cell was tenantless. The witch had left the castle quite as mysteriously as she had entered.

On the floor was a little slip of parchment, with some words upon it.

"See," said one of the men, " there is the charm by which she forced her way through the doorway. It must be something terrible to have power over the horseshoe."

"Bring it hither," said Witherington.

The man, who was a brave soldier, hesitated. Had it been any number of human foes, French or Scotch, he would have rushed into the fray right manfully ;

but the little slip of parchment, in his eyes, represented the powers of darkness.

" I touch it ? Nay, good captain, I have no desire to burn my fingers by meddling with the fiend or his works."

Witherington gave the speaker a black look as a reward for his disobedience, and then took up the parchment himself— with the point of his sword. Even he had no desire to " burn his fingers," and carefully kept his precious relic between himself and the suspected document.

In this manner he carried it to the earl, followed by all his men-at-arms.

" Where is the witch ?" demanded the noble.

" I know not, my lord, whether this be she, or only a token she has left behind," replied Witherington, holding out the letter on the point of his sword ; " at all events this is all that is left of her."

" What says the scroll ?"

" I know not, my lord."

The earl took it and read the following words :—

" Hitherto I have protected and aided you in many things ; henceforth my hand is against you. I sought your castle for no evil purpose ; but, instead of hospitality, I found a dungeon—though its bolts and bars were powerless to imprison me. But wrong rankles in my heart. Earl of Northumberland, dread my revenge !"

The earl crushed the parchment in his hand without saying a word. Had he made those around him acquainted with the contents of the letter, in all probability he would have been deserted by nine-tenths of his followers.

For some minutes he sat in silence ; but, at length, addressing Witherington, he said—

" If this woman falls into your hands again, hang her without delay upon the nearest tree. Let these orders be known."

Witherington bowed, and he, with his followers, left the hall.

The old soldier designed to seek out Hotspur, and severely take him to task for two or three pieces of bad science exhibited in the tilt-yard. He designed to make his young knight the most finished soldier in Christendom ; and history furnishes tolerable strong proofs that a fair amount of success attended his efforts.

Hotspur became one of the most

successful leaders in England, and there is little reason for doubting that he would have been still more successful had he not often allowed his personal bravery to overcome his prudence.

Old Witherington on this occasion sought in vain for his pupil. Harry Percy was not to be found in the tilt-yard or in the riding-school; neither was he to be found in the armoury, as was often his wont, practising the fence of sword and buckler.

Hotspur was not to be found, and the stout old soldier was obliged to content himself with giving a severe lesson to Ralph Percy and young Witherington, assuring them, by way of consolation, that they would eventually become far superior to the young noble—"a lazy young rascal," he muttered aside.

But where was this "lazy young rascal?"

He was in far better society, according to his own opinion, and, no doubt, in the reader's also.

When Hotspur rose that morning, it must be confessed he was a little flushed and feverish. But it was not altogether the unusual quantity of wine he had swallowed the previous night that caused his temples to throb; there were other reasons.

Had he not been hailed victor in the lists? had he not sat at the head of the board? and, above all, had not Lady Katherine Mortimer answered, by blushes and tender glances, the many soft speeches he had poured into her ear?

This latter circumstance had as much effect upon the youth's brain as anything else, and now in the early morning he paced up and down a little grass plot in the private garden through which he knew the fair one would pass on her way to the chapel of the castle to perform her morning devotions.

Hope burned brightly in his bosom, for ever sanguine, he had no fear that his addresses would be repulsed.

At length a side door opened, and Lady Katherine appeared—her face radiant as the morn, her cheeks suffused with blushes, and her eyes sparkling like dewdrops in the rays of the sun.

She looked more exquisitely lovely and loveable than ever.

Hotspur gallantly doffed his cap as he advanced to meet her.

"Good morrow, fair lady," said he, "you have rested but ill, one would fancy, as you rise so early."

"Surely some horrid vision must have frightened you from your couch, my gallant knight?—at least, ever since I arose, I have seen you pacing up and down, to the utter destruction of my favourite daisies."

"Do you grieve much that they should be destroyed?"

"Aye, I would not see the most simple thing in nature injured. But I must away to the chapel, fair coz. We shall meet again ere long."

"Meet again? May I not accompany you?"

Lady Katherine said nothing—the blushes on her cheek became deeper, and the eyelids drooped to veil those sparkling orbs.

No word passed between them as they entered the holy place.

Hotspur stood behind Lady Katherine as she knelt, and in silent prayer addressed the Deity.

But when her devotions were finished he stepped forward and stood by her side.

"You come here every morning, dear Lady Katherine?" said he.

"I do."

"Then we shall meet often."

"Why, is there no other place where we can converse?"

"None so well suited as this, no place that so well accords with the words that I am about to utter. Lady Katherine, young though I am, I love you; I love you more fervently than words can express. What place, then, so well fitted for this declaration of my love than here in this holy place, within sight of that altar, where, ere long, our hands and hearts may be united? If you refuse me not, Lady Katherine, you, who felt for the daisies, can surely bestow your pity upon me."

For a few minutes the fair girl was too agitated to reply, her cheeks changed from pale to red, and from crimson back again to the purest white.

But she did not attempt to withdraw the hand that Hotspur held in his own.

"Say, dear cousin, shall my heart be crushed like the petals of the daisy ?"

"No ; I love you."

Slowly, and with faltering accents, the words came from her trembling lips, upon which the impetuous youth at once pressed a kiss, the first kiss of love, of which poets have so often sung.

"And now, dearest, come kneel with me at this altar, and let us there plight our faith to each other in the sight of heaven only," said Percy, leading her forward.

Together they knelt hand-in-hand.

"Here, before this altar, I solemnly pledge my faith to you, Lady Katherine Mortimer, and solemnly vow that my heart shall be yours, and yours only, for ever to remain, firm, faithful, and constant," said Hotspur, in low tones.

"And I return the pledge," said the fair Lady Katherine, earnestly, "for here I vow to be yours and yours only."

For a moment longer they knelt together, and then rose.

"I fear I did wrong, dear, in allowing you to come hither with me," said Katherine.

"Wherefore ?"

"The servants of the chapel often come her in the morning ; we might have been overheard. Holy Virgin ! what is that ?"

She started back in alarm, pointing towards a picture suspended over the altar.

The sun shone brightly upon it, but across the centre of the canvas was a dark and well-defined shadow—the shadow of a hand holding a huge sword.

At the same moment a deep, sepulchral voice was heard, sounding as though it came from the tombs beneath their feet.

It said—

"You have plighted your faith at the altar, but the sword shall separate you."

CHAPTER XXXII.

A FIGHT WITH A SCOT.

THE sword shall separate you !"

The words were deep, hollow and mysterious, as though a dead prophet had spoken from the tombs to prophesy evil to the living."

And then there was the shadow !

That fearful shadow, which like the sword of Democles, seemed to hang, a threatening, uncertain danger over their young heads.

When would it fall, and in what manner ?

The strange scenes he had witnessed in the underground home of Gunara had given Hotspur's mind a shade more of superstition than it had orignally possessed.

But the undaunted courage of the house of Percy still remained.

Winding one arm around Lady Katherine's waist, the young noble laid his disengaged hand upon his sword.

"Who speaks ?" he asked, looking around.

The tapestry on one side of the altar seemed agitated, but no answer was returned.

Hotspur rushed to the spot, threw back the curtains which concealed a window, and, sword in hand, searched through the nook.

But no one was to be seen, and on returning to Lady Katherine, he perceived that the shadow had disappeared.

But the voice once more sounded.

"Resist not the decrees of fate," it said.

"Heaven preserve us ! This is very terrible !" said Lady Katherine as she heard the sound.

"DANGER!"

The continued excitement, the revulsion of feeling proved more than her nerves could endure.

With a low moan, she fell senseless at the foot of the altar.

Alarmed beyond measure at this circumstance, Hotspur hastily sheathed his sword, and catching up the inanimate form of his betrothed, rushed with her into the open air.

"Help ! help !" he shouted.

"What is the matter, my son ?" exclaimed the countess, who was on her way to the chapel.

"Lady Katherine has fainted. Order your attendants to bear her to her chamber."

"But what has caused this sudden illness."

"Some sound in the chapel alarmed her," replied the young lord.

The countess summoned her attendants, who had remained a few paces behind, but just as they were about to apply the remedies deemed most efficacious in those days, the fair girl opened her eyes and looked languidly around.

"What ails you, sweet ?" asked Lady Percy.

"I heard some sound—I was very much frightened ; but I fear you will be angry with me for being so foolish."

"Foolish you may be, sweet niece, but I am not angry as I know it is natural for the young to be timorous and easily frightened. But hasten to your chamber, love ; my women shall attend you ; and you, my son, seek your noble father, who would have some moments to talk with you."

Hotspur would have preferred to remain with Lady Katherine, but obedience to the parental authority was always most strictly maintained at Alnwick, and therefore he wended his way to the great hall, where the earl still sat in state, as was his custom in the morning.

"You desired to see me, my lord ; I am here," said Hotspur.

"On a matter of very slight importance, my son. Seek Witherington, and he will inform you of two or three slight errors in the management of your steed and weapons. Let his instructions be remembered."

Hotspur hastened away, but the old captain of the castle and the other youths were not to be seen.

A casual inquiry, however, soon revealed the path they had taken.

The old warrior and his two pupils had, after completing their morning lesson, strolled down into the village to learn if anything had been seen or heard of the witch, the strange knight, or the monk during the past night.

Hotspur walked after them.

His blood was still boiling with excitement, and he fancied the walk would perhaps cool his fevered brow.

The pathway took him through a lovely landscape.

Meadows, stream, and grove, with hills rising abruptly on either hand.

But the young noble was too much occupied with his own thoughts to heed the beauties of nature.

What cared he for the shining river ?

It was dull and muddy compared with the bright eyes of Lady Katherine.

The odours of the sweet-briar, and thousands of wild flowers had not half the perfume of her breath.

The white clouds in the sky to him seemed far less pure than her fair skin.

The lark's morning carol discordant compared with her silvery notes.

Nor did even the sun itself seem to shine more brightly than Lady Katherine's golden locks.

Deeply engaged in a mental review of the physical and mental beauties of the lady of his love, Hotspur almost forgot the object of his journey, nor did he wake from his reverie until he came to a narrow brook, over which he had to cross on stepping-stones.

The slight stoppage this occasioned recalled his mind once more to the things of this earth, and he began to wonder, as no doubt does the reader, what had become of his brother, his old military tutor, and his esquire.

When these last-named persons left the castle they proceeded to the village, and on reaching the little collection of houses paused, to make their first inquiries at a little inn, of which some mention has been made.

In answer to their question, the host informed them that he had not heard anything of either the knight, the witch, or the monk, but that there was a stranger in the house who could no doubt give them the latest information.

Old Witherington, after a short consultation with Ralph Percy, strode into the house in order to obtain from the stranger any news that might be learned, not only of the persons he was in search of, but also of the general movements of his hereditary foes—the Scots.

For, in those days, when printing was not invented, newspapers were unknown, and the only method of circulating intelligence was by word of mouth.

The stranger was seated at a table, his hands spread before his face.

In fact he seemed to be asleep, nor did he take the slightest notice of the new comers, until Witherington laid a hand upon his shoulder.

"Good morrow, fair sir. You have travelled far, and are fatigued with your journey, I should guess," said the old soldier.

"You have guessed rightly, sir," was the short reply.

"You are from the north ?"

The youth nodded.

"A Scot, perhaps ?"

Again the stranger nodded, adding with a smile—

"I am travelling with a safe protection, granted by the Earl of Northumberland. Here it is."

As he spoke the youth drew from the breast of his doublet a folded parchment, which he held out towards the old soldier.

Witherington shook his head.

"You take it, my lord," said he, addressing Ralph Percy. "These letters in writing are so much alike that my old eyes are unable to tell one from the other."

The lad assented, and began to read the parchment document.

"It seems from this," said he, "that you come from the neighbourhood of Jedburgh."

The stranger nodded.

"A spy, no doubt !" exclaimed young Witherington.

The unknown turned and bent a look of anger upon the English youth.

"I am a Scot, and of good family. It is not my custom tamely to submit to insolence."

"Pshaw ! do not think to frighten me with your angry looks and big words, Sir Scot."

"My house has been renowned for deeds as well as words. Provoke me not too far."

"I do not tremble although I have raised your ire," replied young Witherington. "The scrap of rusty iron you carry by your side for a sword has no terrors for me."

The young Scot rose from his seat, and laid his hand fiercely upon the hilt of his sword.

"Do you wish to quarrel, Sir Saxon ?" he asked, half drawing the blade from its scabbard.

"I am indifferent, Sir Gael," replied the young esquire, drawing his weapon towards him in readiness.

During this altercation old Witherington had been attentively listening to Ralph Percy, who slowly, and word by word, gave him to understand the contents of the document.

But now hearing angry voices he turned towards the hostile youths.

"What is this, in the name of Heaven ?" he exclaimed. "Return your swords, boys. We have no fighting in Alnwick ward."

"This youth has cast an affront upon me. I will wash out the insult with his blood unless he forthwith retracts his words," said the Scot.

"Let us first hear the nature of the affront."

"He said I was a spy."

"Is this so, Harry ?"

"It is ; and I care not to withdraw what I have spoken."

"Then the duello must take its course. Out to the green, lads, and fight it merrily ; but ere you cut my son's throat, Sir Scot, let me ask if during your journey you saw or heard anything of a certain strange female called the Witch of Wooler ?"

"I have heard many strange tales of her in days gone by."

"The spy equivocates, and will not give a direct answer," said young Witherington.

"If he answer not that remark with his sword, I shall think he is both spy and coward, Harry. You seem determined to force him to a combat."

"Lead on, sir. You shall find me ready enough to answer insult."

With these words the indignant young Scot strode from the tavern, followed by Ralph Percy and the young Witherington.

At first sight it seemed that they were a most unequal match; for the stranger, whose name, according to the parchment, was Malcolm Ogilvie, stood at least three inches taller than the young esquire, was much broader across the shoulders, and more stoutly made.

But the Northumbrian youth was one of the most agile lads in the Border country, and had been trained almost from his cradle to the use of weapons.

Few of his age could equal him in the use of the sword.

In the present instance, too, young Witherington had no supernatural being to combat with; the Scot was a being of human flesh and blood.

So on the green before the little hostelry they stood facing each other, their blades drawn, foot advanced.

Then with a clash the blades met.

The Scot led off the combat with a rapid succession of heavy blows—a mode of fighting for which his heavy broadsword was best suited—while young Witherington for a time contented himself with receiving them upon his blade.

His object was to allow the stranger to exhaust his strength and wind, then, by straight thrusts, a style of fencing not much known or understood at that time, to disable or kill his adversary.

But Ogilvie's arm seemed a machine, and the shower of blows flagged not.

Witherington saw this, and saw, moreover, that if he hastened not to inflict some wound upon his opponent he should certainly be compelled to yield.

He drew back a pace, and, as Ogilvie stepped forward to follow up his supposed advantage, lunged forward, and with the point of his sword slightly grazed the Scot's ribs.

But he did not escape unharmed himself, for the broadsword of his adversary drew blood from the young esquire's left shoulder.

"Well fought, lads," exclaimed the old soldier.

"And now let the fight cease," said a voice, and at the same time, Hotspur, catching hold of young Witherington, dragged him back a couple of yards from his adversary, placing his own body between the two.

"There has been enough fighting. Put up your sword, good sir, unless you are the knight who yesterday encountered me at the castle, in which case turn it against myself."

"I have never been to your castle; but I have been insulted by yon youth."

"You have both proved your courage sufficiently. Sheath your sword, Witherington, we have much to do."

The young esquire returned his sword to its scabbard.

"Have you heard aught of the monk or of Douglas?" continued Hotspur.

"I have heard nothing of either, if it be Douglas you mean who met you so stoutly yesterday."

As these words were uttered, young Ogilvie sheathed his blade and returned to the inn; nor did the others notice his departure.

CHAPTER XXXIII.

A RIDE TO THE RUINS.

WHEN Douglas followed Father Abel out of the tilt-yard he had no very definite idea of what was the cause of the sudden summons.

All he knew was that the monk brought a strict injunction from his father to cease fighting, and that command he dared not disobey.

Father Abel led the young Scot through a side door into the tapestry chamber before mentioned.

There they saw standing before them Gunara, the weird woman, with whose dress and features both were acquainted.

"So far you have performed your duty well," said she, addressing Father Abel. "Now, read this scroll."

Father Abel glanced over the document, which was signed by the "Moody Forester."

It ran thus :—

"When you have succeeded in extricating the young Earl Douglas from Alnwick Castle, you will conduct him to the ruins on Elvedon Hill. There a message awaits him."

"Can you tell me what all this means, holy father?" said Douglas, when the monk had communicated to him the contents of the letter.

"Not I. I am only a messenger."

"Can you tell me, wonderful lady?" he continued, addressing Gunara.

"Your noble father desires your return to his camp. At Elvedon Hill you will learn where you may find him."

Douglas heard, and bowed his head.

"Away," said Gunara. "This avenue will lead you from the castle."

As she spoke the witch touched a small brass nail which appeared to suspend the tapestry.

A huge block of stone moved out of its place, revealing a vaulted passage, into which the monk stepped, followed by young Douglas.

The passage was long, narrow, and dark.

Had it not been for a lantern Father Abel had concealed beneath his serge gown, they would have had some difficulty in finding the way.

At length they came to the end, and Father Abel, by pressing another spring, opened a way for them to pass out into the open air.

They found themselves in a ruined building, some little distance from the castle walls, and concealed from it.

The monk pushed back the secret door into its place.

A spring was heard to snap, and then the young Scot spoke—

"Why have you closed the passage ? How can we return if it be necessary ?"

"My instructions say nothing of returning, Lord Douglas," replied the monk.

"If the Northumbrians follow us, what means of escape have we ?"

"We have horses in yonder thicket," said Father Abel, pointing towards a small copse at no very great distance. "Hasten, my lord, for I have no mind to fall into the hands of the Lord Percy or his hot-headed son."

Concealed within the thicket they found two powerful horses, fastened to the branch of a tree.

Douglas untied them, and nimbly leaped to the back of one, while the priest more slowly mounted the other.

"Away with you, father ; show me the road !" exclaimed the young Highland lord.

Father Abel gave his steed the rein, and they commenced their journey.

For some miles they travelled in silence over a beautiful and picturesque country.

The landscape was tinted with richly variegated hues, and the declining sun, which streamed upon the hills, produced a beautiful and spirited effect upon the scenery.

The rich golden corn fields glowed through the dark green of the surrounding foliage, and the prospect seemed lighted up with a brilliant luxuriance.

Then they entered a deep valley, along the bottom of which flowed a clear stream, whose banks were adorned with thick groves of waving trees.

At length the valley became merely a narrow dell, while the trees and the hills on whose sides they grew overshadowed the path, to the almost total exclusion of the light, for the sun had disappeared, and a deep twilight cast its gloom upon the track they were pursuing.

After traversing this route for some distance, the monk turned off to the right, and pulled up his horse before the entrance of a cave.

" Here we will rest," said he. " We are not expected at Elvedon Hill until after to-morrow's sun has set."

" But my father ?"

" He knows all. Enter ; let us eat, drink and sleep, for I am instructed that we shall find refreshments here."

Douglas assented, and entered the cavern.

All was darkness at first, but a flint and steel soon furnished a light for Father Abel's lantern, and by its rays the two travellers saw they were in a not uncomfortable place.

A huge curtain or screen of thick cloth hung at one side, and could be drawn right across the mouth of the cave, thus excluding cold winds and hiding the light from the monk's candle. In the corner a quantity of dried sticks were piled up before a place which was evidently the fire-place of the establishment, while in a second nook was a bundle of fodder for their steeds. Before the fire-place above mentioned were beds of sweet heather and moss, on the ground a huge basket, from which protruded the neck of a leather bottle. Creature comforts had been carefully provided.

Douglas little cared to enter into conversation with his strange guide. He helped to light a fire, and partook moderately of the food contained in the basket, then, throwing himself on the bunch of heather, gave himself up to thought.

Father Abel soon perceived that his conversation was thrown away, and com posed himself for sleep.

It was nearly sunset the following day when the monk gave the signal to proceed.

They mounted their steeds, and made their way once more into the narrow dell they had quitted. The path soon began to grow steep and rugged, the trees more scattered, and at last, just as darkness began to encroach upon the light of day, Douglas perceived at some distance up the long vista before them the ruins of an old tower or mansion.

The gloom of the trees partly concealed it from his view, but, as he drew nearer, each forlorn and decaying feature of the fabric was gradually disclosed to view.

" These are the ruins of Elvedon," said Father Abel, turning to his companion.

The aspect of the building, or rather ruins, well accorded with the melancholy mood of the young Scot.

The broken battlements enwreathed with ivy proclaimed the fallen grandeur of the place, and at the same time reminded him of the broken hopes which had once possessed his heart. The shattered, vacant windows, which exhibited their desolation, and the high grass, which, overgrowing the threshold, seemed to say how long it was since mortal foot had entered, had their counterpart in the desolation and emptiness of his bosom.

The young Earl Douglas had loved Lady Katherine with an impetuous, fiery love, which frightened her gentle soul ; he had seen how her heart had been won by another ; the splendid temple erected by love had crumbled away and left nought but shattered ruins behind.

The more Douglas gazed upon the place the more it seemed to him fit only for dark deeds done by desperate people.

A few yards from the ruins they dismounted from their steeds, and tied them up to a tall pine tree, through whose branches a hollow wind echoed in melancholy tones.

The monk then led the way towards a gate which, instead of swinging upon hinges, lay flat upon the ground, and entered the building.

Douglas looked with a feeling akin to awe, upon the roofless, cracked walls, green with damps ; upon the Gothic points of the windows, where ivy, briars, and spiders' webbs had long since supplied the place of glass, and upon the festoons of green hanging from the broken capitals of some columns which had once supported the roof.

Suddenly the monk stumbled upon the broken pavement, and his voice, as he uttered a sudden oath, was returned in strange hollow echoes, that made the scene seem still more wild.

At length they reached a flat block of stone, which had all the appearance of a tomb. The monk paused.

"Here we must wait," he said.

Douglas nodded and seated himself upon the slab, saying nothing ; and the monk, having failed on several previous occasions, did not attempt to enter into conversation with his moody companion.

For a long time they sat thus, long after the sun had set, and the moon had arisen, only to veil her head behind clouds.

Bats and owls fluttered noiselessly about amongst the ruins ; toads croaked amidst the long grass and ivy.

This was the only sound heard, but suddenly the two watchers became aware of a dark form gliding without sound across the open space.

CHAPTER XXXIV.

THE SPIRIT OF WAR.

"HIST! what is that?" asked Douglas. "I know not ; let us watch," replied Father Abel, who, to tell the truth, felt very ill at ease.

The dark figure was joined by another and then by a third.

As the eyes of the watchers became more accustomed to the darkness, they perceived that the strange forms had the appearance of ancient females, dressed in tattered garments.

"By the mass ! this smacks strongly of the sin of witchcraft," muttered Douglas.

"You are right," said a voice close behind.

Both turned, and beheld Gunara, the Witch o' Wooler.

"You are right ; those are the strange beings called witches. But fear them not, they are obedient to my command."

At this moment the three old crones became aware of the presence of Gunara, and immediately advanced towards her.

"Hail ! hail ! great mistress !" they exclaimed, in harsh, cracked voices. "Why have you brought us hither ?"

"Back ! question me not, but await my commands. First of all to you, Douglas, I must deliver this missive."

The witch handed a letter, as she spoke, to the young chief.

"Little use is this to me, unless you were also to give me a light by which to read it."

"A light you shall have," said Gunara, as she brandished her staff around her head, at the same time repeating some strange words.

In a moment the end of the staff was tipped with a lurid flame, which continued to burn steadily.

The young Scot, after a look of surprise, conquered the awe he felt, and, by the light of this strange torch, read the letter :—

"Obey the strange woman in all things, my son ; look upon the wonders she will show you, and then return with a full report to me at your best speed.
DOUGLAS, Earl, his X mark." *

---

* To be able to read and write was, in the fourteenth century, accounted a great accomplishment.

So ran the letter, which the son consigned to his pouch when he had read it.

"What more would you?" she asked, when the young Scot once more turned his eyes towards her.

"Great lady," said he, "I have once beheld your power, but would fain look upon the skill for which you are famed again. Show me, therefore, if you can, the spirit that shall rule my destiny."

"You shall—if it be any of those who obey my call. Come."

So saying, she led the way to the spot where the three hags were busily engaged in preparing a fire. Over this hung a huge cauldron.

As the fire burned up, the three crones hobbled round and round the cauldron, from time to time throwing various substances into it. Gunara stood by, looking on, while, a little distance behind her, were Father Abel and Douglas.

As the steam began to arise from the cauldron, Gunara, in a loud tone, uttered the following lines:

> "Spirits of earth and ocean rise,
> Spirits strong, and spirits wise,
> Ye, who taught my feeble tongue
> How to rule you, wise and strong,
> Spirits return to this earthly sphere,
> Be ready, and when I call, appear."

The same rushing sound was heard that Douglas had noticed in the cave of Gunara.

"Are you prepared to look upon the spirit who shall guide and rule your actions during life?" she asked.

"I am."

> "By the seven mysterious burning words,
> By the seven enchanted magic swords,
> Arise from beneath, or descend from on high,
> Thou who dost rule his destiny."

As the Witch of Wooler finished speaking there was a fearful clap of thunder, and with it a blinding flash of lightning.

At the same moment a shadowy figure seemed to ascend from the cauldron, the figure of a man with features like those of a fierce demon.

The brow of this strange figure seemed to be encircled with a crown, in its hand a glittering sword.

"It is the spirit of war," said Gunara; "speak not, or his rage may be turned towards you."

The witch then made some motions with her staff, and the figure disappeared.

"Is there aught else you desire to see?"

Douglas shook his head.

"Then hie away. Five miles beyond the good town of Jedburgh your noble father's camp is pitched. Away, ye foul hags, I have no more present need of your services."

With a shrill yell the crones vanished, seeming to soar up into the air, while the cauldron and fire disappeared with similar rapidity.

"There lies your road; four hours' hard riding will bring you to your journey's end. Away."

The monk was glad enough to be off, for the scene he had just witnessed was by no means a pleasant one to a person of his uncertain nerves.

They mounted their horses and galloped off at full speed; the moon shining out, it seemed, purposely, to light them on their path.

In less than four hours the town of Jedburgh came in view, but they passed aside instead of entering, and keeping at no great distance from the walls soon found themselves on the road to the camp.

That they had taken the right direction was very certain from the numerous hoofprints.

At length they reached the camp itself.

"There is my father," said young Douglas, pointing to a gigantic warrior, clad in armour, over which he had thrown a wolf-skin cloak, and who stood surrounded by inferior nobles—inferior both in dignity and size.

Father Abel looked with awe upon the huge soldier, over whose shoulder appeared the hilt of a great two-handed sword little inferior in length to the rifle of one of our modern soldiers.

But the youth hastened forward, and the monk was compelled to follow.

Arrived in the presence of his father, who held an open letter in his hand, the young Scot threw himself on one knee before the old earl, exclaiming—

"Noble father, I am here; pardon my long absence!"

CHAPTER XXXV.

FATHER AND SON.

WELCOME, welcome, my son," said the Earl Douglas, as he raised his boy from the ground.

"Am I then forgiven, father?" asked the young chief.

"Most freely, most heartily, my son. But who is yon priest who stands at your back?"

"I know nothing more of him than that he brought your first letter to me at Alnwick, where I met the proud young Percy lance to lance, and sword to sword. Would he had lingered on his journey, then I might have avenged all the insults the English lord hath put upon our nation."

"My first letter? I sent one only."

"Two have been delivered to me ; one commanding me to quit the lists at Alnwick, and the other directing my return to your camp."

"Come hither, Sir Priest. Explain this matter."

"It is as the young lord says," replied Father Abel. "Two letters were given him by me ; though I know not from whom they came, if not from yourself."

Although he spoke thus boldly, the friar was in reality filled with fear ; for he knew that the great Scottish lord was, if possible, more absolute and uncontrolled in his dominions than the Earl of Northumberland.

The name of Douglas was a tower of strength to the Scottish monarchs, who sat securely on their thrones if they could win the love and esteem of the powerful nobles of that house.

Like the English Earl of Warwick, the Douglas family could make and unmake kings ; aided by their numerous vassals, they could set all other chieftains at defiance.

"Show me these letters," said the great man, sternly.

The young chief took the two packets from his breast, and presented them to his sire.

The earl looked at them with a puzzled air, turning the documents round and studying them from every point of view.

"This is the one I sent you," he said at length, selecting the one he had commanded to be written, more from knowledge of its shape, size, and seal, than from ability to read its contents. "Come hither, Lennox—read me this as it is written."

As these words were spoken, a youth of the noble house of Lennox came forward, and took the paper from the earl's hand.

Young Lennox, though second son of a powerful baron, thought it no degradation to act as page to Earl Douglas, and to learn the art of war under his command. Being a little better educated than most of the Scottish nobles of the time, he also occasionally performed the duties of secretary.

In a clear voice the youth read the note which had been given Father Abel by the strange forester he had met.

"From whose hand did you receive this?" asked the earl.

"From a man known as the 'Moody Forester.'"

A look of anxiety passed across the earl's face,

"What motive had he for thus forestalling my purpose?"

"I know not, my lord."

"Are you in reality a priest, or only a man-at-arms in masquerade. Speak the truth, or by my hopes of salvation, your tongue shall be torn from your mouth."

"My lord, I am a humble member of the church, for which it is said you have a great reverence."

"They say well who tell you I have great reverence for the holy church. But come to my tent, my son, I will consult with you on matters of importance. Merchistoun, see that the priest is properly lodged and fed."

With these words, the earl led his son away to the principal tent in the camp, before which floated his banner.

The pavilion was well furnished, though not with the iron bedsteads, camp-stools, and other articles with which your more foppish soldier of the modern day encumbers himself in the field. But there were piles of skins which formed soft couches ; there were arms and armour in abundance, and there were provisions in plenty.

"Sit down, my son, and tell me how *you* have prospered in your suit. Has the English lady looked with an eye of favour upon you?"

The youth heaved a deep sigh, and his cheek became pale, as he replied—

"Alas ! no !"

"How is that?" demanded the earl, with a frown. "Did not your romantic schemes of knight-errantry suit her?"

"For a time all went well ; but when the young Percy became an inmate of his father's castle, Douglas was forsaken. His courtly fashions newly brought from London pleased her more than all my ardent devotion, burning love."

The elder Douglas swore a great oath.

"Malediction on all the Northumbrians ! I, too, have failed in my treaty with the earl. But they shall bitterly rue the insult they have put upon our house."

There was a long silence.

"They shall bitterly repent, I say," continued the earl. "The house of Douglas knows how to wipe out an affront as well as to reward a faithful friend. Within six months I will sweep through the north of England ; fire and sword shall mark my progress ; weeping and mourning shall follow in my path ; war, in all its horrors, shall proclaim my vengeance, and force them to the alliance they now decline."

"And I?"

"Thou shalt ride beside me, no more a humble suppliant praying for a fair lady's favour, but a proud conqueror demanding a bride as the price of peace."

"It can never be as you wish. I have learnt my fate."

"How ?"

"From the Witch of Wooler."

Another long pause followed these words.

The all-powerful noble was more superstitious than his son, though the bravest of brave Scotland's warriors.

"What said the wise woman?" he asked, after a long pause.

"That Lady Katherine Mortimer could never be mine. But has my henchman Ogilvie returned yet, noble father? I would speak with him."

The earl caused inquiries to be made, and then commenced a conversation with his son, the subject of which was the best mode of making a sudden inroad upon English territory.

It was while this conversation was in progress that young Ogilvie entered the camp and was at once informed that his presence was required by his master, the young Lord Douglas—"the young earl," as he was generally called, though he could not legally assume that title until the death of his father.

Ogilvie made his way thither, and bowed low as he entered the tent.

"Welcome, Ogilvie ; I began to fear you had deserted me," said the young chief.

"When did ever an Ogilvie desert his friend and patron ? It was you, my lord, who deserted me, and left no tidings by which I could trace your steps."

"But how comes that blood upon your dress, Ogilvie? You are wounded."

"A slight scratch, received in a skirmish with an English coxcomb. But I gave as good as I received, my lord, and would have slain him had not the fight been stopped by some meddling springalds from Alnwick."

"What news of the southern?" asked the old earl, taking his gauntlets from the floor as though determined to march into Northumberland without a moment's delay.

"Nothing of importance, my lord, though I have heard that a hunting will take place in two days' time."

"Let them beware how they trespass upon Scottish ground."

"That they will scarcely do, my lord,

since my Lady Mortimer, a guest at the castle, takes part in the sport."

"Then they may hunt in peace; I war not upon unarmed men."

"Would that I were earl," muttered the young lord, as he arose and stalked to the tent door. "Then I would prevent their sport, and be revenged upon the faithless lady."

Hasty words which produced much evil.

They were overheard by Father Abel!

The priest had just received a letter, the contents of which were, that as his services would not be required by the "Moody Forester" for at least a week, he might remain during that time in the Scottish camp.

It was to request the earl's permission to take up his abode with the Scottish soldiers that the priest had wandered up to the tent and overheard the words of young Douglas.

"So, so," thought the crafty friar. "Here is a fine opportunity of winning the favour of this young lordling. I shall yet triumph; for this Scot will aid me if I assist him. And by his help I will so avenge our outraged church upon the Earl of Northumberland, that whatever I request in the way of advancement shall be granted!"

Full of these thoughts he entered the tent to make his petition, which was at once granted.

CHAPTER XXXVI.

THE CRYSTAL PHIAL.

LATER in the day Father Abel received a summons to the tent of the Scottish earl.

On repairing to the spot he found the owner of the pavilion and his son seated at supper, along with two or three of the subordinate commanders.

A seat was placed for him at the board, the earl motioned him to be seated, and a conversation commenced.

"By your speech you should be a Saxon, Sir Priest?" said the earl.

"I am, my lord."

"Then, how comes it that you travel thus boldly to the camp of the Earl Marshal of Scotland? Had you no fears for your own safety of body?"

"The dress of my profession is a sufficient passport in any land," replied Father Abel, "and you already know, my lord, by whose directions and in whose company I came hither."

"Yet it has been whispered to me that the priest's frock may cover a spy."

Father Abel began to quake and tremble.

In spite of his boastings about the protection afforded by his professional garb, he doubted not that the Earl Douglas would hang him if he suspected treason.

With great difficulty he managed to answer.

"Should you suspect me of falsehood, my lord, it easy enough to set a watch upon my actions."

"I suspect you not. Had I any fears, you would not be sitting on my left hand."

"I am, indeed, highly honoured, my lord," replied Father Abel, with a low bow.

"But how comes it that you have left your native land, priest?"

"Through zeal for the church, my lord."

"How? What are we Scots, then, all heathens in the opinion of your English holiness?"

"Not so, my lord. Not one can entertain more respect for the piety and learning of the Scottish church than the priesthood of England."

"Then, in Heaven's name, explain."

BEHOLD THE FIEND OF WAR.

"Through zeal for the church, my lord, I incurred the enmity of the Earl of Northumberland."

"Humph!"

"Who is sorely suspected of encouraging the abominable heresies of the Lollards, and other religious sects, who have lately given us of the true faith much trouble."

"And it was to escape him that you crossed the Tweed ?"

"It was, my lord."

"Have you any knowledge of the Earl of Northumberland's household ? What kind of state does he keep at Alnwick, Warkworth, and Bamborough ?"

The subtle priest hesitated to consider how this question should be answered.

If he over-estimated the number of retainers kept by his late master, the Scottish lords might decline the attack.

If he undervalued them the northern warriors might advance to the attack with a small force and defeat might ensue.

So he resolved to tell the truth.

"For many a long year I was chaplain and confessor to your foe, my lord, so therefore can speak from knowledge. The castles held by the Earl of Northumberland are well fortified and well provisioned, good knights and men-at-arms throng the hall, scores of English archers line the ramparts. Many great officers are maintained by him, for he keeps a state more befitting a prince than a baron."

"If you have told me the truth, Sir Priest, you shall see how Douglas rewards his friends ; if, on the contrary, you bring false news, beware, expect no mercy.'"

"I have told you the truth, my lord."

"It is well. Ho! page! some wine."

The earl hammered impatiently upon the table with his fist, but there was no response to his call.

The page in attendance had quitted the tent.

Again the earl shouted for wine.

"The page has left his post, my lord," said young Lennox.

"Then henceforth let him do horseboy's duty. Provide some other youth to take his place."

"Let me be your cup-bearer, my lord," said Father Abel. "The wine will taste none the worse for coming from a priest's hands, I'll warrant."

Without waiting for a reply he arose, and proceeded towards the sideboard, on which stood several goblets of wine.

His loose dress and wide sleeves concealed his motions.

The Scots suspected no treachery, nor did they see the false monk extract a small crystal phial from his pouch.

The vessel contained a perfectly colourless liquid, a few drops of which were allowed to fall into the goblet of wine.

With such dexterity was this action performed, that no one in the tent had the slightest suspicion of foul play.

The wine sparkled more brightly as Father Abel brought the goblet to the earl, who, raising the cup to his lips, took a deep draught.

Another page had by this time taken up his station in place of the deserter, and the banquet went on.

Once, indeed, the monk took occasion to perform another of those feats of dexterity which oftentimes did him as much service as bodily strength and physical courage.

He threw the crystal phial under the before-mentioned sideboard, without attracting any attention.

Ere long a change was visible on the face of the Earl Douglas.

His cheeks became pale, his lips twitched convulsively, his eyes glittered with a glassy lustre.

Frequently, too, he pressed his hand upon his stomach, as though to keep down by force the pains he felt.

For some time he made no complaint. But at length the pain became serious.

"Lennox," said he, "call me the surgeon."

"Surgeon, my lord ?"

"Aye, and that quickly, too, for I am in pain."

Half-a-dozen men at once rushed away to call the medical attendant.

In the meantime the agony of the earl increased.

He writhed in his chair, low moans

escaped his lips, and his eyes became bloodshot.

The surgeon or physician hurried in, and taking up his station by the earl's side, began to suggest such remedies as his very limited knowledge and experience suggested.

"It is poison," he said, in low tones, when all the symptoms and pains had been described. "It is poison, and a deadly one."

"Who hath done this foul deed?" asked the young Lord Douglas, looking sternly round.

The assembled nobles met his gaze in silence.

They were innocent.

Father Abel passed round to the side of the earl, who was now nearly insensible with pain, to assist the surgeon in applying such antidotes as were then known.

"Come hither, my son," said the earl.

The youth knelt by his side.

"Find out the traitor who has done this, punish him, but let his death be less painful than mine."

"Oh! my father! speak not of dying. Tell me, each one, are you innocent of this crime?" he continued, addressing the nobles.

"I am innocent," said every one, and then all was again hushed, save the moans of the victim of treachery.

The silence was broken by Father Abel, who, in an audible whisper, desired the page in waiting to bring him the small phial which was plainly visible.

"You ask who can have done this deed, my lord," he continued. "Who can it be but the guilty one who, ere he fled from his post, forgot to conceal this evidence of his crime?"

As Father Abel spoke, and held the phial on high, the knights around no longer doubted.

"It must be the page! He has fled to avoid the punishment of his crime," they said.

At that moment the youth in question appeared at the door of the tent.

"Accursed villain! Have you come to look upon your handiwork?" said the young chief, clutching him by the throat.

Astonished at such an unusual reception, the poor lad could not find words to explain the reason of his absence.

"See!" exclaimed Father Abel, snatching a dagger from the wall. "He dares not deny his guilt. The lie refuses to come from his tongue. Traitor! Thus your master is, ere dead, revenged."

With these words he buried the weapon to its hilt in the bosom of the unfortunate youth, who, with a groan, fell—dead.

The groan seemed echoed, and, as the barons and knights turned towards the earl, they saw with sorrow and astonishment that he had breathed his last sigh.

The brave Douglas was dead!

"You were too hasty, good father," said Lennox. "You should have left the page for torture. Now we know not who instigated him to the crime."

"'Twas love for the noble earl that nerved my arm," replied the priest.

But his face was ashy white, and every limb trembled.

The young lord—earl now—threw himself by the corpse of his parent, and gave way to a passionate outburst of unfeigned sorrow.

CHAPTER XXXVII.

ON THE BRIDGE.

ALL that night Father Abel remained on his knees at the entrance of the tent which contained the corpse, repeating in monotonous tones the prayers and other forms ordained by his church for the occasion.

Not that the monk had much faith in the efficacy of his own petitions, but h deemed it the best way to remove any suspicion that might have been excited against him.

On the following morning when the young earl had become more calm, Father Abel besought permission to journey to some monastery, in order to make arrangements for a fitting and stately funeral.

"Make what arrangements you will, but see that they are suited to the dignity of my noble father."

So Father Abel rode away, accompanied by young Lennox, the squire of the deceased earl.

The squire, however, did not journey long with the monk, who despatched him on an errand to a Benedictine convent.

This done, the paltry assassin rode off towards the border at full speed, his object being to communicate, if possible, with certain brigands, who would, if he offered a good reward, undertake, without the slightest hesitation, the capture or assassination of Lady Katherine Mortimer.

"And be revenged upon the faithless lady."

These words, spoken by the young Douglas, were his guiding star, for, judging all men by his own vile nature, he had no doubt that the death or captivity of Lady Katherine would be very acceptable news.

He rode on and on, crossed the border without meeting any adventure, and then began to descend a rather steep hill.

The road was rough, and therefore, not very agreeable to the nerves of the traveller.

At the bottom of the hill was a rapid stream, too wide to leap, and too swift to be forded with ease or pleasure.

It ran from right to left, towards the sea.

The monk sat upon his horse undecided which way to turn.

But his actions were hastened by a noise which fell upon his ear.

Far away to the right he could hear the sounds of horns, dogs, and men in pursuit of some kind of game.

Fearing it might be the Percys and retainers, the monk at once turned his head eastward.

Fear lent swiftness to the monk's flight.

But just as he was congratulating himself on having escaped all dangers, an accident occurred which nearly brought his wicked life to an abrupt conclusion.

The steed Father Abel bestrode was hurrying at a brisk gallop along a path which was bounded on one side by a tall rock, while, on the other hand, was a steep declivity of thirty or forty feet in depth.

There were many large stones, roots of shrubs, and other impediments along this path.

And the horse several times stumbled enough to give Father Abel a very severe shaking.

At length, however, the animal went to the ground headlong, sending the monk flying several feet beyond.

Such an equestrian feat the holy man had never performed before, nor had his body ever received such a shaking as it did on coming in contact with mother earth.

But worse than that fared the horse.

In its struggles to rise it rolled over, and went crashing down over the bushes and boulders till it reached the bottom of the declivity and the brink of the stream.

Its groans as it lay there were fearful to hear, but the monk could render the poor animal no assistance, nor was there a being within call to aid him.

He hurried away on foot as fast as possible, trusting ere long to fall in with the ruffians whose society he sought.

The continued clamour of the horns and hounds alarmed him.

After walking or rather running, for a couple of miles, Father Abel began to feel exceedingly warm and scant of wind.

But at that moment, just as he was on the point of seating himself he caught sight of the hunters who were riding in a line parallel to his own path.

The dresses they wore were those of the Percy family, and the priest could very plainly distinguish the forms of Hotspur, Ralph Percy, and Lady Katherine Mortimer.

He at once concealed himself amongst some bushes and lone rocks that grew a few feet over a wooden bridge which crossed the stream.

From this point he could see all that transpired.

A noble buck was in view of the hounds, who, with loud-mouthed clamour, pressed forward.

The hunters spurred their steeds and cheered on the dogs.

Hotspur was foremost in the chase, though his brother was not far behind.

Lady Katherine seemed not inclined for such reckless riding, and suffered even the menials to pass her.

"Oh, that I had a dozen trusty followers," thought the monk, "then should the fair one journey perforce to the camp of our young Earl Douglas. Curses on her, and on her knight, and on all related to her by ties of blood."

We are certainly told on the highest authority that the causeless curse falls upon the head of the utterer ; but for a moment or two, it certainly seemed as though the monk's maledictions had taken effect upon Lady Katherine Mortimer.

Her horse, like the monk's, stumbled, and the fair rider was thrown.

"By St. Satan, she is killed !" thought the monk ; " and there is no one to help her, for the headlong hunters have galloped into yonder wood, and are lost to sight."

He was wrong, however, for Lady Katherine had received no material injury, excepting in dress, and she arose nimbly to her feet.

Her horse, however, bounded off after the hunters, and by this accident she was left standing alone in an open glade at the foot of the Cheviot Hills.

It would be folly to say that Lady Katherine was not alarmed. She well knew the unsettled state of the country, and that hordes of banditti, both Scotch and English, lurked about the border.

She determined to walk towards the stream, of which she had caught several glimpses while on horseback, for the purpose of quenching the thirst produced by exercise.

Father Abel, however, was not aware of her object in coming towards him, and he nestled down the more closely behind the bush which sheltered him.

His eyes eagerly watched her every motion.

The bank of the stream on Lady Katherine's side, was very steep, and she was unable to obtain the clear draught she longed for.

The rude bridge, however, caught her eye, and she resolved to cross it.

Father Abel's eye glittered with a fiendish glare as he saw her set foot upon the bridge.

The busy spirit of murder whispered that the moment had arrived.

He quietly rose, and taking up a huge stone, poised it in both hands over his head to dash down upon her.

At that moment Lady Katherine looked upwards, caught sight of the monk's features distorted as they were with evil passions.

She started back, and uttered a loud shriek of horror.

"Help ! help !" she screamed. " Oh, vile, base monster ! What have I done that you should seek to injure me ?"

" I hate you—I hate your house—I hate those whose power has protected you. Die, then, and let my hatred be avenged !"

Down came the ponderous mass of rock, with a frightful crash, upon the frail wooden structure.

Lady Katherine gave a second leap back, and so avoided being crushed beneath its weight.

But the bridge gave way, and the helpless girl narrowly avoided being plunged into the swift stream beneath.

" Thank Heaven ! Oh, how can I have offended the priest ? Why should he attempt to take my life ?" she murmured, as she reached the shore on the opposite side.

The destruction of the bridge proved her safeguard, for Father Abel was unable to follow, as otherwise he would, no doubt, have done.

After a brief, fervent prayer of thanksgiving, Lady Katherine rose to her feet, and made the best of her way to the wood where she had last seen Hotspur and the other hunters.

The monk followed her with curses and imprecations, throwing stones after her as far as his arm could hurl them.

But, luckily, his aim was untrue, or it

might have fared ill with one of England's loveliest daughters.

Father Abel was thoroughly maddened by the exciting scenes he had passed through, and having once allowed his passions to take their course, little cared what ensued.

To her intense joy, Lady Katherine saw Hotspur and a groom emerge from the wood, the groom leading her truant steed by the rein.

A few words explained to them the events that had taken place, and the knight, with his followers, set spurs to their horses to overtake and punish the rascally priest.

Father Abel saw them coming, and at once started off to evade them.

At the top of his speed he careered along the path, while Hotspur and his followers kept on the other side of the stream, which was too rapid to swim and too wide to leap.

Suddenly he halted.

There in the path before him he saw a party of armed men.

Father Abel fancied he had seen those Scottish dresses before, nor was he mistaken.

He turned with the intention of retracing his steps, but, to his horror, saw that Hotspur had succeeded in crossing the stream.

The torrent beneath went tumbling down a rock, down a deep gorge, and, as Father Abel set eyes upon it, he muttered to himself—

"I will disappoint them of their prey."

With these words, he threw himself into the foaming stream, and was carried over the cataract.

CHAPTER XXXVIII.

THE ROBBERS.

MALEDICTION on the priest! he has robbed us of our vengeance!" exclaimed Hotspur, when he beheld the body of Father Abel go plunging down the foaming cataract.

"He may not be dead, my lord," said the groom. "Had I not best go down the stream to see that he escapes not?"

"Best go over the fall yourself and see how long you survive afterwards. What living being could survive after being carried by the tide through that fearful and rocky passage?"

With these words the impetuous youth turned about and rode back to the spot where he had left Lady Katherine.

He had not seen the Scottish soldiers, nor did they perceive him till he was once more in the open plain.

Then just as Hotspur was rejoined by his companions in the hut, Lennox and Ogilvie, who were in command, caught sight of the English hunters, and followed hard after them.

But not too swiftly at first.

The young Scots knew not how many Englishmen might be concealed in the forest, nor how many more might be waiting within sound of the notes of Hotspur's bugle.

Young Percy and his companions in the hunt entered the wood, the Scots keeping just far enough behind to escape observation.

Lennox and Ogilvie had seen the monk plunge over the cataract, and that confirmed the suspicions they had previously entertained that Father Abel was in reality guilty of the murder of Earl Douglas.

Lennox had been so struck by the vague and evasive replies of the monk when they parted, that, instead of proceeding to the convent as directed, he returned to the camp, communicated his suspicions to the young earl, and obtained permission to take with him six men to pursue and capture the treacherous priest.

Ogilvie had obtained permission from his young lord to accompany the party, and now, having seen, as they imagined the last of Father Abel, they meditated vengeance upon the Northumbrians, hastily concluding that no one but a member or friend of the house of Percy could have instigated so foul a deed.

They followed the Northumbrian hunters into the wood, and there for a time lost sight of them. At length they found themselves in an open glade, and discovered that Percy had been reinforced by a band of at least two score archers who had been roving through the forest to drive the deer and other game up towards the noble young hunters.

"Shall we strike a blow for Scotland?" asked Ogilvie, half drawing his sword.

"Faith I feel much inclined; but the odds are sorely against us."

"We are eight, well mounted and armed."

"They are, I should fancy, fifty in number."

"True; six to one at least," observed Ogilvie.

"So it was at Bannockburn, yet Scotland gained the day. Ah! Ogilvie, would that you and I had seen that glorious field."

"Saint Andrew! but that is a day that shall never be forgotten while Scottish lads have tongues to tell each other of the feats performed there. But touching these English?"

"I fear that we must even let them escape; they may have friends in the copse yonder to which they are making their way."

"They have no lances."

"Right."

"We have, and know well how to use them."

"Their archers have bows, and can shoot right swiftly and strong. Hark!"

A horn was heard at some distance.

Hotspur blew an answering signal on his bugle.

"There are others, then, in the wood. Back, my men."

So said young Lennox, heaving a deep sigh as he spoke. He would willingly have risked an encounter, but knew not how far the young earl might approve of such an action.

The Scottish men-at-arms looked sullen as they heard this order; but true to that spirit of strict discipline, for which they have ever been noted, did not attempt to disobey.

They retraced their steps and recrossed the little stream, without Hotspur, or any of his retinue, being aware that a Scot had crossed the border on an hostile errand.

As they passed by the cataract, they looked along the foaming surface of the stream; but no sign of Father Abel's body could be seen.

"Homewards!"

The Scots then returned to their camp.

But what had become of the monk? Was his body dashed to atoms upon the sharp rocks, or did it float with the tide out into the sea?

Neither one nor the other.

There can be no doubt the assassin meditated this when he thus found himself between his foes; but he was not destined for such a death.

The force of the water carried him beneath the surface for several yards, when he reached the bottom of the cataract; but when he rose to the surface, it was beneath the shadow of some overhanging bushes, which threw their branches far over the stream.

Father Abel was half stunned by the concussion, deafened by the roar of the water, and bruised severely by violent contact with various masses of stone he had encountered. But the first taste of death by drowning was sufficiently bitter to make him cling with more desperate energy than ever to the slightest chance of life.

The first chance, if we may so term it, that presented itself to Father Abel's bewildered senses was the vine of some creeping plant which had its roots in the bank, and sent several branches to float upon the stream.

This he clutched, and by holding it,

saved himself from being swept farther down the torrent.

Thus clinging, he waited for a short space of time to regain his breath, and to consider how to escape.

The bushes he was under were thick, and their branches nearly touched the surface of the stream, so that he was completely hidden from the observation of both parties, but he could see all that passed at the head of the fall.

He saw Percy, with his groom, come and glance down the stream, then turn back.

He saw the Scots and heard them, as they passed within a few yards of his hiding-place, consult as to the advisability of following the Northumbrians.

Then, when they had all disappeared, he gently drew himself to land by the aid of the bushes, and after a very careful glance round, walked off as fast as his bruised limbs and wet garments would allow along the path in an opposite direction to that taken by Lennox and his Scots.

The road seemed clear enough, no foes no obstacles of any kind.

When he had gone half a mile or more a source of perplexity arose, however, for the path divided into two.

A moment's reflection convinced the monk that his best chance of safety was in not being seen.

"The road which is the least used is the best," thought he, and forthwith began to ascend a rude path made by sheep and their keepers in ascending the side of the rough hill.

The country again began to look wild and desolate.

"What excuse shall I now have for seeking these robbers?" thought Father Abel, as he walked along. "Lady Katherine was in my power; but, pshaw! I had forgotten that they know nothing of the scene on the bridge."

The sound of horses' feet far down below fell upon his ear, and by mounting a huge block of stone by the side of the path, he was able to see that Lennox was conducting his men homeward.

Then, when the retainers of Douglas had passed, a keen, wild whistle was heard—a whistle much resembling the cry of the plover, and other wild birds frequenting the northern heaths.

But Father Abel thought not of plovers. He only heard a shrill whistle blown three times, and answered by three whistles from a distance.

Conscious of his own guilt, the wretched priest began to dread the idea of meeting men whom he had always looked upon as bloodthirsty monsters, regarding crime as an accomplishment, and murder as something to be proud of.

"Should they know what has happened I am doomed. The Scots robbers will slay me for the sake of their earl, whilst the English banditti will hang me for even thinking harm of their young countess that is to be."

So thought the monk, and upon casting up his eyes after finishing his mental speech, he found himself face to face with half-a-dozen men, whose faces would have sufficiently proved their profession had Abel felt any doubts upon the subject.

Father Abel, however, at once understood that he was in the presence of some of the robber tribes he came to seek, and a most villainous set of rascals they were, with thick brows, large coarse mouths, fierce and cunning eyes, and faces full of wickedness, as well as, in some instances, scored with the marks of wounds.

"Give you good day, father," said one.

The priest bowed.

"Your reverence will not refuse us your blessing," the man continued.

"You have it, my son," said the priest, raising his hands.

The men grinned, and then their leader continued—

"You have not yet told us whither you journey, holy father."

"I heard not the question."

"Ah, I may have forgotten to ask; but we expect every wayfarer who travels amongst these hills to give an account of himself."

"Does your rule extend to the church?"

"Aye, that it does. The fact is, good father, we live by the tolls we levy upon travellers, and as you priests will not let us into heaven without payment, neither do we allow either priests or laymen to pass through our midst without contributing towards the support of our little territory."

" You are robbers ?"

" We are."

" Then I can trust in you."

" It little matters whether you trust us or not since you must perforce go with us.   Seize the priest!"

At these words the men surrounded Father Abel ; his hands were bound, his valuables taken from him.

This done they tied a rope round his neck, and led him away up the hill.

" What have I done ? Of what crime am I guilty that you treat me thus ? Have respect for my office," said the priest.

" We have respect for your office, holy father, though none for you. But silence would profit you more than such shouts and cries."

" May I not know whither you would take me, and what is your purpose ?"

" That you shall know. You are being conveyed to our home, there to await our leisure to take you to the camp of Earl Douglas."

" But I was on my way hither."

" You speak falsely, sir priest ; you fled after poisoning the good earl."

" No, no, no, not so ! I beseech you put no fai h in such idle stories."

" Idle they may be, but I fear it will be a serious matter for you when the young earl strings you up to the gallows ; that is, unless he takes off your head in playful mood with the Lochaber axe of one of his followers,"

" Why should you deliver me up to him on such slight grounds ?"

" Slight ! ha ! ha ! Why we have good hopes of a reward, father, more especially as two gallant pages and a company of soldiers have been searching for you. It was from their conversation in our place of concealment that we heard of the murder."

" I am not the monk they spoke of."

" That is a question they must decide. But it was certainly a bold expedient to throw yourself over the fall. For a poisoner, you certainly have more courage than I should have imagined from looking at your face."

The priest was silent for some time.

It seemed very evident to him that his captors possessed a certain amount of information, and he feared he might criminate himself by contradictory statements.

But his mind was busy, and, after an interval, he again spoke.

" I fear, friends, that your trouble will be for no purpose. Earl Douglas will scarcely reward a band of robbers otherwise than by a dungeon."

Hope shot through the monk's heart as he saw that this speech had made some impression upon the men, who at first looked at, and then whispered, to each other.

Father Abel resolved to strike while the iron was hot, and continued—

" No worldly reward will you gain by giving me up, but much spiritual good by restoring me to liberty. Do as I ask, and I will grant absolution, as well as perform mass without any fee or reward whatever. Thus, you will benefit by my freedom, while, on the other hand, my death will avail you nothing."

" Hist !" said one of the men, who walked a few paces in advance. " To cover—to cover ! a score of Scottish men-at-arms are coming up the hill."

The robbers at once darted amongst the bushes and tall ferns by the road-side, dragging Father Abel with them.

" Silence, for your life, priest," said the chief of the band. " The slightest sound seals your death-warrant."

As he spoke the man held a long, keen knife at Father Abel's throat, to prove that his words were not meaningless, but that the robbers would certainly purchase silence at the cost of life.

The troop came by within a few yards of the spot where the robbers were concealed ; but not the slightest rustling of the bushes betrayed them.

CHAPTER XXXIX.

A SHARP COMBAT.

FOR a long time the robbers lay thus concealed—long after the horsemen from Scotland had descended the hill, crossed the brook, and entered the forest glades of Northumberland.

Two scouts were then sent out, who, after a brief survey, reported that the road was clear.

"Forward, then, my men," said the leader; "and you, sir priest, thank Heaven you are not yet in the hands of those angry men who are now going to kill every Northumbrian they lay hands upon because you were clever enough to drug the earl's wine."

They walked forward again, though with more caution, and at length came to a wild, desolate glen, where big rocks were piled up and scattered about in profusion.

Two of these stones—of the largest size—lay close together, and from top to top were laid long poles, upon which a quantity of branches of trees, dried fern, and long grass had been piled, so as to form a roof. This was the home of the banditti, as was testified by the heap of embers where a fire had recently been burning, bones and fragments of food lying about, with shreds of cloth and tattered articles of wearing apparel.

The robbers evidently considered that they had done their day's work, for they began to rekindle the fire and prepare food.

Father Abel was kept bound; but when the meal was ready, one of the robbers sat down and gave the monk his share, though the meat was not very dainty, nor could the captive force himself to swallow a very great portion of it.

Then two of them departed, their object being to follow the Scottish men-at-arms, watch if a conflict took place, and appropriate any plunder that might be left upon the scene.

Nor were their hopes frustrated.

The Scots seemed animated with a strong desire to avenge the death of their chief upon the Earl of Northumberland, and pressed forward hastily till they nearly overtook the English hunting party.

Then a hasty consultation took place.

Hotspur had just brought down a noble deer, and was standing by his quarry contemplating it with all the pride of the youthful sportsman. His huntsmen and followers were gathered round, some leaning upon their bows, some attending to the panting horses.

Suddenly the sound of trampling horses' hoofs was heard, and looking up, they saw the Scottish men-at-arms approaching at full speed.

"Look to your bows, my men; out with your blades!" cried the young leader. "Remember we have to fight in the sight of a fair lady!"

The archers and grooms, with a shout of defiance, prepared their weapons and awaited the charge.

"Ralph, do you conduct Lady Katherine homewards, while we protect her from pursuit," continued the youthful hunter.

"Not I. Not that I would see her exposed to any danger; but I must exchange one blow with these fiery Scots."

Hotspur looked round in perplexity.

The Scots were approaching at a hasty gallop, and another minute would bring them upon the hunters.

"Oh, that I could exchange a score of these archers for half their number of lancers!" he exclaimed. "Witherington, haste home with the lady."

But the young squire did not, or pretended not to hear.

The thunder of hoofs became more rapid, and at length the opposing bodies met.

The English being armed lightly—for they were, as must be remembered, on a hunting party—had not the advantage their superior numbers would have otherwise given them.

Many of their number fell beneath the long spears of the Scottish riders.

Hotspur himself was unhorsed, so was his brother, Ralph Percy ; but they continued to fight bravely on foot, drawing their men closely round Lady Katherine so as to protect her.

The archers, so much despised by Hotspur, now began to make themselves conspicuous.

Their long, sharp shafts went crashing through Scottish shield and breastplate.

"Bravely shot, my men !" exclaimed Hotspur. "Here, Tim of Tynemouth, send me an arrow through the tall soldier yonder who unhorsed me !"

The archer drew his bow, saying, with a look of confidence—

"He shall level spear no more, my lord !"

Then the shaft sped, and, piercing through the tall horseman's right arm, completely nailed that limb to his body.

The man fell dead without a groan, for the arrow had pierced his heart.

"Bravely shot, Tim ! Fight on for St. George and merry England !"

"For England, for Percy !" responded his men, as with their swords they strove to parry the lance thrusts of the furious enemy.

"For Scotland, and for the murdered Douglas !" responded the Scottish soldiers.

"Ha ! did you hear that, Ralph ? The Earl Douglas murdered ! By my faith, we have been treacherously deprived of a noble foe !"

Hotspur's words were heard by Ogilvie, who was one of the number ; he, Lennox, and the six men who started with them, having joined a larger party, whose object was vengeance.

"Yes, and murdered by your vile artifices, Henry Percy ! Assassin as you are, I dare you to combat, though it would be no honour for the pure sword of an Ogilvie to be sheathed in the black heart of a murderer !"

"By the blood of my ancestors !—by the lion on our crest, such a bold challenge shall not remain unanswered. You lie, villain Scot, if you say I had aught to do with the death of Earl Douglas."

With these words he seized upon the horse of one of his followers, and leaping upon its back, urged the animal forward.

A blow of his sword severed the iron head of Ogilvie's spear from the shaft.

The Scottish youth at once dropped the useless wood and drew his claymore.

As if by mutual consent, the two conflicting parties drew back, so as to allow clear space for the combat between the two champions.

Ogilvie had scarcely time to grasp his broadsword firmly in his hand before Hotspur was upon him.

Furious blows were exchanged, the swords clashed, and sparks of fire glanced from their blades.

Ogilvie made little attempt to ward off the blows of his adversary—his breastplate and steel cap in a great measure protected him ; while Hotspur, who wore no defensive armour, had to parry all the heavy strokes made by his antagonist.

It was this ill-advised confidence in his armour that proved Ogilvie's ruin, for the young Percy, watching closely, soon found an opportunity to plunge the point of his sword beneath his foeman's breastplate.

With a heavy sigh the brave young Scot dropped from his saddle, another victim to the violent feuds that then raged along the borders.

"Forward ! ride them down ! avenge our comrade's death !" exclaimed Lennox.

"Draw your bows, my men ; send every shaft home to its mark !" cried Hotspur, waving his bloodstained weapon in the air. "Ha ! what spears are those above the brushwood ? On, gallant men-at-arms !"

The Scots saw the advancing reinforcement, and made a desperate charge.

Several of the archers were transfixed by their long lances, but still a solid phalanx remained, with Hotspur and Ralph Percy at their head.

"Away, away !" shouted Lennox, when he saw that the last charge had failed. "To the mountain pass, there we may defy pursuit !"

His followers wheeled about, sorely chagrined at being compelled to quit the field.

THE RETURN TO THE SCOTTISH CAMP.

They would willingly have remained to face the whole of Percy's forces; but their young commander, having shown his valour in the combat, judged that the time had arrived to prove his generalship in conducting a retreat.

He himself rode last of all, as though his single arm would suffice to protect his gallant band, now reduced from twenty to thirteen.

They made their way towards the hills, and the English men-at-arms, after making a show of following, judged it prudent to allow them to retire unmolested.

CHAPTER XL.

THE YOUNG EARL.

IT was about an hour before sunset when the robber scouts returned, and reported to their chief that the Scottish men-at-arms were riding homewards.

The leader of the banditti climbed up to the top of the cliffs, at the foot of which their camp was situated, and from that situation gazed along the pathway which ran along the other side of the range of rocks.

"Ha, ha!" he exclaimed, as he saw the party. "They have found the difference between hunting priests and lions. The lion has turned upon them it seems."

The Scots passed by as before, wholly unaware that a nest of banditti lay concealed within a few paces of their spear points.

Had they known it, or, still more, had they been aware that Father Abel was a captive amongst the robbers, they would certainly have paused to exterminate the "nest of hornets," and transfer the prisoner to their own safe keeping.

For these robbers were outlaws—social pests—acknowledging no rule save that of their own chief, who had, by violence, attained his rank.

They belonged to both kingdoms, yet owned neither sovereign; robbed the poor and helpless of both nations, and were in consequence hunted down by the border rulers, both Scottish and English.

But in those rude days of constant warfare it was not difficult for a man known to possess a certain degree of physical strength and courage to gather round him a company of reckless villains, and thus it was that as soon as one band was cut to pieces or dispersed, another started up in some other glen or forest.

The robber chief, having seen the Scottish men-at-arms pass by, hastily summoned his followers, and marched off at their head at a good speed.

Father Abel was with them, his hands still bound, and a gag thrust into his mouth, as an additional precaution against noise.

The robbers took a course nearly parallel to the path of the men-at-arms; but at times were enabled to make short cuts, by which they managed first to overtake then pass the clan Douglas soldiers.

The leader at length paused, and posted his men on each side of a deep gully, through which the bridle way ran.

"He means to attack them," thought the monk. "Yet surely he would not drag me all this way to see him kill the foes he threatens to give me up to."

The robber chief's designs were soon very plainly understood.

As the twelve men-at-arms approached the gorge, they heard a loud voice exclaim—

"Halt!"

Instinctively they paused, and beheld, the figures of several archers, with bent bows and arrows fitted to the string, standing among the bushes on either side of the pass.

These were the robbers headed by their chief.

"What want you ?" demanded Lennox.

"A conference," replied the robber.

"For what purpose ?"

"To deliver up to you a certain prisoner ; the monk you rode in search of this morn."

"A truce to jesting, and call your archers away, or it will be the worse for you. The monk is no more, for did not I see him swept down the cataract ?"

"Aye, true enough. Yet behold him !" and with these words, the robber dragged Father Abel forward by the collar, holding him in sight of the Scottish soldiers.

"Behold him ! All the waters of the Tweed could not drown the man destined to adorn the gallows."*

At the sight of the monk, several of the Scots leaped from their saddles, and were about to rush up among the bushes. But the voice of the robber chief was once more heard.

"Stay your men, fair sir, or I no longer hold my men from shooting."

"Halt, men, to your ranks !" said Lennox.

"Twelve pieces of gold, and a promise not to molest or follow us, and the priest is yours."

"You shall have it," replied Lennox, whose pouch happened on that occasion to be pretty well lined. "Send down two of your men with the priest, and they shall take back the gold without hindrance."

"Order all your men, except one, to fall back, and we will meet you."

"Fear not," replied Lennox, who, nevertheless, complied with this very reasonable request.

The robber chief himself, and two of his men, then scrambled down the bushes, dragging Father Abel between them. Lennox counted out the money and placed it in the hands of the robber, while his attendant soldier laid hold of the rope fastened round the wretched monk's neck.

"We wish you good joy of your bargain, fair sir ; the scoundrel was scarce worth taking for the sake of the money in his purse, but we judged a reward might be obtained."

Lennox made no reply, but beckoned up his men ; the two robbers in the meantime scrambling up the rocks again, and vanishing behind the hill where the sun had just gone down.

"Set the priest on a horse," said the young Scot, when his men came up.

The order was obeyed.

"Now tie his legs under the beast's belly, and look to it that he escapes not."

This command was carried out to the letter, and in such ignominious state was the priest compelled to ride back along the pathway towards the camp of the young Earl Douglas.

At length the camp was reached ; but as it was discovered that the young earl was asleep, Lennox committed the priest to the care of twenty trusty men, and then sought his own tent.

Father Abel, as may be imagined, passed a sleepless night.

The morning dawned, and a bright sun shone in the cloudless sky, but its rays could not cheer the heart of the hapless monk.

It was indeed almost a relief when a guard of soldiers arrived to conduct him to the tent where his foul crimes had been committed, and where the son of his noble victim was waiting to see the slayer of his father.

Father Abel shuddered as he passed into the pavilion where the young earl was seated, with his allies and vassals grouped around him.

For some minutes Douglas looked sternly at the priest without speaking. At length, however, he said :

"Vile murderer, prepare for death ! Yet ere the executioner touches your neck, confess all, and tell me—Who instigated you to so foul a deed ?"

Father Abel trembled ; his tongue at first refused to perform its office, but after several attempts, he managed to stammer out—

"I am innocent—I am innocent !"

Douglas made a gesture of impatience.

"Confess—trifle not !"

---

* The proverb, "A man who is born to be hanged cannot be drowned," is of very ancient date.

"I am innocent."

"Away with him to the castle, and let torture wring the truth from his lips!"

"No, no! Mercy, mercy!" screamed the poor monk. "Oh, my lord, I entreat you not to torture me. By the love of Heaven—by your own hopes of mercy—spare me."

"Confess then, vile wretch!"

"I am innocent. But, Earl Douglas, dread the wrath of holy church, and lay not a hand on one of her ministers."

"The church will disown a murderer. Away with him; conduct the scoundrel with all speed to the castle; chain him in the deepest dungeon."

The monk made another attempt to obtain a remission of the sentence, but without avail.

Four men seized him, dragged him from the pavilion, and led him away.

They were soon joined by young Lennox, to whom had been entrusted the task of seeing Earl Douglas's orders properly carried out.

Six stout horses were prepared.

Four of these animals were mounted by the soldiers, the priest was lifted to the back of the fifth, while the charger of young Lennox was the sixth and last of the cavalcade."

Thus guarded, and followed by the curses and execrations of the whole camp, the monk was hurried away towards the strong castle of the Douglas, which was half a day's journey distant.

"Good youth," said the monk, when he had so far overcome his tears and his terrors as to be able to speak, "good youth, I have a word for you in private, if it will please you to order these soldiers to fall back a few paces."

"I have no desire to hear you," replied Lennox, sternly.

"But I can make you as rich as any prince in Christendom. I can show you how to obtain eternal fame."

"Silence! Soldiers, gag the prisoner if he again attempts to speak."

Thus rebuffed, Father Abel had no alternative but to hold his tongue.

The road seemed short enough to him, though the soldiers thought it a wearisome journey; but, then, they were journeying with different destinations in view.

Father Abel knew the end of his journey to be a gloomy dungeon, with, perhaps, a still more fearful torture chamber adjoining, while the soldiers had their hearts fixed upon the castle buttery, where good ale might be obtained to refresh their dry throats after a long and dusty ride.

At length the towers of the castle rose to view, situated on a rocky height by the side of the ocean.

It was a place of great strength, and although the sun shone brightly, and the blue waves sparkled and foamed merrily, the hold had a stern and forbidding appearance.

"Thank the saints, we are nearly at our journey's end," remarked one of the soldiers.

"Amen," responded his comrade, "though the prisoner here looks anything but pleased at the termination of his ride."

A steep and rugged path led from the plain up to the rocky promontory on which the stronghold was perched.

The horses were compelled to proceed at a slow pace, so that Father Abel had plenty of time to contemplate the external appearance of his future abode.

But for how long a time was it to be his abode?

That was the great question which kept the brain of the unhappy prisoner at work.

It was a question he could not solve.

The postern gate was reached at length, and the foremost soldier knocked loudly.

In reply to the summons the steward of the castle made his appearance with a guard of axe men, armed with the fearful weapon which made the Scottish soldiers so terrible before the invention of fire-arms.

To this steward, Lennox in a few words explained what had transpired.

"Bring the prisoner this way," said he, leading the party down a winding staircase.

Down, down forty feet at least into the heart of the rock, and then a low arched door was reached.

The steward took a key from his girdle, and in a moment Father Abel saw before him his prison.

CHAPTER XLI.

THE TORTURE CHAMBER.

A GLOOMY-LOOKING dungeon was that which presented itself to the view of Father Abel, the pillars which supported the massive roof being festooned with huge iron chains by which prisoners were secured.

The soldiers dragged Father Abel to one of these pillars and fixed a chain round his body.

The huge links clanked together most dismally as the fetters were riveted ; the sound seemed to say that hope had fled.

The locks were very large, and apparently strongly made, although in reality so clumsily put together that any modern burglar could have got the better of their fastenings without much trouble.

But then Father Abel was not a picklock, and, although tolerably well versed in the dogmas of the Romish creed, was profoundly ignorant of the principles of mechanism.

The daylight only found its way into the dungeon at noon, and then through a passage purposely made tortuous, so as to exclude the rays of the sun, while it presented no obstacle to the ingress of wind and rain.

Nor were comforts of any other description provided in those days, for the general idea was to consider prisoners as guilty until proved innocent, instead of considering them innocent men until proved guilty ; so that Father Abel was left with only a heap of straw on which to repose himself, a jug of muddy water, and a loaf of coarse bread, to serve for refreshment.

Thus passed a night, a day, and a second night.

On the evening of the second day of his confinement, some time after the sun had gone down, Father Abel heard loud shouts in the castle courtyard.

These sounds announced to him the arrival of the young Earl Douglas.

"My fate will soon be decided," thought he, as with restless step he paced backwards and forwards as far as his chain would allow him.

Nor was he deceived in his calculations, for about an hour after he heard steps approaching, and a murmur of voices at the door of his cell.

He at once understood these to be the voices of the persons come to summon him to the torture.

"I will maintain my innocence," he muttered. "When they see I am firm they will release me."

The door was unbarred, and two persons in dark-coloured garments appeared.

They were well-armed, and without saying a word advanced towards the prisoner.

Their faces were concealed beneath black masks.

"Who are you, and what do you want?" demanded the prisoner.

They made no reply, but throwing over the prisoner a singular kind of cloak, drew their swords, and led him from the dungeon.

They passed along many galleries and avenues, but not a person was to be seen, and the shouts in the courtyard having ceased, it seemed as though death had already anticipated his work in these regions of horror, and had laid his hand alike upon the torturors and the tortured.

After making many turns and ascents, they found themselves at length in the great courtyard, where Father Abel had been received by his present gaolers on the night of his arrival.

From thence, they passed along an avenue, and down a long flight of steps that led to subterranean chambers.

During all this time his conductors had not uttered a word, and Father Abel held his tongue, believing that asking questions would bring on the anger of his guides, and subject him to greater severity when he reached his destination.

One of the guides bore a plain-looking though large iron key, with which he opened the various doors through which they had to pass; while the other man bore a torch; indeed the passages were so dark and gloomy, that even in day-time it would have been difficult to find the way without one.

They then crossed a vault, which seemed to contain graves; but the extent and obscurity of the place did not allow this fact to be ascertained, and, having reached another door, they came to a halt.

The guide who bore the key tapped the door three times with it, while the unhappy monk trembled with fear, as he pictured to himself the horrors to be found beyond that door.

Having waited a few minutes, the door was opened, and Father Abel was ushered into a spacious chamber, the walls of which were as dark and gloomy as those of his own dungeon.

Then a voice from the other end of the apartment said in a loud tone—

"Bring lights, and lead forward the prisoner."

Several torches were at once produced, and the two men hurried Father Abel forward.

Three persons were seen seated under a canopy, upon chairs, raised a step or two above the floor. These seemed to be the judges, and, on looking, Father Abel perceived the faces of Douglas, young Lennox, and a third person, who appeared to fulfil the duties of secretary or reporter.

At some little distance from this tribunal was a kind of bench, covered with a ragged cloth, but beneath it could be seen certain wheels and levers which bespoke the fearful character of the concealed object.

"Once more we meet, father," said the young earl; "and so convinced am I of your guilt that I beg of you to confess, without compelling me to put you to the rack."

"I have nothing to confess," replied the monk.

The young earl motioned with his hand, and four men instantly seized the luckless priest.

"Now bind him to the rack."

The words fell like a death-knell upon the ears of the victim.

He writhed and struggled in the hands of his executioners.

"Mercy! mercy!" he screamed.

"You showed none; yet confess and mercy shall be granted you."

"Innocent! innocent!" shouted Father Abel, exerting his strength to the utmost.

"Put him to the torture, then," commanded the young earl. "But," continued he, in a whisper, "stand by, Lennox, and see that they do not kill the poor wretch."

"I will, my lord, though had I command over those four men he should be torn limb from limb," replied he.

In spite of his struggles, Father Abel, was lifted from the ground; the cloth which shrouded the horrid rack was thrown aside, and the dreadful engine stood revealed, with all its cranks, handles, levers, pulleys, and wheels.

The gaolers bound him to the instrument of torture, which was then set in motion.

The engine groaned most fearfully, as the wheels turned.

The monk's limbs were dragged out to an unnatural length, and a loud scream broke from his lips.

"Mercy! I confess!" he cried, "I confess; but save me from this fearful torture."

The young earl raised his hand, and the torture ceased.

"Take down the monk's confession," said Douglas, addressing his secretary.

The scribe dipped his pen in ink, and waited; but not a word came from Father Abel's lips.

"Confess, rascal!" said Lennox.

Still there was silence on the part of the prisoner.

"Then rack him again," said the young esquire in decisive tones.

Again the engine of torture was set in motion, and Father Abel's bones were dragged farther from their sockets than before.

Groans succeeded screams, and then, as had been anticipated, came the cry for mercy.

"I confess! Mercy! Have pity, good gentlemen."

"Your confession instantly, or your vile body shall be torn in pieces," said Lennox, fiercely.

"I poisoned the earl."

"How did you accomplish the fiendish trick?"

"I put the poison in the wine I handed him."

"What was your object?"

"Love for the young lord who now holds the honour of the house of Douglas in his keeping."

"And who, no doubt, will order the four quarters of your body to be set up in four different towns where his rule is acknowledged."

The secretary whispered a word in the ear of young Lennox, who resumed his examination.

"Had you any assistants or confederates in your design?"

"No."

"Have you acknowledged your crime elsewhere than in this apartment?"

"No."

All these questions and answers were duly noted by the secretary, who continued writing after Lennox had concluded his interrogations.

He then, in a hurried manner, read over the following confession, which he had drawn up :—

"*I confess myself guilty of the great crime of murdering, by means of poison, the most noble earl, James of Douglas, in which heinous crime I had no associates or accomplices.*"

"Unbind his right hand," said Lennox.

This order was obeyed, and the secretary thrust his pen between the trembling fingers of the prisoner.

"Sign there!" said he, pointing to the foot of the document.

The monk, with difficulty, managed to write his name, and the document was then carried to the young earl, who had averted his face from the scene of torture.

After reading it, he turned towards the prisoner and thus addressed him—

"You, Abel, the monk, being guilty, by your own confession, of the crime set forth in this document, are little deserving of pity at our hands ; nevertheless, we will so far extend our clemency as to grant you your life——"

"Thanks! Thanks! most noble earl!" cried the monk.

"Though, that the murderer may not escape unpunished, we adjudge you to be kept a prisoner in the dungeon from which you were brought hither, until death sets you free. Away with him! Chain him to a pillar! Let bread be his only food, water his only drink, and straw his couch."

As these words were concluded, the men at the rack unbound their prisoner, and hastily carried him back to his gloomy dungeon—carried him, for his limbs were so strained and dislocated as to be useless.

The old fetters were removed, lest time and rust should have weakened them sufficiently to afford the prisoner means of escape, and in their place bright new chains were brought.

With these he was fastened to the pillar as before, the heap of straw was kicked up together by one of the men, who then laid the monk upon it, with about as much gentleness as the butcher uses towards the lamb when he lays it upon the ground before killing.

"I feel half inclined to finish the work," muttered one of them, laying his hand on his dagger.

"That would be a pity. Let him live, and if he succeeds in making himself happy in this dungeon, we can rack him again."

His companion's answer convinced the individual who had proposed putting an end to Father Abel's life, and, after casting a parting glance round to see that all was secure, they left the dungeon.

CHAPTER XLIL

A MYSTERIOUS MURDER.

THE Earl of Northumberland sent out several parties to scour the hills and woods when he heard the news that his sons and his fair ward had been attacked while hunting.

A rescue had been accomplished, as our readers already know, by a party of men-at-arms, who were constantly patrolling the borders ; but this force the earl at once decided to be insufficient, and sent out fresh parties. But though they sought, they found not.

But, if angry at this casual invasion of his territory, the earl was positively furious when he learned that his own name and that of his sons had been coupled together with an accusation of murder.

"By the bones of St. Cuthbert, these revilers shall rue the day that they dare accuse me of so foul and unknightly a crime. The lion is aroused, and will chase these Scottish hares."

"And, I too," said Hotspur, "do vow a deep revenge. The rash youth who used those words fell by my sword ; but I hate the whole nation, and like the Roman Emperor, I wish they had but one neck, that a single blow might suffice to kill them."

"But," said Ralph, who had joined the group, "is it not natural that they should suspect us, being their bitterest foes and at deadly warfare with them ?"

"No true noble would use such vile arts to slay even his bitterest enemy. Twice did I meet the dead earl in fair field, and never shrunk from any blow his arm could bestow ; twice did I meet him at courtly banquet, but never thought of poisoning his cup. The young earl has accused me of a crime, of which, if guilty, my spurs should be hacked off by the hangman, and my body delivered up to die a felon's death upon the gallows."

So spoke the earl, who therein uttered the true sentiments of his mind. He then turned away into his chamber to devise the campaign upon which his mind was bent.

Hotspur after a few minutes' conversation with his brother, left the hall, intending to steal round by the garden to a side-door, which would admit him to Lady Katherine's boudoir.

The gallant youth was rapidly becoming an impassioned lover and gave unmistakable symptoms of it by neglecting all out-door sports which she could not witness or participate in.

As he softly crossed the garden, he saw a female figure advancing towards him. At the first glance he imagined it was Lady Katherine, but a second look showed him his mistake.

It was her servant.

Hotspur was about to walk on, when he saw the figure of a man emerge from the shelter of a cluster of bushes, and advance swiftly towards the girl.

The servant, it seemed, was not aware of the man's approach until he was close by her side.

She turned then, and gazed at him with amazement, for he was a perfect stranger.

Hotspur, however, stood aside, fancying that it was one of his father's numerous retainers who had made an effort to win the good graces of the girl.

"Who are you ?" she asked.

"You shall first of all tell me who you are ?" replied the man.

"I am Lady Kath——"

"Ha !" exclaimed the stranger and his hand made a rapid movement.

Then came a fearful gasp, a sound that spoke of the most fearful of earthly terrors.

The girl remained motionless for a moment, and then fell to the ground.

Not so the stranger, who rushed away amongst the trees, while Hotspur, who began to see that a crime had been committed, hurried forward.

But he was too late to secure the stranger, who disappeared in the direction of the out-building.

He turned his attention to the woman, who remained lying on the turf just as she had fallen.

Hotspur took hold of her arm to raise her up, but his hand slipped from her wrist; he felt something warm and sticky, and he knew well that it was blood.

Her face was pale, and it needed no cunning physician to tell that life had departed.

He knew well that murder had been done, and that his hands were wet with the blood of the assassin's victim.

He held them out as far as possible from his body.

But what could be the reason for such a fearful crime? What motive could have prompted the murderer?

These were questions Hotspur could not solve; but there was the weapon, his eyes caught sight of its hilt!

The blade was buried in the bosom of the unfortunate woman!

A shudder crept over Hotspur's frame as he drew the dagger from its human sheath, hoping to find by its means some clue to the murderer.

But a still more awful spasm convulsed his heart as he eagerly read the following lines, which were written on a scrap of parchment attached to the hilt of the weapon.

Those words he had heard once pronounced by a voice which filled him at the time with vague alarms—

"*You have plighted your troth, but the sword shall separate you!*"

Outside the document was addressed to "Lady Katherine Mortimer;" and there could be little doubt but that the death blow was intended for her.

For a moment Hotspur's tongue was silent with a vague fear.

The next moment he rushed to Lady Katherine's apartment.

She was safe, unharmed, knowing nothing of the fearful crime which had been committed.

Pressing one ardent kiss upon her lips,

the youthful noble rushed out of the room as hastily as he had entered.

"Percy!" she cried, wishing to recall her lover.

All was silent; but that silence endured only for a minute.

Then arose a wild cry, a terrible and fearful sound, fatal words which echoed round the towers and battlements of the castle, and were repeated again ere its sounds died away.

"Help, here, help! a foul murder has been committed!"

Then came the rush of feet, the glare of torches, and the hum of many voices as men crowded to the spot from all parts of the castle in answer to that cry.

"Carry her away, some of you. The rest aid me to find the murderer!" said young Hotspur.

"Who is the assassin, my lord?" asked old Witherington.

"I know not. He fled this way. Torches here! Search out the bushes!"

They searched; but no trace of the felon perpetrator of the vile deed could be found.

"Who goes there?" shouted a sentinel, who had his station on the summit of a little postern-tower.

Hotspur and half-a-dozen men rushed to the spot, but ere they could reach it the sentry's challenge was repeated.

Looking up, they saw the soldier with his cross-bow levelled, they heard the twang of the string as a heavy bolt whistled through the air.

A few words sufficed to explain.

The sentry had seen a man on horseback emerge, as it seemed, from the tower beneath him; he had challenged him twice, and receiving no answer had discharged a bolt from his crossbow without harming the fugitive.

The hoofs of the horse were at that moment heard clattering along the path leading from the castle.

Two minutes more, and Hotspur was on horseback in hot pursuit, leaving orders for his men to follow at their swiftest speed.

Sparks of fire flashed from beneath the hoofs of Percy's horse as he goaded the animal forward.

Should he overtake the unknown assassin his life would be of little worth.

Though the servant had suffered instead of the mistress, Hotspur looked upon it as an attempt upon the life of his fair lady, and was determined to punish it as such.

As the fiery steed rushed along the road the landscape swam around him in all its clear and moonlight beauty.

There were clear, sparkling streams that leaped merrily along beneath the silver rays, there were dark woods slumbering on the sides of the ancient hills, there were fields of golden corn, over which the night breeze rustled with a peaceful sound.

Overhead was the silvery moon, attended by a host of stars, all sailing majestically through the blue vault of heaven, whitening the clouds, and steeping the still landscape in a perfect flood of bright, cold beams.

Occasionally Hotspur caught sight of the flying figure he was pursuing, occasionally he heard the clatter of the distant horse hoofs above the sullen trumpeting of the flying beetle, the merry chirrup of the grasshopper on the long grass, and the scream of the owl, as it sailed over the surface of the earth in quest of its prey.

The path they were following—the pursued and the pursuer—led to the cave of the hermit before mentioned.

In a few minutes after commencing his headlong ride, Hotspur entered the ravine which led to the cave.

He felt certain that the murderer had passed through it, and that he could no longer follow by ear. The echoes of the hoof-strokes of his own horse drowned all other sounds.

And besides that, the bed of the stream became more rocky, the waters dashed from stone to stone with great violence, keeping up a roaring sound that could be heard at a considerable distance.

But Hotspur knew that if his destined victim had entered that ravine he must keep in the path, for the rocky walls on either side prevented any turning to the right hand or to the left till the extreme end of the gorge was passed.

As the gallant young horseman entered the pass, the moon, which had hitherto been shining with unrivalled splendour, disappeared beneath a cloud bank, and left the scene in comparative darkness.

But Hotspur knew the path, and rode forward as swiftly as his steed could go along the rugged, uneven path.

Big thoughts of vengeance were in his mind; he would slay the cowardly assassin whose design was to plunge a dagger into the bosom of his betrothed.

He neared the hermit's cave, and began to consider whether he should make inquiries of the reverend inmate, when a new sound was heard.

Not the scream of the owl, the howl of the wolf, or the roaring of the flood, but a strain of deep harmony, which, mingling with the voices of nature, softened their harsher tones and echoed grandly through the rocky glen.

The holy tenant of the cell was chanting his evening devotions, and reining up his horse, the young noble reverentially lifted his cap.

CHAPTER XLIII.

THE MONK'S DREAM.

WE return to the monk, who was left in his gloomy cell by the gaolers who had taken so prominent a part in applying the torture.

His reflections—if reflections they can be called when thoughts, hopes, curses, and resolutions rushed through his brain in a bewildering chaos—added to the discomforts caused by bodily pain and inconvenience.

He had failed—not in crime, but in

reaching the object which had first prompted his guilty mind to imagine such foul deeds.

He had imagined from those words, " Would I were earl," that the young Douglas possessed a heart as black as his own ; he imagined that no one would hesitate to connive at or share in the perpetration of a sin by which personal advantage might be obtained.

" Oh, fool that I was !" he muttered, " Had I but remained, and watched the sorrow of the young chief with unmoved countenance, all would have been well. It was my hasty departure that brought suspicion on me."

In the midst of such reflections, with others of a deeper dye, he fell asleep.

Exhausted nature asserted her supremacy, and he was soon in the land of dreams.

But such dreams !

The horrors of his position in waking moments were not half so fearful as the terrible scenes through which he mentally passed while his body was at rest.

He imagined himself at the bottom of a precipice ; upon its brow he saw a host of white-clad figures, headed by one who bore a striking resemblance to Lady Katherine Mortimer.

At a signal they all hurled down large stones upon him. He could see their mocking faces as the sharp, jagged masses struck him to the earth ; he could feel the pain as the heavy missiles crushed his bones and tore away the flesh.

He shrieked for mercy, but the only response was a mocking laugh.

Again the scene changed.

The pavilion of Earl Douglas once more met his view. The earl was there, with his knights and courtiers, but all had the appearance of death in their faces.

A flagon of wine was set before the monk, and the earl, with a stern gesture, bade him drink.

" Drink, and be one of us !" said the phantom, in deep tones, and his words were echoed by a sepulchral laugh from the ghost-like company.

" Drink !" they cried.

In vain did the monk endeavour to keep the poisoned draught from his lips —an unseen force compelled him to swallow it, and in a moment he began to feel the burning effect of the deadly potion.

He writhed and struggled, turning over and over in his sleep as he lay upon his couch of straw.

His tortures were excessive ; he would rather by far have been stretched upon the rack again than endure such supernatural agony.

" Water, water !" he cried, the words actually issuing from his lips as he slept, so strongly was his mind impressed with the reality of the scenes he had witnessed.

" Ha, ha, ha !" laughed the spectres, as they witnessed his tortures, " there is no water here ; nothing but fire !"

Then a form advanced, knife in hand, and the wretched being recognised the page he had slain to conceal his own crime.

He struggled to his knees, and begged for mercy.

" Oh, spare me !" he muttered, " spare me, by the remembrance of the sufferings you endure."

" Ha, ha, ha !" laughed the phantom of his excited brain, and the knife descended.

Father Abel awoke.

The laugh still seemed to ring through the vault.

As he opened his eyes he saw that it was day, that he was on his knees, and the Witch of Wooler stood before him.

" Ha, ha, ha !" laughed the weird woman, looking with scorn and contempt upon the wretched prisoner.

ON THE BRIDGE.

CHAPTER XLIV.

THE HERMIT AND THE ROBBER.

HOTSPUR waited until the hermit had finished his devotions, then rode forward to the cell.

He reached the flight of steps, and, alighting from his horse, ascended to the grotto.

The hermit was still upon his knees, nor did he at first perceive the youth, who made a slight noise to attract his attention.

"Benedicite !" said the old man, rising, and holding his hand over young Percy's head.

"Father, a foul crime has been committed. I came to seek the murderer," said Hotspur.

"But wherefore in this cell, my son ?"

"I sought him not here, father ; but he must have passed along the ravine below."

"I saw no one ; since the hour of sunset I have been engaged in prayer and meditation, for my sins are many, and need earnest supplication."

"But what of his horse, good father ? The assassin was mounted, and must have passed at a gallop."

"I heard no sound, my son, except the dash of those ever restless waters, which by their hoarse voices, as they hurry onward to the ocean, remind me of life's swift river and the haste with which it speeds away to the great sea of eternity."

"Then I am foiled, and the murderer escapes, for long ere now he must have reached the end of the pass, and plunged into the forest."

"You say a murder has been done ; who is the unhappy victim ?"

"A serving woman who waited on the fair Lady Katherine Mortimer."

"Mortimer, my son ?"

"Aye ; have you not heard, good father, that she resides in our castle ?"

"My son, so little interest take I in the things of this world that I knew not whether your noble father kept his state at Alnwick or Warkworth. But tell me how this happened ?"

Hotspur, then, in a few words, related what had occurred in the castle gardens.

"Who is the assassin ?" asked the hermit.

"I know not, father, neither can I divine his motive in attempting so foul a crime as the murder of a fair lady who never wilfully injured any human being."

"Strange."

"Strange, indeed ; but I must mount and away to the end of the pass, to see if any traces yet remain of the course taken by the murderer."

So saying, he hurried down the rocky stairs, and in a few seconds was again upon the back of his staunch steed.

Onward again, past rock, tree, and bush, till the ravine was passed, and a little green sward appeared.

This open glade was surrounded on all sides by a dense wood.

Hotspur leaped to the ground once more, and by the moon's light, carefully examined the turf.

There were horses' tracks in numbers, some leading in one direction, some another.

It was impossible to tell which path the murderer had taken.

More than once Hotspur thought of riding into the forest on the bare chance of seeing or hearing something of the criminal.

But, on more mature reflection, such scheme seemed to him a useless waste of time.

He mounted, and was about to return, when he caught sight of two men who were in the act of emerging from the wood.

Percy at once reined his steed behind the shelter of a clump of thick bushes which grew on one side of the mouth of the ravine.

The approaching strangers were on foot ; they seemed well armed, each bearing sword and dagger, while the taller of the two carried a short hunting-spear in his hand.

"Who can these be who roam through the woods so leisurely at night ?" thought the youth. "I must wait and hear the subject upon which they converse so earnestly, though it little suits me to be playing the part of spy."

The strangers had not seen Hotspur, who stood behind the bushes, one hand upon his sword the other on his horse's rein, prepared for fight or flight, as either might prove necessary.

"He is there, then ?" said the hindmost of the two, halting as they approached Percy's hiding-place. "Are you certain ?"

"Yes ; my spies never fail me."

"And we must release him ?"

"Unless we would be ruined."

"But is he in possession of so much information as to injure us ?"

"I have not trusted him very far ; but he could set those upon our track whom we should find it difficult to evade."

"But you have not yet told me from whom you heard this news," continued the shorter of the two.

"From a certain robber——"

"Ha, ha, ha ! Never mind the name or the profession. Is our own calling a honest one ?"

"It is. We fight and we plot for political purposes, which raises us to the rank of warriors."

"With the same objects in view—namely, gold, and the power gold gives, which objects again drag us down to the level of common banditti."

"Well, it little matters what we style ourselves. The priest is in the hands of young Douglas, and we must rescue him. The Moody Forester never deserts one of his followers."

"But the Douglas keeps a strong castle, with well armed vassals on the walls."

"And, therefore must we recruit our band, which was sorely shattered and reduced by that ill advised attack upon Berwick. Poor Graham ! with the best

of intentions and a good strong arm, he was, after all, but an indifferent plotter."

"Perhaps Du Bois was as much to blame as Graham for that unlucky event ; the herald had a wily tongue, which he well knew how to use. But to business. How do you intend to recruit your forces ?"

"By purchasing strong arms and willing swords with gold."

"An excellent plan— with one drawback."

"What may that be ?"

"We have no gold."

"It was to procure that precious metal, so very necessary to the successful issue of our scheme, that I brought you down to this rocky glen."

"How ? Have you some secret store, or have you discovered the philosopher's stone, by which you intend to transmute flints into marks ?"

"A secret store."

The short man looked inquiringly in the face of his tall companion, who, striking the staff of his spear upon the ground, replied—

"I have a secret store, or rather the hermit has, who dwells down this glen. His cave contains golden vessels of great value ; those we will take to re-furnish our exchequer."

"What, rob a hermit ?"

"Aye."

"It is sacrilege to do so."

"And ruin not to do so. Come, forward ; no time should be lost."

The short man hesitated a moment, and then walked on with his companion, saying—

"Well, be it so ; one crime more or less makes little difference in the course of so black a life as mine. But if the hermit resists ?"

"We have weapons, and know how to use them."

"Humph !" was the reply, as the Moody Forester walked on with his companion.

"A nice conspiracy I have overheard." murmured Percy, as he moved after them, keeping beneath the shadow of the rocks as much as possible, and leading his horse by the bridle.

He was determined, since he could not

overtake and punish the perpetrator of one crime, to prevent the other, if possible.

"They are two," thought he. "But, what of that? I know how to use my sword, and, in such a case, it surely would not be accounted cowardice to fall upon them without warning. Besides, my men will be here ere long."

He carefully kept in sight of the would-be robbers till he saw them halt at the bottom of the rocky steps which led up to the cave.

Then he tied his horse to a bush, and, with more caution than before, crept forward to prevent the ruffians from carrying out their design.

But, before he reached the bottom of the steps, the robbers had dissappeared in the mouth of the cave, and the next moment young Percy heard the voice of the hermit calling for help.

"Help, for the love of Heaven! Have respect for a harmless hermit."

"Silence, old man; your screams are not likely to bring any one to your aid, so be quiet and give us up peaceable possession of the gold and silver vessels you keep so carefully."

"I have neither silver nor gold."

"Confess, old man, and so save yourself much needless injury."

"I have nothing, only the coarse food you see, and the earthen vessels which contain it."

"Then, since you are so obstinate, die! and allow us to search the cell at our pleasure!"

So said the shorter of the two confederates; at the same moment lifting his sword to take the hermit's life. But, to the robber's intense surprise, his weapon encountered a sword instead of a helpless body.

Hotspur had swiftly, yet quietly, ascended the steps, just in time to save the old man's life. He parried the thrust, and, with a dexterous turn of his wrist, jerked the robber's blade from his grasp.

"Ha! what means this?" exclaimed the Moody Forester, instantly springing forward from the corner of the cell he had been searching.

But ere the tall man could draw sword, or lift spear, Hotspur's blade had passed through the man who attacked the hermit, who, with a loud yell, rushed from the cave.

Not so the Moody Forester; he stood firm, and resisted the impetuous attack of the young noble. Their swords met, and gave forth a deadly sound as the blades glided along each other.

Hotspur found in a moment that he had an antagonist both powerful, skilful, and brave; but he flinched not from the contest.

It was lucky, he thought, he had managed to disarm the ruffian who fled in such haste. One antagonist of this stamp is sufficient, without being exposed to the murderous attack of a coward.

Clash, clash, went the swords; both blades shivered at the hilt.

In an instant, Hotspur threw the useless weapon aside, and, rushing forward, grappled with his huge antagonist, to prevent him from drawing his dagger.

A fearful struggle took place. Hotspur, though but a child in the arms of his powerful adversary, held fast. In the midst of their wrestling, the dagger dropped from the Moody Forester's belt. and was at once secured by the priest.

"Strike, father!" cried Hotspur, "Surely this is a time when you may lawfully use weapons?"

"Not so. Oh, heaven, forgive them!"

As these last words were uttered, the two combatants disappeared from view. They had stumbled at the mouth of the cave, and rolled over the steps down into the glen beneath.

The first thought of the hermit was to fall on his knees; the second to rush down the steps to assist his gallant young champion.

It was lucky he did so, or Hotspur would have been slain. The Moody Forester was about to raise a huge stone, with the intention of dashing out the youth's brains, when he saw the hermit coming down the steps, still holding the dagger in his hand.

"Foiled this time," he muttered, rising to his feet, and dashing off down the glen. "Curses on the coward who deserted me!"

'Are you hurt, my son?" asked the

hermit, as he stooped by the side of young Percy.

"It seems as though every bone in my body had been broken," replied the gallant boy, as he attempted to rise.

"Give me your hand, my son. Let me assist you up these rude steps."

Aided by the hermit, Hotspur managed to stagger up the steps, and then fell fainting upon a bed of grass and leaves.

CHAPTER XLV.

THE WITCH'S SECRET.

SORELY astonished, indeed, was Father Abel, when he awoke from his sleep in the dungeon, and found himself kneeling before the witch.

"Ha! ha! you little expected company, good father, I imagine," said she.

"What mean you? Are you, too, a prisoner?"

"A prisoner, forsooth! It must be, indeed, a strong dungeon that can hold me. Have you forgotten how easily we passed through Alnwick Castle? And think you that this building could detain me?"

"If you can escape you can set me free."

The weird woman shook her head.

"There are secret doors and passages in this castle known only to me ; over them I have power ; but over your fetters I have no control," she added, with a sneering smile, "for you yourself blessed and sprinkled them with holy water, long ere you took service with the proud Earl of Northumberland."

"Save me! Oh! release me from this fearful place !"

"I cannot."

"Then, why come hither to torture me with the knowledge that you are free, while I remain a prisoner?"

"I came here to question you——"

"Well, speak."

"You have spared me the trouble, since, in your sleep, you confessed every black action of your wicked life. Oh! disgrace to the priesthood! was it to commit all those crimes that you took upon you the garb of religion ?"

"Religion—aye, and religion shall rid me of your tormenting presence! Avaunt thee, Sathanas !"

"Hush! your curses are harmless. Blasphemy would only add to the dark list of evils already attached to your name."

"Liberate me."

"I have already said I cannot. Now I add that I would not set you free, even had I the power. Your foul attempt on the life of a fair being who never did you harm, deserves that you should receive the utmost punishment your captors can inflict."

"Douglas does not punish me for that."

"Then your vile assassination of his brave father demands that your life should be the forfeit."

"For that he has condemned me to remain here for life ; but I shall escape."

"You will not escape, or, if you do, it will only be into the hands of the Earl of Northumberland, who has vowed a heavy vengeance against you. Nevertheless, that he may know where you are confined, I will hie off to Alnwick to impart to him the joyful intelligence."

"You said you came here to question me," said the monk, after a long pause. "What is it you desire to know ?"

"I wished to satisfy myself from your own lips that it was you who administered the poison to the good earl. You informed me while you slept, and in this case I can believe you."

"I did."

"Then, farewell. But first of all let me deliver you this letter."

With these words the weird woman tossed a packet at the monk's feet, and glided behind a pillar.

Father Abel rose, and looked about the dungeon as far as his chain would allow him, but Gunara had disappeared.

The priest then opened the note, and made himself acquainted with its contents.

"Though you acted without orders in doing the deeds of blood for which you are imprisoned, you are not forgotten. You shall be rescued if possible, or, if not, shall be avenged. To-morrow night your intended victim, Lady Katherine Mortimer shall die. *This letter will be delivered by the hand of your mother.*"

"My mother!" shrieked the priest. "No, no, that cannot be! Surely I am not the son of a—a—witch!—a being whose soul and body are both lost!"

"Ha! ha!" sounded the mocking voice of Gunara. "A fine greeting the son gives his parent!"

"Oh, say, is this true?" cried the priest.

"True! Aye, true," replied the woman, again stepping forward. "See, here is the document given me by the monks of Lindisfarne, when they took you, a child of scarce three years old, to rear up in the doctrines of their creed. Read it, for they taught you, even as one of their fraternity taught me, to curse."

With trembling hands the monk held to his eyes the paper, in which was duly set forth the reception into the establishment of Abel, son of Gunara Alleyn, as well as the particulars of his baptism.

"True! true! But since I am your son, is it fit you should leave me to die in this dungeon? Why not help me to escape?"

"I placed you in a convent that you might learn the good I had lost. But had I known my son was to be a murderer I would have placed him in a grave."

"But I never harmed you?"

"Never harmed me! Do you not recollect that some four years ago, before you became tutor to the sons of the earl, you pronounced a deep curse upon me and all my kindred? Ha, ha! you were fulfilling your priestly duties; but you little knew that *you* were my nearest kin, and that upon yourself was to fall the heaviest portion of your own curse."

"I knew not."

"No, you knew not how your curse harmed me—how peasants, who before gladly gave me food and shelter, shunned me as a malignant being—how, in consequence, I was left to wander and starve upon the mountain sides, without even a roof to shelter me from the storm and the wind. That was your work, my son! Your words changed me from a harmless to a baneful being, and now you reap the fruits. Reflect well upon what I have said; my words will give you food for meditation many a long, dark and lonely night."

With these words she again disappeared, and although Father Abel called at the top of his voice she did not return.

His guards, however, heard the outcry, and hastily entered to know the reason.

"The witch has been here; she passed behind that second pillar."

The men strode to the spot, looked around, and carefully searched out every corner, but no one save themselves and the prisoner could be seen.

"Let us have no more of this," exclaimed the soldier, giving the monk a hearty kick, which set every one of his bones aching. "If you play me such a trick again, beware the rack!"

CHAPTER XLVI.

ALNWICK GARDENS.

A VERY slight examination served to convince the good old hermit that Hotspur had broken no bones in his encounter with the Moody Forester, A few drops of water poured down the lad's throat revived him ; he sat up, and then attempted to rise to his feet.

"Not yet, my son ; your strength has hardly returned sufficiently," said the hermit. "Sit awhile, and swallow this draught, which will ease your pain and give you nerve for any further exertion it may be necessary to make."

With these words the pious, benevolent old man poured out a draught from a phial and held it to the lips of the youth, who swallowed it readily.

In a few minutes the pain he had felt seemed to die away, his blood seemed to course freely through his veins, and he jumped to his feet.

'Come father, my horse is behind the bushes yonder. Let us go."

"I cannot quit my cell, my son."

"But if you remain those robbers will take your life."

"My term of years draws to a close : why should I seek to prolong my days ? Let them have my life ; it is of little value."

"To yourself it may, perhaps, seem worthless, holy father ; but not so to others. Everyone in Northumberland knows and reveres the hermit of the glen, and I, who have just witnessed an almost miraculous display of your healing powers, am anxious that your life should be preserved for many a long year, that you may do good to others."

The monk smiled feebly, and Percy continued.

"Therefore, good father, gather up your vessels of silver and gold, or aught else you may possess, and come with me to Alnwick, where you will be more secure than in this lonely cave."

"The way is long, my son, and my limbs are feeble," replied the hermit.

"But my horse is close at hand, and his limbs are sturdy enough ; I will bring him to your door."

In a few minutes this was done, and the hermit then made his appearance.

"I will go with you, my son, and, by my advice, endeavour to check those passions which, I fear, will have an evil influence upon your future life. I have no gold or silver, as the robbers imagined, nor aught to burden me save these three books."

The young knight then doffed his cap as he helped the aged hermit to the saddle.

He remembered the day—not long past—when he had felt the same deep respect for Father Abel that he now did for the hermit ; but his old tutor had proved a robber and assassin, and this circumstance, though it did not shake his faith in the religion he had been trained in, brought him to the conclusion that *all* priests were not necessarily good men because of their holy calling.

"Thank Heaven," he thought, in his heart ; "Such men as Father Abel are indeed rare ; never before have I met with so much villainy concealed under the cloak of piety."

He then took the horse by the bridle, and led it along the path in silence.

The hermit said but little, for, old and experienced as he was, he could not help feeling a little regret at leaving the grotto which for so many years had been his home.

Ere they had travelled far they met a party of the men who had been directed to follow the assassin.

Hotspur gave the word to return, at the same time springing to the back of a horse, one of the soldiers having dismounted in order to accommodate the young lord.

The same soldier took the rein of Hotspur's charger, on which the hermit still sat, and in this manner they returned to the castle; the soldiers wondering to see the hermit thus travelling with their young lord, though they did not openly express their surprise.

Alnwick was reached at length, and the whole party dismounted before the great hall.

Henry Percy in a few words related to his father and brother what had happened —how he had saved the hermit's life, and induced him to come to the castle for protection.

The earl joined with his son in requesting the holy man to reside in the castle, to which he at length acceded.

A place was prepared for him at the table; but the hermit declined to partake of the meal, on the pretence that he had already taken sufficient food for the day.

"1 crave your pardon, my lord, if I offend, but I am hardly yet accustomed to the noise of all this multitude. I would ask permission to walk in the gardens of the castle awhile."

"Do as you list, good father," replied the earl. "And you in the hall, be every one of you obedient to the voice of our reverend guest."

With slow and stately steps, the hermit passed out, first of all inquiring of one of the servants in what part of the gardens the murder had been committed.

The man volunteered to show the spot, but, this offer being declined, directed him which way to proceed.

The night was now far advanced, but still the silvery moon held her sway in the sky, and the good hermit thought, as he stepped out upon the terrace of the garden, that he had never beheld so lovely a scene.

For some time he paced up and down in deep meditation.

Suddenly he paused and stood erect beneath the shadow of a tree, for a dark figure was seen slowly approaching.

"Surely the murderer cannot wish so soon to revisit the scene of his crime; or is it possible that the criminal has discovered his mistake, and is come to perpetrate a second deed of blood? It must

be—it is a woman, old and haggard looking. Ah, now I know her."

So thought the hermit as he watched the figure, which was indeed that of the witch, who, as our readers know, we left in Father Abel's prison the morning before these strange events took place at Alnwick.

As she approached, the hermit stepped from his concealment to meet her.

"What seek you here?" he asked.

"Stand aside!" she replied, haughtily. "None in this castle dare bar my path, or question my right to wander where I please."

"That I do! and, by this holy symbol, I command you to depart without injuring any person or thing within these walls."

As he spoke, the hermit held aloft his crucifix, and, as the weird woman saw it, she drew back, shuddering and averting her face from the holy emblem.

"Enough," said she, "I acknowledge your power."

"It is not enough that you acknowledge my power, or rather that of my holy calling," replied the hermit, "you must inform me why you wander round the castle at this dead hour of night with intent to injure or alarm its inmates. What wrong have they done?"

"Many. But I am not here for vengeance."

"Your object, then."

"What if I refuse to tell?"

"Then, by this sign of my faith, I will compel you to speak."

As the hermit uttered these words, he again laid his hands upon the crucifix.

The woman drew herself up to her full height, and looking the hermit fully in the face, replied.

"I, too, have a power at my command. Beware how you provoke me."

"I know you, and yet I do not fear. Tell me instantly, what dark errand brings you hither."

Instead of replying, the witch turned upon her heel, and was about to walk away, when the hermit drew a bottle from the breast of his robe, and sprinkled its contents upon her.

The features of the woman assumed a

look of intense pain, but she remained motionless.

" By this holy water," said the hermit, " brought from the sacred river of Jordan, and blessed by a holy bishop, I command you stay, and answer all questions I shall ask."

" I obey," said the witch, in hollow tones.

" Your object in coming hither ?"

" To see the Earl of Northumberland, or his son."

" For what purpose ?"

" To tell them that one they hunted has been caught."

" Who is this one ?"

" A certain monk, Father Abel by name. The man who attempted the life of Lady Katherine Mortimer."

" Who has captured him ?"

" The Earl of Douglas. He is now confined in the Douglas castle."

" Enough ! Now you may depart."

With these words the monk lifted up his hand, and the woman hobbled away ; occasionally casting back pained and angry looks towards the spot where the hermit was standing.

" Father Abel," he murmured. " The name seems strangely familiar to me :— I must have heard of this man long before the strange events of these few days past ! Captured by Earl Douglas— perhaps it is as well—for sad indeed would be his fate if he fell into the hands of Northumberland. I must return to the hall."

So saying he retraced his steps, and made his way towards the great room where the earl and his son were seated at supper with their dependent knights and retainers.

" These sounds of rude mirth and revelry jar strangely upon my ears," thought he. " It is long since I mingled in such stirring scenes : ah ! those were times, but it would be well could I forget them. Those were times, indeed, when I wore bright armour instead of monkish robe, a sword girded around my waist instead of this crucifix, a helmet and plume where now sits the serge hood."

He sighed deeply, pressed his hand to his brow, and walked to and fro for a few minutes.

" And *she*," he continued, " once the heiress of a castle as noble as this, mistress of a fortune almost as large as that with which Earl Percy endows his sons— what of her ? Forgotten ? No ; for even in my lonely hermit cell, at the dead hour of night, would visions of that fair form arise before my eyes, to renew in my heart that wild passion which once inflamed my whole being. Lost, lost, lost—for ever lost ! And I—I know not where lie buried the remains of one whose beauty and fame this arm once upheld at every fete and tournament. But away vain thoughts ! Let me be the hermit once more."

He drew his hand across his brow, and with his usual stately, solemn step, re-entered the banquet chamber.

Amongst other customs of past date which the Earl of Northumberland still preserved in his household, was that of having an attendant musician to play on his harp and sing during meals.

This custom, imported from the North by the Saxons and Danes, was peculiarly grateful to the descendants of those warlike nations, who formed the majority of the Percy tenantry.

The skald, as some of the poorer classes still called the harper, adhering pertinaciously to their northern tongue, was seated at the extreme edge of the table, chaunting a song of fierce encounters in which the Percy family had won great renown.

Every eye was fixed upon him—every ear listened eagerly to his strains.

But the song ceased abruptly as the hermit entered the room ; faces were turned from the harper to the monk, whose face was pale, and whose features seemed agitated.

" How now, father ?" said the earl, motioning his reverend guest to a seat. " Has aught occurred to alarm you ?"

" My lord earl, my soul is little given to fear ; yet an adventure has befallen me which I would fain tell in your private ear."

" These are stirring times, indeed. Fall back, gentlemen, beyond the sound of the holy man's voice."

In a moment the platform was clear.

"In the gardens of your castle, my lord, I encountered a strange being, known as the Witch of Wooler—"

"What again? Now, by the mass, she shall suffer for it if she fall into our hands."

"This woman, in answer to my questions, replied that the purport of her visit was to inform you that a certain Father Abel is now a prisoner in the hands of Earl Douglas."

"Then I swear by the holy rood he shall come thence, despite the Douglas and all his, to the deepest dungeon of Alwnick Castle."

"Your resolution is soon formed, my lord."

"It is, though not easily changed. Ho! there, my secretary, be in attendance in my chamber; and you, sir seneschal, see that the reverend hermit is properly bestowed for the night."

The charm was broken, and in an instant the bustle of human life was once more heard.

CHAPTER XLVII.

FATHER ABEL ATTEMPTS TO ESCAPE.

FOR more than a fortnight Father Abel remained in the dungeon, chained to a pillar, walking wearily to and fro, as far as his chains would permit, revolving in his mind various projects for escaping.

But none of his plans seemed feasible, for the simple reason that he could not disencumber himself of his chains.

Had he been able to free himself from these bonds, the monk imagined that he would very soon be able to walk out of his dungeon.

His gaolers brought him food and water day by day, and sometimes examined his fetters to see that they were secure.

One day—nearly three weeks after he was tortured—a warder came as usual to bring him his allowance of coarse bread. The monk observed that the man seemed considerably overcome by liquor.

"Here, monk, take your food. It is more and better than I would give you if my will were law in this castle."

"I know not what I have done to earn your anger, my son."

"Silence! Stand up, while I see that these rings are properly secured about your feet."

Father Abel rose, while the man knelt to examine his chains.

The gaoler's back was partly turned towards the priest, and the hilt of his dagger was thus within easy reach of Father Abel's hand.

In a moment the monk secured the weapon, and raised it in his hand to strike.

Never was man so near a sudden and violent death as that unsuspecting gaoler. But a slight movement he made alarmed the priest, and, instead of sheathing the weapon in the man's back, he carefully concealed it beneath his own robes.

The goaler was saved without even being aware of his danger.

Again Father Abel was left alone.

His scheming mind was now in a much greater state of turmoil than before. Confinement seemed ten times more irksome now that he had, as he imagined, the means of freedom in his possession.

Yet he dared not attempt to escape during the daytime, for he was liable to be visited at various hours by the officers of the castle.

About half an hour after this affair the door of his prison was opened, and two men appeared.

One of them was an officer of high authority in the garrison; the other was a surgeon. Without speaking a word, this latter personage advanced to Father Abel, and examined his limbs to see whether he had recovered from the effects of his torture.

"What think you ?" asked the officer.

"He is better."

"Is he well enough ?"

"Yes, provided the torture be not applied excessively."

"Then to-morrow morning, he shall go upon the rack again."

"Oh ! in Heaven's name, good sirs, do not torment me any more. I have suffered much ; spare me a repetition of those fearful agonies."

"Ha, ha ! you little care what torments you inflict upon others ; but, good sir monk, it is our turn now ; and, though our young lord will have your life spared, you shall not escape the rack."

"Mercy ! show mercy !"

"Not I, so prepare yourself for the rack to-morrow. Come away, master surgeon ; and pleasant dreams to you, sir monk."

The two men then left the cell, and as soon as they were gone Father Abel gave vent to his rage in curses and imprecations.

"Fiends they must be to torment me thus," he exclaimed "may everlasting torments consume them ! But I will baulk them of their sport ; I can die but once, and death shall now free me from their tyranny."

So saying he drew the dagger, and held it for a moment with the point resting upon his breast.

But then came the thoughts of that dreadful unknown future, that mysterious after life so little understood, and therefore all the more feared by him.

"I dare not die," he moaned, dropping the weapon upon the straw which formed his bed. "I must remain the victim of their devilish cruelty."

He sat himself down, and began to moan over his hard fate.

Then the dagger again caught his eye.

"Why should not this weapon free me from my chains ? It is of good steel, its edge is keen. I will essay the task."

He took up the weapon and examined it narrowly. It was, as he had said, of good material and workmanship.

He then knocked one of its edges against his iron manacles till it was full of notches like a saw.

It would be used as a file.

"It will be strange, indeed, if I cannot cut through my chains with this," he muttered. "But let me see where is the weakest portion ?"

After a careful examination of his fetters he came to the conclusion that the links nearest the rings which encircled his legs and his waist were most worn, and therefore the points which promised him most hope of freedom.

Father Abel at once commenced to use his file. He knew he had no easy task to perform, and that if he could not accomplish his task before the morning his hopes of freedom would be dashed to the ground.

For a long, long time he worked as hard as possible, only pausing occasionally to listen whether anyone was approaching his dungeon.

No one came, however ; his gaolers seemed perfectly satisfied that their prisoner was safely secured.

Darkness came on soon after he began his task ; but that proved no impediment to his exertions. He could saw away in the dark as well at in the light.

"One leg free at last," he exclaimed, as the chain fell to the ground. "I can get rid of this ring when I have more time to spare."

At that moment footsteps were heard approaching, and rays of light from a torch or lantern streamed beneath the door of his gloomy dungeon.

Father Abel threw himself upon his couch of straw, concealed the dagger in his sleeve, arranged the chain so that no one could see it had been severed, and then pretended to sleep.

With a harsh grating sound, the dungeon door rolled back upon its hinges, and two men entered.

They were gaolers, who had just taken place of others, and had come at the commencement of their term of duty to see that the prisoner was safe in his prison.

"The monk sleeps soundly," said one.

"Aye ; though, had I my will, he should sleep still more soundly," replied the other.

"VILE MURDERER PREPARE FOR DEATH!"

"How ? What do you mean ?"

"He should sleep in his grave."

"That, perhaps, would be less punishment than to let him live in this dungeon, with nothing to cheer him save the thoughts of his crime."

"And an occasional stretch upon the felon's bed—the rack."

"Aye ; of which we have to give him notice."

So saying, the speaker gave the monk a kick with his foot.

"Hullo ! wake up, monk."

"No, no, it is not time yet," exclaimed Father Abel, feigning to wake, though in reality he had heard every word.

"Ha ! ha !" laughed both the men, " it will, as you say, be time enough for that in the morning."

"Time for what ?"

"For the rack, father. We have orders to warn you that such is to be your fate in the morning."

"Ah ! then it is no dream ; but surely the Earl Douglas cannot be so cruel."

"No ; our young lord is a very tender-hearted chicken over such matters, though, in a fight, game enough ; but that is no reason why his followers should show you any mercy. Good night, father. Prepare yourself for a wholesome stretching in the morning."

With these words the men took up their light, and left the dungeon without stopping to examine the priest's chains.

Father Abel then arose from his couch.

"They will search in the morning but I shall not be found," said he, and immediately set to work to sever the chain attached to his other leg.

The task was a long and wearisome one ; but at length it was accomplished.

"One more link to cut through, that which holds me by the waist,—and then I can say I am free."

He was free from his chains at length, and moved carefully towards that side of the dungeon where he knew the window was situated.

This window was a sort of loophole, guarded by an iron bar.

Father Abel's heart felt some misgiving as he felt the obstacle which barred his exit from the dungeon.

It was of great thickness, and should he be compelled to cut through it, would probably keep him in his prison till daybreak.

The monk took it in both hands, and shook it with all his strength.

To his great joy it seemed to give way at the top, and upon making further investigations, Father Abel discovered that instead of being set in solid stone, it was simply set in a kind of cement of the the same colour as the granite of which the walls were composed.

With the point of his dagger he quickly picked the cement away, and found that he was able to move the bar far enough aside to admit of his body being passed through the opening ; for the priest had been kept upon coarse and scanty fare for some time, and had lost much of that corpulence which distinguished him when our readers first made his acquaintance.

But having made this discovery another thought presented itself to his troubled mind—

"How far beneath the window was the ground ? Or was there any ground at all on which to alight ?"

He could hear the waves dashing against the rocks not far below, but the night was too dark to allow of his seeing whether there was any ledge of rock below to save him from plunging down into the sea.

How, then, was the discovery to be made ?

Father Abel had a stout cord passed twice round his waist, and tied girdlewise in front—in all there were about ten feet of good stout hemp, knotted at either end to keep it from untwisting.

The monk took it from his body, and made one end fast to the iron bar of his window.

Then with great caution he began to slide down the rope.

In a very short time he reached the end, but could not touch the ground, nor could he, through the darkness of the night, discover how far it was beneath him.

"I must ascend again," thought he. "It would be unwise to risk a fall from an uncertain height, not knowing whether land or water was beneath one."

But that was easier to think of than to do, for Father Abel was by no means an agile man, nor had he ever practised the art of climbing ropes.

He found himself, in spite of all his efforts, unable to ascend a single inch.

Worse than that—far worse !

He was gradually losing his hold of the rope—the cord seemed leaving his grasp !

In vain he clutched it with all the force remaining in his half-benumbed fingers, while beads of perspiration, caused by intense fear, stood upon his brow.

At length he could hold on no longer ; the rope slipped from his grip, and with a loud scream of despair he fell !

CHAPTER XLVIII.

THE HERDSMAN'S DAUGHTER.

I MUST and will have possession of that traitor's body," thought the Earl of Northumberland, whenever the recollection of Father Abel's evil deed crossed his mind.

" I would rack the vile monk for attempting her life," thought Hotspur, whenever his eyes fell upon the fair form of Lady Katherine.

The impetuous youth knew not that Father Abel had already been subjected to the torture, or his speech and thoughts would have been tempered with mercy.

The Earl of Northumberland meditated an inroad upon the territories of his Scottish neighbours, for the express purpose of capturing the monk, though, as a preliminary step, he sent a knight and herald to demand that the culprit should be given up peacefully.

But, in order that he might not be unprepared should warfare be necessary, he also sent out several scouting parties, with instructions to penetrate as far beyond the borders as possible, and bring back all the information they could as to the numbers and positions of the Scottish troops stationed in the Lowlands.

Hotspur took command of one of these parties.

His youthful activity would not allow him to sit quietly at home when fighting, or anything likely to lead to a fight, was to be done.

Old Witherington was not one of the party on this occasion, nor was his son, the young esquire.

It was early morning when they set forth, and for a few miles they rode at a good speed.

But when the castle was hidden from their eyes Hotspur began to slacken his pace, and debate in his own mind whither he should lead his men.

There was no one in the band with whom he cared to converse.

The soldiers were all as ill-favoured ruffians (half-a-dozen in number) as could be met in England or Scotland.

After some deliberation Hotspur resolved to follow the same path that he had taken when Lady Katherine was carried away by Graham and his companions.

He intended to learn if possible whether any troops were still in the town of Roxburgh, and whether the convent of St. Agnes was still garrisoned by the foreign banditti employed by the lady superior.

They continued their way for a long time through the narrow glen and across the heath which followed that glen.

The summer had merged into mid-autumn.

The sun was extremely powerful, and the heavy armour worn by the English rendered the journey anything but a pleasant one.

At length they reached a grove of trees on the extreme edge of the heath, near the fence which separated the waste ground from a few rudely cultivated cornfields and pastures.

Here Hotspur proposed a halt, that his men and horses might rest themselves until the sun's rays were less powerful.

He imagined that his movements had not been noticed, and that the party had entered the grove unseen. In this, however, he was mistaken.

A certain herdsman, who had once been threatened with death by old Witherington, had, from the door of his little hut, seen the horsemen enter the grove.

He recognized the horse which carried young Percy, and at once resolved to take measures for the capture or destruction of the whole band.

Not far distant, though hidden from the main road, was a village, the inhabitants of which held their little farms by military service from the Earl of March, a friend of the house of Douglas, and a sworn enemy to all Englishmen.

Thither the herdsman resolved to take his way, to call up from amongst the villagers a force sufficient to overcome the mere handful of Northumbrians.

"See ye stir not out, lassie," said he to his daughter, as he stood in the door, "unless the Saxons march. Then haste with your best speed along the road, and tell me what path they take."

The girl, a good-looking lass of about eighteen, promised obedience, and the herdsman started at a swift walk.

But before he had been gone long the natural curiosity of her sex worked its way uppermost in the mind of the girl.

She resolved to look at the English soldiers, and see whether they were at all like her own countrymen.

She had never set eyes upon Saxon troops; the tide of war had rolled past and around her cot without alarming her; and besides all this, when was not a soldier sufficient cause to awaken all a woman's curiosity?

Even Venus preferred the stalwart god of war to her limping spouse, Vulcan; and can it be supposed that a simple Scottish maiden could repress the feelings to which even a goddess was compelled to yield?

"They will not harm me," she said, as she cautiously stepped from the cottage door, glancing behind her occasionally to see lest her father should suddenly return.

Poor simple-hearted Minnie! She little knew that there were men in that rude band who had no respect for aught on earth—no fear for aught beyond the grave.

So, with pitcher in hand, she slowly paced along, as though only intent upon procuring a draught of cool water from a sparkling spring, which had its rise beneath the shadows of the trees which concealed the English soldiers.

Hotspur had fallen fast asleep, so had two of his men.

Four of them remained awake, however; two, whose duty it was to watch over the safety of the party, and two who, in a low voice, planned scenes of violence and robbery whenever they should come at any unprotected Scottish household.

Even they little thought that an adventure was so near at hand.

But one of the villains, blessed with sharper eyesight than his companion, caught sight of the pretty maiden as she tripped towards the grove.

"We are in luck already, friend Robin," said the man who had fixed his eyes upon her.

"How mean you?" asked his comrade.

"A prize—a tartan petticoat."

"Pshaw! such a prize is not worth the trouble of capture."

"What! and thou darest to say this since the miller's daughter refused to be seen in thy company?"

"Well, where is this Scottish lassie? Has she any golden pieces in her pocket?"

"That I cannot tell; but she has golden locks around her face. See, yonder she comes!"

"But not towards us?"

"No; she shapes her steps to the other end of the grove, where we shall be less liable to interference."

"Come along, then."

So saying, the two ruffians stole off towards a part of the grove, towards which Minnie appeared to be making her way.

The fair girl reached the spring, just at a spot where it fell with a boisterous rattle over a shelving rock some five and twenty feet in height.

She filled her pitcher, and with it was about to return by another path when she was suddenly seized from behind by two ill-featured men, completely armed.

"Holy Virgin! help!" she shrieked. "What want you, good gentlemen?"

"Silence!" said the one called Robin, as he drew his dagger. "Silence! or I will cut your tongue from your mouth!"

"You are a prize, my fair one ; a lawful captive to our swords and our spears," said the other.

"Help! help! Duncan! for Heaven's sake help me!"

At that moment footsteps were heard hastily approaching, and a voice said—

"I am here, dear Minnie."

Then was seen the tall, stalwart form of a Scottish youth of scarce seventeen summers, a poorly clad, but noble-looking young fellow, whose eyes seemed filled with anger as he saw Minnie between the two ruffians.

"I am here, dear sister," he repeated. "Ah! release her, dastards."

All unarmed as he was—unless the knife at his waist could be called a weapon—with bare feet and uncovered head, he leaped forward to save his sister from the ruffians.

The one called Robin fled, without caring to stand the charge of the valorous young Scot ; but the other, though as great a villain, was not quite so cowardly.

He drew his sword, and made a furious thrust at young Duncan.

Our young Scot parried the thrust with his bare arm, and then, catching the weapon in his hand, plucked it from the soldier's grasp.

Another instant, and the steel blade was snapped in two across his knee.

"Thus much for safety, now for vengeance!" he shouted.

Making another bound forward, he caught the astonished Northumbrian by the throat, and, after a short struggle,

hurled him back over the ledge of rocks before mentioned.

The man gave a fearful yell as he fell, then came a dull, heavy thud, as his heavily-armed body reached the earth.

"Oh, save yourself, dear Duncan, save yourself by flight, ere his companions come!" exclaimed pretty Minnie, ringing her hands with sorrow.

"What, and leave you here at their mercy? Never, dear Minnie!"

Even had he felt disposed to do so it would have been too late, for some of the other Englishmen, warned by the screams of the girl, came running up just in time to see the unfortunate man disappear.

"Cut down the Scottish rascal! Hew him in pieces," shouted one.

"Riddle him with arrows!" shouted a second.

"Or pitch him down head foremost to bring up poor Mat."

"Oh! do not harm him," screamed Minnie, throwing her arms round her brother's neck.

"Bind them both together and throw them down," said the first speaker, as they all made a rush upon the brother and sister.

Duncan made a stout resistance ; but he was overpowered, and there is little doubt that both would have been condemned at once, had not a voice arrested the hands of the scoundrels.

"Hold there, villains!"

It was Hotspur who spoke.

"Our young lord, Hotspur!" they exclaimed, as reluctantly they released their prizes.

"What is the meaning of this strange scene?" demanded the youth.

"My lord, we were about to take vengeance for the death of our comrade, Mat," replied the man called Robin.

"How did he meet his death?"

"He was slain by this young Scot, my lord."

Hotspur turned fiercely towards Duncan, and laid his hand upon his dagger.

"Is this true?" he demanded.

"It is true."

"Rascal! your doom is sealed, since you have slain a follower of the house of Percy."

"Oh, be merciful to me, my lord!"

cried Minnie, dropping on her knees before the young Englishman. "He did but protect me from the ill-usage of the man who is dead, and his comrade yonder."

As she spoke, the fair girl pointed with her finger towards Robin theRuffian, as he was named familiarly by his companions.

"Ill-usage, did you say, girl?"

"Yes, my lord; such as Scottish man never offered to defenceless stranger whether man or woman."

"Is this true?" again asked the youthful leader, this time bending his frowning brows upon his own soldiers.

One or two of them made answer in the affirmative.

"Release your prisoner," said Hotspur.

Robin trembled, his face changed from red to white, and from white to red, while his lips quivered, so as to deprive him of the power of speech.

"I—I—thought, my lord, we might kill any Scots we met."

"Rascal! You, a soldier, owing service to the Earl of Northumberland, have dared lift your hand to maltreat a girl. Disgrace to the name of Englishman—never again wear our livery! Strip him, men, take away his weapons, his helmet, his breast-plate, and tear off his jerkin."

This was quickly done, and the crestfallen soldier stood a prisoner in the hands of his comrades.

"Now bind him up to yonder tree."

The soldiers knew not what fate their young lord had in store for Robin, but they hesitated not to obey his commands, lest Hotspur's wrath should fall upon them.

In a few moments the man was fixed securely by cords and thongs to the trunk of a huge beech tree which grew close by the spot.

"Oh, do not kill him, Lord Percy! Enough punishment has already befallen his companion for the insults they offered me," said Minnie.

"I will not kill him, girl; but I will teach his nation as well as your own, that English soldiers war not upon defenceless women."

"Release him, I pray," continued the girl.

"Nay, I must punish him, if it only be for a breach of discipline in attacking any one without word of command from his leader. Bring hither that sword belt which sustains the rascal's weapon."

One of the men immediately presented him with the article required.

Hotspur then approached Duncan.

"You are the brother of this fair damsel?" he asked.

"I am."

"Did you see this man lay hands upon her?"

"I did."

"Then revenge is within your reach. Take this broad buff belt and lay on his shoulders till you are satisfied."

Duncan took the belt, looked for an instant at the writhing victim before him, then raised his arm.

But the blow fell not, for the bold Scottish youth cast the belt to the ground as he exclaimed—

"Not so, Lord Percy. I have never raised my hand against a defenceless foe."

"But he may escape if you do not satisfy your vengeance now."

"Then let him escape; or, if it please you, lend me a sword, restore him his weapon, cut his bonds, and set us face to face. I will, by the aid of St. Andrew, take such vengeance that he shall never again harm man or woman!"

"It shall be done," said Hotspur giving the necessary directions to his followers.

"Dearest Duncan, do not risk your life. The Englishman is used to arms."

Minnie put her arms round her brother's neck as she uttered this petition.

"I must fight," said the Scottish youth. "These English would call me a coward did I now retract my challenge."

So saying, he gently pushed her away, and took a sword which was offered him by Hotspur.

Robin the Ruffian had also been provided with a weapon, though he showed little inclination to use it.

The two then faced each other, awaiting Hotspur's signal to commence the conflict.

CHAPTER XLIX.

MUTUAL DEFIANCE.

LAY on!" said Hotspur, giving the two combatants the word to commence.

The swords clashed, and blood was seen to flow from the right shoulder of the English soldier.

"Have a care, Rob," bawled his comrades.

But the warning came too late, for the sword of Duncan descended upon his head with fearful violence, levelling the ruffian to the earth.

"By the mass, the Scot hath conquered," said one of the band.

"Aye, and here comes his countrymen to follow up his victory," replied a second.

"Where?" asked Hotspur.

"There, my lord. You may see them winding along the road at the foot of the hill yonder, a goodly company with bright spears and swords."

"How many are they, think you?"

"At least a hundred, my lord."

"And we but five men. But I must break a spear with their chief ere we turn."

"It would be madness, my lord. Besides, now they approach nearer, I can see they are not knights or men-at-arms, but peasants, armed with scythes, oxgoads and implements of husbandry."

"Peasants! But by the rood I will so tame this wild land, that I will hunt in it for three days without hindrance."

"And I in the name of the Earl of March, whose liege man I am, do defy you to do so," said Duncan, stepping forward.

"I fight not with peasants," replied Hotspur, in haughty tones.

"The Earl Douglas, our warden of the marches, is no peasant. He shall meet you if you trespass upon Scottish lands again."

"That I will do in four days' time."

Hotspur rejoiced in the idea of bringing matters to a crisis. He hated Douglas, because he still suspected him of a secret participation in the abduction of Lady Katherine, as well as the murder which we described as having taken place in Alnwick gardens.

Duncan said nothing more, but, taking his sister by the hand, walked away.

"Shall I send a shaft after him, my lord?" asked one of the soldiers.

"By no means. He fought bravely for his sister and his life ; he shall have both."

He then gave the word of command, and his little band began to retrace their steps.

Duncan and his sister were observed on their return by their father, who at once hastened towards them.

"Ye look angry, Duncan, and the lassie is pale ; what means this?"

"I saw her insulted by the Saxons in yon grove."

"And you did not kill the fiends? You allowed them to escape, and triumph over their brutality?"

"Not so, father ; I slew the ruffians who dared lay hands upon my sister. Their leader, the young Earl Percy, gave me a sword and a fair combat."

"What doth young Percy here?"

"I know not, but he swore that in four days' time he will come again, or as often as he pleases. He will hunt these fields and woods."

"Then word of this must be sent to Earl Douglas, since our own lord, the Earl March, is in high disgrace at court. Hie away, Duncan, be first to bear him the news, so shall you be rewarded."

Off sped Duncan, not stopping for food or drink, though he had a journey of at least thirty miles before him. But he knew that when hungry it would be easy enough to procure food from any of his countrymen.

All that day he walked, till about an hour after sunset, when he halted at a little cottage by the wayside.

Its inmates received him hospitably and would have pressed him to stay, but Duncan refused.

After about two hours' rest, he again started though it was nearly dark. He knew well enough that there would be a splendid moon to light him through the night, and strode on manfully.

He reached the castle about the same time that the sun rose up from behind the waves of the sea.

A single knock at the great gates brought a porter to learn his business.

" I have a message for the noble earl."

" You must wait two hours at least ; and even then he will most probably receive the English knight and herald before he hears what you may have to say."

" I must see him before these English, so that we may defeat their plans."

" Well, well, my good youth, I will try and manage that it be so. But come in here and rest ; you look travel-worn."

Duncan waited for no second invitation, but in a few minutes was fast asleep.

It seemed to him that he had been upon his bench but a few minutes when the porter aroused him with these words—

" Wake, my bonnie lad ; the young earl will now give you an audience."

Half sleeping, half waking, Duncan was hurried into the presence of the young noble ; but once in the presence his natural self-possession returned.

He stated the intelligence he had collected, adding to it young Percy's threat that he would hunt or march wherever he pleased upon the borders.

" Then, by St. Andrew, we will prevent him. Ha ! what noise is that without ?"

" The English knight and herald, my lord, request immediate audience," replied a servant.

" Admit them."

In another instant the two Englishmen stood in the midst of a room crowded with their Scottish foes.

" We are here once more, Earl Douglas," said the herald, " to demand of you the body of a certain traitor monk, known as Father Abel, who hath been guilty of murder, and of treason towards his liege lord and master, the most noble Earl of Northumberland."

During this speech the English knight leaned upon his sword, calmly surveying the Scots. He knew no fear and had he been attacked, would willingly have encountered the whole assembly.

" The monk is not here, Sir Herald ; he hath escaped from our dungeons. But in thus stating our inability to comply with your request, we do not acknowledge your right to demand from us one who has been guilty of foul practices towards Scottish subjects ; nor, had we the monk in our castle, would we deliver him up to you."

" Well spoken, my lord !" muttered the Scottish chiefs and nobles.

" Furthermore, tell your young lord, who is called Hotspur, that if he shall presume to molest either Scottish men or venison, Douglas will take such speedy vengeance that his sport shall be turned into sorrow and mourning."

" All this will we faithfully report, Lord Douglas ; yet doubt not that, if Hotspur has promised to hunt, he will do so."

With these words the ambassadors withdrew, and in a few minutes their horses were heard galloping across the drawbridge of the castle.

" Now, my lords and gentlemen," said Douglas, " shall we tamely submit to be thus invaded by the English ? or will you aid me in this quarrel, which is not of my seeking ?"

" Arm, arm, and march at once !" was the general cry ; and immediate preparations were made to encounter the Northumbrians.

Ere many hours had passed, a body of nearly two thousand Scottish soldiers were on their way to the southern border of their kingdom.

Full of hope and confidence, they marched bravely forward ; alas ! how few of them were destined to return !

CHAPTER L.

THE WAR CLOUD GROWS DARKER.

WHEN the English knight and herald returned, they duly reported all they had heard.

"I will keep my word," said Hotspur, "and let Earl Douglas prevent me if he dares. Who marches with me?"

"I—and I—and I!" resounded from all the knights and gentlemen present in the hall.

Then prepare your men. Let them take their bows, and quivers full of arrows, and we will hunt these Scottish deer back to their highest hills."

The warlike preparations were soon made, and on the following morning, a beautiful calm Sabbath day, the little army set out.

Percy and his companion knights, were, of course, attended by their squires and pages, bearing the heavier portions of their armour; the men-at-arms were nearly fully equipped, and the archers carried swords and bucklers as well as their bows.

Ralph Percy was there in high glee.

He, too, thought of winning golden spurs.

Amongst the pages was one who seemed to keep aloof from the rest, attended upon no knight, and appeared to be a stranger to all the rest.

Young Witherington spoke to the lad, but obtained no response, nor could he catch a glimpse of the stranger's face, which was shrouded beneath a hat of foreign shape and make.

An advance guard, under old Witherington, preceded the party, keeping about five miles ahead, and occasionally sending back messengers to report progress.

For a time all went well, but shortly before sunset one of the advanced guard was seen galloping back in great haste.

Then came another and another.

"What means this?" sternly demanded Hotspur.

"My lord, our party has been attacked by the Scots, and your flag, borne by De Witherington, is taken by them."

"Forward, my men!" roared the young leader. "By the rood, I return not without my pennon."

With all haste they hurried forward, and at length reached a spot which bore evident signs of recent conflict. The grass and bushes were trodden underfoot, and dead bodies lay scattered about. Old Witherington was among the slain.

"But where are the Scots?" demanded the young warrior.

"Surely they must be wizards, my lord; they have vanished without leaving a trace behind to show which path they took. But we cannot follow them to-night as it grows dark, and the mist which gathers will hide the moon from our eyes."

"Then we will camp here, and to-morrow, by the aid of the saints, will hunt for men and for deer."

'Twas soon done, and the ruddy fire-light from the camp gave a grotesque aspect to the surrounding forest.

Sentinels were placed, and a strict watch kept; but the night passed without alarm.

As soon as the first beams of returning day began to show in the eastern horizon, the English were in motion. Hounds were uncoupled, and a hunt commenced, though, in reality, the game sought was human.

More than one man present who had taken part in the first hunt we recorded, remembered the words of the Witch of Wooler—

"Blood like a torrent shall flow down the glen,
Death shall be hunter, his quarry be men!"

But Hotspur had forgotten that circumstance, and only thought of the business on hand.

His hounds were of the best breed, his archers the truest in all the north country, and he soon became excited with the sport.

In the words of the old ballad—

> "Long time before high noon they had
> A hundred fat bucks slain ;
> Then having dined the hunters went
> To rouse the deer again."

Yet Hotspur did not forget the threat sent by young Earl Douglas, and sent scouts around on every side to report if the Scots made an appearance.

"For what purpose does the Douglas delay ?" he said. "He promised to prevent my sport, and yet we hunt here at pleasure. Is he satisfied with the honour of defeating a small body of my men who numbered scarcely a tenth part of his own army ?"

"Depend upon it he will be here, my lord," said Sir Robert Ratcliff, a renowned knight. "And as I live, here he comes round the grove of trees yonder, as goodly an array of foemen as any Christian knight might wish to encounter."

"Form beneath your banners ! bowmen to the front !" shouted the young lord. "My friends, we shall win great glory to-day."

The English soldiers formed up in battle array very swiftly, leaving the slaughtered deer lying upon the ground in all directions, and awaited the approach of Douglas, who halted the main body of his troops, and then rode forward with two or three of his personal attendants.

"How is this ?" said he, as he approached the English line. "What bold men are you who dare thus to kill deer upon Scottish ground? These woods and hills belong to the King of Scotland, and I, by birth his Chief Ranger, command you to retire."

Hotspur had drawn down his vizor, and made answer in these words—

"We care little for the King of Scotland or his ranger ; but we will hunt through these woods when we please, for they belong to us."

"Percy, I know thee ! But, since we have thus met, let not any of these innocent men suffer. If our own arms cannot decide the question, may I forthwith be unbelted !"

"By my patron saint, such welcome words never issued from the mouth of Scot ! Ho, Witherington, my lance and breastplate. Gentlemen, fall back, I pray you ; give us a fair course."

"My lord, you shall not arm for a single combat," said the young squire, striking his foot resolutely on the ground. "Are we not English and are not these men Scots? why then should we be deprived of a share in the glories of the field ?"

"You have spoken truth indeed, Witherington," exclaimed Ralph Percy. "Harry, this single fight cannot be allowed."

"Then, look well to yourselves," said Earl Douglas, retiring to his own men.

The English bugles sounded, the English bows were bent, and a flight of arrows went hissing through the Scottish ranks.

Thus commenced the famous battle of Chevy Chase, a conflict which Froissart describes as the "hardest and most obstinate battle that was ever fought ; for the English and Scots are excellent men-at-arms, and whenever they meet in battle, they do not spare each other nor is there any check to their courage so long as their weapons endure. And when they have well beaten each other, and one party is victorious, they are so proud of their conquest, they ransom instantly their prisoners."

"Advance my banner !" shouted the young Earl Douglas, who was impatient of winning renown.

With a shout of "Douglas ! Douglas !" the Scottish pikemen rushed forward, thinking to disperse the archers of Northumberland ; but in this they were mistaken, for the English kept them at bay with their swords, while the men behind poured in fresh flights of arrows.

"Ha ! ha ! well shot !" screamed a wild discordant voice. "Said I not, truly, that blood should flow down this glen? Douglas, remember the vision in the glass ! Percy, prepare for death. You have both persecuted me and mine ! My son, the monk, was treacherously slain in your castle, Douglas !"

"Thy son, the monk !" exclaimed Tim

of Tynemouth, an archer before mentioned. "Then here goes a shaft to avenge the son's villanies upon thy hell-doomed carcase."

With these words, he discharged a shaft, which pierced the weird woman's heart, and for ever stopped her speech.

"Thank Heaven for that!" exclaimed Hotspur. "But, forward my friends. Percy! Esperance!"

The shouts resounded, and, like a whirlwind, the impetuous English youth, with his companions in arms, burst upon the Scots, trampling the foot soldiers beneath their horses, and penetrating almost to where young Douglas sat in the midst of his knights with his banner displayed.

But here they met with a stouter resistance ; spears were shivered, swords gleamed high in the air, and heavy blows clanged with incessant din upon helmets and shields.

But wherever Hotspur turned he noticed that the strange page kept near his side, not seeking to distinguish himself, but apparently contented with warding off any blows that were aimed at the young Percy.

"Who are you, my lad?" said he, while still hotly engaged with a Scottish chief. "And why take you so much care for my safety and so little for your own?"

"You may find another as pleasing in your eyes, but I shall never see another Lord Henry Percy."

"That voice! Katherine, what madness brought you here? Depart instantly!"

"No, I cannot leave you."

"For Heaven's sake quit the field instantly! The fight will be a desperate one, and Scottish spears are no respecters of persons!"

"I must fight by your side!"

"What, against the Douglas?"

Lady Katherine's face became crimson as she remembered how, in times past, she had listened to the voice of the young Scot, and had even provided a ladder of ropes for his use.

"No—I go, Henry—I go, but still am true to you. Heaven's blessing attend your arm!"

"See her safely beyond the crowd, Witherington, and then seek me where you shall see the thickest fight."

So saying, he clenched his teeth, and, driving his spurs into his horse's flanks, pressed onwards in search of Earl Douglas.

The young Scot was no less eager to meet his foe, and ere long they found themselves face to face.

Their lances splintered ; Hotspur drew his heavy sword, while Douglas unslung the axe he had worn suspended from his neck.

"Well met, my foe," said Hotspur. "I am right glad you have kept your promise, and interfered with my hunting."

"And well pleased am I to have an opportunity of thus avenging the many injuries practised by you and yours towards my poor countrymen upon the borders."

No more time was wasted in words ; blows, and heavy ones, were the order of the day.

The champions were fighting with different weapons, so that each had a certain advantage. Douglas, with his axe, could deliver crushing blows ; but Hotspur's weapon, being more manageable, was better fitted for parrying.

Both were wounded, though not seriously, the first minute of the encounter, Hotspur having a slight wound on the left shoulder, while Douglas had felt the point of his foe's sword in the side. But had not their armour been of the very best manufacture, they would have hacked each other to pieces.

"Percy, I see you are wounded. Yield, and you shall be well treated by myself and our king, at whose court I must present you."

So said Douglas, thinking that his foe was weary of the fight.

"Not I. I care not to visit your king's court; and if you take me there, it must be when my arm can no longer wield weapon."

So responded Percy, and the fight continued. The knights of each party were anxious to continue the fight so long as they could hold spear in hand.

Cowardice was a vice then little known, and the most splendid courage was everywhere exhibited by the gallant youths of England and Scotland. They were so closely intermixed, that the archers' bows became comparatively useless, and each party fought hand to hand in a grand *mêlée*.

THE WITCH OF WOOLER VISITS FATHER ABEL IN HIS CELL.

The English began slowly to press the Scots back, their leaders still engaged in a most furious conflict. Douglas saw that things were coming to a crisis, and collected all his energies for a mighty effort.

With a terrific blow aimed at Hotspur's head he sent that young knight's steed rolling in the dust, and then swinging his battle-axe over his head began like a brave chief to rally his men.

He dashed into the midst of his foes, shouting his war-cry, " and gave such blows on all around him that no one could withstand them, but made way for him on all sides, for there were none so well armed with helmets and plate but suffered from his battle-axe."*

---

* Froissart's Chronicles, by Thomas Johnes.

In the meantime Hotspur quickly provided himself with a second horse and spear, with which he again charged furiously upon the young Scot, and at his side were two other English knights, each anxious for the honour of conquering the Scottish Chieftain.

But ere they could touch him a shaft from Tim of Tynemouth's bow came hissing through the air, and, finding its way through the armour worn by young Douglas, was instantly buried in his heart, causing instant death.

The next instant three spears struck him, one in the shoulder, another on the stomach, and a third entered his thigh ; thus was the gallant young Scot slain, and borne under foot.

But he fell covered with glory, and his name lived after him !

CHAPTER LI.

HOTSPUR'S FALL.

THE death of their youthful leader only added to the desperate courage of the Scots.

Five or six of them, headed by Sir Hugh Montgomery, a Scottish knight renowned for deeds of arms, vowed to revenge the death of Douglas.

With a brief prayer they charged the three English knights whose spears had borne the dead earl to the ground.

So impetuous was their advance, that all three were hurled from their horses.

Hotspur alone rose, being unharmed and clad in lighter armour than his companions.

Montgomery leaped from his horse, drew his sword, and at once engaged with Percy, whose sword, shivered in his combat with Douglas, flew into halves the moment it touched Sir Hugh's armour.

" Hold him, my friends ; we have a prize of value !" shouted Montgomery ; and at the same time he pushed the young Englishman into the midst of his own troop.

Hotspur was faint with many wounds and had no weapon.

" I yield myself your prisoner, Sir Scot, rescue or no rescue."

" And I, at all events, will rescue thee, my lord," cried Witherington, as he rushed headlong upon the foe, hoping to release his young lord.

But the efforts of the young esquire were in vain, for he was struck down by a huge iron mace, while at the same time a big two-handed sword lopped one leg clean off at the knee.

Even then, with his last strength, he raised himself on the other knee, to aim a farewell blow at his foes.

Ralph Percy had been in a different part of the field, but he too had fought with all the manly courage of an English boy of the period.

He had overthrown foe after foe, though

but a boy in years ; for he was well-grown and strong, and his limbs rendered supple by constant practise in all martial exercises.

But in his ardour he advanced too far ; he was wounded, disarmed, and being hardly pressed, surrendered himself.

"I surrender myself, Sir Knight," said he. "If I mistake not, you are Sir John Maxwell."

"That is my name ; and you, by your shield, should be of the house of Percy."

"I am called Ralph Percy, second son of the Earl of Northumberland.

"By St. Andrew, were all English lads as expert and valiant as yourself, we Scots should indeed be compelled to look well to our laurels."

Ralph smiled faintly, and then said—

"I pray you, Sir John, bid your men pay me some attention, for I am sorely wounded."

"Aye, that will I. Come with me to my Lord of Moray, who is close at hand."

The war-cry of Moray was heard close at hand, and towards that spot did Sir John Maxwell conduct his prisoner.

The Earl of Moray was leaning upon his sword, watching his men, who, though reduced to about one-fourth of their original number, were beginning to beat the English back.

"My lord," said Maxwell, "allow me to present you with Sir Ralph Percy as a prisoner ; but let good care be taken of him, I pray you, for he is badly wounded."

The Earl of Moray gravely saluted Ralph, and gave orders that his surgeon should attend on the youthful warrior.

The fight continued to rage for a long time, though nearly all the leaders on both sides were slain or wounded.

But, at length, as night came on, the English were compelled to retire, which they did slowly.

As victory declared itself for the Scots a page was seen to ride wildly off from a grove of trees, from which he had witnessed the fight.

The page's horse was fresh, and sped swiftly towards Alnwick.

That page was, as our readers may have guessed, Lady Katherine Mortimer.

Ralph Percy, though wounded and a prisoner, continued to watch the fight, so long as it could be seen, from the midst of his enemies.

The last thing he saw was the gallantry of a youth who had attended him as esquire.

This youth, whose name was Felton, was a very handsome and robust lad, about a year older than his young lord.

He was surrounded by a body of Scots, but would neither fly nor surrender.

On the contrary, he made a rush towards the standard of the Earl of Moray, and endeavoured to capture it.

This attempt, however, was repulsed by the superior numbers of the foe.

Many Scottish knights called upon him to surrender, so much did they admire the youth's courage, but he refused, and, after a stubborn conflict, was slain.

Down went the sun and up rose the moon over as gory a field as ever its beams glistened upon.

The fight was nearly over, saving in places where some scattered groups still kept up the combat. As the ballad says—

"This fight did last from break of day,
    Till setting of the sun ;
For when they rang the evening bell,
    The battle scarce was done.

"Of fifteen hundred Englishmen,
    Went home but fifty-three ;
The rest were slain in Chevy Chase,
    Under the green-wood tree."

 *   *   *   *   *

Ere Lady Katherine had travelled many miles on her journey back to Alnwick she fell in with a party of men from the castle under the command of the earl himself.

The fair page reined in her steed when she saw the earl.

"Ah ! is it you, my sweet ward ? Pray what mad pranks have you been playing ? How come you with this helmet, breastplate and gauntlet ?"

In a low trembling voice she told the earl all that had happened, and that his two sons were prisoners.

"But surely you did not venture into the fight   Yet it must be so, for there is the mark of a sword plainly written upon your helmet ; your gauntlet is sprinkled with blood ? Are you wounded, Katherine ?"

"But slightly, dear uncle. I can return with you."

"Tut, tut! What would my mad-cap son Harry say did I take you into the combat? He would surely say that his hot temper had come to dwell in my old head. Here, Redman, Clifford, take some half dozen spears and escort this fair lady safely back to my castle."

The two men called were esquires who had grown grey in the service of the Percy family.

Perhaps the earl thought that their old arms would be less missed than those of younger soldiers.

With a hasty farewell to his niece, the earl rode forward to avenge the captivity of his sons.

Nor had he long to wait.

He soon fell in with some few of his own men, pursued by a larger body of Scots, under the command of Sir John Maxwell.

A sharp decisive conflict followed.

The Scots were unable to stand before the newcomers, and left their leader a prisoner.

"Ha! Sir John of Maxwell is my prisoner. But, good Sir John, tell me have you encountered my sons?"

"The youngest is my prisoner; the eldest when dismounted and disarmed, yielded to Hugh Montgomery. Both are now with the Earl of Moray, who treats them very courteously. But he has marched back from the borders, leaving only me and the men you dispersed to finish the fight."

"For the sake of my two sons, Sir John, you shall have gentle treatment."

"You may be well assured my lord earl, that the youths will be well used."

"Aye; but tell me, Sir John, how did they bear themselves in the fight?"

"Never in Scotland or England did I behold more gallant lads, if with them I mention our own young Lord Douglas."

"What of him?"

"He fell! and Scotland mourns."

"Well may Scotland mourn for the loss of her brave son!" replied the Earl of Northumberland, who then gave his troop the word to march.

CHAPTER LII.

LIBERTY!

LIBERTY may well be called the greatest of human blessings.

Without it riches are useless, fine clothes hang miserably upon the limbs, and a splendid palace has no more joys than a dreary dungeon.

So thought Harry and Ralph Percy, as they passed the hours of their captivity in dull silence.

Since the battle they heard no news of their friends and kindred.

The Earl of Moray could not or would not give them any information, and in fact Hotspur felt very doubtful whether Lady Katherine had escaped or not.

Their captors, indeed, had given them this much information, namely, that the Earl of Northumberland had retired to his own land, after following the Scottish forces for a few miles.

Five days thus passed.

Ralph Percy was unable to leave the chamber his captors had prepared for him, and Hotspur was too fond of his brother to think of leaving him.

The sixth day was ushered in with the noise of a small party of men entering the castle of Haddington, where the two brothers were kept in captivity.

"There seems an unusual stir amongst our hosts, or gaolers," said Hotspur.

"What is the meaning of such excitement?" asked the invalid, Ralph.

"I know not, unless it be that our

noble father has sent to demand our release."

Ralph sighed heavily.

"The fortunes of war are sorely against me. In my first field I am wounded and captured."

"Cheer up, my brother! Many more experienced warriors than yourself fell in that fatal fight."

There was a long pause.

"What strange circumstances led us on to that combat?" said Ralph.

"Strange indeed. But the monk—the monk was at the bottom of it all. It was his treason that set Scots and English in hostile array against each other."

"But what of the monk?"

"He died, so I have heard, in an attempt to escape from the dungeon in which our foeman, the young Douglas, imprisoned him."

A hasty step was heard approaching the room in which the two brothers sat.

"It must be a message from home," said Ralph. "I feel certain it is. The very thought gives me new strength and health; my limbs have their suppleness restored, and I feel a different being."

A servant entered.

"My lords, your presence is required in the great hall by my noble master, the Earl of Moray."

"Lead on," said Ralph. "To-day I am able to follow you, though I could not have done so twenty-four hours ago."

It was the hope of freedom strong within his bosom which urged the youth on to a physical exertion of which he would have been incapable under any other circumstances.

On reaching the great hall of the castle they found there the Earl of Moray, with several of his retainers; but the sight that most of all gladdened their hearts was the presence of three individuals with whom they were well acquainted.

The principal person of the three was a certain Sir Edward Withers; the others were squires from Alnwick.

All gave the young lords a stately greeting as they entered, and seats were prepared for them.

"Lord Henry Percy," said the Earl of Moray, "I have sent to request your presence, in order that you may hear the terms of your ransom."

"Name the terms, my lord. Doubt not that we shall be glad enough to leave your castle in spite of your hospitality."

The Earl of Moray smiled, and said—

"By the mass, Sir Hotspur, you are as impatient to leave Scotland as you were to enter it."

A frown crossed the youth's brow.

"I may come back again in a very different manner, Lord Moray."

"You know the warm reception you are likely to meet. But now to the conditions of your release; this good knight, Sir Edward Withers, is fully empowered to act on behalf of your noble father."

"Sir Edward is a true knight; I can well put my trust in him," said Ralph.

"Then, the conditions are these, which Sir Edward, for the Earl of Northumberland, may accept or refuse, as he shall think fit.

"First. The Earl of Northumberland shall build, or cause to be built, a strong castle, in such place as the Earl of Moray shall consider fitting within a distance of forty miles, English, from the boundary between the kingdoms of England and Scotland. This castle to consist of moat, inner and outer courts, drawbridge, portcullis, keep and dungeons, with suitable habitations for those to whom its defence shall be entrusted.

"Second. The Earl of Northumberland shall complete this work within the space of three years from the day on which the Earl of Moray shall notify to him the spot where the castle is to be built; this to be fixed within one month from this date.

"Third. The Earl of Northumberland shall place within the castle sufficient armour for four knights, forty men-at-arms, and one hundred archers.

"Fourth. The Earl of Northumberland and his sons, the Lords Henry and Ralph Percy, shall make no war or inroad upon Scottish territory for the space of four years.

"Fifth. Failing the due observance of all and each of these conditions, the Lords Henry and Ralph Percy shall, as good knights and true, deliver up themselves to Thomas, Earl of Moray, at such place as he shall appoint."

There was a long silence when the earl finished reading these conditions.

Both the youths looked at Sir Edward Withers, who in return, made a slight motion with his head.

"Do you accept these conditions, noble sir?" asked Moray.

"I do accept them on behalf of the most noble Earl of Northumberland, whose seal I will presently affix to that parchment," said Withers.

The Earl of Moray nodded and turned towards the brothers.

"And you, young lords?"

"I pledge my faith to the fulfilment of the conditions you have offered," said Hotspur.

"And so do I," exclaimed Ralph.

"Then, noble sirs, you are at liberty to depart; yet I hope that ere you turn your backs upon my castle, you will so far honour me as to partake of a banquet which now awaits you. This good knight, Sir Edward Withers, has travelled far and must need rest."

Hotspur bowed in acknowledgment of the earl's hospitality, though he would have preferred starting at once.

However, he had sufficient of knightly breeding to know that he must accept the offer thus hospitably made, and so restrained his impatience.

The banquet seemed slow and tedious, though it boasted all the luxuries of the period, and was enlivened with the rude music in which our ancestors so much delighted.

At length, to Hotspur's great joy, it came to a conclusion, and the earl gave his guests permission to retire.

Need we say how eagerly the two youths availed themselves of this permission?

A litter was prepared for Ralph; Hotspur and Sir Edward had good steeds and the dozen men-at-arms who had accompanied the knight were also well armed.

With joy in their hearts they turned their horses' heads towards the south; they were homeward bound, and almost forgot their late defeat in the joys of liberty.

CHAPTER LIII.

A FUNERAL AND A FEAST.

AFTER a long journey and a night's rest upon the road, the little party came in sight of the well-known and welcome towers of Alnwick.

From the top of the tower floated a black banner, token that a death had been busy in the late fight, and that mourning had found its way into the castle.

"It must be for old Witherington," said Hotspur; "he was slain, I remember."

He was right; but it soon became evident that, in spite of the sorrow occasioned by the death of the good old squire, preparations had been made to welcome home the captives.

Numerous parties were seen ascending and descending the slope which leads to the castle.

There were mendicants by the dozen, many of whom, by professing to be disabled soldiers from the Crusades, gained no small amount of small coin from sympathetic souls.

Well might Hotspur and his friends gaze with astonishment upon the scene, which was one of extreme confusion.

Mirth and mourning seemed strangely mixed; the emblem of death overshadowed a scene of busy life.

There were wandering minstrels and bards, some chanting a mournful ditty on the death of Witherington, while others took a more joyous view of things, and shouted forth loud notes in praise of the glorious doings of their young lord, Harry Percy, and all that noble family.

Inside the great gate the scene was something similar, though diversity was given to the appearance of the place by a crowd of cooks, scullions and cellarmen, who were bustling about in every direction, some cooking huge oxen and sheep, while others were placing casks of ale in such positions as would best suit the convenience of both mourners and holiday makers.

Such was the scene in the courtyard of Alnwick Castle, when Hotspur, with his brother and friends, re-entered it, after an absence of nearly ten days.

The warders at the drawbridge had taken but little notice of the crowds of inferior persons passing in and out ; but when they saw the cavalcade approach from the northward, they shouted loudly for the seneschal or steward.

This officer soon made his appearance, habited in garments partly military, partly civil, and partly heraldic ; a gold chain was slung round his neck, and a white wand of office tipped with gold was in his hand.

"Welcome home to Alnwick, my lords," said he bowing low.

Then, flourishing his staff, he marched on before the little party, shouting—

"Room for the most noble and valiant knight, the Lord Henry Percy ! Room, my masters ; stand back !"

With these words he thrust back the crowd, and conducted the brothers to the entrance of the great hall where the earl was waiting to receive them.

Hotspur's eye took in the little assemblage at a glance.

There was his father, the earl, his mother, and a few warriors whose faces were familiar.

But, alas ! many well-known countenances were not to be seen.

They slept beneath the greenwood tree in Chevy Chase.

"Thank Heaven, *she* is safe !" muttered the youth, as his eye fell upon the fair form of Lady Katherine, who stood rather behind the other members of the group.

"My son, my son, welcome home !" said the earl as his first-born leaped nimbly to the ground.

"How fares it with you, my gallant boy ?" said the countess, "and where is your brother ?"

"He is in yonder litter, wounded, and still weak, but fast recovering, thanks to the free fresh air of Northumberland."

"Thou canst now see the danger of rushing into war unadvisedly," said the earl. "But, by the rood, you fought so well that you have my forgiveness for all that has taken place."

"Thanks, noble father ; I shall benefit both by your pardon and the experience I have gained."

The attendants then lifted Ralph from his litter and bore him carefully into the castle.

The long journey had fatigued him, and his wounds were beginning to give pain.

So Hotspur was left alone with Lady Katherine.

"At length you have returned, truant," said she, pretending to look very angry.

"I have, to give you the severe lesson you so richly deserve."

"Ah ! how have I offended ?"

"By risking your precious body in a fight which shall always be remembered. Katherine, that was indeed a rash action."

"Are your own actions always thoughtful and well considered, Sir Hotspur ?"

The youth smiled.

"They are not, I grant ; but when you consider the love I have for you, I fancy you should have refrained from putting your life in peril."

Lady Katherine smiled ·faintly as she made reply—

"This is no time for words of love, Henry, for hark, the bell proclaims that poor old Witherington is about to be borne to his last resting-place."

As Lady Katherine spoke, the tones of the castle bell fell upon the ears of the young pair.

Again and again the sullen sounds were heard, following each other in rapid succession, and leaving but sufficient space for each clang to die away in distant echo ere the ear was again filled with a repetition of the iron knell.

The sound, the signal of the approaching ceremony, had the effect of drawing away the attention of the menials from the jugglers and minstrels.

Awe chilled the hearts of the assembled multitudes, whose eyes were now turned towards the chapel where the body of the old squire had remained before the altar ever since the fatal fight in which he fell.

Hotspur hurried away to make such change in his dress as was suitable for the occasion.

From the chapel to the vault where the squire's grave had been dug was a good distance ; nevertheless, the head of the procession had nearly reached the tomb before the end of the band had left the gates of the church.

First of all came a man, bearing the banner of the Earl of Northumberland, with another by his side, who carried the pennon of the Witherington family.

Then came all the knights and squires who did military service to the house of Percy.

Behind them two heralds, and then the coffin on which the helmet and sword of the dead warrior had been placed.

Next came a sorry spectacle.

Young Witherington, borne upon four men's shoulders, as chief mourner.

The youth had insisted upon rising from his bed to pay the last honours to his father, and many tears were shed as the bystanders gazed upon the mutilated form of the gallant young esquire.

Then came the earl, the countess, Hotspur, and other members of the family, two men with black wands closing up the procession.

The coffin was lowered into its last resting-place ; the priests recited their last prayer, and the heralds snapped their wands as, in loud tones, they proclaimed the rank and style of the deceased.

" He died fighting for his liege lord !" said a hollow voice, that of the only Witherington who remained.

The youth could say no more, but was carried in an insensible state from the gloomy vault.

After a long silence the earl gave the signal to return.

" You see, Harry, how your hot temper has caused the death of the best retainer who ever did homage to the house of Percy."

Thus spoke the earl.

" I see, noble father. But if my own death could have preserved his life, I would willingly have died for him. But cease to upbraid me, I implore you."

The earl made no reply, but returned to his own apartment.

Hotspur, on the other hand, took his way to the apartment in which he knew Lady Katherine was seated, and without much difficulty prevailed upon her to name a day upon which, with the earl's sanction, their hands, hearts, and fortunes might be united.

CHAPTER LIV.

THE FALL OF THE CURTAIN.

A FEW days passed away in peace. All traces of war had vanished from the castle of Alnwick ; archers and men-at-arms walked about on the battlements in a listless manner—their occupation was gone.

Hotspur found more delight in the sweet society of Lady Katherine than in the clash of arms, and for a time neglected all his old warlike habits.

Ralph, under the care of the good old hermit, rapidly recovered his health and strength, for the recluse had in the solitude of his cell learned many secrets of healing, which made his presence always welcome in the castle.

One day, about two weeks after the return to Alnwick, the brothers were walking together upon the terrace which overlooked the main gateway when a man was seen approaching.

His dress was semi-military, but the man himself had a worn, jaded appearance.

He walked with difficulty by the aid of a staff in his hand.

"What is your business here?" demanded the porter at the gate.

"I would see the Earl of Northumberland."

"And think you that the earl will grant an interview with every lame beggar who comes to the gate for alms?"

The stranger drew himself up proudly, as he replied—

"I have not asked for alms, nor would I take a crust from one of the Percy race to save myself from all the pangs of starvation."

The noise of the altercation reached Hotspur's ear, and he commanded the warder to allow the unknown to enter.

"Who are you that would see the earl?" he demanded.

"It matters not, my young lord, my business is for his ear alone."

"Go, tell my noble father that a stranger desires to see him," said Hotspur, to a soldier.

The man departed, and in a few minutes the earl was seen approaching, leaning upon the arm of the hermit.

The stranger gravely saluted the noble.

"I have news for your private ear, my lord," said he. "Will it please you to desire these gentlemen to retire?"

The earl made a motion, and in a moment was left alone with the stranger.

"Now, what have you to say?"

The man bent forward, as though to whisper, but at the same time drawing a poignard from his dress, aimed a desperate blow at the earl's heart.

"Ha! traitor!" exclaimed the earl, grappling with the would-be assassin. "Your vile purpose is defeated."

At the same moment he hurled the stranger from him with such violence as to pitch him over the low parapet on the terrace, and send him rolling down to the paved courtyard below.

Hotspur and Ralph, who had seen the attempt, came running up with drawn swords, and would have despatched the stranger.

"Hold, my sons! Let us learn, if we can, who this bold stranger is," cried the earl.

A dozen attendants were upon the spot in a moment, and the assassin was raised up.

"I am dying!" said he ; and a torrent of blood gushing from his mouth confirmed his words.

"Die, and save the hangman a dishonourable task," said Hotspur.

"What object had you in thus attempting to take my life?" asked the earl.

"Ha! ha! you seek information, do you, Earl Percy? You shall have it. Know, then, that I am called the Moody Forester, and was, till now, head of a band which had for its object your death."

"For what reason?"

"Three reasons ; to preserve the influence of the church, which you are suspected to despise in your own heart ; to avenge the death of a member of our band, Father Abel ; and to prevent, if possible, any farther union between the houses of Percy and Mortimer."

"Then it was you who murdered a helpless serving woman in the gardens of this castle?" said Hotspur, hastily jumping at an idea which flashed through his brain.

The man nodded.

"That dagger was for—"

Hotspur raised his weapon, and was about to plunge it into the bosom of the dying man.

"Hold! slay him not!" said the earl.

"He is dead," said the hermit, solemnly, as he stooped down to examine the man's face, "he is dead, and thus

Providence has removed from your path a powerful and unscrupulous foe."

"Remove the body," said the earl, "and, in future, let all who seek admission be more strictly examined."

"My presence seems to bring with it war and bloodshed," said Hotspur. "I must carry with me some strange fatality."

"Hush!" replied Ralph. "Here comes one whose presence brings with it peace and sunshine."

He pointed, as he spoke, to Lady Katherine, and the two youths walked towards her.

*　　*　　*　　*　　*

The gloom soon died away, the attempted murder was forgotten, and all seemed *peace and sunshine* on the day when the bold Hotspur, still a boy in years, saw himself united for life to the fair Lady Katherine.

Would that *peace and sunshine* had always gladdened their hearts; but it was not to be so, for the clouds of war soon again darkened the air.

Wherever trumpet-call was heard, there Hotspur was seen, foremost in the field; till, at length, on the fatal field at Shrewsbury, the hero of the north fell in a fight which has been celebrated by England's greatest band.

Many wept his fall; none more than the fair wife he left behind, and who, as she contemplated all the fatal incidents of that day, recalled to mind some of the circumstances which gave rise to the less celebrated though almost equally fatal battle of CHEVY CHASE.

THE END,